Ice King

By

GEOFF WOODLAND

MDW PUBLISHING

Ice King
by Geoff Woodland

Copyright ©2010 by Geoff Woodland

All rights reserved under all Copyright Conventions.

No part of this book may be reproduced, stored in a retrieval system, or transmitted by any means, electronic, mechanical, photocopying, recording, or otherwise, without written permission from the author.

Published by MDW Publishing
ISBN 13: 978-0-9808201-0-2

First Edition

For Maureen, Sara & Mark.

Prologue

The masthead of the *Margaret Rose* was bathed in the ghostly blue glow of St Elmo's fire. The light danced and sizzled as First Mate, William King, breathed a sigh of relief. The eerie light was a sign that the storm was abating.

Within the hour, the wild movement of the *Margaret Rose* eased. The blackness of night gradually surrendered to the dull grey of first light.

A perceptible change in the vessel's movement told him the seabed was shallowing. William sensed they had entered Liverpool Bay.

Captain Loper had insisted on sailing from Dublin on the evening tide. His eagerness to return to Liverpool with the *Margaret Rose* crammed with Irish immigrants had cost him his life. The storm, when it hit, was worse than anyone anticipated.

It was during the fight to keep the ship's bow facing the oncoming sea that William witnessed his Captain washed overboard. There was nothing he could have done to help. It would have endangered the lives of all on board to attempt to put the *Margaret Rose* about.

The cry 'Land ho!' brought staggering, ashen-faced passengers on deck. After many hours suffering below, the promise of dry land was a welcome reprieve from the tortuous journey.

- CHAPTER ONE -

Father's House

Commissioned.
Liverpool June 1804

William pushed open the front door of his home on Tythe Barn Street and dashed upstairs to the first floor, where his father, George, ran the family business; King Shipping.

George King leaned forward over the sideboard to check the chafing dishes of hot food. Studying the older man as if it was the first time he had really seen him, William noticed the thinning dark hair and white streaks on top of his father's head. His rounded face denoted success, a success that allowed him to indulge in drink. ('After all', his father would say, 'haven't I earned a little extra?') His face showed thin red lines where the alcohol had taken hold. He was also, even as a large man, running slightly to fat—but then one expected a little extra weight on a successful businessman.

The lack of hair on his father's head did not stop the growth of his facial hair. His upper lip was bare, but thick side-whiskers extended from just in front of his ears to just below his chin. George was wearing a long black coat with matching knee britches. A silk shirt and silk stockings proclaimed the final touches to the uniform of a successful Liverpool trader who controlled his own shipping company.

'Good morning, William.'

'Good Morning, Sir.'

'Shall we talk over breakfast?'

'If that is your wish.'

'Sit. Sit down. What would you like? Can I get you something?' He waved his hand towards the food on the sideboard.

William sat midway down the long dining table and felt like a schoolboy again. He steeled himself for the coming argument. He knew the request he was about to make would not be granted but he had to ask nonetheless.

'Just coffee, thank you.'

His father would take the seat at the head of the table. William couldn't remember when this had not been the case. Seated there, his father could see everything that went on in the room. The long sideboard behind the chair held food only at breakfast time.

'Should eat more, William,' said George as he placed a cup of coffee in front of his son.

'Thank you,' said William.

The clang from the covers on the chafing dishes was the only sound as George King scooped fried potatoes, beef and eggs onto his plate before sitting in his chair at the head of the table.

William glanced down at his coffee and realised he was more nervous than he originally thought.

His mother had died giving birth. George, never having remarried, had dominated William's life. Tired of being overshadowed and having his wishes ignored, William decided, as he entered his teens, to be his own man.

In his childhood so many different women had been hired to tutor and look after him, he'd lost count. No one had lasted long. When his father returned from sea, he either caused so much friction that the tutor left, or he dismissed her for some minor infringement.

Each time his father returned home he would always bring a gift, but all William ever wanted was his father's time. The few short weeks his father was home were usually spent conducting business as he prepared for another voyage. His father couldn't change from being a sea Captain with authority of life and death over his crew, to a loving father. William had a feeling that his father blamed him for his mother's death.

When William was twelve, he knew he would follow in his father's footsteps and go to sea. He hoped this would please his father, and perhaps they would then have something in common, other than his mother.

'Well, my boy,' boomed George as he cut into a large piece of fried beef.

'Well, Sir,' said William, sipping the hot black coffee, 'we have held this conversation before, but I just wanted to make sure nothing has changed.'

'If you're talking about being appointed to your own ship as Captain then nothing *has* changed. I appreciate you brought home the *Margaret Rose* safely, after the death of Captain Loper, but you must be aware the French are attacking English merchant ships in the Mediterranean and we can't obtain insurance at the right price. You're also aware times are not good, not as they have been, but at least we're able to trade to the west and use the *Margaret Rose* on the Irish emigrant trade instead of the

Mediterranean——'

'But——'

'Keep silent, Sir! I am speaking. You have just completed a year as first mate on the *Margaret Rose* with emigrants from Ireland and we have turned a nice profit. Not a lot, but at least we are not in danger of being sunk.'

William opened his mouth to speak but his father stopped him with his hand held palm out. In a more reasonable voice, George said, 'Let me finish, William, after which I will listen to your thoughts on the matter. It is my wish that you spend more time as first mate and also time in the office. You need more experience.'

A silence fell while George cut another large piece of meat, smothered it in mustard, and pushed it into his mouth. He wiped the fat that dripped from his lips with a flourish of his napkin. He signalled to William that he had finished speaking and silently chewed his food.

'I was afraid you'd not have changed your mind and that the reason you'd give for not giving me command would be that I lacked experience.'

George nodded his head and swallowed. He attacked the meat again.

'Taking this into account, I am pleased to inform you I have taken steps to gain much more experience in the future than I have gained on the *Margaret Rose*.'

George stopped chewing. With his knife and fork gripped in his hands, he asked in a quiet voice, 'How so?'

'Yesterday I was commissioned Lieutenant in His Majesty's navy.'

'What! Commissioned! What nonsense is this?'

He watched his father's face turn a bright red and then a dull purple. Scraps of food sprayed from George's mouth as he made a supreme effort to get his words out.

'You will resign immediately – tell them it was all a mistake.'

'I will not resign, and there is nothing you can do to make me.'

'Isn't there, by God. We will see about that. I am your father and you will do as you are told!'

William rose slowly from his seat, placed his hands on the table and leaned towards his father.

'I am doing as I am told, Father,' he said softly. 'Our King, our Sovereign, has commissioned me to join the fleet. Not even you can go against the King. He is not someone who can be bullied. I hoped I'd receive your blessing and you'd be pleased your son is ready to fight for his country.'

'Fight for his country? You have done this to spite me!'

'Spite you? You are the one who said I needed more experience. You made me, Father, and you have moulded me, so don't be surprised that I have made my own decisions. Do I have your blessing?'

'No! You, you, you, I'll see you damned first.'

William straightened himself and returned his chair to the correct position. With sadness in his heart and a small lump in his throat, he faced his father and said, 'If that is your last word, Sir, then there is nothing to keep me from attending the Admiralty in London. I bid you, good day.'

He stared at his father, whose eyes became bright with tears, although his lips were set in a hard line. This was a look William couldn't remember seeing before. Nothing in the past could match the look he now saw on his father's face.

William walked to the dining room door and could sense his father's eyes following him. He opened the door and stepped through into the hall and closed the door gently.

November 1804-HMS Belleisle off the French coast

Lieutenant King blew on his hands as he gazed across the spume-flecked water at the coastline of France. It had been some months since he had reported to Captain Whitby of HMS *Belleisle,* the day before they sailed for blockade duty off the French coast. For weeks they had sailed close into the French shore at dawn and back out to the safety of the ocean at twilight. Captain Whitby would not allow himself to get caught on a lee shore in the dark. The French were as bored watching the *Belleisle* sail up and down their coast as the crew of the *Belleisle* were, watching their shoreline.

Only a year ago, William had cursed the lack of support from the Navy. He had sailed the Mediterranean on his own or in company of one or two other traders, but never with a Navy escort. Now he realised that the Navy completely lacked the vessels to offer support. Merchant vessels had to take their chances while they relied upon the Navy to bottle-up the French ships in their homeports. He was uncomfortably aware some French ships did occasionally break out in the Mediterranean and make a dash for an unescorted and undefended British merchant vessel. It did not matter what the merchantman carried, everything was valuable to the blockaded French.

William's hands were still cold. Winter had come early this year. As the weeks became months on blockade duty, he knew conditions on the *Belleisle* would get worse. Unless they received fresh orders, Christmas 1804 would be a cold celebration off the enemy coast.

'Watch your heading,' said William curtly, standing behind the helmsman to check the compass.

'Aye, Aye, Sir.'

William was tired and knew that he shouldn't have been so sharp with the helmsman. Hands behind his back, he resumed his steady tread in an effort to keep warm.

'Mr King, if you please.'

William turned quickly as he recognised the voice of the Captain. He hurried across the deck and touched his hat. 'Sir.'

'Mr King, according to the fishing boat we intercepted earlier today, a French brig is hidden behind Penmarch Rocks.'

William remained silent, though his spirits rose at the possibility of a battle against the French, and perhaps prize money.

'All officers to my cabin in one hour, if you please, Mr King, and I wish you to attend, so arrange a relief.'

'Sir.' William touched his hat and turned to the young midshipman who shared his watch. 'Midshipman of the watch, all officers to the Captain's cabin in one hour.'

William entered the Captain's cabin, removed his hat, and joined the other junior officers, who were trying to be attentive yet inconspicuous at the same time. He couldn't help but compare this giant cabin of a ship of the line to the cabin of a small merchantman.

The *Belleisle* measured over 168 feet from bow to stern; the *Rose* had been 80 feet. In terms of weight the *Belleisle* displaced 1600 tons, eight times that of the *Rose*.

He glanced at the deckhead; unlike in the *Rose,* here in the Captain's cabin he could stand upright without trouble. Daylight from the large windows behind the captain's desk flooded the whole cabin, eliminating the need for oil lamps during the day.

The First Lieutenant saluted the Captain. 'All officers present and correct, Sir, except for two officers on watch.'

'Thank you, rest easy gentlemen. You know I received information about a French brig at anchor in waters behind Penmarch Rocks. It is my intention to cut her out.'

An air of excitement ran through the cabin, action at last.

'This is what I propose. The First Lieutenant will be in overall command and in charge of the launch. Mr King will be in charge of the pinnace and second in command.'

William felt pleasantly surprised at being given such an honour. The Captain continued, 'I don't normally explain why I so order, but in this case I will. Mr King has years of experience as First Mate on traders so if he gets lost he has a better chance than the other junior officers to find his way home.' A ripple of laughter ran around the junior officers. Perhaps it was their way to cover their disappointment at not being picked to be involved.

The pinnace had eight oars so if he double banked, he would have sixteen men plus the coxswain and himself.

'A midshipman will be in command of a cutter and will act in support in case the First Lieutenant or Mr King meet strong resistance. At dusk we will turn and sail away from the coast. The French have been watching us for months as we sail close in shore at daylight and out to sea as darkness falls. Tonight, however, when it is dark, we will sail back to the coast under reduced sail and drop the boats close in by the entrance to the Rocks. Any questions?'

Captain Whitby looked around his group of officers and waited for a question. All were silent.

'It appears there are no questions so I will not delay you gentlemen. Make ready and pick your men but don't let the French see any of your preparations. Good luck and God speed.'

—⚓—

The overcast sky threatened rain as the three boats clustered together a short distance from their mother ship.

William leaned forward to hear the whispered commands from the First Lieutenant in the launch.

'We will aim for the shadow of the island', and he indicated the darker area of the island, 'that way we should be able to blend into the island and avoid any lookouts.'

William in the pinnace, and the young midshipman in the cutter, nodded. Their orders were not to speak unless in an emergency.

'Mr King will take station astern of me and the midshipman will be in the rear. A shielded lantern shown intermittently astern from the forward boats will give some guidance to those behind. Give way together,' ordered the First lieutenant to his boat's crew.

William touched the shoulder of his coxswain. The men bent to their oars as the pinnace followed the launch. He glanced over his shoulder and was pleased to see the Midshipman's boat keeping station behind.

Rounding the southern point of the island, William could just make out the French brig anchored ahead.

The First Lieutenant stood carefully in the stern of the launch and scanned the area for guard boats. William also stood and peered into the blackness ahead. He could see an area darker than the rest and realised that it must be a second ship anchored near their original target. It was a two-masted schooner.

'First Lieutenant's boat is stopped, Sir,' whispered William's coxswain. William switched his gaze from the schooner to the first boat in their group. 'Oars', whispered William. His boat slid quietly to a stop near the First Lieutenant's launch.

'Mr King,' whispered the First Lieutenant, 'there is a second vessel at anchor. I believe she is a schooner. I want you to capture her and sail her out to meet the *Belleisle*.'

'Aye, Aye, Sir,' replied William in a low voice. 'Coxswain, aim for a point ahead of the bow of the French brig.' William eased himself to the bow of the pinnace to determine the schooner's exact position. 'We'll go over the bows, men,' whispered William. 'Coxswain, cut her anchor cable as soon as you board.' He pointed to the first two oarsmen. 'You two make sail when the cable is cut. If the French feel the ship under way, I hope they'll become disheartened and not cause us too much trouble. Coxswain, when the cable's gone, you take the wheel.'

'Right, lads, time for the armbands, but keep it quiet.'

Each of his crew produced a small strip of white cloth in the shape of a circle and pulled it up their left arm. 'Remember, lads, anyone with a white armband is a *Belleisle*. No white band means he's French! I don't want any pistol cocked until you're on board. An accident will be the end of us all.'

The boat slipped quietly through the black water, the oars dipping rhythmically. A sudden flash of lightning from the forbidding sky lit the anchorage for a split second. The crew stopped rowing. William caught a glimpse of the schooner but could not see any guards. 'Give way together. Steer for her anchor cable,' he whispered to the coxswain.

A deep rumble of thunder shook the air.

That will hide any noise we make, thought William, as he glanced at the sky and hoped the rain would hold off until after they had boarded the schooner.

The boat gently nudged the schooner's mooring cable and eager hands grabbed the rope to steady the pinnace. William signalled to the bowman who grasped the cable and began to climb. To ease the strain on his arms, the bowman wrapped his feet around the slippery rope and pushed his body higher. When the bowman reached the hawse pipe, William grasped the rope and began to climb. He wished he were as agile as the sailor before him. His arms ached with the effort of pulling himself up the mooring rope as his sword flapped against his left leg. A final heave and he was over the gunwale and collapsed on the deck. His heart thudded with the unaccustomed effort.

He peered around to check if his noisy arrival had alarmed the French. All appeared quiet. Then he saw, suddenly, a body dressed as a French sailor next to him. The Frenchman's throat had been slit. The pinnace's bowman sat calmly, a few feet away, wiping his bloody knife on a piece of cloth cut from the Frenchman's shirt. William started to rise as two more of his crew dropped gently onto the deck. Keeping low, they ran towards the schooner's stern.

Each minute saw two more of his boat's crew drop to the deck and silently take their positions.

'Ready, Sir,' whispered the coxswain, his axe held high over the anchor cable. 'Ship's boat secured alongside in case we have to make a run for it.'

'Thank you, coxswain. Hold off cutting until I give the word. It is a lot quieter than I expected.'

'Johnny Crap-'ards don't like to get wet, Sir, and it feels

like rain.'

William smiled. 'Crapaud, in French, is pronounced krap-o, Coxswain, so if you wish to insult a French sailor, make sure you pronounce it correctly or he won't realise you're insulting him,' whispered William in return.

He knew his little speech about the mispronunciation of a British sailor's name for a French sailor, Johnny Crapaud or Johnny Toad, was due to his nervousness.

'Aye, Sir,' answered the Coxswain.

William watched the man's face.

It was obvious that the man didn't know what William was talking about.

William left the coxswain and joined the rest of his crew, who waited near the foremast for orders. 'Sails ready?' he whispered.

'Aye, Sir,' said one of the two men designated to deal with the sails after the cable parted.

As William turned to speak to the rest of the men, the peace of the night was broken by the sound of shots from the brig.

'That's it for silence, Coxswain. Now!' he shouted as he drew his sword.

A dull thud of the axe signalled the cable had parted.

'Haul those sails. Coxswain, take the wheel,' shouted William.

The sound of running feet and the noise of the French crew as they poured from below put an end to any further speech. The French and the British were now in a bloody hand-to-hand fight. William sensed the vessel begin to list as the wind caught her sails. He could hear the sound of pistols discharging, and hoped they were British and not French.

A large Frenchman swinging a two handed axe charged through the knot of British sailors. William ducked and felt the wind from the blade as it passed close above his head. The man grunted and tried to correct the momentum of his swing as William thrust upward. He felt the blade slide under the man's arm and into his side. Though wounded, the Frenchman was not finished and swung the axe back at William in an attempt to cut him in half. William stepped back as the axe brushed his chest and embedded itself in the mast. As the French sailor tugged to free the axe, William thrust his sword at the man's chest and ran him through.

The sound of steel on steel, oaths, grunts and the occasional scream rang across the small ship as the enemies fought for control of the vessel.

William looked around for any indication of the Captain or an officer but couldn't see anyone in such a uniform. His heart beat fast as he parried a wild stroke from one of his own crew.

'Pay attention, damn your eyes.'

The wild eyes of the crewman told William the man had lost control and would hack at anybody who got in his way. Before William could do anything about him the crewman turned and charged back into the fight.

The motion of the schooner told him they had reached the open sea. Spray now splattered across the deck and she buried her bow into the Atlantic waves. The fighting was diminishing as his crew gained control.

William trying to avoid further and unnecessary bloodshed, shouted 'Capituler, capituler' to the French. The only word he could think of and hoped he pronounced it correctly.

The fighting eventually stopped. William could make out a small group of about fifteen Frenchmen gathered aft of the mainmast. The schooner's Captain must have allowed half of his crew to go ashore but each second meant the ship was sailing further from the shores of France.

His boat's crew, gasping for breath, threatened the Frenchmen from a few feet away.

'Capituler,' shouted William again.

First one and then another Frenchman dropped his weapon, until eventually all surrendered. Not until the final weapon had dropped did his heart begin to slow. He sheathed his sword and waited while his crew pushed the prisoners into some order. They were a sorry sight. His emotions stirred as he realised, but for his good fortune, the roles might easily have been reversed and he might have become a prisoner of the French.

A voice broke his reverie.

'*Belleisle* on the starboard bow, Sir.'

'Thank you, Coxswain, come under her lee if you would.'

'Aye, Aye, Sir.'

'Davenport, search the prisoners.'

Davenport pushed the French prisoners as he began his search.

'Search a vois, search a vois,' he shouted and patted various prisoners for hidden weapons.

The pinnace's crew laughed, being aware of what Davenport meant. The consternation on the faces of the French, and their lack of response, brought further laughter. The prisoners stood in a huddle and watched Davenport as they tried to work out his question.

William stood behind Davenport and studied the prisoners. He wished to find out who was in charge.

Davenport pushed a young man against the gunwale and bent to tap his pockets and waistband for a weapon. William finished inspecting the prisoner's faces and began to turn away. He would never know why he turned back, but as he did, he saw the flash of a knife. The young Frenchman had drawn his hand back and plunged a short knife into Davenport's throat.

Davenport screamed until the knife cut his voice. William pulled out his pistol, aimed, and shot the Frenchman in the face. The Frenchman dropped to the deck, a bloody hole where his nose had been and half his head missing, much of which had splattered on Davenport's now collapsed body. William felt aghast; this was the first time he had shot a man in cold blood. Strangely, he didn't feel any sorrow. The man's attack after he had surrendered, in William's mind, sealed his own fate.

The remainder of the French prisoners moaned and dropped to the deck and cowered.

'Bind their hands,' William ordered.

Indicating the dead Frenchman, he addressed two of his boat crew. 'Throw that piece of rubbish overboard.'

Two sailors grabbed the dead man and heaved him over the side.

William knelt beside Davenport and checked for signs of life.

The Frenchman's knife had severed an artery. Davenport was dead.

'Pick up our shipmate,' said William, as he stood, ' and we'll take him back to the *Belleisle* and give him a decent burial.'

The Captain's plan had worked with great success. The captured brig, *Le Tigre*, and the schooner, *Desiree,* would be sold into the British Navy on their return to England.

Captain Whitby was in high spirits. Although the money received for the two French vessels would be split amongst the officers and crew of the *Belleisle*, the majority would go to him.

'A fine episode, Mr King, and we all benefit from it.'

'Aye, Sir, we will.'

'In the meantime I will use the *Le Tigre* to scout for us while you, Mr King, will command the schooner and take my dispatches back to England.'

William was overjoyed at being given his first command. If the action was gazetted, would his father be pleased at seeing his son's name in the newspapers or would he still be angry?

- CHAPTER TWO -

A Ship to Command

Leaving HMS Belleisle for England. November 1804

The voyage back to England became one that William would always remember. The *Desiree*, a lively craft that sailed fast and steady, had become his first command. The feel of her riding the waves gave him the greatest pleasure. He had to make an effort not to smile each time the crew referred to him as Captain.

On arrival in England, William reported to the Port Admiral at Spithead from whom he received orders to sail to Falmouth, in Cornwall. While off Falmouth he was to take on fresh water and stores and await further orders.

The Port Admiral read Captain Whitby's dispatches. As a reward for her capture, the Admiral confirmed William's appointment as commander of the *Desiree*. William's heart felt as if it would burst with pride; he had a ship to command at last.

His crew consisted of a sailing Master, Master's Mate, a young Midshipman from Edinburgh named Peter McCall, and thirty crew. The broad Scottish accent of the tall, gangling, red-haired Midshipman was evident during his normal speech but when he raised his voice over the wind, the accent disappeared. The midshipman's red hair and fair skin could become a problem in the Tropics, thought William. At least the crew would understand him when he gave orders, even if they couldn't when he spoke normally.

While they awaited orders, the *Desiree* was bought in to the navy and re-christened *HMS Nancy*. She was a fine new vessel for his Majesty.

Falmouth December 1804

HMS Nancy lay at anchor off Falmouth for three weeks before William's orders arrived. William had hoped the crew of the *Nancy* might celebrate Christmas in England, but when Spain declared war on December 12th, he knew that Christmas at home was a lost dream.

The messenger handed over a package from the Admiralty addressed to Commander, *HMS Nancy,* together with a weighted sealed sack. William signed for the package and dated it 16 December 1804.

He studied the sealed package with its fouled anchor and couldn't help thinking that the symbol should be changed. If ever a symbol needed change, it must be the fouled anchor. After all, Britain ruled the waves, and a fouled anchor as a symbol of the Admiralty seemed totally out of place.

He slit open the package and quickly scanned the contents. His orders indicated he should sail forthwith for Cape Town and report to the Admiral in command of the Cape squadron. William picked up the large canvas bag, which contained the dispatches, and felt the weight of the sown-in shot. If they sighted an enemy vessel, and could not outrun her, and there was a risk of capture, the dispatch sack would go overboard. The weight of the shot would carry it quickly to the bottom. He placed the dispatch sack under his small bunk for safekeeping, and after refolding his orders, locked them in his desk drawer.

'Bosun!' yelled William, making his way from his small cabin to the poop deck. 'Make ready to weigh anchor! We sail within the hour.'

'Aye, Aye, Sir,' answered the Bosun, taking a final look at the English coastline.

Once clear of Falmouth, William set course southwest. He wished to take the *Nancy* out into the Atlantic to avoid other ships, French and British. If he met an English ship he might be required to heave to, or even be diverted from his current instructions. It would be difficult, if not impossible, for a mere Lieutenant to refuse to carry out a senior officer's instruction even if he did carry urgent dispatches from the Admiralty.

'Bosun, muster the crew aft.'

The Bosun grasped the small silver whistle that hung around his neck and blew the call to muster all on board.

The Bosun's Mate walked the main deck, his voice competing with the Bosun's call.

'All hands muster aft, lively there!'

The crew tumbled up from below, aware that the Bosun's Mate carried a small cane or starter, and would use it on the last man.

They assembled below the poop deck, their upturned faces waiting for their Captain to speak.

The dreariness of the sea, as each wave marched relentlessly towards the horizon, infected the mood of the men. Heavy clouds hid the warming rays of the sun. They were tired and cold after spending two days tacking back and forth to escape the Channel into the Atlantic. Some blew on their hands; others hugged themselves in an effort to keep warm. They swayed as one, countering the *Nancy's* movement, as she rolled in the Atlantic swell. The men were unhappy.

William paced the small deck until they were silent.

'Men, I thought I'd bring you into my confidence as to our destination.'

A ripple of whispers ran through the crew. Their mood changed to interest, as they waited for their Captain to speak again. Thirty pairs of eyes watched William in anticipation.

Not many officers would tell their crew their destination.

'The Admiralty felt a little sorry for us, stuck in the River Fal for three weeks, growing colder and colder.'

A few of the crew laughed.

'So, to make amends, they have ordered us to Cape Town in South Africa.'

A long silence ensued as they absorbed the news. Not many had sailed so far south. Their usual destination was the English Channel or the Bay of Biscay to beat back and forth, day after day, in cold damp weather. The Bosun raised his hand indicating that he wished to speak.

'Yes, Bosun, what is it?'

'Is it warm in South Africa, Sir?'

'Yes, I am pleased to tell you, it can be very warm.'

The Bosun nodded his head and smiled at the thought of some sun and heat. The crew saw his face and deduced South Africa would be a good destination. The cheering started.

'Men, I have one last thing to tell you,' shouted William over the cheering. 'We are now at war with Spain, as well as France, so we must keep a sharp lookout for any ships. We do not want to be taken by a Frog or a Dago, do we?'

'No!' yelled back the crew.

'Treat every sail as an enemy. Dismiss hands, if you please, Mr McCall.'

William drove the *Nancy* hard, knowing that the Cape squadron desperately needed the information he carried. Without knowing if war had broken out, any of the squadron meeting a Spanish warship could be fatal.

He took his little command well out into the Atlantic to avoid any encounter. After three days of good wind, he altered course south for the Cape.

Each time he heard the lookout's cry of 'Sail!' he altered course away, hoping the *Nancy* would not be followed. He would not come close to another ship for thirty-five days, until he closed on Cape Town.

William marked the noonday site on his chart and felt proud of his navigation. Although the Master, Mr. Hargrove, carried out the daily navigation activity, William took his own noonday sight and plotted the track of their voyage separately.

During the voyage he demanded all Petty Officers gain the respect of the men by example, rather than by fear. He also made it clear to the men that they did not have a choice but to obey any order given by the Petty Officers.

At the beginning of the voyage there were a few problems from the new hands. They argued or answered back to the Petty Officers but a day or so at the masthead, in freezing weather as they crossed the Bay of Biscay, fixed the problem. A landsman, seeing the ship roll and sway beneath him, soon came back in line. Seasickness was a far greater punishment to the uninitiated than a striped back, which only caused resentment and festered ongoing fear of the navy. He had heard it said—a flogging would spoil a good man and make a bad man worse.

The cold weather in the Channel became a memory as they voyaged towards the Equator. William used the time for daily gun practice and sail drill. He devised competitions between the watches to keep them busy. Most of the crew were *Belleisle* men, with a few new hands collected in Falmouth. He'd hoped to sign volunteers, but no able-bodied man would hang around a seaport to read notices. The fear of the press gangs made sure they were miles inland, well away from the smell of the ocean. Five of his original crew had run, but he managed to get nine hands from the local debtors prison. At least they would eat, and if they were careful and survived, they would earn some money, perhaps even enough to payout their debts on their return. In the meantime they were immune from prosecution. The constant training and the example set by the old hands soon integrated the crew into a well-oiled machine.

The crossing of the line allowed him to loosen discipline a little. The tradition of asking King Neptune and his wife, Amphitrite, to come aboard and proclaim the Pollywogs, or those members of the crew who had not crossed the Equator before, to be trusty shellbacks made for an eventful day and night.

Sitting on an upturned barrel, with his trident as his badge of office, King Neptune, who was the Bosun dressed in a rope skirt, wearing a wig made from unpicked ropes end, had the Pollywogs dragged before him. He ordered that each should be purified before crossing the Line by having his head shaved and the bald area greased. The greasing would make it easier for the Pollywog to slip over the Equator and not cause ripples in their Majesty's domain.

Midshipman Peter McCall, as Queen Amphitrite, dressed in a canvas dress adorned with short pieces of rope made to look like seaweed, was very generous in daubing each bare head with a liberal amount of grease. At the conclusion of each Pollywog becoming a Shellback he was hosed down with saltwater.

The relaxation of the day allowed the crew to see that even the Petty Officers and Midshipmen were human. One of the crew, having an artistic nature, drew up a fancy parchment for each of the new shellbacks. As Captain, William signed on behalf of Neptune and awarded each new shellback a tot of rum along with his certificate. The whole day was allocated to 'make and mend' and a double tot of rum for each hand capped the celebrations.

Late January 1805

Dawn broke over a cobalt-blue sea speckled with the occasional breaking wave. As the sunlight lit the ocean, the crew of the *Nancy* watched the dark mass on the horizon harden into Table Mountain.

Lieutenant King studied the mountain with its peak topped in white mist, the sun not yet hot enough to burn the cloud away. He remembered the quote in the Admiralty notices, attributed to Sir Francis Drake after he had sailed around the Cape in the *Golden Hind*: "This Cape is a most stately thing, and the fairest Cape in the whole circumference of the earth".

HMS Nancy drew closer to land, allowing William to focus

his telescope on Cape Town at the mountain's foot. He felt a sudden concern that the Spanish may have already landed, and perhaps captured this outpost of Empire.

'A beautiful sight, Sir.'

'Yes indeed, Mr McCall, a fine landmark for the navigator.'

'The clouds seem to roll down the mountain from the top like smoke. It isn't smoke, I suppose?'

'There is a legend my father told me, when I first went to sea, one of his many stories. The smoke effect of the cloud is supposed to be a Dutch man called Jan van Hunks. He retired from the sea to live on the mountain. He loved his pipe and spent all day smoking until one day a stranger asked him for a fill. They passed the time of day and decided to have a smoking competition. This lasted for some days but eventually van Hunks won. It turned out the stranger was the Devil. The legend is that the smoke you see rolling down the mountain is the two of them competing again. In reality it is the southeast wind in the summer which causes the clouds to roll down the slopes.'

'Ships at anchor in the bay, Sir,' yelled the lookout at the masthead.

'A man in the chains, if you please, Mr McCall, we don't want to run aground.'

'Land on the larboard bow,' came the voice from the masthead.

William refocused his telescope and realised it was Robben Island, the prison island.

The warm air pushed the *Nancy* into the Bay. As the sun climbed higher it became hot enough to melt the tar in the deck seams. The British flagship floated above a duplicate of itself in the clear blue water.

'Mr McCall, make the private signal and our number. She

must answer the private signal correctly. If she doesn't, we'll know she's been taken.'

William raised his glass once again and studied the anchored vessel as flags rose to the top of its halyard.

'Private signal answered correctly, Sir.'

'Thank you, Mr McCall, standby for the salute.'

HMS Nancy eased her way into the safety of the harbour with her ensign and number flying from her masthead. William was not taking any chances-- not in a French-built schooner entering the harbour of an English base.

The *Nancy* slowly approached the anchorage near the flagship. When he was satisfied William waved his hand and shouted 'Let go'. The splash of the anchor brought them to the end of their long voyage. The sails dropped smartly. All eyes would be on the new arrival, and the crew knew it.

'The flagship's signalled, Sir. Captain to repair on board immediately.'

'Thank you, Mr McCall, make the boat ready if you please, and Peter, while I'm away arrange for a water boat and fresh fruit and vegetables. I doubt we'll be allowed to stay any longer than necessary.'

'Aye, Sir.'

William quickly changed, and climbed down into the *Nancy's* small boat to the sound of the single bosun's pipe. The boat left the shelter of the *Nancy* as soon as he had settled in the stern. Although it was still morning, William could feel the heat of the sun through his thick, English designed, uniform. The only breeze was self-generated as the *Nancy's* boat moved through the water. Sweat gathered beneath his hat. He could feel it as it started to run down the side of his face. He envied his boat's crew in their loose fitting clothes as they effortlessly rowed towards the flagship. The oily calm water reflected the cloudless sky.

His boat glided in to the relative coolness of the shadow cast by the flagship. The heavy dispatch bag between his feet was a reminder that he didn't want anything to happen to it in the last few minutes in his charge.

'Hold water starboard, oars up larboard,' commanded the coxswain and the *Nancy's* boat came to a halt beneath the towering wooden wall of the flagship.

William stood in the boat and judged the timing of his step to the bottom rung of the Jacob's ladder. With the dispatch bag slung over his left shoulder he slowly climbed the swaying ladder. Eventually he came to the entry port.

He stepped through the port to the sound of the Bosun's call and doffed his hat in respect to the flag. Even though he was only a lieutenant, as a commander of one of His Majesty's ships he was entitled to due honour.

A middle-aged, immaculately dressed, Flag Lieutenant doffed his hat in reply.

'Lieutenant Spring, Sir, Admiral Popham's Flag. May I take the dispatches? Mr Dignan, one of our midshipman will show you to the wardroom.'

William turned to Midshipman Dignan and nodded his thanks. The midshipman looked about thirteen. His face was tanned from the tropical sun and he was obviously uncomfortable in his uniform under the hot sun. His family must have influence, thought William, to be so young on a flagship. . The Flag Lieutenant accepted the canvas bag and hurried off to open it in front of Vice Admiral Home Popham.

William was aware of Admiral Popham as the man who

devised the Royal Navy signal system of flags the previous year. He was a man who would not suffer fools. His reputation as a fighter was well known having fought against the French and the Americans and had then taken the Royal Navy to court after they seized his trading vessel.

'Will you follow me, Sir?' asked the young midshipman. 'I will conduct you to the wardroom for refreshments.'

'Thank you.'

William knew that it could be a long wait while the Admiral read the various dispatches.

Below deck the open wardroom windows allowed a gentle breeze to waft through the cabin. The glass of cool white wine and the breeze soon took its toll. William slept.

'Sir, Sir, the Admiral wishes you to join him,' said a young voice, as a hand gently shook his shoulder.

Jolted awake, William pulled out his watch. He had been asleep for an hour and a half. 'Why didn't you wake me?'

'No point, Sir. You were tired and there was nothing else for you to do until the Admiral wanted to speak to you.'

The Midshipman and smiled, at least this officer could think for himself thought William.

'You'll go far young man.'

'Thank you, Sir, please follow me.'

William climbed to the quarterdeck to see the Admiral sitting at a small desk in the shade of a large piece of sail rigged above the stern of the flagship.

The wooden deck, stretching forward from the Admiral's desk, was sun bleached white and without blemish. It was obvious that the liberal use of salt water and holly stones, by the ship's crew, was a daily event. The only colour, apart from the dark blue uniform of the Flag Lieutenant, was that of the armed scarlet clad marine at attention. His normal position would be outside the Admiral's cabin, but as the Admiral was working on deck, he stood just under the shade of the canvas screen.

The flag lieutenant greeted William and accompanied him to the Admiral. The Flag Lieutenant saluted and stepped to one side. William halted in front of the Admiral and saluted.

The Admiral had removed his wig and placed it at the end of the table, where it sat like a large grey-haired cat. He leaned back allowing his frock coat to fall open for coolness. He was forty-two years old and was starting to lose his hair. He had a pleasant face, and although his hair was turning grey, his eyebrows remained black making his face appear younger than his years. The smile he gave William carried to his dark eyes.

The interview, as William expected, was straight to the point.

'You are aware, Lieutenant, that we are at war with Spain?'

'Yes, Sir, it happened just before we sailed.'

'Sight many other vessels?'

'No, Sir, we avoided all contact as soon as we sighted a sail. My orders were to deliver the dispatches as fast as possible.'

The Admiral grunted as he flicked through the papers on his desk.

'I will have replies for you tomorrow,' said the Admiral, 'and I'll expect you to sail for England as soon as they're on board. What do you require in the way of provisions?'

'I need water and fresh vegetables, and to replenish my powder.'

'I thought you didn't meet any other vessel.'

'I didn't, Sir, but I have used some on practice. I wanted my crew to experience as close as possible a live situation.'

'Ahem. See to it, Flag.'

'Aye, Aye, Sir.'

'I want the *Nancy* out of here by the 22nd.'

'Yes, Sir.'

'Thank you, Lieutenant, you may go.'

On his return to the *Nancy*, William ordered the ship's boat crew to row him around the ship so he could see how she sat in the water.

If he stowed some stores aft, the *Nancy* would sail closer to the wind and travel faster.

Before dawn next day William and Midshipman McCall organised the crew for the loading of fresh water, fruit and vegetables.

He went ashore to make certain of the quality of the fresh produce that was to be supplied. He did not want rotten or overripe fruit. It wasn't unusual for quartermasters to fob off second grade stores on a young commander.

He watched the water barge make its way from the shore and amused himself as he compared it to a water beetle, the oars replacing the beetle's legs. The *Nancy's* water barrels had been cleaned and were now ready to accept the sweet fresh water. He even managed to scrounge a few barrels of beer for the crew.

Periodically William had the boat crew row him around the ship to make sure the *Nancy* sat correctly to her anchor.

Mid-morning on the 22nd January, the final supplies of vegetables were loaded and the Admiral's dispatches signed into William's care. The Flag Lieutenant's boat cast free of the *Nancy*, which released William to order the anchor hove short and the sail made ready for sea.

'Anchor's aweigh!' came the cry from for'd as *HMS Nancy* sprang into life, now free of the land.

'Lay a course to round the headland, Mr Hargrove, and then steer nor'–nor'–west.'

'Nor'–nor'–west after we've rounded the headland. Aye, Aye, Sir.'

The *Nancy* heeled over with the wind on her larboard bow. William allowed his legs to bend just a little to compensate for the list of her deck.

The bright blue sky was sharp and clear, as if freshly painted. The sun beat down to suck what moisture it could from the bodies of the *Nancy's* crew.

'Call me when you are ready to alter course to round the headland, Mr McCall. I am going below to get out of this uniform. Feel free to dress down on your next watch.'

'Aye, Sir,' smiled Midshipman McCall.

They were headed back to England. The days passed in a routine of watches between William, the Midshipman and the Master. William and the Bosun inspected the vessel from stem to stern. They checked the stores and made sure the *Nancy* was trimmed to her Captain's satisfaction. Barrels of meat and water were shifted, which altered the trim a few inches. William even had some barrels re-stowed to the lee side when he set her on a course for some days. The wind blew from the South-West day after day so the miles slipped below the *Nancy's* keel.

They re-crossed the line again, without ceremony this time, King Neptune having been acknowledged on the outward voyage.

As the strange craft became easier to see, William could make out her rigging and the dirty condition of her hull. He thought he could see weed clinging to the hull, but as he refocused his glass, he realised the hull was painted dark green under the dirt. A cold chill ran down his spine as he pointed his glass to the masts and saw that the lower part was a buff colour, whereas the upper part was white.

A dark green hull to allow the vessel to hide in tropical rivers and the top of her mast painted to match the sky. Most expected the topmasts would be blue to match the sky. Frequent rain in the tropics meant the sky would be broken with white clouds. The topmast painted white blended in to the clouds. A slaver!

'By the look of her, she is not a navy ship,' commented the Bosun. 'The muck all down her sides tells me she's not navy. Could be a Dago.'

'I think you may be right, Bosun,' said Lieutenant William as he closed the glass with a snap. 'Distribute small arms but don't let them be seen. I think she is a slaver.'

'A slaver, Sir?'

'Aye, and we're about to put a stop to her dirty traffic.'

The crew filed past the arms box under the wheel to take their pick of cutlasses, swords and bludgeons. Each man picked his weapon and swung it in anticipation.

'Keep those men quiet and make them keep the weapons out of sight. I don't want to scare her'.

The Bosun touched his knuckle to his forehead. 'Sir.'

The stranger was not more than half a mile away when Midshipman McCall shouted in alarm.

'They're throwing things overboard.'

William lifted his glass and checked the items that floated in the water. They were alive!

'She is a slaver! By God, I'm right. If we'd been down wind of her, we'd have smelled her hours ago. I've smelled slavers in the past. The stink sits in one's nose for days.'

'He's throwing the slaves overboard, Sir,' cried the young Midshipman.

'Bosun, put a shot across her bow and signal her to heave to.'

'Sutton,' cried the Bosun to their best gunner, ' a shot across her bow.'

Sutton positioned the gun carefully and sighted along the barrel. The weather was relatively calm and he did not need to make too much of an allowance for the state of the sea. He satisfied himself, stood and pulled the firing cord. The sound of a loud cough, rather than a bang, carried across the water. He'd used one of the four-pounders, more for image than effect.

They all watched as the ball splashed about a hundred yards ahead of the slaver.

'He knows we're here now. Run out the guns and show our colours.'

- CHAPTER THREE -

The Slaver

Atlantic Ocean, February 1805

Midshipman McCall tugged on the flag halyard and released the colours.

William studied the vessel and watched the crew running around in panic. They could not mistake the *Nancy's* intentions now that she had shown her teeth. Slowly the flag of Spain rose to the slaver's masthead.

William conned the *Nancy* closer and closer to the Spaniard. The stench from the slaver was oppressive. They were still throwing slaves overboard. The Spaniard, in an effort to gain more speed, was willing to jettison even his cargo of slaves.

'Mr McCall, take the smaller of the two ship's boats and see if you can pick up some of the people in the water. Make sure you and your crew are armed and don't forget that those people do not speak English, but don't allow any of them to gain the upper hand.'

'Bosun, four armed men to the ship's boat,' shouted the young midshipman.

William's stomach gave a sickening lurch as he contemplated anyone who would steal people from their homes and sell them in a foreign land, like cattle at a market.

To trade in slaves was legal in England, but William knew of a strong movement, led by William Wilberforce, to have slavery outlawed. He had read with interest some of the speeches made by Wilberforce, a Member of Parliament representing Hull in Yorkshire.

As more slaves were thrown overboard, he remembered John Newton. Like many in Liverpool, William knew of Newton, the ex-captain of a slave ship who converted to Christianity and turned from poacher to gamekeeper by advocating the end of the slave trade.

The influence of John Newton and others managed to persuade Wilberforce to lead their anti-slavery group in Parliament. In the past eighteen years Wilberforce had become famous as the public leader for the anti-slavery movement. William wished the advocates of slavery were here now to see the result of their desire for profit.

'Heave to, damn you,' shouted William as he came within a few yards of the slaver. ' Anyone speak Spanish?' he asked of his crew. More than one language amongst the older hands was common in the Navy. Perhaps not the sort of language one would use in polite society, but at least he could make himself understood to a slaver.

'I think they understood what we wanted when we ran our guns out, Sir,' commented the Master.

'I think you're right, Mr Hargrove. He's at least taking in his sails. The stink is unbelievable. Bosun, lower a boat and I'll go across and speak to her Captain. Ten fully armed, experienced men are to come with me.'

'Mr Hargrove, you are in command until my return, and if the Spaniard tries anything, blow him out of the water and we will take our chances. He must not be allowed to escape.'

William and his men dropped from the deck of the *Nancy* in to the larger of the ship's boat.

'Shove off!' called William as the last man scrambled aboard. 'Oars out, pick up the stroke.' He pushed the tiller down and headed towards the Spaniard a short distance away.

The *Nancy's* boat skimmed across the short distance to the Spaniard. William, followed by nine of his men, boarded the slaver. One crewmember had been left to secure the boat.

'Round everyone up and make sure that any slaves are secure. I don't want them to be able to attack us because they think we are Dagos.'

A tall thin man, dark-haired, dressed in a creased uniform jacket and a pair of dirty white duck trousers, stepped forward. In halting English he demanded why they, a friendly power, had fired on a Spanish vessel.

'Where have you been, Captain? What is your cargo?'

'I loaded slaves from Benin for His Catholic Majesty's possessions in Cuba. It is a legal trade and you have no right to stop me.'

'It is a legal trade, Captain, even in my country, and slaves are classed as cargo according to both your country and mine. Your vessel is now my prize.'

'Prize? What do you mean, prize? You are a pirate stopping an innocent vessel on the high seas and boarding her. I will complain to the Spanish Government when I return.'

'When were you last in Spain, Captain?'

'November last year, why?' the last word said very quietly. It was as if the Captain already knew the answer to his question.

'I regret to inform you, Captain, that Spain declared war on England in early December. This ship and her cargo are now my prize!'

'But, Captain, this is all I have. This ship is all that my family has. If you take my ship, my family will starve.' Tears began to roll down his cheeks.

Johnson, the senior hand of *Nancy's* crew, knuckled his forehead. 'Crew secure, Sir. Fifteen mustered on deck and we've used their own swivel gun to guard them. They fixed the swivel gun to guard against a slave breakout from the hold, now they can sit and watch it.' His gap-toothed grin brought a smile to William's face.

'Put the Captain with the crew. I'll go below to see what I can find.'

Johnson grabbed the Spanish Captain by the arm and pushed him towards his crew at the base of the mast.

The humidity, heavy with the smell of humanity and filth, greeted William as he made his way below. He tried to breathe lightly so as not to suck in too much of the fetid air. The Captain's cabin was small and it did not take long for him to go through the few papers, and to investigate the chart. If the marks on the chart were correct, it appeared that the Captain had told the truth. William didn't have a reason to disbelieve the chart; the Captain hadn't had time to produce a dummy one, even if he'd wished to hide anything.

William understood enough Spanish to read the ship's manifest, which informed him that the Spaniard had bought two hundred and twelve slaves. They were a mixture of men, boys, and a few girls. The girls would be for house servants and the men and boys for fieldwork. He glanced up as he heard the low moans of the slaves locked in the hold.

There was nothing more of interest in the papers. Closing the door of the cabin behind him, he stepped into the entrance area and noted that there were three doors. One was a weather door leading to the deck, the second was the door he had just closed and the third was a door to a second cabin.

He opened the door to the second cabin as Johnson shouted down that the boat had picked up just one survivor from the water. Sharks following the slaver had made short work of the remainder. William turned his body to hear Johnson so only his left shoulder and side had entered the second cabin when it happened. He sensed he was not alone. He began to turn when he caught sight of something. The flash of light was all he saw before the knife sliced across his left cheek and down his body. The pain in his shoulder felt like he'd been stabbed with a hot iron. The knife glanced off his collarbone and opened the flesh on the upper left side of his chest. His right hand grabbed the attacker's wrist as it drew back for a second strike. The wrist was small like a child's, the black fingers bloody where they gripped the sharp edges of a large piece of glass.

William fell into the cabin against a spitting screaming woman still attempting to bite and stab him. He forced her back with his right elbow under her chin and twisted the hand in which she held the weapon. The cabin was too small for him to use his sword so he had to grapple with her hand to hand. He brought up his left arm and hit her across the face. The woman screamed and fell to the deck. Blood ran down his face and his chest throbbed with pain. Still gripping her blood-covered weapon, the woman began to rise. William kicked her in the stomach; the woman's attack forfeited her right for him to act in a chivalrous manner. She gave a great gasp and opened her fingers, allowing the glass dagger to drop to the deck, where it broke into three pieces. William stepped on all three to make sure they could not be used again. The broken window over the small bunk told him how his attacker had obtained her weapon.

Blood dripped down his arm as he leaned against the bulkhead to get his breath back.

'Are you alright, Sir?' cried Johnson as he rushed into the small cabin. He saw the woman on the deck curled into a ball.

'Thank you, yes,' whispered William. The pain throbbed across his face and shoulder. 'If you hadn't called out to me when you did, she would have stuck her glass weapon in my eyes.'

William looked down at his assailant and saw she was naked and black. 'Now I know why they didn't heave to when we fired. The captain was too busy to give the order. He was trying to rape one of the slaves! Take her up top and be careful, she is a vixen.'

'Aye, Aye, Sir. You should get your shoulder and face attended to. She's cut you badly. In this climate it doesn't take much for an infected wound to kill a man.'

'Thank you for your advice. I will bear it in mind.'

On deck, William stripped off his shirt and inspected his wound as best he could. They were clean cuts, but the shoulder wound burned in the hot sun.

'Johnson, see if you can find some clean cloth to bind this. I think I saw some clean clothes in the Captain's quarters. Use them if you have to.'

William leaned on the taffrail and called the Spanish Captain to him. With his dark sunburnt skin, and blood running down his shoulder, William was a man who would not deal in niceties.

'Captain, tell me about the slave in your cabin.'

'I refuse to speak to a pirate.'

'Be careful, Captain, pirates hang their prisoners, as do the English navy for anyone who rapes a woman.'

'She is not a woman! She is a slave!'

'She is a woman. She was your prisoner and you took advantage of your power.'

'It happens all the time. We must have some distraction on such a long voyage. All those in the African trade take a woman to help pass the time.'

'So now you admit she is a woman.'

'No, no, you misunderstood me,' cried the Spanish Captain, who feared a trick.

'And the slaves you threw overboard when you realised my ship was near?'

'They were dead, and we cannot do anything but put them over the side.'

'I saw them in the water. They were not dead! You put live men in the water knowing they would drown or be attacked by the sharks that have followed you for days.'

'No, no, Senor, they were dead! I swear they were all dead!'

'Then a miracle has occurred, Captain. My ship's boat has just picked up one of your dead slaves very much alive. You threw them overboard to lighten this ship in an effort to get away from us.'

The captain fell to his knees and clawed at William to implore 'the gallant English Captain' not to hang him, but to treat him as a prisoner. As a Spanish gentleman and an officer, he would offer his word not to try and escape.

William leaned forward with his hand across his face in an effort to stop his cheek from bleeding. Some of the blood dripped on the Spanish Captain.

'You disgust me!' shouted William and shoved the Spaniard away with the sole of his shoe.

The Spanish Captain fell on his back and cursed William and all his family, the speech so fast that William only managed to grasp the outline of the curses.

Midshipman McCall's boat pulled to the slaver. McCall climbed aboard accompanied by his three crewmen and the rescued slave.

Johnson, with white linen from the Captain's cabin, gently wiped William's wound and tied clean strips around his Captain's shoulder and chest. He made sure the strips were tight enough to hold a wad of linen in place over the long open wound.

'Thank you, Johnson, that feels good. Please help me on with my shirt.'

'Your orders, Sir,' said McCall, saluting.

'Midshipman McCall! Take that excuse for a man,' pointing at the still cursing Spanish Captain, 'and put him in irons on the *Nancy*. I want him and his officers to experience what it is like to be locked away on a small ship at sea.'

The Midshipman seized the Spaniard and dragged him to his feet.

'Johnson, you are now acting petty officer. Check the hold and be careful of the slaves. I want to know how many slaves, and how much water and food there is on this scow. Search the rest of the vessel for arms and anyone else who may be in hiding. Do we have a helmsman amongst us?'

'Yes, Sir, Jones the Welsh.'

'Put him on the wheel and steer nor'- nor'- west, and tell Mr Hargrove on the *Nancy* to do the same.' His voice faded as his head spun and he felt himself falling into a black hole as he collapsed on the deck.

William was delirious with fever. Wild dreams filled every hour of his existence. His body passed from freezing cold to tropical heat. He felt gentle hands sponge him as he sweated and battled with his demons.

Eventually his mind cleared and the wild dreams stopped. He felt his head being held as someone spoon-fed him some broth. It tasted good and it warmed him.

'How do you feel, Captain?'

'What's happened? Where am I?'

'Don't fret, Captain. This is Hargrove, the Master'

'The slaves?'

'Don't worry, Sir, all is in hand. Mr McCall is in charge of the slaver and is doing a good job. She is still near us, but we have lost some more slaves. With the number thrown overboard by the Dago, Captain, plus the twelve who died since we captured her, I estimate we have about one hundred and thirty left, if the manifest was correct.'

'How long have I been here?'

'Three days, Sir. You collapsed on the slaver and we brought you back to the *Nancy*. We bled you to bring down the fever and we have fixed the wound on your face. I am afraid you will have a jagged scar, but perhaps the ladies will find it attractive. We had to dig a little for some glass in the shoulder wound. I think we have most of it out but it wasn't a clean cut. We poured in rum to clean the wound. It looked feverish, so we used maggots to clean out the shoulder wound, because we feared gangrene. The area around it is still hot to touch and puffy.'

'Help me up.'

'I would not suggest that, Sir. You are weak and you may tear the stitches. I did my best, but I am not a sail maker.'

'Help me up, damn your eyes!'

The Master placed his arms under William's good arm and heaved him up to a sitting position. William allowed his legs to fall over the side of the bunk and pushed himself upright. His legs gave way as he placed weight on them. Only because Hargrove held him was he saved from falling to the deck.

'I appear to be too weak to walk, Mr Hargrove. You were right and I am sorry for my abuse.'

'We have passed Gibraltar, Sir, and I thought we may have called in to put you ashore, but Mr McCall said we should try for England, and that you would wish us to keep you onboard.'

'He did right. I stay with my ship. Perhaps in England they may be able to fix the wound.'

'Lay back, Sir, and let me change the bandages and then I will give you something to help you sleep.'

'Change the dressing, and then I want to speak to Mr McCall.'

―∞―

Midshipman McCall sat in the only chair in the Captain's cabin and brought his Captain up-to-date on what had happened since the capture of the Spanish slaver. The two ships had sailed in convoy, Hargrove and Johnson taking turns in command of the Spanish vessel. McCall ordered the prize crew to be changed frequently as the smell from the confined quarters of the slaves caused friction amongst the *Nancy's* crew.

The Spanish crew had been used to clean out the human waste from the hold of the slaver. The process was part punishment for the Spanish sailors, but mostly to keep them busy, and to not allow them time to plot and try to recapture the ship.

The slaves were allowed on deck in small numbers, and the sea-pump rigged to wash them down in an effort to keep them clean. There were two deaths amongst the Spanish crew. The slaves caught and killed them before the *Nancy's* crew could come to their aid. Because of the low number of guards, every eventuality had to be planned. The Spanish Captain and Master were still in irons on the *Nancy*.

'It appears, Mr McCall, you have done very well, and I have little to worry about.' William smiled and then winced as the movement pulled at the wound in his cheek.

'I could not have done it without the full support of the Master, and crew, Sir. We have been fortunate. The weather has been kind to us as well, but we are now close to the cooler latitudes and have the Bay of Biscay to contend with, in the next few days.'

'I will note all you have told me, together with my praise, in my report to the Admiral. We must get to England.' He fell back into his bunk and closed his eyes. He felt exhausted. The strain of talking had been too much.

- CHAPTER FOUR -

Proposal

June 1804

A few days after William left for London, his father, George, decided to visit his club, the *Athenaeum*, a short carriage ride from his home. He wished to consider his company's future without his son's involvement.

The club was relatively new, having been built in 1799. He made his way to the reading room, nodding at some other members reading the local newspaper or the days-old London papers. He made his way to his favourite dark-green wing-backed leather armchair. It was near the window and from it he could watch the traffic along Hanover Street. A waiter silently approached, eyebrows raised.

'Brandy,' whispered George.

Within minutes the waiter had placed a balloon glass of brandy on the small table alongside George's chair.

George swirled the bowl gently, allowing his hands to warm its contents before he sipped.

Should he send the *Margaret Rose* back to the Mediterranean and risk losing her to French attacks, or leave her on the Irish run for safety's sake? The Irish run was not as profitable as it used to be, thanks to other ship owners following his example.

He sipped his drink again and watched the people in the street below as they hurried about their business.

A small movement at the periphery of his vision made him conscious that someone had sat in the chair near his own.

He recognised the man by a sudden snort. A person only had to hear that sound once to remember it forever. The stranger made a habit of blowing sharp bursts of air down his nostrils.

'Morning, King,' whispered the man, and snorted again.

'Morning, Nicholson,' replied George in the same low whisper.

'Would appreciate some of your time.'

'Now?'

'If it is convenient,' replied Nicholson, snorting again.

If Donald Nicholson, or should he call him Alderman Nicholson, wanted to talk to him, George had best be on guard.

George waved his hand for the waiter to replenish his glass, and held his own glass towards Donald Nicholson in an unspoken offer of the same.

Alderman Donald Nicholson was a legend in Liverpool. He had started with a few pounds, and through trading sugar, built that small sum into over five hundred pounds. In addition to his good fortune in trading, Donald Nicholson, or lucky Nicholson, as he was called behind his back, had won twenty thousand pounds in a lottery. He had used his winnings to set himself up in business. He had married well, became involved in the African trade and made a fortune. To crown his business success, he had been voted on to the Liverpool Council.

Nicholson and a few other slave traders, along with some

abolitionists, had founded the Athenaeum Club. It was strange, but William Roscoe and James Currie, who hated the African Trade, were also founder members. It was odd how the personal requirements of the members for a club such as the Athenaeum overcame their likes or dislikes of the African trade.

George accepted a fresh glass of brandy from the waiter and indicated that another was required for the Alderman.

'I understand your son has gone and joined the Navy.'

'News travels.'

'I also understand the *Margaret Rose* isn't making money.'

George kept his face blank and looked at Nicholson. Who let that piece of information out onto the streets?

'What makes you think that, Donald?'

'I'll be honest, George.'

George did his best to keep a smile off his face. The idea of Donald Nicholson being honest was a joke in itself.

'I pay a lot of people a lot of money to keep me informed of bits and pieces, which by themselves may be trivial, but when mixed with other pieces of information can be of great value to me.'

'Are you telling me someone in my company has accepted bribes?' demanded George, his voice rising. The last snort had got on his nerves.

'George, George,' said Donald, in a low whisper, and held a hand up in submission. 'No, no, George, you have me wrong. I haven't bribed anyone, but people talk. They talk in taverns, and at the docks while they work the ships. I have a number of sources, but none of them are your people.'

The explanation sounded logical to George, but he also knew there was little chance of him ever finding out if anyone did accept bribes. For the sake of peace he would allow himself to believe Nicholson.

'Now you have this information, what do you intend to do with it?'

'Nothing, George, but I do have a proposition for you. By the way would you like to be proposed for the committee? We are always on the lookout for new blood, people with new ideas.'

'I am very flattered, Donald. May I think it over?'

'Of course, my dear fellow, of course.'

'You spoke of a proposition.'

'The *Margaret Rose* is still in Liverpool?' a snort emphasised the point.

'Yes, she arrived from Ireland a couple of days ago.'

'Very fortunate I met you today. I had planned to go to your office tomorrow, but I think this is a more pleasant environment than any office, be it yours or mine.'

George remained silent and waited for Nicholson to carry on.

'You know I have been involved in the African trade for some years. I did have a ship lined up for my next venture to Africa, but she is late and I am not sure when she will arrive. Perhaps the French have taken her, who knows. I don't wish to wait any longer. As you have the *Margaret Rose,* do you wish to join me as a partner?'

'What would be required of the *Margaret Rose?*'

'I can rely on your confidentiality, of course, George.' Snort. 'We do not want this to get about too much, not until after our ship has sailed. Then it will not matter. I intend a run on the African trade. I have many of the sale goods already in a warehouse near Canning dock, and a First Mate who has much experience of the trade, along with knowledge of the various loading areas in West Africa. He is also aware of the type of African required in the West Indies. Would it interest you to change the Irish trade for the African trade, George?' asked Nicholson, with a smile on his face—slightly disfigured by a snort for good measure.

George sipped his brandy.

He was losing money on the Irish trade. Few people failed on the African trade, and he knew that Donald Nicholson had made a fortune shipping slaves to the West Indies. George could not find any negatives in the proposal, plus he may end up on the Club committee if things went well. Nicholson had a First Mate to replace William and would also contribute to the cost of chartering the *Margaret Rose,* as well as sharing the profits.

His decision made, George held out his hand. 'King and Son will be happy to do business with you,'

Nicholson smiled and gripped George's hand to settle the arrangement.

'Excellent, excellent, come around to my home at the end of the week to discuss the details. This place has too many ears and eyes for my liking.' His comment ended with a final snort.

- CHAPTER FIVE -

Liverpool

Liverpool, December 1805

Donald Nicholson, his wife Sarah, son Henry, and daughter Charlotte, sat wrapped in their cloaks in the carriage. The two women also shared a rug that had been packed around their knees when they left their home on Rodney Street. It was a cold December night, two weeks before Christmas.

'I trust Mother dear, you will make an effort to enjoy yourself,' said the younger of the two women.

'Charlotte, my manners and upbringing would not allow me to show any displeasure as a guest in someone's home, and I am surprised you would even comment on such a matter.'

'Please Mother, don't get upset. I just want us both to have a pleasant evening at Mr King's. I believe he always has a very nice table.'

'Nice table, indeed! He has his eye on you, and him old enough to be your father. I do not know what the world is coming to. In my day——'

'Yes, Mother,' interjected Charlotte, 'in your day you worked long hours to help father build the company, I know. You have mentioned the fact a number of times before. But I like Mr King, and he is rich enough to take a wife.'

'A wife,' snapped Charlotte's mother. 'It is not a lady's position to consider marriage without first being asked by the gentleman.'

'Mr King works hard, and since his son disappeared into the navy he is lost.'

'I suppose you will find him? I do not know what you find wrong with the young men of Liverpool. It is not as if you do not have a large choice of suitors. There has been plenty of young men from good families presenting their cards, and asking us to family dinners.'

'I know, Mother, but now I find the young men a little crass. I like a mature man who knows how to treat a lady.'

'Treat a lady, indeed. What exactly do you mean by that? Remember, young lady, you are only eighteen, and you still need your father's permission to marry anybody, especially an old man like Mr King.'

Donald sighed as he felt that he was about to be drawn into the conversation between his wife and his daughter. He closed his eyes and thought of his daughter. She was a very attractive young woman with clear skin, bright eyes and long dark hair that was teased into curls. Many a young man had come to call, but he had made sure most of them realised they were not fully welcome. He'd always believed that if your only daughter was to marry, it should have the result of furthering the company, and the family. One should not waste such an asset on just any man, especially one with poor prospects or limited contacts.

He extracted a long black cheroot from his cigar –case, clamped one end between his teeth and lit the other. Closing his eyes once again, he tried to ignore the chatter of the women.

George King and the ventures they'd handled together in the past year or so had been profitable with little risk. Most of the ships they'd used were chartered, which allowed great savings and afforded them peace of mind.

The three vessels Donald did own gave a very good return, particularly the *Liverpool Lass* captained by his son, Henry.

Donald opened his eyes and studied Henry. At twenty-five, and Master of the *Lass,* he was known for his strict discipline. He was a big man, well over six feet tall, with a shock of coal-black hair. Regardless of what he did to his hair, it always grew like wild grass. Due to a large flat area across the bridge of his nose, his eyes appeared to be much wider apart than normal.

The flat area had been caused by an accident some years earlier on the *Liverpool Lass*. Donald had then been Captain of the *Lass*. While in a storm, a block fell from the rigging and struck Henry, who was first mate, across the bridge of his nose. The power of the blow had forced the soft bone into Henry's skull. Donald had patched up his son's smashed face and eased the broken nose bones out from the skull. At the time he was frightened because he knew that if he made a mistake, the boy could die. The wild motions of the vessel, due to the storm, did not make it easy to retract the bone. In desperation, Donald decided it would be best if he closed the broken skin and secured the damaged bone. He had worked under the most difficult of circumstances, and had done his best. The result was a larger than normal spread of skin between Henry's eyes. The accident also left him with a deep growl of a voice, which sounded as if it came from his nose rather than his mouth. The economic use of his lips in his speech enhanced the impression that he spoke through his nose. Then there were his other unusual features: his black hair was set off by very fair skin, which, in the tropics, bore an abundance of small brown freckles. At a certain distance it appeared that Henry had some form of disease, similar to smallpox.

While some may have interpreted his son's odd face as a sign that Henry was simple, however, they soon realised their mistake. Henry was not averse to taking his fists, or a knife; to any person he felt insulted him.

Donald watched Henry through curls of smoke. He knew that his son was never happier than when he was on the deck of the *Liverpool Lass*. His face didn't matter to his crew, especially as a number bore the scars caused by similar accidents at sea.

By Henry's acceptance of the invitation to dine with George King, Donald knew the two would become better acquainted. He was aware that Henry harboured a concern that George may be a threat to his own future, when his father retired.

Donald Nicholson smiled. A little fear of the future might keep Henry in line.

The prattle of the women was beginning to get on Henry's nerves and he considered calling the evening off. He should return to the city for a night with friends in the local brothels. His face lightened as he thought of the pleasure he'd recently sampled with the new Irish girl at the Hill Street Gentleman's Club near Toxteth Park.

He was fortunate to live in such times. The mills of Manchester attracted many young Irish women, as there was little work in Ireland. The women had heard that Manchester mills paid over seven shillings a week, and they thought that if they could just reach Manchester, all their worries would be over.

Ironically many of the girls with whom he dallied arrived from Ireland on the *Margaret Rose,* which belonged to George. If only George knew, thought Henry, and made a mental note to thank him for all of the pleasures he had unwittingly supplied.

The coach rocked him gently as his mind drifted.

The cost of advertising in Ireland, to encourage the girls to come to England, was cheap. They arrived in Liverpool not realising Manchester was a further thirty miles inland. They had little money, so with subtlety and some cunning, the proprietors of the Hill Street Gentleman's Club would offer the girls work in the Club. They were told it was a temporary position, just to help out until they saved enough for the remainder of their journey. Of course many never saved enough after they'd paid the Club for a bed and food.

After a few weeks these unfortunates would be given notice to leave. Their bed was required for new girls. Henry knew that many would do anything rather than be stranded in the street. This is when they became playthings for Henry and his friends.

His investment in funding the Club was one of his better ideas. As the major shareholder, he had nothing to do with the management of the Club. He simply wanted a return on his money and a regular supply of new girls whenever he visited Liverpool.

Some of the girls were frightened of his face, and he often chose those who appeared the most frightened to enhance the evening's pleasure.

A simple arrangement with staff in the club saved him a lot of trouble. If the staff thought one of the girls would stand a little pain, she would be given a small bouquet of flowers to pin to her dress. Henry had suffered inconvenience in the past when taking girls to bed, only to find they did not like pain and screamed their heads off. He found a sharp slap would calm many of them, but on one occasion he had slapped too hard. She had fallen and broken her neck. He gave out a long sigh as he remembered how expensive that evening had become. The staff at the club managed to get rid of the girl. Henry didn't care how they did it, as long as he didn't become involved. The river was an easy place to lose a body.

'A long sigh, Henry,' said his mother.

'I am bored and wish I'd never agreed to attend the dinner.'

'Not long now,' she said, and tapped his knee in affection.

Henry lapsed into silence. It appeared more and more gentlemen leaned towards the supply of strong discipline. There were many who liked a little punishment from a lady, whether she wielded a cane or a ropes end. It didn't bother him as long as they paid.

Strange desires meant high prices for the user and more profit for the supplier. The potential brought a smile to his face.

Donald Nicholson watched the scene between his wife and his son. He thought about his son's smile and would have liked to know what he was thinking.

Even though he was Henry's father, he had to admit Henry could be cruel. He had heard tales of the 'houses' visited by Henry, and the monetary cost when things went wrong. He remembered when eighteen-year-old Henry sailed as his First Mate to Africa. He could not fault the running of the ship, but he had seen his son's cruelty first hand. Henry made sure that at all costs the profits returned to Liverpool and the Nicholson family. Lord Nelson had scanned the horizon with his blind eye, so too did Donald turn a blind eye at his son's Trade activities.

Donald knew that Henry's methods on the African coast were close to being illegal. Henry always packed a few more slaves than was allowed to offset the losses during the Middle Passage. The first time any slave caused trouble, Henry would make an example of the troublemaker, along with those slaves shackled on either side. The use of the whip soon brought the remaining slaves to submission.

The slaves were simply deemed to be cargo. Donald insured them against drowning. If a slave died from old age or sickness, the insurance company would not pay any compensation, but if the slave drowned, the insurance company would pay out on the value of the slave. In Africa the basic cost of a slave was twenty-five pounds – equivalent to the cost of a specific amount of chintz material, flint, shot, gunpowder, muskets, beads and brandy. For twenty-five pounds one expected to buy a healthy full-grown male. The cost of a female or youth dropped in proportion to the overall value of a healthy male. The sale price of the male slave in the Caribbean was sixty pounds, or almost two years' wages for the average English workingman. Donald, like other slavers, considered insurance companies to be thieves. They would only pay out the cost of the goods, not the final sale price, so any death by drowning meant a twenty-five pounds payout, against nothing if the slave died from sickness. Regardless of how a slave died on the Middle Passage, Henry made sure they were all logged 'Drowned attempting to escape'.

Sick slaves were simply heaved overboard as the value of a sick slave could drop as low as one or two pounds. No Caribbean plantation owner wanted the trouble of nursing a slave back to health. Twenty-five pounds from an insurance company was better than a pound from a plantation owner, and there was the cost of food and water for the sick slave while at sea. It was good business in Henry's eyes simply to throw overboard the sick, or those who looked as if they would not last the voyage.

Donald had some concerns at the number of deaths Henry reported, but as long as he sailed into Liverpool with a profitable cargo of sugar, having sold the slaves at a profit in the Caribbean, he would not investigate the deaths too closely.

Lately the women's arguing had become more frequent due to the friendship between Donald and George King. Charlotte had set her eyes on George, and Donald surmised that George had strong feelings for Charlotte.

―∞―

An uneasy silence fell between the two women. Charlotte peered out of the window of the carriage and shivered. The bare branches of the trees that lined the road appeared to wave at her. The wind caused the carriage light to flicker, and the shadows caused in her a child-like fear that each tree would try and hold on to the vehicle.

The wheels rattled over the cobbled stones of Duke Street as the coach drew nearer to their destination. Charlotte could make out the shape of a large home set back from the street, with lights shining from all of its windows. The entrance area had a Greek theme. Large Corinthian pillars supported the stone roof, which protruded from the house to cover an area of the drive. Guests would not have to step down from their carriage in the rain as the large covered area accommodated two horse and carriage at the same time. The Nicholson carriage swayed as it turned into the driveway.

Charlotte couldn't help but admire the large house set on the corner of Duke and Kent Street, a very fashionable part of Liverpool. When she was a child, her father had showed her the outside of the house. It had been built, he told her, in 1768 by Richard Kent, a Liverpool shop owner. She liked the use of local sandstone. The house dominated the crossroads.

The carriage halted before a footman. He stepped forward and opened the carriage door, allowing a set of steps to unfold. He stood near the steps and offered his arm.

George King waited at the entrance to his new home. He watched his manservant, Alfred, bow each lady from the coach.

Alfred, a black man from Africa, was one of a number of slaves captured on the West African coast. The *Elizabeth Rose's* Captain had taken a liking to him, and kept him rather than sell him in the Caribbean markets. During the return voyage to England, Alfred was trained in the basic skills of being a steward.

George kept the steward and named him Alfred, the name being easy for the African to pronounce. Over time Alfred learned English and became more useful around George's home.

Donald stepped down from the coach, flicking away his half-smoked cheroot before striding up the stairs to George. The ladies followed in his wake.

'A fine house, George, a much better residence than the city combination of offices and home.'

'Glad you like it, Donald.'

'Henry, glad you could come,' said George, offering his hand to the young man. Henry shook hands and grunted an unintelligible greeting. George hesitated to ask him to repeat himself. Henry always made him uncomfortable.

'Good evening, ladies, thank you for coming,' said George to mother and daughter, while another servant helped them with their cloaks.

George bowed over Sarah's hand to kiss it lightly. 'I trust you are well, Mrs Nicholson?'

'Tolerably. Thank you, Mr King. I am well.'

George raised his face. 'Good, good, such a cold night.'

He turned as Charlotte extended her hand to him. 'Good evening, Mr King.'

'Good evening, Miss Nicholson,' and he bent to kiss the daughter's hand.

'Welcome to my home ladies.'

'Thank you, Sir, the honour is all ours,' said Sarah, a slight smile on her lips as she looked at Charlotte.

Charlotte inwardly sighed with relief as her mother's smile confirmed she was enjoying herself.

George turned and presented his arms so that each lady could link her arm with his, and strode into the main part of the entertaining area.

The noise of the other guests rose and fell as George and his new guests entered the large room that was abuzz with the talk of business and making money. A small orchestra played in the far corner of the room, but few heard the music. George surveyed the fifty or so people who had gathered in his new home to help him celebrate his good fortune, and felt at ease with the world. He had arrived and was now part of the society elite in Liverpool. The house, with its manicured lawns to Duke Street, had cost him a large proportion of his profits from the African trade, but it was worth every penny. From the master bedroom, George could see the haze of grey that hung over the city of Liverpool.

His new house was close enough to the city to allow him to be in his office within half an hour, yet far enough away to avoid the heavily polluted air of the 'Pool. Other great houses (George liked to think of his house in this manner) had been built along the same street as the more influential and wealthy settled further out of town. The African Trade had helped Liverpool become very prosperous, and the families involved had built most of the larger homes around the area.

His guests' acceptance of his invitation to visit indicated that the more prominent traders considered him an equal. By inviting everyone who was anyone, George had laid the foundation of a strong business network.

'Alderman and Mrs Nicholson, Mr Henry Nicholson and Miss Charlotte Nicholson.'

A few heads turned, and some of the guests waved.

'May I offer you both a glass of champagne?'

'Thank you,' said Sarah, accepting a glass from the bewigged servant. 'It appears the partnership is profitable.'

'Indeed it is, Ma'am, and this small gathering is evidence of the result of our successes.'

Charlotte accepted a glass from the waiter and raised it slightly in a silent toast to George.

Donald sipped his champagne and allowed his eyes to roam over the chattering crowd. In a few moments he had summed up the guests in order of business importance.

The waiter offered the tray to Henry. 'Make it rum, a large one,' Henry told him. The waiter found it difficult to take his eyes off Henry's beaten face. He stood like a rabbit in the glare of a light.

'I said rum,' Henry said, 'Are you deaf?'

'Fetch the gentleman a large glass of rum, and be quick about it,' said George, in an effort to forestall any trouble.

The waiter, released from his frozen state by George's barked order, rushed off to do as his master bid.

'A good gathering, George,' sniffed Nicholson, and followed it by a snort.

'I think so, Donald. Some of the guests have come from Manchester. They are mainly our trade goods suppliers, who naturally hope we will buy more off them.'

'If we can make the same profits, I don't care where we buy the trade goods.'

He pulled out a large 'kerchief and sneezed. 'Dashed cold outside.'

'Could not have put it better myself about the trade goods, Donald. Sorry about the weather, though, couldn't control it,' smiled George. 'This may not be the time nor place, Donald, but I would like to have a talk with you in the library some time this evening.'

Nicholson looked at King and smiled. He realised George had a slight heightened colour on his cheeks and felt that it was not from the drink.

'I am at your pleasure, George.'

'Perhaps after dinner, when the ladies withdraw?'

'Fine, fine,' said Nicholson, drifting off to take advantage of some of the guests. A talkative merchant with a belly full of wine was a good target.

George turned to see Sarah Nicholson in conversation with the wife of one of the older members of Liverpool's society. The Dowager, many called her.

'Are you well?' whispered Charlotte as she sidled up to

George and placed her hand on his arm. George could feel his arm suddenly hot from her gentle touch. Her perfume filled his head with the scent of summer flowers and days wasted under a warm sun. He glanced around in case anyone realised the effect Charlotte had on him, and noticed Henry leaning on the side of the fireplace, a large glass of rum clasped in his fist, as he half-listened to a small group of businessmen.

'I am always well when I am in your company,' he whispered to Charlotte, his eyes on her smooth neck and shoulders. Her blue silk dress clung to the tops of her arms, yet managed to show an expanse of pale smooth skin from her neck to the tops of her perfectly shaped breasts. The dress allowed just a hint of décolletage before it cascaded down her body to emphasise her narrow waist, and finally covered her small feet encased in dark blue silk shoes.

'I heard you ask father for some time later this evening.'

'Yes,' he said, and withdrew his arm from her light touch.

'May I ask if it is a subject I should know about?' said Charlotte, flicking open her fan.

'I would prefer to meet with your father before I tell you what it is about.'

She pouted and sharply snapped her fan closed and gazed into George's eyes.

'I didn't know we kept secrets from each other?' she said, allowing her gaze to fall from George's face. Her top lip gave a slight quiver as if she was on the brink of tears.

'It is about my feelings for you, Charlotte dear.'

Her quivering lips stopped and her mouth turned into a small smile. She gazed up at George.

'Feelings, Mr King, what feelings?' she stressed the last word and replaced her hand on his arm.

'Ahgmm!' said George, as if about to make a speech.

Charlotte allowed her gaze to focus on him as she waited for a few romantic words from her George. She had never told anyone she considered George to be hers. She knew George was a successful businessman and quite rich, and he would be able to maintain her level of comfort. She doubted if the young men of her own age would be able to offer her the same niceties. She was unwilling to waste her youth waiting for success. She wanted success now.

Her Mother annoyed her by inviting suitable young men for approval. Charlotte's one thought was that when she married, she would not have to see any more young men or listen to chatter about their backgrounds.

'Yes, George?' prompted Charlotte.

'Well——'

'Mr King, when will you introduce me to your young friend?'

George jumped as if stung. He whirled around to confront the Dowager.

'Ahgmm, yes, Mrs Johnston, may I ask how you are?'

'You have asked me already, Mr King. I want to know who this young lady is and why you have kept her all to yourself?'

'Mrs Johnston, allow me to introduce Miss Nicholson, Donald Nicholson's daughter.'

'Does she have to be identified as Donald Nicholson's daughter, or does she have a Christian name?'

'Of course, I'm sorry. It's Charlotte, Mrs. Johnston, her name is Charlotte.'

'How do you do, my dear, I know your dear Mother' said Mrs. Johnston, and held Charlotte's hands while she peered at her.

'My, my, you are a lovely young thing.'

'Mrs Johnston,' said Charlotte, and dropped a small curtsey while bowing her head, her face hot with a slight blush.

'Come over here, my dear, and tell me all about yourself. Obviously George does not wish to share you with anyone else.'

Mrs. Johnston propelled Charlotte towards a group of women who were ensconced on a row of chairs from where they could watch the other guests and gossip the time away until dinner. One of the women in the group was Charlotte's mother.

'Not as young as I used to be, my dear,' said the old lady, and used Charlotte to lean on in place of her walking stick.

Charlotte smiled politely, while busily working out how she could escape the clutches of her mother's group.

'I want you to meet my nephew, Charlotte dear,' the Dowager added. 'He has been speaking about you all evening.'

'Oh,' said Charlotte, and looked more closely at the old Dowager's friends.

They reached the group, who made room for Charlotte to sit next to the Dowager. Mrs. Johnston said to Charlotte's mother, 'Would you mind, Sarah, my dear, finding my nephew, Owen. Please tell him I wish to speak to him.'

'Certainly, Mrs Johnston,' said Sarah, and stood to peer around the room for the missing nephew.

Her temper rising, Charlotte sat next to the Dowager. She wanted to know what George meant earlier when he spoke of 'feelings'.

When I rule this house, she thought, this old crow would no longer be welcome. She flicked open her fan and waved it to cool herself.

Then she saw her mother accompanied by a small man. She

supposed he must be the elusive nephew. He walked in an agitated manner that caused his arms to flap backwards and forwards in a jerky motion.

Please Lord, she thought, not him. I couldn't bear to spend time talking to a pixie. He cannot walk and carry a glass of wine because of his odd gait.

'I found him, Mrs Johnston,' called her mother in triumph.

'Ah! Yes, so I see. Thank you, Mrs Nicholson.'

'Owen, I wish to introduce you to Miss Charlotte Nicholson. I believe you wish to speak with her?'

The young man wrung his hands in embarrassment and muttered in anguish. 'Aunt, please.'

'Never mind all that, Owen. Miss Nicholson,' she called, 'my nephew, Owen Johnston,' and waved her hand as if she had produced him from thin air.

Charlotte extended her hand. 'Mr Johnston.'

'Miss Nicholson,' replied Owen. He bowed and raised her hand to his lips. Charlotte could see he suffered from extreme shyness.

He released her hand and raised his head to speak. At that moment, the double doors at the end of the entertaining room opened and the butler entered and struck a gong with a flourish.

'Ladies and Gen'lemen,' he said, 'please take your partner for dinner.'

The sound of the gong brought silence to the room. A great bustling occurred as men crossed the floor to their ladies.

Charlotte stood and bent a little to brush her dress and free it from any creases. Owen Johnston was shuffling from one foot to the other. He suddenly stopped moving, stood erect and offered his arm to Charlotte. The difference in height between her and

Owen became obvious. At his full height he was just short of her shoulder. He tried to look at her face but shyness caused him to drop his eyes, which then focused on the gap between her breasts. He blushed, which caused his face to turn deep red.

Donald Nicholson sauntered across the floor and smiled as he offered his arm to his wife.

'Shall we go, my dear?' He then noticed Owen with his arm out for Charlotte.

Sarah watched her husband's face change from that of a smiling, dutiful man to an angry one, as he saw in which direction Owen's eyes were focused.

Charlotte saw the change in her father. He was about to give this little upstart a verbal thrashing. Fortunately, George King suddenly appeared before her and bowed. He offered his arm and murmured loud enough for Owen to hear, 'You promised to allow me to escort you to dinner, Charlotte. Would you honour me, and take my arm so that we may join the others?'

The small play came to an end when Charlotte smiled politely at Owen, and on George's arm, glided across the now empty floor to enter the large dining room. 'Well timed, Mr King,' she whispered. 'Who is that dreadful little man?'

'You looked like you required a little help before you either fainted or your father hit poor Owen. He is part of the Johnston family. They supply us with trade goods. He is the only son of the family, but I think his father despairs of him. I have heard that Owen is strongly against the African trade, but while his father makes money from selling us trade goods, he will be kept in line.'

George stopped behind his chair at the top of the table and offered Charlotte the chair on his right. While a waiter drew back the chair and helped her to sit, George surveyed the scene. This had the promise of a very pleasant convivial evening.

George had come a long way from the initial meeting between himself and Donald Nicholson at the *Athenaeum* Club. He had met Donald's family and, in particular, he had met Charlotte.

She was a pleasant girl, only sixteen at their first meeting. He had not spent much time talking with her, as he was usually locked away with her father developing their buying and selling opportunities.

As time passed, the two partners became close friends. George received a number of social invitations to join the Nicholson's at various functions around Liverpool. Sometimes Charlotte would attend but on other occasions it was just George and Donald.

Usually the two men met at the club or with the merchandise sellers from Manchester or Leeds. Occasionally Henry would join them, if he were home from one of his trips.

A few months ago George and Charlotte were alone for the first time. He and Donald had visited the *Margaret Rose* to discuss the forthcoming voyage with Captain Parker. At the end of their meeting, George wanted to stay on a little longer to discuss with his Captain further detail of the ship's management. Donald excused himself to attend a meeting in town. Shortly after Donald departed, Charlotte had arrived looking for her father.

She wore a cream-coloured dress and a matching hat, which sat daintily on her head. A small silk parasol, which kept the sun off her face, complemented the whole effect. She ordered her coachman to wait while she went to find her father. She stepped lightly across the dock to the *Margaret Rose,* and walked up the small gangway to the main deck. One of the crew, realising she was a lady and not a shore-side doxy, rightly assumed she would be looking for either the Captain or one of the two visitors. He removed his cap as he approached her respectfully.

'I am Mr Nicholson's daughter. Can you tell me where I may find him?'

'Yes Ma-am, he be below with the Cap'n. I'll show you the way, if you'd like to follow me.' He turned to make his way to the companionway that lead to the Captain's quarters.

'No need, thank you, I will find him. Down here?'

The crewman stopped and stepped aside. 'Yes Ma-am, but mind your head. The deckhead is low at the bottom of the stair.'

'Thank you, I will be fine.'

The crewman turned to resume his duties and Charlotte collapsed her parasol. She stepped cautiously down the steep stairs until she reached the bottom, where she bent her head slightly as advised.

As she groped her way along the companionway, her body blocked the sunlight. Her shadow darkened the way ahead as she walked the few yards to the far door, which could only be the Captain's cabin. Just before she reached the door, she failed to see a low deckhead beam. She felt it when her head made contact. The pain caused her to let out a scream as she recoiled and collapsed on the deck, sobbing from pain. The Captain's door burst open and George appeared. Now that she was sitting, sunlight lit the passageway and she saw him coming towards her, angry at being disturbed.

George first assumed she was one of the dockside women who had taken a wrong turn, wandering aft instead of going forward to the crew's accommodation. He was about to remonstrate with the woman when he recognised Charlotte. His anger evaporated as he dropped to one knee beside her.

'Charlotte,' he exclaimed in surprise, 'are you hurt, did you fall? What are you doing here? Is everything all right?'

'So many questions, Mr King, I can hardly think which one to answer first.'

'Are you well enough to stand?'

'Oh! I think so. Just a sore head when I hit that piece of wood in the ceiling.'

George's head turned to follow her finger as she that pointed to the wooden beam. 'Deckhead,' he said unthinkingly.

'What ever it is called, I hit it,' said Charlotte, and rubbed her head.

'If you are well enough, allow me to help you up.' Charlotte moved slightly towards George as he reached out. He could feel the roundness of her breast. The narrow passageway brought them into close contact. She felt a shiver when his left hand pushed against the side of her breast. They were so close she could smell the cigar he had smoked. She could smell something else as well. He did not smell like her father and certainly not like her female friends. She could only think it must be the smell of a man who is not a relation. It awakened something in her. She enjoyed, yet feared the feeling. It confused her. She felt excited to be so close to a mature man. George was not at all like the men Mother invited home.

'Mind your head, my dear,' said George as he guided her towards the captain's cabin.

'Captain Parker, the use of your cabin, if you please.'

The Captain removed charts from his favourite chair and made room for George to help Charlotte sit down.

'Captain, would you get some water and a clean cloth so that I can bathe Miss Nicholson's injury?'

'Aye,' answered the Captain promptly.

On the Captain's return, George gently washed the bruised area of Charlotte's head.

'I think you'll live.' He smiled as he gently dried the skin around the bruised lump. 'The skin isn't broken, but you'll have a bump and a sore head for a day or so.'

Charlotte tried to smile. She had to admit to herself she'd enjoyed the feel of his hands as they ministered to her head. Suddenly she felt faint and began to slowly slide off the chair towards the deck.

George noticed the sudden change and called, 'Charlotte, look at me!'

'Brandy, Captain, I think she is about to faint!'

Captain Parker had seen the blood drain from Charlotte's face. He quickly grabbed one of the glasses of brandy on the table and handed it to George.

With his right arm around Charlotte's shoulder to stop her slipping to the deck, George handed the glass to Charlotte. 'Here, drink this, it'll make you feel better.'

Charlotte took a mouthful. The liquid burned and caused her to have a fit of coughing, but it brought the blood back into her face.

'Have some more, Charlotte, but don't gulp it, sip it,' advised George gently.

She drank half of the measure before he took the glass from her hand and said in a mock stern tone, 'I think that will be enough, young lady, or else you'll not be able to walk off this ship. Do you have a carriage?'

'It's waiting on the dock.'

'Can you stand?' he asked gently.

'I think so.' Charlotte rose and held onto George's arm. 'If you'd be so kind as to help me to my carriage, I will be fine,' she said.

'Meeting is over, Captain, thank you for your help. I will take Miss Nicholson home. You and I can continue our meeting tomorrow, if that's agreeable with you.'

'Aye. Sir, I'll see you tomorrow.'

The walk to the carriage was long for Charlotte. The bump to her head caused a dull ache and the brandy soon made her sleepy.

George managed to get her into the carriage and climbed in alongside.

'Home,' he ordered the coachman.

The carriage sped through the Liverpool streets. Charlotte, close to sleep, flopped against George. The smooth skin on her arms, and the memory of her breast, sent the blood pounding through George's body. She smelled of flowers, clean and sweet. George felt very protective of her. It had been a long time since he felt protective towards a woman, not since his wife died all those years ago. He placed his arm around Charlotte's shoulders in an attempt to cushion her from the bumps of the ride. She half smiled as her eyes closed, and he felt her settle into his shoulder as she drifted into sleep.

The coach stopped in front of the Nicholson's house on St. Anne Street. The coachman jumped down and ran up the steps to bang on the front door, which was almost immediately opened by the butler.

George climbed from the coach, and dropped the small steps

to assist Charlotte from the coach.

'Fetch Mrs. Nicholson!' called George to the butler, as he supported Charlotte up the short flight of stairs to the front door.

Sarah Nicholson appeared, demanding to know the cause of the noise and disturbance

'Myrtle, put two warming pans in Miss Charlotte's bed quickly,' called Sarah to one of the housemaids.

George and Sarah laid Charlotte on a chaise longue near the fire in the sitting room. As Sarah arranged Charlotte's head on a cushion, she sniffed and smelt brandy.

'Why does she smell of brandy, Mr King? Have you been plying my daughter with intoxicants?' demanded Sarah, her glare implying that he was the smallest and nastiest thing she could imagine.

'Madam, I assure you I only gave her a drop of brandy, and that was for purely medicinal reasons.'

'Medicinal reasons!' repeated Sarah loudly. 'I perceive that she has a large lump on her head, which I can only surmise is the result of falling down drunk like some common street woman.'

In as controlled a voice as he could manage, George replied, 'Madam you judge us both wrong. Let me tell you what happened.'

'I do not wish to discuss this any further. Kindly leave my home. I will inform her father of today's happening. I expect he will wish to know why his business partner is supplying his daughter with intoxicants, why she can hardly stand, and why she has marks on her face. Good day, Sir!'

George rose from the side of the chaise longue.

What a wicked woman, he thought, thinking I would harm Charlotte or take advantage of her in any way.

He glanced at Charlotte, who was asleep, and turned and marched out of the room.

The hall full of servants watched as George closed the door of the sitting room. They had heard everything between their mistress and George King.

'Your hat and cane, Sir,' said the butler coldly from the top of the steps. He offered the articles, which he had recovered from the coach, to George.

'Thank you,' said George, and placed the hat on his head. The butler turned his back and walked into the house. The door closed loudly behind him.

The incident was now months ago, and the misunderstanding had been cleared up. When Charlotte had awoken the following day with a dull headache, she explained to her mother how George had looked after her and brought her home.

Her mother had sniffed loudly. She still held doubts about George's involvement and intent.

Donald was more understanding and commented to George that it would be some time before Sarah would warm to him, but he would do his best to smooth things over.

Tonight's dinner was going well and he had received some warmth from Sarah.

He glanced at Charlotte and smiled. 'Are you comfortable, my dear?'

'Thank you, George, I am,' said Charlotte, and glanced down the long table to see wine glasses and cutlery sparkle in the light from the cut-glass chandelier above the centre of the table. The murmur of voices rose and fell as the guests carried on their conversations.

George picked up his spoon, and tapped his wine glass to attract his guests' attention. The chattering subsided as George pushed back his chair and stood.

'Ladies and gentlemen, I would like to propose a toast before the main course. I wish to thank you all for coming to help me celebrate my new home.'

He raised his glass and glanced from one guest to another all around the table and said in a loud voice, 'Thank you all. A Merry Christmas and profitable 1806 to one and all!'

As George sat down, Donald Nicholson stood and said in a loud and booming voice:

'As your partner, George, I think it only right I answer your toast on behalf of us all. We are all pleased to be here tonight and I am sure we all look forward to a profitable 1806. Nevertheless, this will not come about if we allow the likes of 'Butterfly' Wilberforce and his anti-slavery friends to lead Parliament down the wrong path. Liverpool is built on the African Trade and there are thousands in the land who benefit from this trade, from Yorkshire through to the second greatest city in the Empire, Liverpool!' The last word was shouted and brought many of the male guests to their feet with rousing shouts of 'African Trade and Liverpool. A pox on the Butterfly!'

George noticed, with some consternation, that Owen Johnston had not drunk the toast, nor did he stand.

George thought him an odd fellow and wondered if he was an abstainer of alcohol. If so, he would have a poor life without a glass of wine to keep him company on a cold night.

- CHAPTER SIX -

The Liverpool Road

Liverpool Coach
December 1805

William King felt fit and well, as he conned *HMS Nancy* into the Fal River under the shadow of Pendennis Castle.

The cooler temperatures of the Bay of Biscay had helped to reduce his fever, and the clean fresh salt air assisted the healing of his wounds.

'Let go!' shouted William to Midshipman McCall on the forecastle.

The anchor dropped through the grey waters of the river as the sails were furled. The voyage was over. The Spanish prize, with the Union flag flying over the flag of Spain, anchored under the guns of the *Nancy*, two ships lengths towards the shore.

'The flagship is signaling, Sir,' called Hargrove the Master.

'Captain to repair on board?'

'Aye, Sir, I'll have your boat made ready.'

'Thank you, I'll go below and change.'

'Come in, Commander, and sit yourself down. How is it with you? I see you have a prize.'

'Yes, Sir, a slaver captured south of the Canary Islands. My report, Sir, and I have dispatches from the Cape.'

'Prize money for you, young man,' commented the Admiral as he accepted William's report.

'Yes, Sir, but she has over a hundred slaves onboard, and in our climate they are suffering from the cold.'

'Damn and blast, what are we to do with a hundred slaves?'

William remained silent. He was only too glad to hand over the responsibility of the slaves' welfare.

'I'll read your report later. Give me a brief outline of what happened in South Africa, and of the slaver. Sit down, sit down, I get a pain in the neck looking up at people.'

'Thank you, Sir.' William chose an upright chair and sat down.

'As ordered Sir, I proceeded to——'

On completion of his report to the Admiral, he had been told of the victory off Cape Trafalgar, and the death of Nelson. His emotions were mixed. He wasn't sure if he was glad because of the victory or sad for Nelson's death.

The final blow came towards the end of the meeting. He was to be relieved of his command and sent to the local hospital for a full check-up. He would then be placed on half pay while the Government decided on the number of officers and seamen required to man the fleet, now that the enemy had lost so many ships.

William doubted he would be retained.

The light rain splattered off his hat and cape as William

entered the inn. He handed both cape and hat to a servant.

'I'll be in the parlour, please fetch some hot tea.'

William stood at the window gazing out at the dull, rain-soaked afternoon. He heard the tray rattle as the servant entered the room.

'Put it on the table, please. I'll serve myself.'

'Yes, Sir.'

It had been three weeks since he collected his back pay. He had obtained an advance on his hundred pound prize money from a London Prize Agent. The agent had charged a small commission for the advance, but William knew he would be better off with most of the prize money now, rather than waiting months or years for the Government to pay him.

With his newfound wealth he moved to an inn near the Strand, in London.

He spent time contemplating his future. The Navy was contracting. Should he stay and hope for a new ship or should he resign and talk to his father about a position on one of the company's ships. If not in command, perhaps he could get a First Mate's position, or even refresh his knowledge of the business and help his father.

After many days of contemplation, he decided to go back to Liverpool and talk to his father. If he couldn't find a position on one of his father's ships he would return to London and petition the Admiralty.

He remembered his last trip by coach from Liverpool to London, before reporting to the Admiralty. It had been a hard trip, though at least it was summer, and he had sat outside with the driver for the four-day journey. Now, as an officer and a gentleman, he wished to ride in comfort.

William noted the Royal Arms emblazoned on the carriage doors, and the upper panels embossed with the insignia of the four principle orders of Knighthood. Unlike the regular commercial coaches, this coach carried a number, not a name, and bore the simple words **Royal Mail,** with the names of the two places at either end of its journey–London and Liverpool.

He climbed into the coach, under the flickering oil lights of the inn's courtyard, and secured a seat inside, facing forward. It was a few minutes before departure time; the last of the mail was being loaded.

On entering the coach he had seen two other passengers - an elderly couple that smiled at him when they saw his uniform. He hoped they would be the only ones beside him. The extra room for his legs would make the higher cost of the ticket a little more bearable.

Glancing out of the window, he saw a large man hurrying towards the coach.

'Wait! Wait!' he was shouting, and waving his hand.

The coach driver–not seeming to notice him–climbed up to his seat and, with great authority, ordered the ostlers to remove the horse coverings. He then turned to the guard behind him, who contemplated his timepiece.

The large man reached the coach and pulled open the door just as the guard called out, 'All ready inside and out!'

William leaned out of the window, looked up at the driver and thumped the side of the coach shouting, 'Ahoy there. You have another passenger!'

'Close that door,' the driver shouted, looking at William. 'We will not be late departing.'

The whip cracked over the ears of the four horses and the wheels began to turn. Chains rattled and the horses' hooves began a rhythmic clip- clopping as they dragged the coach over the cobbled stone yard.

William slammed the door shut as the sweating man collapsed into the seat in front of him. The man pulled out a large handkerchief from his sleeve and mopped his brow, while his lungs dragged in the cold night air in short gasps.

'I am much obliged, Sir, thank you,' gasped the man. 'I cannot afford to have missed tonight's coach.'

He sat for some time with his carpetbag clutched to his knees. Eventually his breathing calmed. He leaned out of the window with his bag and swung it high over his head so that it landed on the roof of the coach.

'Guard, watch my bag, if you please. There will be a shilling for you at the next stage!'

At the mention of a shilling, the guard grabbed the bag as it rolled on the coach's roof.

The older couple sat quietly, fascinated by the little spectacle they had witnessed. It was evidently all part of the journey's entertainment.

'Madam, Sir,' said the large man as he flopped back into his seat, 'my apologies for such an entrance, and I hope I have not disturbed you too much.'

'Not at all, Sir, not at all,' smiled the elderly man.

The large man smiled back, and then faced William.

'Thomas Clarkson, at your service,' and held out his hand.

'William King, destined for Liverpool.'

'As I am! I am sure we will get to know each other in the

next couple of days. I have visited Liverpool a number of times, and find the time goes faster when one meets strangers to chat about everyday things. A naval officer, I see. Is it business or pleasure that takes you to Liverpool?'

'I am on my way home. On leave,' responded William.

The coach shuddered as the horses took the strain while the driver navigated down Lombard Street towards the Great North Road.

'Oh!' said the elderly lady, and rolled down the canvas curtain near her seat. She dabbed a small perfumed handkerchief under her nose, the smell from the streets too much for her.

The miles clicked by, during which, William found out that Thomas worked with William Wilberforce, the anti-slavery advocator. Thomas spent weeks on the road gathering evidence from thousands of sailors who had sailed in slave ships. He also collected leg irons; handcuffs, branding irons and instruments to force open a slave's mouth. These instruments he would produce in evidence to persuade Parliament that slavery should be illegal. William could feel the passion of Thomas's conviction that slavery was immoral and against God's order. The conversation between William and Clarkson continued until they arrived, after two hours, at the first stage. On the approach, the guard blew his horn to warn the stage that the mail coach was near, and for them to have any northbound mail ready.

The change over of horses took less than three minutes, which was enough time for William and his talkative new friend to walk around the yard and relieve their cramped muscles.

Back in the coach, conversations resumed until both men fell silent, and eventually slept.

It was the sound of a horn that woke them – the coach was near another stage. William pulled his watch from his pocket and squinted in the low light to study its face.

'Good morning,' said William, as Thomas Clarkson slowly awoke, 'it appears to be almost half past six, and the horn has gone again.'

'I heard every one of the blasts last night. I never get used to sleeping in coaches. Takes me a day or so to get over this type of journey.'

Soon the coach pulled into the *Cock Inn*, at Stony Stratford, which was near to halfway between London and the North.

The air was filled with the cries of drivers and ostlers as they changed horses. Passengers wandered restlessly to ease the stiffness in their joints. Others entered the building in search of hot food and drink. Lit torches cast flicker pools of yellow light across the courtyard. The smoke from the torches mixed with the smell of sweating horses and unwashed humanity.

The *Cock Inn* was one of the more popular inns that lined the main street of Stony Stratford.

The driver pulled the coach to a halt outside the main door and yelled down to his passengers, 'Twenty-five minutes. We leave at five minutes to seven.'

'Perhaps a hot drink, William, and some food.'

William dropped to the ground and stamped his feet to help the circulation. 'A hot drink and breakfast sounds a capital idea.'

The two men entered the inn and were greeted by a hubbub of noise. Waiters ran from room to room with plates of hot food. A barber and his mate walked around shouting, 'Shave, first class shave!'

Boot-boys climbed the stairs two at a time to deliver cleaned boots to their owners.

'It appears we have entered a madhouse,' cried William over the noise.

Thomas opened a nearby door marked Parlour and glanced in. 'In here, William, there are only a few people, so it should be a little quieter.'

The smell of cooking wafted through the inn and made both men's mouths water. The large warm room was about a third full, but the area around the roaring fire was free. Thomas rubbed his hands together.

'I thought I'd lost all feeling in them. At least the heat reminds me that I am still alive,' he laughed.

Thomas watched a young lad push into the room, his arms full of balanced plates stacked with hot food.

'Boy!' he called.

'Be with you in a minute, Sir,' answered the boy, and skilfully slid the plates across a table where a family group sat.

Thomas turned to William, 'Coffee, chops, roast potatoes and a small brandy for medicinal purposes, I think, William.'

'Sounds appetising; it will fill a gap,' replied William, 'but will they be able to get it to us in time? The coach leaves at five minutes to seven.'

'Boy, take this order and have it to us within three minutes. There'll be sixpence for your trouble. We'll have chops, roast potatoes, coffee and brandy for two!'

'Yes, Sir,' said the boy, and rushed from the room. The sixpence was as good as his. The food order had been cooking for some time as it was a regular favourite of travellers, and was prepared ahead.

William and his companion sat near the fire and resumed

their conversation from the previous evening.

'You were saying about the slave trade being immoral and inhuman,' prompted William.

'Ah! Yes, it is a trade I have spent my adult life trying to stop. We have taken a number of votes against the trade in the House, and all but one was successful. The blockage has always been in the House of Lords. I have travelled everywhere to collect information to prove the Trade's wickedness, and I am on my way to Liverpool to meet some like-minded people. We hope to try and persuade the shipping company owners that the slave trade is reprehensible and morally wrong. We now have the Commons convinced, and with God's help, it is only a matter of time before we get the Abolition Bill passed. Regardless of current setbacks, we grow stronger all of the time, and we will see a stop to this terrible trade.'

The boy entered the room with plates of food.

'Ah! Breakfast,' cried William, as the boy set a plate before each man. They both fell silent and ate quickly.

'Liverpool mail coach departing in three minutes,' came a cry from within the inn.

'Our call, William,' said Thomas through a mouthful of food. 'How uncivilized we have become, with our desire for speed. I can remember when the London to Liverpool journey would take nearly a week, and we would enjoy the experience of travel. I must say, not all of the hostelries were of a standard one would recommend to one's friends, but at least we did not get indigestion!'

William quickly drank the hot coffee, followed by the brandy. The heat from the fire, the food and drink had warmed him. He was ready to face the next stage of the journey.

- CHAPTER SEVEN -

Liverpool Arrival

Liverpool
December 1805

The grey sky became lighter as the sun began to climb across the heavens.

'I wrote some pamphlets about the abominable trade. You are welcome to read them, and perhaps they will better explain my ideas,' said Thomas, as he passed William several pamphlets.

'Thank you, with your permission I will read them now. It's light enough.'

'My pleasure, I'll not disturb you.'

William began to read the pamphlets and realized how little consideration he had given to the African trade in the past. He felt grateful that his father was not involved.

The rattle of the wheels over the frozen ground was the only noise to disturb the silence within the coach. Even the constant clip-clop of the horses seemed a little subdued, as the mail coach drew ever closer to its destination.

After an hour William finished reading and rereading the pamphlets. With a sigh, he raised his head and looked at Thomas

Clarkson, seeing the man in a fresh light. He was a man with a mission, a mission of mercy.

'How can we reject what has been written about this evil trade?'

'It is out of sight and therefore out of mind for many people. They want their sugar, but they do not think of the pain and damage inflicted on their fellow human beings to obtain it at a price they are willing to pay. In an effort to influence the plantation owners, we have persuaded many people to forgo their use of sugar. If the owners cannot sell their sugar in the English markets, they will have no need for slaves. You no doubt saw the picture of the chained slave? We have used it as our symbol for some years. It is called *'Am I not a man and a brother?'* Josiah Wedgwood produced it in 1787, and it has such a strong impact that we have used it ever since. Wedgwood has been one of our members for a long time. We believe the image, that he produced, aptly and emphatically depicts the brutality of the trade, and appeals to the better instincts of those who view the picture.'

'We?'

'Yes. *The Society for Effecting the Abolition of the Slave Trade.* We have many members, and we grow stronger by the day. Have you seen the image before?'

'I have, but to my shame, I always considered it as someone else's problem. I am aware that the image was reproduced on medallions and became very popular.'

'Excuse me, gentlemen, but I could not help but overhear your conversation,' said the elderly man from the corner of the coach. 'Surely, if the plantation slaves are set free, they will no longer have any reason to work or grow and harvest the cane. Is it not God's will that we civilised races control the lesser forms of life on Earth? You will find it so in the Good Book; Leviticus and Exodus in the Old Testament, and Colossians and Corinthians in the New.'

Thomas Clarkson retorted, 'Because the African's skin is black, Sir, cannot possibly give us the right to enslave him. He is the same as ourselves, and in the eyes of God we are all the same. Are we not created in His image?'

'Indeed we are, Sir, but it is quite evident that the African is a lower species than the white races. Just consider his face; note how his nose and his lips are different from ours. So is the shape of his skull. He does not feel pain as we do. He does not have the same concern for his family, so the removal of healthy specimens to the Indies, to work in the fields for our benefit, is surely no different than breaking a horse to pull this carriage.'

Thomas gave out a snort and spluttered. He tried to get his words out in a cohesive manner without yelling at the elderly man.

'How can you say such a thing? It is preposterous to say the African does not feel pain in a similar manner to a white man. It is ridiculous, and unscientific, to think that the African is not a human person the same as you and I! How can you misquote the Bible on such a serious matter? Regardless of our colour, we are all God's children!'

'The next thing you will be telling me,' said the elderly gentleman, 'is that a Chinaman is as good as my wife, or myself, just like the African! And to think you are in Parliament.'

'Don't stress yourself, my dear, his words just show his ignorance and that he has not read the Good Book,' said the elderly man's wife as she patted her husband's hand in a motherly gesture. 'We will be leaving this coach at the next stage.'

'Quite right, my dear, as usual, I should not let myself be stressed about a matter that cannot be changed. We should take comfort that the good people in Parliament have rejected all the efforts of this misguided anti-slavery group. How they think we will manage without slaves in the Fever Islands is beyond my comprehension. Obviously, God did not create us to work in the heat of those islands, whereas the African was born to such heat, and does not notice the difference between that of Africa and the islands. I believe they want to work for us, because they know we will take care of them just as we do our dog. If a dog knows this, the African will know it also.'

Thomas was turning red as he listened to the elderly man. It was a discussion he had heard before from so many ignorant and misguided people.

'This is ridiculous. I refuse to discuss the matter for a minute longer.' He sat back in his seat, breathing deeply to calm his temper. After a minute's silence, he turned to William. 'It is a long time, William, since I lost my temper, and I apologise to you. Perhaps I will close my eyes for a few minutes.'

William smiled and nodded his understanding. Perhaps he should also rest his eyes he thought and avoid the embarrassing contact with their fellow travellers.

The blast of the horn as the coach approached the next staging jolted William awake. The coach turned into an inn's yard and was met by a man who was almost bent in half, as if he were carrying an invisible weight on his back. Two young men ran from the stable and began unharnessing the sweating horses.

The four passengers alighted from the coach and stretched their cramped muscles. The elderly man passed a few coins to the guard to ensure his cases would be unloaded carefully. His wife glanced at Thomas, who raised his hat in a polite gesture, and nodded his head.

'Ma-am,' he said in a quiet voice, 'I trust you have a safe journey home.'

The woman nodded, linked her arm with her husband, and guided him towards the main door of the building.

'Come, my dear,' she said, 'I am cold and I don't like it out here.'

'Is it any wonder you have problems getting slavery declared illegal when people hold such opinions,' William commented, and nodded at the couple entering the building.

'Public opinion is one thing, but if I can persuade just one shipowner not to do business in the African trade, it will be worth all the heartache.'

'Gentlemen, a small repast or a glass to keep out the cold?' asked the half-bent man.

'Coachman, how long do we have here?' asked William of the coach driver.

'About five more minutes, Sir, we have to make Liverpool by this evening.'

'Thank you.'

Turning to the stooped man, William said, ' Perhaps some cold chicken, bread and a bottle or two of your wine. We will take it with us, so please be quick, because if we leave without our hamper, you will be short of a few shillings!'

'Aye, Aye, Sir,' snapped the man, and knuckled his hand to his head.

'What ship?' called William to the retreating figure.

The man paused, turned and retorted, 'The *Orion*, seventy-four, gunner's mate under Captain Duckworth, Sir, on the Glorious First.'

William returned the knuckled salute, smiled and said, 'Carry on, Gunner's Mate.'

The figure hurried into the building.

'What was all that about?' queried Thomas.

'That man's bent back made me think perhaps he'd served at sea in the past. He indicated he'd served under Lord Howe, of Ushant. His bent back is a sure sign of the lower deck. Did you see the marks of powder burns on his face? A sign of the gunners' trade.'

The two men watched as the ostlers backed fresh horses in to the coach shafts.

'All aboard,' called the driver as he climbed up to his seat. He settled himself into a comfortable position; then flicked the long whip to alert the horses they were about to leave.

At the same time the gunner's mate arrived with a basket containing the food and wine. William paid for the food and added a generous tip. A gunner's mate deserved more from life than a bent back in the service of his country.

'Thank 'ee, Sir, God bless you,' said the old sailor, stepping back quickly as the coach lurched forward to begin the final part of its journey.

The conversation between the two men recommenced. They enjoyed their meal as Thomas Clarkson detailed the trials the Society had been put through to become the champion of the African. The corks had been drawn from the cold wine that together with the food and the extra space inside made for a more pleasant journey.

The coach rattled to a halt at the turnpike gate at Prescott, the final toll before Liverpool.

'Perhaps an hour, or an hour and a half, Thomas, and we will be in Liverpool.'

'I feel as if I have pulled this coach most of the way on my own,' replied Thomas. 'My back is so stiff.'

The crack of the whip, and a cry from the driver, heralded the start of their entry into Prescott. The pace of the horse's hooves on the cobbles quickened. The horses knew how close they were to the end of the journey.

Eventually Prescott dropped behind as the horses increased their speed. The road descended gently towards Liverpool.

'At this rate we will be in Liverpool before dark,' commented Thomas.

It didn't seem any time at all to William before the coach passed the *Old Swan Inn*.

'Half an hour at the most, Thomas; we have just passed the *Old Swan*. I can smell the river from here. Some believe it to be a wretched smell, but to me it is the smell of Liverpool.'

William leaned out of the window to get a clearer view of his hometown. He could see yellow flares chasing away the darkness as people lit lamps in their homes. The constant smoke hanging over the town turned the last of the daylight into an early dusk. The nearer they got to the river, the more people they passed on the road. He heard the hawkers as they shouted their wares, and the aroma of roasted chestnuts made his mouth water.

Darkness was upon them when the journey ended in Castle Street, near the site of old Liverpool Castle. A few urchins met the coach in the hope of making a copper or two from carrying a passenger's bag. They were disappointed when they realised the coach was the Mail coach, and not the regular coach. They knew the Mail Coach never carried many passengers. They could make a shilling or more from the regular coach, with its twelve or fifteen passengers. The naval officer appeared strong enough to carry his own bag, so all but one boy drifted away.

'You, boy, carry my bag for thre' pence.'

The young boy grinned and ran to collect William's bag.

'Captain,' saluted the urchin in an exaggerated manner. He sat in the dust next to the bag and waited for William's directions.

'William, will you be going to your parent's home tonight?' asked Thomas.

'I'll get a hackney and surprise father. Thank you for your company, Sir, I have learnt a great deal from you. My new knowledge will be shared with others.' He shook hands with Thomas and gestured to the urchin to follow. The boy and William crossed the road to where a hackney cab waited.

'Driver, do you know the Kings' residence in Tythe Barn Street?'

'Aye, Captain, I do.'

'Take me there,' said William, and climbed into the vehicle.

The boy handed William's bag to the driver, turned and saluted. 'All stowed, Captain,' he cried in a voice that mimicked the driver.

William laughed and dropped some coins onto the boy's outstretched hand. 'Thank you, lad.'

As the cab pulled away, the driver gave a slight flick to his long whip and caught the boy on the thigh of his leg. The boy yelped like a small dog.

'Don't you mimic me, you little pimp; next time you'll get a thrashing.'

The horse clip-clopped its way towards Tythe Barn Street.

William watched the boy pick up a lump of horse dung and throw it at the driver. It fell short, but the scene made him realise he was back in Liverpool.

His head nodded in sleep as the cab came to a halt in front of the building of King and Son, Ship Owners and Trade Merchants.

'We have arrived, Sir,' said the driver. William alighted and accepted his bag from the driver. He studied the home he had known from his childhood, remembering how it was always bright and light. Now it was in darkness and only a small light was visible downstairs.

He banged on the door and shouted. Only then did the small light approach the front door. The door opened a little to allow a pair of sagging eyes to peer at him.

'Open up, man. It's cold out here.'

'We are closed, Sir. Please come back in the morning.'

'I am William King, George King's son,' said William, pushing at the door. It gave under pressure and the sagging eyes disappeared as the watchman was pushed back.

'Here, you cannot come in here. We are closed, Sir, and if you don't leave, I will have to call the Night Watch.'

'Give me the light, please.'

The old man, too old and frail to challenge the officer, handed over the lit candle.

'Thank you. Who are you?' William asked, allowing the light to fall on his uniform.

'I am the Company's watchman.'

William held the light towards the watchman.

'You're new.'

'Not new, Sir, I've had the honour to work for Mr King for

two year past, come this Christmas.'

'I am your Master's son, Lieutenant William King. Where is my father?'

'Oh dear, Mr King will not be back until tomorrow.'

William could see that the layout of the offices appeared much the same as before he left. Perhaps there was a little more style, and the office did appear a lot cleaner than he remembered. He made his way to the stairs. Using the candle, he lit a number of the wall lights, which allowed him to take in the whole scene. He remembered the game he used to play called stair jumping.

Start on the bottom step, jump down, and climb up an extra step, jump down again, and then add another step, and then another, until he could jump down ten or twelve stairs. The sound of the thud each time he landed at the bottom, eventually brought his father out of his office to shout about the noise. The clerks didn't like the jumping either, because each thud vibrated their inkbottle and sometimes caused a spill. A manifest of inkblots, or mistakes, would mean staying back in the evening to rewrite the whole sheet. A jumping child was a great distraction.

He blew out the candle and picked up one of the lit lamps. The watchman watched William while wringing his hands in a repeated washing motion.

William took the stairs two at a time and soon found himself in the corridor of the first floor.

This floor contained the dining room, library, and kitchen. He walked along the corridor to the next flight of stairs. On the next floor were his old bedroom and his father's bedroom and study. The level above contained the servants' quarters. He thought it unusual not to hear the chatter of the servants. There used to be much more furniture than he could see, and the atmosphere gave the impression of abandonment.

In his own bedroom, he held up the light and saw that his bed and furniture were as he had left them so long ago. Except for the dust over everything he might not have been away. He thought that this was the only room that appeared normal, apart from the company offices at street level. He felt chilled and pulled his cloak tighter around his body. He was unsure whether the atmosphere of this apparently deserted house, or the temperature caused the chill.

William made his way back to the office area and the old watchman.

'The house doesn't feel as if anyone has lived here for some time.'

'Aye, Sir, Mr King, took all the servants, and left to live in his new home. I have been left here to keep an eye on the place.'

'Where has my father gone?'

'He is in a big mansion outside of town.'

'Whereabouts?'

'I do not know, Sir, I have never been out of town. I only know the river and streets hereabout.'

'Does the *Pen and Wig* still rent rooms?'

'Aye, Sir, they do.'

'Will you get a hackney to take me there?'

'I'll go and fetch one now,' answered the old man, and limped his way slowly to the door.

After the watchman left, William wandered from office to office inspecting the few papers available. He found papers that provided enough information for him to note that things had changed. He had a strange sensation that the changes were not for the better.

The records he'd seen showed that the Company still exported manufactured goods from Manchester, but they also shipped out a lot of gunpowder and muskets.

Strange, he thought, there is little call for this type of cargo on the Baltic trade. The Irish emigrant trade is more a passenger service than a trading voyage, so why the weapons?

He put the papers back when he heard the watchman return.

'Captain, Sir, I have a hackney outside,' puffed the watchman. The man was gasping for breath after his efforts.

'Thank you,' said William, and slung his bag over his shoulder and made his way to the front door.

'I'd be obliged if you would not mention my visit to Mr King. I wish to surprise him tomorrow.'

'As you wish, Sir, my lips are sealed,' grinned the old man, knuckling his forehead.

'For your trouble,' said William, and dropped a shilling into the claw-like hand of the watchman.

'Thank ye. Sir, thank ye very much'

William pulled his weary body in to yet another cab. '*Pen and Wig,* driver.'

'Sir,' answered the driver, and touched his horse with the end of his long whip.

- CHAPTER EIGHT -

Prodigal Son

*Liverpool
December 1805*

Thomas Clarkson peered through his bedroom window at the *Pen and Wig* and scratched an itch on his chest. Why did it always rain when he visited Liverpool? Perhaps the rain was a reflection on the meanness of the people. No matter how many churches they built, even God hated the place. The African Trade was the largest business in town, so was it any wonder God made it so dreary? The window rattled as the wind blew the rain against the glass. He turned from the window, allowing the curtain to fall back into place.

Nobody was beyond redemption, so if he could help stop the wicked trade and perhaps bring some of the Liverpool people to Christ, he would gladly suffer the rain.

Opening his bedroom door, he called for hot water. Some would be used for shaving, and the remainder for making tea. He preferred coffee, but slaves produced coffee, so he would not drink it.

He sluiced himself in cold water and thought of the reasons for coming to Liverpool. He knew the Society of Friends, commonly called the Quakers, was active in Liverpool against the African Trade. He had arranged to meet William Roscoe and Edward Rushton, and believed Mr Rushton had a surprise for him.

After breakfasting, Thomas sat reading a newspaper in the small dining room, and waited for his visitors. The gentle murmur of the other diners was the only background noise.

The dining room door opened. Thomas glanced up and saw William enter the room.

William looked around the dining room for an empty chair. He saw two tables close to each other, each with a single occupant. One table was occupied by a brutish, looking man whose eyes appeared further apart than normal. His expression did not encourage anyone to share his table.

A man reading a newspaper occupied the other table. He couldn't see his face. William decided to forego breakfast and turned to leave. As he did so he heard someone call his name.

'William,' called Thomas, folding his newspaper as he stood, 'please join me.'

'Good morning, Thomas, I didn't realise you were staying here.'

'I have business here later today. I thought you would be at your father's home.'

'Father has moved! After I have breakfasted, I intend to try and locate him. The old man at the office didn't know father's new address.'

They shook hands and sat across the table from each other.

'At least——' said William, pausing as he watched a well-dressed man enter the dining room. At first glance he did not seem any different to everyone else, but something wasn't quite right. Only as the stranger, holding the hand of a small boy, drew near to their table, did he realise the man was blind. Thomas rose and the small boy guided the man to a seat at their table. Suddenly William recognised the blind man. It was Edward Rushton.

'Edward,' said Thomas, 'allow me to introduce William King, of this town. He and I were on the same coach from London.'

The blind man extended his hand across the table and William shook it gently.

'An honour, Sir, I have heard so much about you.'

Everyone in Liverpool knew Edward Rushton. He hadn't been born blind. He had been at sea, as an apprentice, from the age of eleven. At sixteen, during a storm off Liverpool, the captain and crew were about to abandon ship when Edward grasped the helm, took command and steered the vessel back to Liverpool. He was acclaimed a hero and his company promoted him to Second Mate. Later he sailed in a slaver, and during a voyage to Dominica, complained to the Captain of the treatment of the slaves. Although he nearly ended in irons himself, the Captain relented and allowed Edward to see if he could help those slaves who were suffering from a highly contagious disease of *ophthalmia*. The disease had spread amongst the slaves due to the crowded conditions. While trying to help the slaves, Edward Rushton succumbed to the disease himself, lost the sight from his left eye and damaged the other to such an extent that he became virtually blind.

'Thank you, Mr King, I trust all the comments in regard to

myself were honest.'

'I am sure they were, Sir.'

Realising Thomas and Rushton would wish to speak in private William rose from the table. He was about to say his farewells when the door opened. In strode a man dressed somewhat like a lawyer.

'Thomas, Edward, my apologies for being late,' said the man.

'You are not late, William, Edward has just arrived, and I have only just finished breaking my fast.'

The man replied, 'I think it would be best if we all adjourned to Thomas's rooms. There are far too many eyes and ears in this place.'

'As you wish,' said Thomas.

Seeing William standing near their table, Thomas said, 'My dear fellow, how rude of me.

William, may I present William?' Thomas said with a slight laugh. 'Mr William King, I would like you to meet Mr William Roscoe. You are both from Liverpool and may already have met.'

'An honour, Sir,' said William. He turned to Thomas. 'I have not had the pleasure of meeting Mr Roscoe previously.'

'Are you of the, King family, in shipping?'

'Yes, I am,' said William, smiling that his name had been recognised.

Roscoe turned to Thomas. 'I am surprised at you, Thomas. Didn't know you knew any slaving families.'

Edward Ruston quickly interjected, 'William, I am sure we all know a slaving family in this town.'

Puzzled, William commented, 'Gentlemen, I think you are mistaken. My family is in shipping. We concentrate on the immigrant trade from Ireland and trade to the Baltic. We also act as selling agents and general traders. We do not deal in slaves.'

'Have you been away long, Lieutenant?' asked William Roscoe as he glanced at William's uniform.

'Approximately eighteen months, why do you ask?'

'Just a general observation, as your face shows signs of hotter climes.'

William touched his face in a self-conscious manner. He felt a sensation of disquiet. Everyone appeared to know something he did not, yet he could not bring himself to ask.

Thomas stood and placed his hand under Edward Rushton's arm to assist him to rise.

'We must be going. Perhaps we will meet this evening, Lieutenant,' said Thomas Roscoe as he pushed a chair away from Edwards' feet to clear a passage.

'Yes, perhaps,' answered William, the disquiet growing.

The two sighted men positioned the blind man between them and they all left the dining room. William could hear them in the hall, speaking in low tones. He heard the name King mentioned a number of times until their voices faded.

William returned to his seat and contemplated what he'd heard.

In what was his father trading? Could he be involved in the African trade? Surely Father would not be involved in slavery after so many years of trading profitably to the Mediterranean and the Baltic. The profit from these two routes would be enough for a comfortable life without resorting to the African Trade.

After breakfast William collected his cloak and hat and went out into the cold wet morning. He decided to walk to his Father's place of business. The cold air and the rain helped him to think.

Pushing open the main door of his father's premises, William shook his wet cloak and surveyed the clerks creating manifests and invoices. The well-lit office and busy staff reminded him of how things were when he worked for his father.

He couldn't see the night watchman of the previous evening. He would be asleep or at another job. It was common for night watchmen to sleep the night away in their employer's premises, and to then work through the day at a different job.

As William unclipped his cloak, a tall thin man approached.

'May I be of assistance, Sir?'

'I am looking for Mr George King,' answered William, inspecting the familiar-looking man.

The man came closer to William, his hands behind his back. The overall impression was of a skater moving over ice. His body swayed as he walked. The odd gait appeared false, so perhaps it was to give the thin man more presence. As he drew near to William, he stopped.

'Mr William, is it you?'

'Yes. Ah! You're Watkins, the shipping clerk!' exclaimed William.

'I am very pleased to inform you that your father has made me Chief Clerk, Sir. I am so pleased to see that you are unharmed, Sir. Have you seen Mr King, Mr William?'

'No, I arrived late last night and was surprised not to find Father here. At least you will be able to tell me what has happened, and where I may find him. The night-watchman didn't know anything.'

'No, Sir, he wouldn't. His duties are to keep the place secure. Please follow me, Sir, to your father's office.'

William followed the Chief Clerk past the scribbling clerks. The smell of ink brought back a flood of memories.

They entered his father's office. William noticed that it had become a lot more imposing.

The large desk under the window commanded the whole room. The leather chair behind the desk gave the impression that one was in the office of a solid profitable company.

'New furniture,' commented William.

'Yes, Sir, Mr King has created a very profitable company, and we are all honoured to be working for such a far-sighted man. He is very generous and we all owe him a great deal.'

'Where may I find him, if he no longer lives here?'

'His new home, Mr William, is on the corner of Duke and Kent Streets. A very salubrious house, if I may say so, and all redecorated inside. It is a beautiful home, very pleasing to the eye. I have visited a couple of times in the course of business.'

'How far out is it, and how do I get there?'

'It is about a thirty minute carriage ride. I can arrange a hackney or do you wish for me to hire a horse for you?'

'Will my father be coming into the office today?'

'I am afraid not, Sir; Mr King will be visiting all day. A number of suppliers from Manchester have arrived to attend Mr King's celebration this evening.'

'What celebration?'

'I think Mr King is keen to show his new home to his friends. I believe around fifty will attend. I arranged the invitations, and at the last count, it was fifty.'

'If Father is not at home and he does not intend to visit the office today, then I think I will return to the inn and visit him at home this evening.'

'I am sure Mr King will be overjoyed to see that you are safe and sound, Sir.'

'Yes, I think I will return to the inn.'

'Allow me to call a hackney for you, Sir. It is still raining, I fear.'

'No, thank you, Watkins, I shall walk; it is a long time since I walked in Liverpool.'

'As you will, Sir,' said Watkins, standing by the door.

'Perhaps,' said William, leaving the office, 'you will not let Father know I am in town. I wish to surprise him.'

'It will be a very pleasant surprise I am sure, Sir. I will not mention I have seen you but I am afraid that if Mr King asks me about you, I will have to inform him of your visit. After all, I am sure you understand, as Chief Clerk, I am Mr King's ears and eyes in the business.'

'Quite,' said William, collecting his cloak from a stand near the main door. He clipped the neck-fastener and jammed his hat on his head. The wind blew as Watkins opened the main door.

'Good day, Mr William, we are very pleased you are safe.'

'Thank you, Watkins, and good morning.'

'Good morning,' said Watkins, slowly closing the door.

William spent the remainder of the day thinking, and re-reading the pamphlets from Thomas Clarkson. He was concerned that his family was apparently involved in the African trade. Now that he suspected this, what was his future? He could not work for his father if the African trade supported the company, yet he did not wish to return to the life of a naval officer. He knew his interest lay in the world of ships and business. He felt sick, as all his plans appeared to be coming to naught.

He could remain in Liverpool, and try for a berth on one of his father's competitors' ships that did not trade in slaves. This would be difficult, as he did not wish to help anyone else to succeed at his father's expense. After all, he was still part of the family, even if he disagreed with the direction of the company.

William calculated that he had enough money to last several weeks. He would have to put some cash aside for his coach fare to London, if he was unable to gain a berth in Liverpool. At least London vessels would not be in direct competition with his father.

His head fell forward as his eyes closed and he soon sank into a deep sleep.

William woke to the sound of the wind rattling the windows. He lifted his head and tried to focus on the origin of the noise. He stood up and rubbed the back of his aching neck. Although the light was fading he could see the rain had eased and the sky was clearing.

The dinner party might offer an opportunity to gain a berth, if not in one of his Father's ships, perhaps with another company. He must appear prosperous, as nobody hired a man who didn't appear prosperous.

The hackney slowed as it approached the front door of the house. A uniformed black man stepped forward to greet this new guest.

'Evening, Sur.'

'Good evening, I wish to speak to Mr George King.'

'I am afraid the Master has guests tonight and will not be seeing anyone without an appointment.'

'I think he will see me,' said William, and unclipped his cloak. He let it fall over the arm of the servant and marched up the steps to the front door to enter the large imposing hall.

Servants, black and white, milled about, tidying the hall and the large adjacent room. William could hear loud laughter from the dining room. The black uniformed servant caught up with William as he reached the double-doors of the dining room.

'Sir, Sir, please do not go in. The Master does not wish to be disturbed.'

'All will be well, and you will see that the Master will be very pleased to see me.'

William pushed open the double-doors in time to hear the answering speech of Donald Nicholson.

His last shouted words had brought most of the male guests to their feet shouting, 'African Trade and Liverpool. A pox on the Butterfly!'

William waited for the glasses to be drained, noticing a small man at the end of the table who had not joined in the toast.

Nicholson's eyes passed from George to the newcomer entering the room. His face changed from triumph to concern and then to caution. George saw the change in Donald, and swivelled in his chair.

His mouth fell open and he let go of his wine glass. Red wine flowed across the white tablecloth.

'William,' said George in a quiet voice.

'Hello, Father, how are you?'

'I am well, William,' whispered George, standing slowly. 'I thought you were dead.'

'No, I am fit and well.'

'I—— I'm so glad.'

George wrapped his arms around his son.

'Welcome home,' he whispered.

William returned the hug. 'Didn't you get any of my letters?

I must have written about six. We used to pass a mailbag to a homeward-bound vessel. I do know of one vessel that was lost to the French. Perhaps there may have been two or more letters lost with her.'

George pulled back and studied his son 'No, I never received any of them. I thought you left with such anger that you didn't want to write.'

'Which is why I never received any letters from you?'

'I didn't write because I thought you didn't want to hear from me after our disagreement.'

'We have both been fools, Father.'

William wanted to change the course of the conversation. The room had fallen silent as his father hugged him. 'You are looking well and from what I hear, the company is doing very well.'

'Yes, yes it is. Donald, do you know my son, William?'

Donald Nicholson pushed his chair back and stood to greet William. 'I have heard of him, but we have never been introduced. How are you, William? I am very pleased to meet you.'

'And I you, Sir,' replied William.

'Alfred,' said George, 'bring another chair for Mr William. Put it near me and set a place for him to eat.'

- CHAPTER NINE -

Estranged

*Liverpool
December 1805*

The noise increased as each guest dragged their chair closer to their neighbour so as to make room for William. He took his seat and glanced around. Some of the guests he knew and others were strangers. The young woman sitting opposite attracted his attention. She smiled a smile of friendship.

'George, aren't you going to introduce your son to your guests?' asked the young woman.

'Of course; how rude of me. William, may I introduce Mrs Sarah Nicholson, Donald's good lady, and his daughter, Charlotte, and this is Henry, Donald's son.'

William stood when his father spoke.

'I am honoured, Ma-am,' said William to the older lady, and bent to kiss her hand. He released Sarah's hand and looked across the table at Charlotte, gave a small bow. 'Miss Charlotte, your servant.'

He nodded to Henry, sitting two down from Charlotte, and

too far away to shake hands. Henry returned the nod, yet William sensed a certain animosity. Where had he seen Henry before?

Charlotte flicked her fan open and waved it to cool her neck and upper breasts. 'Mr King,' she replied, and nodded her head, her eyes never leaving his face. The charade with the fan, William realised, was designed to make him look at her. Certainly, she made a pleasant sight, after many months at sea. He smiled slightly, the suddenly more livid scar on his cheek making his discomfit evident. Realising she may have gone too far, Charlotte brought the fan closer to her neck.

George noticed the little pantomime and glanced around to see if anyone else did. They all appeared to be chattering with their neighbours.

'Did you hear, my dear, William captured a French ship?' said George, in an effort to break off the by-play.

'Really? Was it very unpleasant for you?' asked Charlotte.

'I have seen and experienced pleasanter things.'

'I'm sure. It will be our job now to help you forget the unpleasant things in life, now you are back with your family, safe and sound.'

'Wine, Sir?' asked Alfred, offering William a decanter.

'Thank you.'

George stood again and tapped his glass with a spoon. 'Ladies and gentlemen, would you join me in an unplanned toast to my son, William, who has returned safe and well from fighting the French!'

'To William,' chorused the guests. 'Welcome home!' shouted some. Henry picked up his glass, raised it to his lips, but did not drink. His eyes remained on William.

The small man at the end of the table, who had not joined

in the previous toast, stood and offered his glass.

He's not an abstainer, thought William, how he is associated with Father?

—⚏—

George King leaned back in his chair and watched his guests. William's arrival, as hero of the hour, could not have been timed better. The reflected glory for George, being the father of a man who had captured a French ship, would help bind many to his Company. A hero would not go amiss in Donald's family either, especially with Donald's political ambitions. The only way Donald could claim William, as a member of his family would be if George married Charlotte.

During the meal William gained much knowledge from the conversations with the other guests. The conversations sadly confirmed that his Father was involved in the African trade.

Could he persuade his Father to give up the evil trade and return to the Mediterranean and Baltic business? The French defeat off Trafalgar meant fewer French ships to harass solitary merchantmen. His Father must know that the seas were clear of the enemy and that he should cease the wicked trade before Parliament made it illegal, and turned him into a criminal.

—⚏—

Eventually the dinner came to an end and the ladies retired to the withdrawing room, leaving the men to their port and cigars.

'Gentlemen, I would appreciate your comments on the port. I used to trade in it before the African trade, which is far more profitable,' George laughed as he poured himself a generous glass, 'but I must admit that we English should learn some of the habits of our Mediterranean friends. I like a glass of port after a meal. It helps settle the digestion. I like to smoke tobacco, or a cigar, as my Spanish supplier would call a roll of tobacco. Please help yourselves, and if you wish for snuff, it is also available.'

George's butler passed from guest to guest, offering a box of cigars and a lighted taper. Most of the men took one of the cigars, allowing it to be lit by Alfred, and sat contentedly smoking and sipping the port wine.

'A fine meal, George,' commented one of his Manchester suppliers, 'and with the return of your son, William, this will be a Christmas to remember.'

George nodded in agreement and looked fondly at his son while drawing on his own cigar. 'You don't smoke, William? I expected you to have picked up the habit in the Navy.'

'No, Father, I don't smoke. Many of my friends in the Navy have stopped smoking in protest to the African trade. The tobacco is produced by slave labour, and my fellow officers, who have seen a slave ship, could not in all conscience support the pleasure of smoking at the expense of so much suffering.'

'Poppycock, you are tired after your journey. I know many naval officers who smoke.'

William carried on, ignoring his Father's interruption.

'Did you know you can smell a slave ship up to ten miles away? You don't have to see them to know when you are close. However, to be fair, I must admit some officers actually took up smoking after boarding a slaver. They took up smoking in an effort to kill the stench that permeated their nostrils and minds, after seeing the conditions in which the slaves travelled. My fellow officers hoped the taste and smell of a good cigar would hide the smell. Apparently it didn't, or so I am informed.'

The scrape of the port decanter across the table as it was passed around was the only sound in the room. Everyone was listening to William.

'William, I wish you to apologise to our guests! That was an inexcusable thing to say. You are implying the African trade is wrong and we are all wrong in doing business in such a way. You sound like that man, Wilberforce, the anti-slaver agitator. He doesn't know what he is talking about, and by the sounds of things, neither do you!'

William hesitated; he didn't wish to embarrass his father in front of his guests. But he was not willing to apologise for his beliefs about slavery. He took a deep breath and began to explain his views.

'Mr Wilberforce is a great man, Father. I have many of his pamphlets and I have listened to a man called Thomas Clarkson, whom I had the good fortune to meet on the coach to Liverpool. I have seen a slaver, in fact I captured it, and I only hope the English navy will return the slaves who were onboard to their homes. The look of despair in their eyes is a remarkable sight and pierces your heart, however cold and unfeeling you are. I have smelled the odour of human misery. How would any of us like it if we were snatched from our bed and sold across the seas, with no hope of ever returning to Liverpool?'

'But the African trade has been a legitimate trade for over two hundred years, my boy,' said Donald Nicholson as he blew smoke to the ceiling. 'This fine city of ours is rich and powerful because of the trade, and your father has built a very good and profitable business. All of us here have built businesses in the trade. Henry,' Donald waved at his son,' is one of our gallant Captains, and has turned a tidy profit from the Trade for all of us. The Trade relies on suppliers of sale goods, ship owners, and many more small businesses in Liverpool, and the surrounding area.'

William's eyes followed Donald's hand as he indicated his son. Seeing Henry as a slave Captain, William realised that he was the man he had seen at breakfast in the Pen and Wig. Henry must have heard the conversation between himself and Thomas' anti-slavery guests. No wonder he felt animosity from Henry. Henry had already placed William as an associate of the anti-slavery organisation.

'It is an immoral trade and King and Son should not be involved!'

The noise from the guests rose as everyone wished to speak in defence of the Trade.

'Gentlemen, gentlemen, please,' said William, 'I do not wish to be rude to anyone; after all, you are my father's guests. I just explained the reason why I do not wish to smoke a cigar.'

A few of the guests laughed to cover their embarrassment at William's outburst.

'Perhaps the Trade frightens some people because they do not have the courage to carry it through,' said Henry Nicholson in a low growling voice.

George King's face turned red.

'Are you saying my son is without courage?'

'I am not saying any such thing, Mr King, just commenting. Some people cannot stomach an honest day's work in the African Trade. It takes real men to handle the slaves and make a profit.'

William stood at the last remark, and was about to speak when his Father said, 'I think, gentlemen, we should rejoin the ladies. Would you lead, Donald? I would like a quick word with William.'

'My pleasure, George; gentlemen, follow me if you please.'

As the guests filed out of the dining room, George motioned

his son to sit down again. 'A word please, William.'

William watched the room empty and the door close quietly, leaving him and his father alone. At least this time he did not feel like a schoolboy; now he was his own man. He did not wish to fight, but he would not back away from any of his principles.

'Henry Nicholson will not insult me in this house again and get away with it,' said William, pouring himself a fresh glass of port.

George studied his son and noted his face drained of blood, which caused the scar to stand out like an angry pink stripe.

William calmed himself and said, 'I am sorry, Father, for upsetting you in front of your guests. It was not intentional. I am very pleased to see you and to be back in Liverpool.'

George pulled at his cigar and studied his son. 'You have experienced things I never have; yet I, in my way, have experienced different things. Both our experiences have been life changing. Without the Trade we would have collapsed as a Company. After you left I was approached to charter the ships to Donald, and we eventually went into a loose kind of partnership. We traded goods for slaves, and the slaves for sugar or tobacco. Then I sell these commodities in England.' He waved his cigar to take in all the house. 'You see, I have been successful, and am now an influential figure in the community. When we ran the trading ships to the Baltic and the Mediterranean, our profit was small, although I was happy with the way we were; I didn't know any different. The war changed everything; perhaps I may be the only man in England to thank Napoleon. The attacks on our ships forced me to make a change, and that change has been very profitable. I am sure you would not wish me to have closed the company and perhaps ended my days begging for handouts.'

'If I had not seen with my own eyes the degradation of the

slaves, I might have agreed with you, but now I have seen and experienced their destitution, and I cannot be part of the trade. They are human beings, the same as you and I, and we cannot be involved in this wicked traffic. You must realise Parliament will outlaw slavery in the near future.'

'Rubbish. Parliament will never outlaw the African trade. How can you say such a thing? You must know how many times the slavery bills have been put to Parliament, and all of them have been defeated. The capital invested in the West Indies in land, slaves and buildings is huge, and it would cause an economic disaster for England if slavery were outlawed. What of shipbuilding, ships' crews and the industries making the trade goods? What you propose is that these enterprises will have their markets closed down. Can you imagine how many men will be out of work? I doubt I will see this trade changed in my lifetime. You will know what I mean when you rejoin the company and help me expand into other areas.'

'I'm sorry, Father, but I cannot join you if you remain in the African trade. I will not be a party to the long drawn-out suffering of people taken from their homes and made prisoners in a foreign land.'

'You have made prisoners of French men, so what is the difference? We make those prisoners work.'

'Father, the difference is we are at war with France, and the taking of prisoners is a legitimate part of being at war; and we don't make French prisoners work in the tobacco plantations.'

'You have just contradicted yourself, you have just told me the taking of prisoners is legal, which is the same as the legal trade in which King and Son conduct business.'

'Father, I do not wish us to argue, nor do I wish us to part under the same cloud we did the last time. I can see now that every stone in every building in Liverpool, including this house, has been cemented together with the blood of an African. I will not be a party to furthering the African trade.'

'What do you intend to do, return to the Navy to fight for the black man?'

'No, I am not sure what I will do. This I am sure of, I will not be involved in the Trade.'

'Do I take down the '*and Son*' from the company?'

'It is your decision, Father.'

'I will think on our talk. I think we should join the others or else they will think the worst.'

George pushed back his chair and stood, remarking in a quiet voice, 'At least we are not at each other's throats as we were the last time.'

'I am pleased we can talk again without shouting at each other, but I will not change my mind. The Trade is immoral, inhuman and against God's law. Henry Nicholson appears to be a fine advertisement for the worst kind of person in the trade. I am sure he enjoys seeing the suffering of his captives.'

'How can it be against God's law? Even in the Bible we are told to look after our slaves, so God obviously agrees we should be allowed to have slaves.'

'I will make you a present of a book I have read called *Practical Christianity*. It will give you a clear understanding on what is required of us by God.'

The two men entered the withdrawing room and rejoined the other guests. The general chatter ceased as all waited for George, or William, to continue the argument.

'Is everything to your satisfaction?' asked George to the

assembled company. His comment broke the silence.

—⚏—

'Do you wish us to speak now George, or wait until later?' asked Donald Nicholson, knowing that George wanted to talk to him.

'If it is convenient, perhaps now would be a good time.' He had a feeling that this evening was going to transform his life. He'd had an unpleasant conversation with his son and was not sure if he had lost William. Now his second conversation, but with Donald, might bring him great happiness or greater sadness than the upset with William.

Donald flicked his near-finished cigar into the fire and followed George from the room.

He closed the library door behind them, giving a friendly nod as George held up a decanter of brandy.

Setting into a large armchair by the fire, Donald contemplated the beautiful room. Two walls were covered with shelves lined with books. How many of the books had George read?

'Thank you,' said Donald, accepting a glass of brandy.

George sat opposite his friend and business partner and raised his glass in a salute.

'I think you know what I wish to speak about,' said George in a slightly hesitant way.

'Perhaps I do, George, but to be sure, I would like you speak your mind, so we are both aware of your thoughts.'

'To come to the point, I wish to marry Charlotte and I am asking for your blessing.'

Donald Nicholson sipped his brandy and allowed his mind to sift the various options. He knew from intuition that this was the question George wanted to ask earlier. He did not wish to offer any suggestions at the moment.

This was how Donald liked to negotiate. George had made the request, which allowed Donald to control the conversation, as well as the decision.

Would joining the two families be advantageous? The return of William might influence George to relinquish the slave trade. Would Donald be able to control William, through George? Could he still influence his daughter if she married George? He had controlled Charlotte, and George, in the past. If George married Charlotte, things should be much easier.

The positives and negatives of joining the two families through matrimony flashed across his mind. William's return could be a bonus. If he did not make too much noise against the slave trade, he could be a real asset, especially for Donald's future.

'My dear fellow, I am delighted that you wish to marry my daughter. Does she know that this is your wish?'

'No, she doesn't, as I have not broached the subject. I am a little old-fashioned in this area, and wished to make sure you and Sarah would be happy to have me court your daughter. After all, you and I are too close to argue, and I thought if you have any objections, we should discuss them on our own.'

'Nonsense, my dear fellow, I am delighted, and I am sure Sarah will be delighted as well, after we have informed her.' He quickly pushed the conversation he had heard on the way to tonight's dinner, between his wife and daughter, to the back of his mind. It was all good business, he surmised.

'When do you wish to speak to Charlotte?'

'I will pick the time and the place, perhaps over Christmas.'

'What do you think William will do, having a mother younger than himself?'

'I wasn't sure that I would see William again, so I never considered his wishes. I assumed he made his choice when he joined the Navy. I was not even sure he was still alive.'

'Will he join you in the company?'

'I am not sure. He can be very strong-minded.'

'Takes after his father,' flattered Donald Nicholson, and was pleased to see a slight blush appear on George's cheeks.

'I only wish he did, and joined me in the company. Perhaps I could make him Captain of one of our vessels.'

'Do not let him blackmail you, George, just because he is family. Perhaps this is what he wants, and all this talk of getting out of the African Trade is to make sure he has a command.'

' I really don't think he would do that. I believe he genuinely thinks the slave trade is wrong, and while he holds that belief he will not join King and Son.'

'Soon to be King and Wife, George,' laughed Donald.

'Yes,' George said in little more than a whisper, and stared into the flames of the fire.

'Come, George, your guests await, and we have been away a long time. People will talk.'

- CHAPTER TEN -

Miss Charlotte

Liverpool
December 1805

Charlotte brushed her hair one hundred times. *'One hundred times and it will shine, and will never fall out'*, or so her nanny told her as a child. Sometimes brushing became very tiresome, but on other occasions, such as tonight, it allowed her to think. The evening had been a success.

Charlotte worked the brush through her hair and smiled at her image in the mirror as she thought of George. He was a gentleman. Her hand stopped in mid-stroke as her thoughts of George faded and William's face filled her mind.

William was a very handsome man, with clear, tanned features after months in the tropics. The scar down the left side of his face added to, rather than detracted from his appeal when he smiled. He had an aura of excitement and danger. Each time he spoke, his voice sent shivers down Charlotte's back.

She heard the raised voices of the men, after the ladies had retired. The voices had become quite heated, and only returned to normal after the men joined the ladies in the withdrawing room. Sadly, George and William had not at first been amongst them.

She resumed brushing her hair.

When George and his son finally did arrive, George whispered something to father, and they had both left the party. William sat next to Charlotte and began a conversation.

Just thinking about William's voice caused her to blush.

She brushed her hair harder in an effort to distract her thoughts from William. It was to no avail. Her mind wouldn't leave William alone. She remembered how much whiter his teeth were against his dark sunburned skin.

During their conversation William asked her if she played a musical instrument. When she mentioned that she played the pianoforte a little, he stood and held out his hand to her.

'There is one in the corner; you must play for us.'

'Oh, I cannot play in public. My skill is not good enough.'

'I will help you,' said William, gently guiding her to the pianoforte.

'How so?'

'I will turn the music for you.'

'How will that help? I thought you would play.'

'It is a long time since I sat at the pianoforte. I did have a nanny who insisted I learn. I remember her telling me, '*To play the pianoforte is sign of a cultured upbringing, and the skill will assist you to gain the hand of a fair maiden.*'

'Where is this lady now?' laughed Charlotte.

'She left. I don't think she agreed with the way father wanted me to be raised. She was very good at playing a number of instruments. She even tried to teach me the harp: all a waste of time. If you sit at the keyboard, I will stand here. People will be able to hear you but they will not be able to see you. Please play, Charlotte.'

'I will try, but you must not allow me to be embarrassed!'

'Upon my honour, I will protect you!' laughed William, opening some sheet music.

'Perhaps this one?' asked Charlotte, pointing to some sheets already on the stand.

'That may be a little risqué,' commented William, after reading the title.

'I have heard Father's men singing it as they weigh anchor. The music does not appear to have any words attached, so I doubt the music itself can be risqué.'

'Quite right; shall I ask them to be quiet, and then announce you?'

'Don't you dare. I will just tinkle a little and see what happens.'

Charlotte played the tune quietly, and began to feel more confident. Some of the men joined in the chorus in a half-hearted way. She finished the piece to a loud round of applause.

'More, more,' shouted some of the guests good-naturedly.

'Can you hear them? Your public demands more,' laughed William.

'This is all your fault!' hissed Charlotte gaily.

'May I suggest you do the same piece, but louder. Let them join in and we will take it from there.'

Charlotte raised her hands over the keyboard and waited until the noise subsided. The only sound now was the low murmur of the older ladies gossiping. Charlotte brought her hands down with a crash and began playing. The guests listened as she played the introduction, and upon reaching the chorus, all the men burst into song. Propriety demanded that the version they sang was fit for ladies.

Charlotte raised her head as she played the final notes, to see her father and George entering the room. George appeared very happy and her father slightly smug.

Turning to George, Donald Nicholson shook hands with him and thanked him for a pleasant evening. Sarah rose from her chair, moved to the pianoforte, and informed Charlotte that they were about to leave.

William walked Charlotte to the coach, kissed her hand, and hoped that they would meet again soon.

Charlotte climbed into the coach, wrapped herself in her cloak, and settled down to try to sleep during the journey home. If she could not sleep, she intended to pretend to be asleep. She expected her mother to chastise her for playing such a tune and she did not want her thoughts ruined by complaints.

Her mother climbed into the coach beside Charlotte and made a comment about the inappropriateness of the music.

'They joined in, and they knew the words,' said Charlotte in her own defence, and promptly closed her eyes to signal that she did not wish to speak again.

She heard Henry give a grunt and made a mental note to have a word with him for being so rude, and not shaking William's hand in farewell. He just climbed into the carriage, made a gruff noise as if to say he wanted to be left alone, and closed his eyes.

She brushed her hair a few more times and decided that she must have reached one hundred.

Is George's attraction fading in the light of Williams's arrival? William didn't have a Company of his own but would he inherit

King and Son, and how long would she wait, she mused. George had the money, position and power now, which is what she wanted. She also wanted to leave home and control her own life, but she knew this would never happen unless she married. If she married George, she was confident that she would be able to control him and perhaps have an input into the running of George's company. If George died early, the Company and the house would be hers.

If she married William (she assumed she could persuade him that marriage was the best thing for him), he would always be second fiddle until his father retired, or died. Did she wish to wait so long for control and power?

William was more exciting than his Father, but he was unable to offer security and the standard of living to which Charlotte was accustomed, or rather, the standard of living to which she considered that she was entitled.

She lay in bed with her feet placed on the hot spot left by the warming pan. How best could she find out William's plans for his future?

If William returned to the Navy, perhaps eventually he could be promoted to Admiral, or even knighted, which would mean that she would be Lady Charlotte. The title had a very pleasant sound. She whispered '*Lady Charlotte*' to her ceiling. Of course they would have to live in London, as Liverpool would be too small for a knight and his lady.

If he was killed in action, or worse, wounded, and could not go back to sea, what would he do?

Her mind wove scenario after scenario as she composed herself for sleep.

- CHAPTER ELEVEN -

The Abolitionists

*Liverpool
December 1805*

William spent days strolling around Liverpool, and down to the small pier near the old 'lither' pool, after which Liverpool was named. The 'lither' pool was a tidal area at the entrance to the dock.

He marveled at the dock, over ninety years old and still being used. It was a great invention, the first of its kind in the world, allowing ships to be worked without waiting for the right tide. At high tide the dock gates opened, and ships moved in and out. After the gates were closed, the ships in the dock could be loaded or unloaded without any consideration of the tide. Before the dock was built, ships anchored in the river and were unloaded into barges. The barges would then be rowed ashore for final unloading, which was an uneconomical way of working a ship.

The temperature had been dropping each day, which brought the only advantage in cold weather; the smell of the city's sewage was minimised.

The wind off the river chilled him to the bone, even though he wore a full uniform and his boat-cloak. He could have stayed in the inn, but found it easier to think while walking, and the cold wind kept him focused. He stood at the small pier and watched the river traffic.

He could go cap-in-hand to his father, or he could return to London and visit the Admiralty in the hope of being appointed to a ship. The first option was impossible if he was to stand on his principles of not being involved in the slave trade. He could not see his father allowing him to rejoin the company. His father would never allow him to stop the Company's trade to Africa.

The anchored ships, waiting in the river to enter the dock, swung to the tide. Perhaps he should approach each captain of the waiting ships for a berth. This option was not pleasant, as he would be admitting that he had failed.

Daylight faded as William felt flakes of snow melt on his face. He pulled out his watch and checked the time. Only three-thirty. The heavy snow clouds had shut out what little daylight was left. He started back towards the *Pen and Wig;* to stand around any longer in such weather was foolish.

The snow fell faster as he began to climb the short muddy embankment from the pier. Suddenly his feet slipped, and he stumbled. Just in time he managed to throw his hands forward to break his fall, and to protect his clothes from the muddy ground.

'Damn and blast,' he muttered, his arms straining to keep from falling face down.

Suddenly a voice from the top of the embankment stuttered, 'Allow——me to assist.'

William gently pushed himself upright in an effort to spare his clothes, and saw a small man shuffling from leg to leg while offering his hand.

William clasped the stranger's hand and pulled in a measured way, not wishing to pull the man down on top of him. The stranger pulled back while digging his heels into the mud. This action gave William a stronger advantage to pull himself to the top of the ridge.

'Thank you, Sir, I am much obliged for your help.'

'M——my pleasure, Lieutenant King,' stuttered the small man.

'How do you know my name, Sir?' asked William suspiciously.

'L——et m——me to introduce myself. My name is Owen Johnston and I attended your father's dinner the other evening, where I m…met you, but at a distance. We did not speak. You and your father appeared to be having a disagreement, and I did not wish to intrude.'

William scrutinised the man and tried to remember the face, and the possibility of seeing him at his father's house.

Owen returned the scrutiny and said, 'I am staying at the *Pen and Wig*. May I offer you a hot drink in this inclement weather? I understand that you are also staying there.'

'Although I am grateful for your help a few minutes ago, I do not remember meeting you, nor informing you that I am resident at the *Pen and Wig*. Have you made enquiries about me?'

The tone of William's voice was the same as he used to a defaulter at sea. It indicated that he would not stand for any nonsense, and that he was suspicious of his benefactor.

'Lieutenant, be assured I have not made enquiries about you. The information about you residing at the *Pen and Wig* has been given to me by a mutual acquaintance, and I assumed it a convenient place to offer you a hot drink!'

'Which mutual acquaintance would that be, Mr Johnston?

I only arrived in Liverpool a few days ago, and have spoken to no one, other than the people at my father's house. I fail to see how we could have a mutual acquaintance who would be aware at which inn I reside.'

'My dear Sir, I do apologise, I have not made myself clear. The gentleman who informed me that you reside at the *Pen and Wig* is Mr Thomas Clarkson.'

'Do you know Thomas?' enquired William in a more cordial tone.

'I have that honour. Mr Clarkson and myself have had a few dealings in the past.'

'My apologies, Mr Johnston, I fear that I have misjudged you. It's just that it appeared unusual to meet someone just at the moment I needed help, who also knew of my private arrangements.'

'I quite understand, but actually I was out searching for you. I have a few matters of business to discuss, if you are interested.'

'Business?'

'I beg your forbearance. I wish to be comfortable when we discuss what I have in mind. This inclement weather is not fit for anybody.'

William noticed when the discussion came round to the mention of business; Owen Johnston's stutter and physical agitation left him. His speech became normal and he spoke in a much stronger voice. The mere mention of business brought out hidden strength in his personality.

The two men increased their speed in a mutual desire to be out of the cold. As they rounded the corner, they saw the warm glow of lights from the inn. The ground had become slippery with the thickening, which brought a hush over the streets, even silencing the rattle of the iron coach wheels over the cobbles. Only the tinkle of the horses' bridles gave warning of an approaching vehicle.

They pushed through the outer door of the *Pen and Wig* to be met by warm air, and the aroma of food and beer. As they shed their cloaks, snow clinging to their shoes soon melted into a puddle of dirty water.

Johnston turned to William. 'May I suggest we repair to my sitting room. It is very private and we can talk in peace over a hot drink, or perhaps something stronger?'

'A capital idea,' replied William, 'perhaps I will have a small brandy to take the chill from my bones. I foolishly stayed out too long, and should have anticipated the snow.'

'Waiter! I would like brandy, and some hot tea, sent to my sitting room.'

'Yes, Sir!' answered the waiter, and hurried away.

'May I call you William, Lieutenant?'

'Please do, and I have just remembered you from the dinner at father's house. You did not join in the toast when I first entered the room. I think my father made a toast to the African Trade.'

'Correct, William; please follow me.'

The sitting room was part of a small suite, with a door connecting to a bedroom.

'This is where I reside when I am in Liverpool,' commented Johnston.

William walked over to the large fire and thrust his hands towards the heat. He rubbed them together to encourage the circulation.

'What kind of business are you in, Mr Johnston?'

'My family's company, in Manchester, supplies the goods for

trade to the slavers on the African coast.'

'What! Without those goods the slavers would find it difficult to trade for slaves.'

'A fact of which I am aware, William, but I cannot change the world in a day. When I realised the connection between our pots and pans and the misery of the African, I tried to persuade the family to change. I wanted them to refuse to sell the goods to people like your father and Donald Nicholson. Unfortunately, I am in the same boat as you; my family will not stop selling to slavers. I think we have a lot in common.'

'So it appears.'

'I, and a few other, have decided to open our own trading and shipping company, to prove we can make a profit in the Americas without resorting to the African trade. We intend to ship the same goods my family make and to offer an agency agreement for other suppliers, and to make a good profit. We plan to return with goods that have been produced by honest labour. We will search out suppliers of crops that have been produced without the use of slaves.'

A knock on the door stopped their conversation. A servant arrived with a tray containing hot tea, a bottle of brandy, and a row of six glasses.

'Put them on the table please, we will attend to ourselves,' said Owen as he extracted a coin from his pocket for the servant's trouble.

'Thank yee, Sir.'

Owen indicated the tray with his hand. 'Help your self, William.'

William moved to the table and poured himself a measure of brandy.

'Can I pour one for you?'

'No, thank you, I will make my own tea. I like to be exact when I pour the milk.'

William held the glass as he leaned on the mantel above the fire. This position allowed him to appreciate the warmth from the fire, with the warmth of the brandy.

He watched Owen make his tea in a very neat and precise manner, and waited for his host to renew their discussion.

Owen placed his cup of tea on a small table alongside a chair near the fire.

'Where was I? Oh Yes! My associates and I intend to show that a ready profit can be made from the buying and selling of inanimate objects between England and the Americas, without recourse to the trade in human flesh.'

'An admirable thought, but how do you propose to carry out this venture?'

'We have the resources, and we have a contact in the Americas, but what we don't have is an honest ship's Captain to act for us. He must be of like mind to us, and not tempted by an easy profit, whether it be by the slave trade, or buying the product of slavery.'

'Have you found such a man?'

'My business associates and I have been seeking the right man for some time. We believe the slavery bill will pass through Parliament within the next two years. It is now Christmas 1805, so by Christmas 1807, we should be able to push through the anti-slavery bill with a majority. We have Prime Minister Pitt on our side, and our support in Parliament has grown. We lost the last vote by a very small majority. We believe we can be the first to trade from Liverpool without the help of slavery, which means we will have a lead on the likes of Nicholson and, I am sorry to say, your father.'

'May I ask who your associates are?'

'You may, and it is my intention to introduce you to them within the hour, which is why I was keen to find you this afternoon. I understood you were still at the inn, until I tried to make arrangements to meet you.'

William moved slowly to the window to consider what he had heard. Is there a chance for him to be appointed as one of the officers on this new vessel? He moved the edge of the curtain and peered out over a white world. The snow was heavy. The dirty smoked-stained buildings, with their dark grey-slated roofs, were changed to virginal white. The city's scars were hidden under a blanket of snow.

He glanced down and saw a carriage stop in front of the inn, and the driver quickly jump from the coach. Three men climbed out and made their way into the inn. Only the tops of their hats were visible, but somehow they seemed familiar. William let the curtain fall, and turned to see Owen lighting the oil lamps around the room.

Owen lit the last one and said, 'I usually sit in semi-darkness, because I like to think on days like this, until the servant comes to light the lamps. My friends will be here any minute and I don't wish us to be disturbed.'

'I will go,' William said, placing his glass on the table, 'as I do not wish to intrude on your meeting. Thank you for your help this afternoon, and for the brandy. Perhaps while you are here I will be able to return the hospitality. I will be here for another two or three days.'

'But William——' said Owen as a steady tap-tap on the door

of the sitting room drew their attention. 'This will be my associates. Please stay a while, I would like them to meet you.' Owen hurried to open the door.

'Gentlemen, please come in. It is so nice to see you again.'

William watched Thomas Clarkson enter the room, followed by William Roscoe, and on his arm, Edward Rushton.

'William, we meet again,' said Thomas in a jovial manner as he extended his hand.

'Thomas,' replied William with a genuine smile, ' it is a pleasure to see you again.'

'You remember William Roscoe and Edward Rushton?' responded Thomas.

'I do indeed, my pleasure to see you both, gentlemen.'

Roscoe helped his friend, Edward, to a seat before shaking hands with William.

'Lieutenant,' he said, and gave a slight nod of his head.

Thomas, standing before the fire, flicked his coat tails to allow the heat to warm his back, and said, 'William, will you not join us? We would value your advice on certain matters.'

'My advice! I doubt if I could advise such gentlemen as you.'

'Do not underestimate yourself, my dear fellow. Will you stay?'

'If that is your wish,' said William, sitting in a chair not too near the fire, yet close enough to benefit from the heat. He did not want to appear to be forward.

'Gentlemen, I call this small group to order and ask for a report on progress.'

Owen spoke first. 'I have found the vessel I believe would be right for our venture. She is a French-built brig, the *L'Harmonie*, which was captured by our Navy. I purchased her from the Admiralty Marshal. She has a copper bottom for protection against tropical worm and has been renamed the *Albatross*.'

'Is the name to imply we are birds of a feather, Owen?' laughed Thomas Clarkson.

'Thomas,' continued Owen, 'Samuel Coleridge wrote a poem a few years ago about an ancient mariner and an albatross. The mariner killed the bird and had to suffer the consequences to himself, his crew and his ship. He felt he was under a curse but he was eventually redeemed by his recognition and love of all of God's creation. Our hope is that we will be redeemed by our recognition that the black man, too, is part of God's creation, and that same God will grant our venture success as we turn our backs on the despicable Trade.'

'Excellent, excellent,' responded Thomas, 'well said.'

'Edward and I have found backers. We have enough money to fit her out, plus we will be able to pay for a crew. We have yet to find officers, but I believe we should leave the crewing to her Captain. He will know what is best for his ship. Now, Gentlemen, I think it is about time we enlightened our guest, Lieutenant King.'

'I agree,' said Edward Rushton.

'William, you know we are all involved in the effort to try and put an end to the wicked African trade. As you now know, we have found the ship and we now have the money to finance the project. We have issued shares in the project to sympathisers, and all we now require is the man to be our Captain, and to run both the Company, the ship, and to advise us in the future. What do you think so far, Lieutenant?'

William steepled his fingers and rested his chin on the peak. He stared into the fire as his imagination saw the sails of many ships moving across the burning logs. He contemplated all he had heard and reasoned that if he said the right thing, he might be considered for the position of Captain, and not just one of the officers. He was confident of his ability to make the project work. The right words now would change his life forever.

He responded carefully, 'I would sincerely recommend that you find a Captain who has not been on the African trade. I believe that this will be critical. Nothing can compromise the reputation of the project.'

'I agree!' called out Edward Rushton, with emotion that startled the others.

With a glint in his eye, Thomas asked, 'Do you have any suggestion, William, as to the right man to command?'

William looked up, and allowed his hands to fall into his lap.

He had a golden opportunity to prove himself to his father. He must be involved. The venture was an answer to his prayers.

Taking a deep breath, he said, 'I beg you not to think me too presumptuous, but the best man I can think of to lead the seagoing side of the project is myself.'

'Hear! Hear! My boy,' shouted Thomas Clarkson, 'I am very pleased with your answer. I have been singing your praises to these fellows since you and I met on the coach. Owen confirmed my feelings with his own comments about you, and your reaction at your father's house to the toast against the abolitionists. May I be the first to congratulate you and to shake your hand? Welcome aboard!'

William felt his hand grasped and pumped up and down with enthusiasm. He couldn't stop smiling as each in the group shook his hand and made happy and welcoming comments. Owen poured brandy into five glasses and passed one to each person.

He raised his glass and said, 'Perhaps I may be allowed the

honour of offering a toast? To Captain William King, our newest member. To the success of our project and to the abolition of the African trade!'

Each raised his glass to William, his face fixed with a grin as they responded together. 'To Captain King, our success, and the abolition of the African trade.'

William realised his greatest wish had come true. They called him Captain and it had a ring to it he would always remember.

He thought for a further moment and interrupted the general happy banter. 'One moment, Thomas, gentlemen, if we dispose of our cargo in America, will there not be a problem of a return cargo? Will we permit any slave-produced cargo at all? Many vessels trade to Boston or New York, and then move down to the West Indies for a return cargo, which may be sugar or tobacco. This cargo will negate our efforts to prove an operation can be profitable without the use of slaves.'

The others quickly discussed William's question. When agreement was reached, Edward responded for the group. 'William, we will not trade in slaves. We're aware we may initially be forced to carry goods produced by slaves, but we would expect you to obtain these goods from plantations that do not mistreat their labour. I do believe there are plantations, owned by Christians, who do not ill-treat their slaves. If possible, we would prefer not to carry any goods produced by a transplanted black man. If you feel you have to obtain such goods, and you are in no doubt that the slaves who produced the goods are well treated, then you may carry slave goods. I don't know if you are aware, but it takes ten times as many slaves to produce the same amount of sugar, as tobacco or cotton. If you must carry produce, please avoid sugar. The least use of slaves is in the production of leather and dried beef. I believe there is a ready market in Liverpool for both products.'

'A concern we do have is that if our efforts are too successful, the plantation owners may decide to do away with their slaves because they cannot sell their produce. This will cause great misery to the slaves. While we are adamant that we want the trade in slaves stopped, and outlawed, we also want to show plantations owners in the interim, that if their slaves are properly treated, a profit can still be made. Certainly this may cause an increase in the cost of certain goods, because plantations owners would have to pay a wage to the people who are now their slaves. If this happens, so be it, but our goal is the abolition of slavery within the British Empire, and to be a beacon of righteousness to the rest of the civilized world. They will follow us, I know they will.'

William watched Owen and William Roscoe nod their heads in agreement. After Edward had finished, silence hung in the room as each member of the group digested Edward's words. William broke the silence.

'Thank you, Edward; I am now clear as to what I can and cannot do on our joint behalf. I will minimise the use of slave-produced cargo, and you may all rest assured that no ship in which I am Captain will ever carry slaves for sale.'

Thomas drained his glass, sat down, and tapped the bottom of his glass on the table.

'I bring this meeting to order gentlemen, we have much business to discuss.'

- CHAPTER TWELVE -

The Albatross

Liverpool
December 1805

Captain William King walked the deck of his new command, the two-masted brig, *Albatross*. He tilted his head back to check the sails furled to the crosstrees. They looked old and in need of replacing. Still, their sad condition could not dampen his enjoyment.

The day after the meeting he had paid an old man in a dory to row him across the river to the *Albatross*. She was anchored off Birkenhead, which was far enough way from any prying eyes in Liverpool. Boarding her had been awkward as the rope ladder, or 'Jacobs Ladder', which normally hung over the side could not be found. He eventually boarded by climbing her anchor cable. The old man was ordered to wait until William was ready to return to Liverpool.

Thick snow on the deck of the *Albatross* muffled his footsteps as he made his way to the Captain's quarters. There he found a half drunk watchman nursing a bottle. The smell in the cabin assaulted William. The drunk had not washed for at least a month. His clothes were filthy and stained. His eyes were unable to focus on the intruder.

William pushed open one of the windows that stretched across the stern of the vessel and let in a blast of cold air, and a flurry of snowflakes.

''Ere, what you doin',' yelled the watchman as the cold woke him from his stupor, 'I'll catch me death from all the cold.'

'Get your gear and get off this ship!' growled William.

'You can't talk to me like that. I am the watchman, and the owner will have something to say if he knows you are aboard.' He clutched his bottle closer to his chest. His eyes rolled in his head as he tried to appear aggressive.

'You have five minutes to get what gear you have and get off this ship. You are a disgrace. I am the new owner, and if you are still here when I get back in ten minutes, over the side you go. There is a dory waiting for me that you may use, he will take you to the Cheshire shore.'

William made his way on deck. He found a lamp and shook it to make sure it held oil, then lit the wick. The lamp threw a yellow light across the white of the snow. He leaned over the gunwale to speak to the dory boatman.

'Boatman, I want you to take the watchman ashore to the Cheshire side and return to wait for me.'

'Aye, Aye, Captain,' replied the boatman as he knuckled his forehead.

Now William could begin his detailed inspection of his new command. He withdrew a strong knife from a scabbard clipped to his belt and began to poke and prod the ship from stem to stern. He wanted to know all he could about her and to find out if she needed to be hauled out of the water.

He crawled through the hold and held the light high as he scraped and prodded the beams and ribs of the vessel. She appeared to be sound. He knew from her paperwork that she was French-built and had been captured in 1803. One hundred and sixty-two tons, seventy-nine feet in length, twenty-six feet in breadth, and she drew two fathoms of water.

He checked her bilges and found only a small amount of water, not enough to worry him. Her holds were dirty but a good crew would put her right within a few days' hard work. He returned to the main deck. With his head right back, he confirmed his previous opinion that some of the rigging would have to be replaced, along with all of the sails. Perhaps he could use the current set for patchwork but he'd leave that decision until they were lowered and inspected.

That afternoon William transferred his personal baggage to the *Albatross*.

Within three days he had hired a small crew of six local men to clean the ship and to help him examine the few stores in the forecastle lockers. He had the pick of the shore men, as it was close to Christmas and work was scarce due to the bad weather.

Ashore, he interviewed potential crewmembers and looked for a good First Mate.

He attended a number of meetings with new partners to discuss outbound cargo and sailing dates. As was the custom, the value of the cargo and ship was split in thirty-two shares. Each of the partners bought a number of shares in the venture, according to their means. William used some of his remaining cash to buy three shares, and the balance to buy trade goods on his own account, which was a Captain's privilege. He persuaded his partners to agree that when he saved enough from his profits, he would be allowed to purchase the *Albatross* for what they had paid for her, plus the cost of rigging her out.

The days passed in a whirlwind of action. The *Albatross* was scrubbed clean below decks, and painted with a whitewash solution to try and purify the hold and sweeten the air.

During one of his visits ashore a Chinaman, one of the many who seemed to be washed up on the Liverpool quayside, accosted him.

'Captain, Captain, you go deep sea?'

William stopped and eyed the fellow up and down. The Chinaman had something about him. His clothes were threadbare, but they were clean and mended. The fine stitching used to mend the clothes showed a certain pride in appearance. His long cue was whipped, sailor fashion, to keep it under control. His face was clean-shaven, without even the trace of a moustache, like many of his race.

'What can I do for you?'

The Chinaman repeated 'Captain, you go deep sea?'

'We are.'

'I werry good steward, Captain, you take me, your steward?'

'We are not going to China.'

'No matter, Captain, I sail wherever you sail, no matter heya.' At the end of his little speech, the last word was emphasized to make the point that he didn't care where he sailed.

William saw a man, not much older than himself, who was tall for a Chinese. Although his feet were bare, the cold didn't appear to be of any consequence.

The stature of the man convinced William to

give this cold, clean man a chance. His eyes, slanted in the normal way of the Chinese, looked honest. The Chinaman was a slave to misfortune and the *Albatross* was to be the first step of ridding Liverpool of slavery.

'Have you any dunnage?'

'Aye, Captain.' The Chinaman answered, and produced a tightly wrapped bundle.

'Can you read?'

The Chinaman nodded, and smiled to show a set of perfect white teeth.

'What name do you go by?'

'Teng Sang, Captain.'

'Well, Teng Sang, meet me in an hour at the entrance of the *Pen and Wig*. I think we may have a berth for you.'

'Thank you, Sorr, thank you, I see you longa time, one hour.'

William could not help but smile as he turned to resume his walk to the inn for another meeting.

—⁂—

The Captain of the *Albatross* and his new steward soon came to an amicable working arrangement. In the three days since Teng Sang joined the *Albatross,* he had organised the Captain's life to such an extent that William wondered how he had managed on his own.

William no longer worried about clean clothes, hot food, or even shaving.

The first morning after Teng Sang joined the *Albatross,* William awoke to the smell of hot tea and the gentle tap-tap of the Chinaman's knuckle on the side of the bunk. 'Captain, Sorr, breakfast and shaving water.'

William rolled out of the bunk, and splashed water over his

face in preparation for shaving. He soaped his face and stropped his razor. As he brought the razor to his face, he heard Sang mutter to himself.

'What's the problem, Sang?'

'Captain, Sorr, it is my duty to shave you. I can dooa.'

William stared at the razor, then at Sang, and debated whether he would do the job properly or just cut his throat and rob him.

Only one way to find out.

'OK, Sang, let's see you shave me.'

Sang's face, lit by a smile, indicated the chair in which his Captain should sit. 'Prease,' he said.

William sat in the chair and rested his head on the back. The razor slid slowly but surely over his face. The gentle touch of the Chinaman relaxed him, allowing him to think over the duties for the day.

Crewing had been completed. He was pleased with his Bosun, a man named Charles Wilson who had served under him, years earlier, on one of his father's ships. He was a family man from Liverpool, which gave William confidence. The Bosun, as the senior warrant officer, would be the link between the crew and the officers. He was a hard man, yet fair, and would keep the crew in line. On signing him on articles, Wilson also signed for part of his wages to be paid via an allotment to his wife. A man with a family was a steady man and would not cause trouble.

William did his best to hire a crew who were not in the hands of the crimps. The crimps were no more than sea-pimps. Crimping, or shanghaiing, was a despicable practice, not dissimilar to the press gangs of the Navy. He refused to deal with any lodging house that offered to supply sailors in exchange for cash, to repay the debt of the sailor. In most cases the lodging house had drugged or cheated the sailor in the first place.

The First Mate, James Austin, was older than William, and prematurely grey-haired. He had been passed over for command, a situation with which William sympathised. Austin knew William was part of the King family, but he also knew the ship was not part of the King family fleet. William's enthusiasm for the future, and that all officers and crew would share in any profit of the voyages, persuaded him to sign. He couldn't afford to stay ashore any longer. The *Albatross* was better than no ship at all.

The Second Mate, David Fuller, was an eighteen year old, who had completed seven years as ship's boy, and sailed as a midshipman in the Navy. Tragically, his family had recently died from smallpox while he was at sea. He found he couldn't settle ashore, now that he was on his own, so decided to return to the sea to escape the pain of his loss.

An apprentice, Dylan Howell, a Welsh thirteen year old with a singsong voice, also signed articles. His voice was yet to break. At times when he raised his voice, it would begin as a high squeak, and then suddenly crack in to a deep bellow. William had to make an effort not to laugh.

The boy's mother had requested a meeting to ask for the apprenticeship for her son.

'An apprenticeship, Mrs Howell, will cost a thirty-pound bond.'

Mrs Howell hesitated at such a large sum and then made up her mind.

'I want him trained officer like, not just to be another deck hand. When he comes back I want him to know his figurin' and his readin'. He has some of it now but I want him trained.'

'He'll be trained, Missus, no fear of that.'

'Thirty pound, you said?'

'Aye, thirty pound, he is not much good to me now. He doesn't know anything, so I have to feed him and train him.'

'All right, Captain, you look like a man of your word. Here's the money.' She slowly counted out the exact amount in a mixture of old paper notes and coins. 'It's all that was left by his grandfather, my father, and I want it to be used to help Dylan to better himself.'

She turned to her son and with a tear welling in her eyes, said, 'Dylan, you're a man now. Captain King is giving you the chance to be a man of means one day. You mind everything he tells you, and make me proud.'

They planned to warp closer to the Liverpool shore and enter the docks to load for America. The weather, cold and snowing, made life difficult on deck, as well as ashore. The snow had blocked roads and disrupted the transport of goods. Fortunately, Owen foresaw this, and arranged for the manufactured goods to be sent to Liverpool by barge. The barge had sailed slowly down the Mersey, and now waited on the Liverpool shore for the *Albatross*.

A knock on the cabin door brought William out of his thoughtful relaxation. 'Come in.'

Having finished shaving his Captain, Sang placed a hot wet towel in William's hand, as the First Mate entered the cabin.

'Good morning, Mr Austin, are we ready to shift to the dock?'

'Aye, Sir, we are. Whenever you are ready. It'll be slack water in about an hour, and the pilot is alongside. The sails are ready, and we have the boats in the water to help guide the *Albatross* to the Liverpool side.'

'Thank you, I will be on deck directly.' William wiped his face of the traces of soap and dropped the cloth on the table.

'Thank you, Sang,' William said, as Sang helped him into his uniform coat.

'Char, Captain,' said Sang, and pointed to the hot tea.

'Is that a Chinese name for tea?'

'No. Sorr, it is a name from India.'

'How did you come to be in India, Sang?' asked William as he closed the final button.

'Long story, Sorr. Please drink your char, or it cold.'

William raised the drink to his mouth and noticed it was not the normal brown colour, but had a greenish tinge.

'Something wrong with the water already?' commented William, looking into the cup

Sang appeared confused.

'The water, Sang, it is greenish. Has it been in the barrel too long?'

'Ayee-yah, no, no, Sorr, it is China green tea,' replied Sang with a smile.

'I didn't order any green tea.'

'No, Sorr, I order small stock when supplies come aboard. I thought you may like to try china tea-ah.'

William sipped the hot brew and found, to his surprise, it tasted very good.

'What about milk?'

'No milk, Sorr, spoil taste. Ayeee-yah!'

Drinking the tea, William laughed at the expression on Sang's face when he asked for milk. Sang was correct; it did taste fine without milk.

He placed the cup down on the table and straightened his coat.

'Hat!' he said in a mock stern voice.

Sang passed his Captain the hat, and watched him place it on his head and check the angle in the shaving mirror.

As William stepped onto the poop deck, First Mate Austin saluted and said, 'Anchor hove short, Sir.'

'Thank you, Mister.'

'Good morning, Pilot.'

'Morning, Captain, weigh anchor, if you please,' responded the Pilot.

'Weigh anchor, Mr Austin, and make sail. I want to enter the wet dock before the tide turns and the current becomes too strong.'

'Aye, Aye, Sir.'

Even the weather was on their side. The *Albatross* slowly drifted in the slack water waiting for its final link with the land to be broken. The snow had stopped, and a light grey sky gave the impression that the whole world had changed from coloured to black and white.

'Anchor's aweigh!' came the cry from the Bosun on the forecastle.

'Make sail,' called Austin to the crew in the rigging. 'Take the strain, Bosun!'

'Take the strain!' repeated the Bosun to the coxswains of the two boats attached, via cables, to the *Albatross*.

William could feel her come alive.

A puff of wind found the few sails set, and pushed her head around.

'Meet her, Helmsman!' called the Pilot.

Slowly the distance from Birkenhead increased and the Liverpool side of the Mersey became more distinct. They drew closer to the area of the old Pool, and the entrance to the wet dock.

'Going well, Mr Austin,' commented William.

'Aye, Sir, much better than I expected considering our raw crew, and the recent bad weather.'

'God favours the righteous, Mr Austin, and our venture is righteous.'

'Aye, Sir.'

The *Albatross* glided into position at the end of slack water. The tide turned and she slipped quietly through the dock gates into the dock.

The two boats released their charge at the last moment, and now lay astern of the *Albatross,* ready to follow her into the dock. Each boat's crew lay across their oars, gasping for breath. Steam from their bodies rose in the still air. The trip across the Mersey had been a little over a mile, and the cry of 'Let go the boats' was a welcome relief. The *Albatross* slowly entered the inner dock, where lines were passed ashore to make her fast.

'When will you sail, Captain?' queried the Pilot.

'All being well, tomorrow afternoon; will you be the Pilot?'

'Aye, Captain, I will. Just let the dock office know, and I will be down to see you on your way.'

'I'll do that, thank you, Pilot.'

William turned to his first mate, 'Secure, Mr Austin, if you please.'

'Aye, Aye, Sir. Bosun, hoist the boats and secure!'

'I am off ashore, Mr Austin. When the cargo arrives, have it loaded, please. It is my desire to sail on tomorrow afternoon's tide.'

'Aye, Sir.'

- CHAPTER THIRTEEN -

Farewell

Liverpool
Christmas Eve 1805

William King walked slowly up the small hill from North Pier, past George's dock, towards the *Pen and Wig* for the final meeting with his partners. He was ready to sail, and felt a little frustrated that he could not sail that evening. His partners had arranged a small celebration to farewell him, and the *Albatross* at the start of their new life.

His partners were already in attendance, along with a few selected guests. Owen's Aunt, Mrs Johnston, held court as usual amongst the ladies, none of whom appeared to be younger than forty years of age. Her voice was in full flight as she announced how pleased her family was to sell goods to anyone who wished to buy. She did not mind if they were sold for slaves, or for cotton or timber, just as long as her family made a profit.

'Aunt, I am sure the ladies don't wish to hear this,' whispered an embarrassed Owen Johnston.

'Perhaps the ladies would like to see the *Albatross*,' said William, coming to Owen's rescue.

'Would it be possible?' asked the old Dowager.

'If you look out of the window over the small rise, you will see a ship in the wet dock. That is the *Albatross*.'

The old lady craned her neck. 'She is very small, Captain.'

'Distance distorts, Ma'am, but if you look closely you will see she is working cargo, the same cargo we purchased from your Company.'

The old lady raised her lorgnette spectacles and peered at the distant vessel.

'Oh, I see,' she said without much conviction. Turning to speak to her nephew, she asked absent-mindedly, 'Where is the boy?' The *Albatross* was already forgotten.

William glanced around to see if he could see Owen, and saw that he was speaking to Edward Rushton. William was about to point him out, but felt sorry for Owen.

He turned and faced the Dowager. 'I am sorry, Mrs Johnston, I cannot see Owen at the moment, but when I do, I will let him know you wish to speak with him. Would you excuse me please, I have a few last minute duties?' William bowed and left the old lady to harangue her female friends once again. Not just Nelson used the blind eye, reflected William with a smile.

As he walked across the room he felt a tug on his sleeve and heard a soft voice whisper to him, 'Will you show me the *Albatross*, Captain?'

William turned and saw a familiar face with large blue-green eyes.

'Miss Charlotte!' he exclaimed, 'I didn't know you would be here tonight.'

'Mrs Johnston asked me to accompany her, because Owen

would be busy.'

'I am indebted to Mrs Johnston.'

Charlotte flicked open her fan and fluttered it across her face. She managed a maidenly blush and looked down.

William took her free hand and kissed it gently. 'I am very pleased to see you again.'

'Thank you, Captain.'

He held her hand just a little longer than custom demanded before releasing it. Charlotte had not made any effort to remove it from his light grasp.

'Will you show me the *Albatross,* Captain?' she asked again, in the same soft voice.

William sensed uncharted waters ahead, but the pleasure of seeing Charlotte again, and the excitement of the last few hours ashore, caused him to push his natural caution to the back of his mind. This evening was a celebration, and a beautiful young woman was smiling at him.

Charlotte had met Mrs Johnston and heard that William had been appointed Captain of the *Albatross.* A word in Mrs Johnston's ear and she had arranged an invitation to the farewell celebration. She managed this without being accompanied by her parents, as Mrs Johnston would be her chaperone.

'We cannot leave,' said William.

'Why not, William? You are the Captain. Why can't I visit your ship with you?'

'We would have to organise a chaperone for the sake of propriety.'

'But you will sail tomorrow and I will not have a chance to wish the ship goodbye.'

'It would be better, if on my return, I arranged for you and your mother to visit the *Albatross*.'

'I thought you liked me?' sniffed Charlotte as she peered into his eyes, allowing her own to fill with tears.

'I do like you, Charlotte, but I can see a problem if just you and I visit the ship without a chaperone.'

'Your crew and the other officers will be on board.'

The look in her eyes unsettled him, as she now appeared distressed.

If she started to cry, it would be difficult to explain. People might get the wrong idea, which could taint the evening. What harm could there be if he took her to the ship and showed her quickly around, then returned to the festivities. It would take less than an hour.

He glanced around and realised that however simple it may seem, it could be a problem for the future. His resolve strengthened. He would not compromise his future for the sake of keeping this young woman happy. She was very attractive, but an unchaperoned visit could become a major problem.

He took Charlotte's hand once again and studied her downcast face. 'Charlotte, you are a beautiful woman, and any man would be very happy to show you around his ship without a chaperone, but it is because you are so beautiful I must refuse your request. I cannot allow you to be placed in a position of compromise.'

Charlotte gazed into his face.

William saw the look in her eyes. She hated him. Her eyes were as hard as stone. Perhaps other men give in to her wants and demands, but he would ignore her little girl charms, even if by doing so, it made an enemy of her. She would be a woman to watch in the future.

'Upon my return, Charlotte, I will be happy to show you and your mother around the *Albatross,* and perhaps take tea afterwards.'

'Ah! There you are, William,' called Thomas Clarkson with a happy smile on his face, quite unaware of the tension, 'everyone seems to be enjoying themselves.'

In a controlled voice that mocked the tears so recently shown, Charlotte said, 'Thank you, Captain King. We will see what the future brings. It may not be convenient at a later date to visit your small ship. My father has a number of vessels and I have been around them most of my life. It seems to me that one ship is the same as the next. Would you excuse me please, I think Mrs Johnston has indicated she wishes to speak to me. My hand, if you please, Captain.'

William released his light grip as she pulled her hand free. Without a backward glance, Charlotte flicked open her fan once more and wended her way past the other guests towards Mrs Johnston.

'Miss Charlotte,' said William, in a manner of farewell. He did not receive a response.

He felt sorry that their short friendship had ended so abruptly, and hoped in time she would realise what he had proposed was the best for them both.

'This is a good moment to give you your orders, William', said Thomas. 'They contain letters of introduction to people in Boston, and also in New Brunswick, in Canada. Read them later, and if there are any questions you may have or suggestions that you'd wish to make, please discuss them with me. We have all signed the instructions and the letters of contact. There is a copy of each for you, and the original is for the recipient. Are you looking forward to sailing?'

William accepted the sealed package and placed it inside his uniform jacket. 'Thank you, Thomas, and yes, I am looking forward to sailing. I have had enough of the land and I am keen to take the next step. I think I may leave shortly and get back to the *Albatross*. There is so much to do before we sail.'

'Poppycock, my boy, enjoy yourself this evening. I am sure Mr Austin can handle the cargo. After all, didn't you pick him?' laughed Thomas. 'Is it good luck or bad luck to sail on Christmas Eve?'

'I never gave it a thought. Some would say good and others bad, but the North Atlantic is not a pleasant place in the middle of winter. If all goes well, we should be in Boston around the end of January.'

'Captain King will sail early tomorrow afternoon, Christmas Eve, to help in our small way to liberate our black brethren from slavery. We will show Parliament that to trade in goods other than black slaves can make good profits for Liverpool. Under William Wilberforce, I am sure we will see the anti-slavery bill ratified. It may not be next year or the year after, but it will happen, and we will be a light to the world. Slavery is wrong, and is contra to the wishes of God. The day after tomorrow is Christmas Day, which is the day God set foot in the world to save us, and show us the way to live. That great act was meant to include the black man as well as the white man, and it is only proper that, on Christmas Eve, our small enterprise under Captain King will demonstrate to England that we can make profit by trade rather than profit by the misery of our fellow man. A toast to Captain King and the crew of the *Albatross;* may they always sail with a fair wind behind them – and let us remember our effort is seed sown and we trust it will grow and multiply anew.'

'Captain King!' The shouts of good wishes and raised glasses brought a lump to William's throat, the road to the future now set.

William raised his glass in acknowledgment and toasted each group in turn. He noticed Charlotte did not drink to the toast, nor did she smile when he raised his glass to the group of guests with whom she stood. The look on her face made her quite shrewish as she squandered her external beauty to her flawed ego.

—⚬—

Donald Nicholson flicked his coat tails to let the heat of the fire warm his back while he watched his son place a glass of brandy on the small table near his chair.

'You have heard of the farewell party for William King?'

''Yes, Father, Charlotte told me of it this morning. I believe he sails on Christmas Eve.'

'So I understand. This enterprise of the abolitionists is a concern to me; it might just work.'

'Never. How can you make a good profit by not carrying slaves?'

'Don't underestimate anyone, Henry, especially William King. He is not like his father, you know. I can twist his father to my way of thinking, but after I heard the speech from young William at his father's house, I will not take any chances with our future.'

'Did George King attend the farewell?'

'I have heard he hasn't seen William since the argument in his house after the dinner.'

'If George is not involved in his son's venture, what do you propose?' asked Henry as he sipped his drink.

'I have a little plan to ruin the reputation of this little enterprise. By the time I have finished, the anti-slavers reputation will smell worse than the river on a hot day.'

'What is it?'

'I have spoken to lawyer Snelgrove and he has arranged to seize the *Albatross.* Snelgrove should be able to tie the anti-slavers in court for years. If he succeeds, the ship will not sail and the cost of defending their scheme will ruin them. I have heard that William King intends to take a share of the profits. If their ship doesn't sail, they will not be able to make any profits.'

'Are you confident that Snelgrove will be able to stop the *Albatross*?'

'If Snelgrove fails to hold King in Liverpool, I propose that you follow him and observe. I will have you try a little trade with our American cousins without the help of slaves. Two can play at being the gentleman.'

'Not carry slaves? What ship? Surely not the *Liverpool Lass;* she is rigged for the African trade and I am to sail in a few days. We are loading trade goods now! You have other competent Captains who can be sent to watch William King!'

Donald Nicholson paused flicking his coat tails and stopped rocking on his heels. He gazed at his son, his eyes cold. He wore an expression Henry recognised as the non-negotiable face from his childhood.

'Henry, you are my son and one of my Captains. I want you to always remember I am Captain of the Company. You will follow my orders.'

The words came at Henry like the sharp stabs he received from his father when he was a child. His father used to stab him in the chest with his finger to emphasise a point. The memory was so real that he felt the physical sensation of his father's finger stabbing him right then. His eyes roamed from his glass to his chest and then to his father, who still stared at him.

'Yes, Sir,' he whispered, feeling a child again.

'It will only be for one trip, so consider it a holiday,' said Donald in an effort to lighten the cloud that had descended on Henry.

'I want you to be his shadow and to find out what he does, where he goes and who he sees. I don't want him to make a success of this venture. I doubt he will, but just in case, I don't want to be without information I can use to stop him and his abolitionist friends. The only person I can trust to do this correctly is you, Henry, which is why I am sending you, and not somebody else. Who else in the Company will have the same desire to make sure the family and the Company are protected?'

Henry nodded, his mind already planning the voyage to Boston. He emptied his glass in a single swallow and proceeded to the decanter for a refill.

'Henry, I have contacts in Boston through one of our slave buyers, so you will be well cared for. The contact's name is Leather. This voyage will not resemble the regular African Trade; it will be easier, so relax a little, but don't let King know you are watching him.'

Henry sipped his fresh drink, turned to his father, a smile on his lips, and said, 'Don't worry, I know what is required, and William King has failed before he sails.'

'That's my boy.'

Henry's mind was now on the girls in town. He had less time to have a farewell romp. Abstinence between Liverpool and Africa was bearable because he knew he would have the use of any female slave on the Middle Passage. Now he would find it difficult to obtain a woman who would allow his special requirements. Boston would be similar to Liverpool; where the women were concerned, they would not allow his special needs, unless they were old and worn out, where a few extra guineas usually sufficed.

William felt the light wind touch his cheek. The air was cold and clear, and for once the clouds had fled Liverpool to leave a clear pale blue sky. A watery sun struggled to warm the air. He didn't really care about the weather as long as he had wind enough to sail from Liverpool. His new venture had begun and he couldn't remember the last time he'd felt so happy.

'A beautiful day, Captain.'

'Aye, Pilot, a great day.'

The *Albatross* had passed through the lock in to the river and was now off the Perch Rock Light on the northern tip of the Wirral Peninsula. William focused his telescope on the Rock Light and could see children playing in the sand at the foot of the framework that supported the light. It would not be long before the pilot would leave, and he would be on his own.

He lowered the telescope, turned to check the Liverpool side of the river and saw a small sailing boat approaching. Its occupants were gesticulating and shouting, though he was unable make out what. He focused his glass on the boat and could see men in uniform.

'What do you make of that, Pilot?' asked William, handing the glass to the pilot, who focused on the boat and studied the people.

'I think they want us to heave to, Captain.'

'Is it safe to anchor here if we need to?'

'Aye, we can anchor just ahead, near the start of the Liverpool side of the channel.'

'They may be from my associates. Heave to Pilot. Mr Austin, prepare to anchor.'

'Aye, Aye, Sir.'

The watch made ready to take in sail and anchor. The small boat drew closer.

'Anchor ready, Sir,' called the Bosun.

'Pilot, are you happy for us to anchor here?'

'As good a place as any.'

'Let go!'

The small boat dropped its sail and drifted slowly to the anchored ship. A Jacobs Ladder was let down.

A top-hatted man in a dark blue uniform climbed over the side and dropped lightly to the deck.

'Captain King?' asked the man as he glanced around.

'I am the Captain,' said William, and walked towards the stranger. 'Who are you?'

'I am Pilcher, of the Sheriff's office.'

'What can I do for you, Mr Pilcher?'

'Sorry, Captain, but your ship is under arrest.' As he spoke, Pilcher took a roll of paper from his pocket and a small hammer and some small nails. At the mainmast he hammered nails through each corner of the paper.

'Your ship cannot sail until it is released by a court.'

'What the bloody hell do you think you are doing?' shouted William.

'I am an officer of the Sheriff and have been instructed to arrest your ship. Good day, Sir.'

William studied the paper and read *'The sailing ship* Albatross *under arrest, together with her Captain, and crew, for trading in slaves.'*

'This is ridiculous. We are the one ship out of Liverpool who will not trade in slaves. We are on our maiden voyage to prove a profitable trade can be conducted without recourse to the slave trade. Who issued this warrant?'

'All I can say, Sir, is that Lawyer Snelgrove, of Liverpool, swore out a statement that you have aboard a black slave, which you took by force in Liverpool.'

'By force? You mean that I am accused of forcing a slave to join this ship?'

'I have been told you have taken a slave, by force, in Liverpool, and you will try and sell him in America. Now I must leave as I have other warrants to issue. Pilot, can I give you a lift ashore? I bid you good day, Captain.'

'Look around, man! You can see all my crew are white, all men from Liverpool, except for the Chinaman, who is listed on the muster as my steward.'

William's mind raced with the sudden change in his circumstances. To think anyone would accuse him of being a slaver was inconceivable. He knew it was illegal to force a man on board a ship with the intention of selling him in the West Indies. A court case in 1772 had shown it to be illegal. He turned from the notice to see the pilot swing his leg over the bulwark in preparation to climb down the rope ladder to the boat below.

'Pilot, can I not persuade you to stay?'

'I am sorry Captain King, but your vessel has been seized, and there is nothing I can do. I have other ships to pilot in and out of Liverpool.'

William watched the Sheriff's boat pick up the wind and head towards the Liverpool shoreline.

- CHAPTER FOURTEEN -

Stowaway

Anchored in the River Mersey
Christmas Eve 1805

William paced the poop deck, deep in thought. The conversation with Pilcher went round and round in his mind. Why would anyone wish to swear out a warrant for the arrest of the *Albatross?* What did they have to gain? They would have to prove that he had abducted someone to be sold as a slave. The authorities would require a witness to prove such a crime had taken place. Without a witness, the only way to prove a crime had been committed was to produce evidence.

Suddenly William realised how the plot must have been implemented.

'Mr Austin, rouse out the crew!''

All hands, all hands muster aft,' yelled the Mate, responding to the urgency in William's voice.

When the crew had assembled, William addressed them. 'Lads, you know the sheriff's office has arrested our ship. While we sit here we cannot earn money, which means I cannot pay you.'

Murmurings of discontent ran through the crew. They didn't mind sitting at anchor anywhere, if they were being paid. If they were not to be paid, they would wish to be put ashore. 'Hold on, lads, I said I cannot pay you; I didn't say I wouldn't pay you. As long as you are with me you will be paid. I guarantee your wages.'

The muttering stopped. Smiles returned to some of their faces.

'I want this ship searched from top to bottom. I don't know what we will find, but my guess is that we will find a stowaway. If we do find someone, I still want the remainder of the *Albatross* searched; there may be more than one. Keep your eyes open and check for anything that appears to be out of place. Mr Austin, take the larboard watch and start the search from the bow to the stern. Mr Fuller, you and the starboard watch search from stern to stem. The weather is calm, so open the hatches and search the cargo. I'll be in my cabin.'

William acknowledged the salutes of his first and second mates, and went below to his cabin. A germ of an idea had come to him. He sat at his small desk and dragged out his chart of Liverpool Bay. He began to study the chart in detail.

It wasn't long before he heard a commotion on deck. The crew had found something. He replaced the chart in the desk draw and made his way to the deck.

'We found this black fellow in amongst the cargo, Sir.'

'Thank you, Bosun,'

The Bosun and a crewmember held the man as William studied him. He was large, with arms that bulged from his sleeveless shirt. His round head was covered in closely packed hair, which showed grey in parts. His eyes didn't show any fear. His canvas duck trousers were held up by a piece of rope that was neatly back-spliced. William noticed that each loose strand had been whipped with fine twine. Who ever made the stowaway's rope-belt was a seaman.

'What are you doing on my ship?' demanded William.

The black man's large round eyes flitted from William's face to the shore.

'Look at the Captain when you are spoken to!' demanded the Bosun.

The black man's head turned as if he had just heard something.

'Can you speak English?' asked William.

The man's eyes still cast about as he looked at the shore longingly.

'He don't speak English, Captain,' said the Bosun.

William watched the black man's eyes. The expression in them convinced him that the man understood the Bosun.

'I have enough trouble at the moment, Bosun, I don't need any more, and this fellow is trouble. I'll not feed anyone who doesn't earn his keep. The *Albatross* has been arrested, but we are not obliged to keep stowaways until we get to land. We have not yet left the river, so he is not my responsibility.'

William's voice rose in anger. The scar across his cheek showed white, as he allowed himself the luxury of venting his anger at his ship's arrest.

'Bosun, reave a block at the end of the yard and make a noose.'

'A noose, Sir?'

'Are you deaf? I said a noose, damn your eyes, do as you are ordered!'

'Aye, Aye, sir,' said the Bosun, and turned to the First Mate for support. Austin stepped forward between the black man and his Captain.

'I trust, Sir, you do not intend to carry out what I suspect.'

'Mr Austin, you will carry out any order you are given, or I will have you for mutiny.'

William turned away from the little group and walked back towards the stern. He clasped his hand behind his back to give the impression he was deep in thought. Half turning, he stared at the group and the now trembling black man.

He watched the man's eyes as he walked slowly back towards him. The man was on the edge of panic.

'Hang him, Bosun, and when he's dead, slide his body overboard when the tide is on the ebb. It will be lost in the Irish Sea by the morning.'

'Ayeeee,' cried the black man, 'no, Mister, no hang.'

'A miracle, Bosun, he can speak English.'

'So it appears, Sir,' said the Bosun, a nervous tone in his voice. He was not really sure if he was still required to carry out the order.

William allowed his body to rock back and forth as he studied the stowaway.

'Why are you on my ship?'

'Mister, I be told to come onboard and hide. I be told you sailin' to Africa and I could go home.'

'Who told you we were bound for Africa? You will refer to me as Sir, understood?'

'Mr Henry, Sir.'

'Mr Henry? Who is Mr Henry?'

'I only know him as Mr Henry, Boss.'

'What did he look like?'

'He a big man, a mean face with wide eyes.'

'Wide eyes?'

'Yes, Boss, the bit of face between one eye and the other is very big.'

'Are you speaking about Henry Nicholson?' asked William, the reason for the *Albatross's* arrest now becoming clear.

'Yes, Sir.'

William slowly walked back again to the stern. His mind was in turmoil.

The black man's existence was the evidence required to condemn William. If William was convicted, he would be ruined, and his partners would lose all credibility in their efforts to make slavery illegal.

'Lock him in the cable locker, Mr Austin, until I decide what to do with him.'

William flopped into his chair at his desk and pulled out the chart of Liverpool Bay to study it once again.

A knock on his cabin door broke his concentration. 'Come in.'

William relaxed when he saw his First Mate.

'James, come in and take a seat.'

'Thank you, Captain.'

'What can I do for you?'

'I would like to know if your anger was real? I don't know if you meant what you said, or if you meant to scare the black man. Would you have hanged him if he hadn't decided to speak English?'

'That is something I cannot tell you, because I don't know.'

'Pardon me for saying this, Captain, but I don't know when you are really angry or if you're just acting for the benefit of the crew. They don't know if you mean it or not either.'

'James, they don't have to know if I mean it or not, all that matters is whether I know if I mean it or not.'

The First Mate realised he would never know if his Captain would have hanged the black man.

'Thank you, Captain, I will return to my duties.'

'Stay a while, James, I have something to discuss with you.'

James waited.

'I think we can weigh anchor and cross the bar this evening on the ebb. I have sailed it many times with a pilot, when I was First Mate on the Irish emigrant run, and believe I have enough knowledge to navigate the channels.'

'But, Sir, we are under arrest.'

'Aye, we are, and I am sure it's because of the black man. If I take him back to Liverpool and hand him over, we will have ruined our chances of sailing. The courts will take their time, and we will be tied up with lawyers for months, which also means the crew, and you, will be on the beach again - without pay.'

'I have been thinking on that, Sir. I need the money. To be correct, my wife needs the money. We have three children.'

'Are you willing to bend the rules a little?'

'How do you mean?'

'Are you willing for us to take a chance over the bar, without a pilot?'

'It's your ship, Captain. What do you have in mind?'

'Bring the stowaway to me.'

It wasn't long before the stowaway stood in front of William. James Austin stood near the door. The two crewmen who accompanied the stowaway were dismissed.

'What is your name?'

'I been told my name is Ben Liverpool.'

'I've told you before to address me as Sir. How long have you been in Liverpool?'

'I brought here when I a young child. I been with Mr. Henry's family for about twenty years, Sir.'

'Would you like to be free?'

'Mr Henry tol' me I free if I hid on this boat, Sir.'

'You did hide, Ben, which means you are now a free man.'

'But I been caught by you, Mister.'

William stood and stared at the black man.

'Sir,' added Ben quietly.

'You have a choice. Go back to Mr Henry, and perhaps he will beat you, or sign on my ship. We will not beat you and you will be free.'

'Lawyer Snelgrove needs to be told we don't have a slave onboard, Sir,' said the First Mate.

'We have done nothing illegal, James, so we will not return to Liverpool.'

'But——' William held up his hand to silence any more comments.

'Ben Liverpool, you are a free man, and as a free man, I can offer you a berth on the *Albatross* as a seaman.'

'Where we goin', Sir?'

'To America, and then the West Indies.'

'Is they near Africa?'

'No, Ben, they're not, but on our return to Liverpool I will guarantee that you do not have to go back to Mr Henry, so he will not be able to beat you. As a free man, Ben, nobody can beat you.'

'Nobody?'

'As a free man, nobody can beat you. You told me that Mr Henry said you would be free if you hid on my ship?'

'Yes, Sir.'

'Have you sailed with Mr Henry before?'

'Yes, Sir, I sailed with him to Africa, but he would lock me up while we waited for the slaves. He thought I would run.'

'I will help you to remain free, Ben, if you sign on to my ship as a seaman.'

'What happens when we in America; they keep black men as slaves?'

'As a British seaman, nobody can touch you. Can you write?'

'I make my mark, Sir.'

William flipped open the muster book, dipped a pen in ink, and handed it to the back man.

'Sign alongside my finger.'

Ben accepted the pen and concentrated on making his mark. When he finished, he stood back with a smile on his face.

'Mr Austin, will you witness the signing on of our latest crew member?'

'A pleasure, Sir.'

'Thank you, James, will you now take this seaman and allocate him to a watch.'

'Aye, Aye, Sir.'

The door closed behind the First Mate and the new seaman. William let out a long sigh. He felt he had held his breath for the past half hour. If Ben had refused to sign, he was unsure what he would have done. The last thing he wanted was to return to Liverpool. The court case would allow the Nicholson family to gloat, and prove that he was unfit for command. He checked his watch and realised it would be dark in less than an hour. The ebb tide would start in about forty minutes.

If he waited for morning he knew the lawyer would be back,

to either order the *Albatross* back to Liverpool, or arrest him and remove him from command.

William waited while Teng Sang fastened the clasp of his boat cloak. The course of the river, and the sand banks, were embedded in his mind, after hours of studying the chart.

'It will be a cold night, Sang.'

'Aye, Sir.'

'Mr Austin, two good men in the chains, each with a lead line; I want soundings both sides.'

Night closed in as William watched two of the crew climb on to the small platforms extending from the deck out over the water. The 'chains' were just aft of the bow, one on each side of the ship. The men's experience and a small length of chain, waist high, were all that would stop them falling overboard. William watched as each made practice casts with their seven-pound lead line. They were finding how high they were from the water. When the *Albatross* began her slow movement down the channel, each man would hang in the chains and cast his lead line ahead of the vessel on their side of the ship. As the ship passed over the vertical line, the men would sing out the depth of the water. It would be dark, so each must know how high he was above the water and deduct this from the reading on the lead line. If it were daylight, it would not be a problem, as they would see the marks on their lines indicating the depth.

Each man plumbed his lead up and down, to test for the bottom. They then touched the line with their tongue or lips, so as to feel the marks. The marks could be linen, bunting, leather or two knots tied together. William knew that their fingers would become useless after a few minutes of handling freezing wet lines.

Their lips and tongue would become their fingers to ascertain the marks on the line.

'Bosun, make sure they use plenty of tallow on the base of the leads. I want to know the type of bottom, along with the depth.'

'Aye, Sir.'

'If we stay in the channel, Captain, surely we will not need to worry about the bottom,' commented Second Mate Fuller.

'Mr Fuller, you may be the newest Second Mate in Liverpool, but believe me, I want to know the type of bottom on each cast. If it is mud, we will be in the channel, but if it is sand, we will be too far over. There are sand banks on both sides of the channel. Didn't you take notice of the buoy about three cables ahead? '

'Yes, Sir, but I'm not sure which one it is, because you were using the chart.'

'Point taken, Mr Fuller: the buoy is Crosby Point buoy. Over there is Crosby Chapel, so we have a reasonably accurate knowledge of our position. When we weigh anchor, I want you to set the jib and foresail only. Your course will be north; and make sure the helmsman is experienced, because if we run aground, we will lose the masts. The ebb should carry us down the channel, during which we will pass another buoy, so keep your eyes open for that marker.

We stay on course until we reach the next buoy. That buoy will be the Formby Point boathouse buoy. We will steer due west at that point.'

William checked the sky and observed that heavy grey clouds had gathered.

'Mr Austin, weigh anchor.'

William walked slowly to the stern and watched the water. It was still, but he could sense the *Albatross* was about to swing and face up river as the tide turned.

'Anchor aweigh,' came the cry from the forecastle.

The jib rose from the deck like a white shroud. The foresail banged as it filled in the wind.

'By the deep six, muddy bottom,' cried the starboard leadsman.

Six fathoms or thirty-six feet of water, and the *Albatross* drew two and a half fathoms. He still had plenty of water under the keel.

'Bosun, cast the log,' ordered William.

'By the mark five, muddy bottom,' cried the larboard leadsman.

'Six and a half knots, Sir,' called the Bosun, coiling down the log line.

'Thank you.'

William's mind calculated the information. If the *Albatross* was doing six and a half knots with the ebb, and the mid-channel buoy was nearly three miles from their anchorage, they should see the buoy in about thirty minutes.

He raised his telescope and focused where he expected the buoy to be, but was unable to see anything.

'By the mark three, sandy bottom!' came the cry from the starboard leadsman.

'What's her head?' shouted William as he hurried to check the compass.

'Due north!'

'Bring her round to north by nor' west.'

The tide was pushing the *Albatross* on to the sand bank.

'North by nor' west,' came the reply from the helmsman.

'By the deep six, muddy bottom,' called the larboard leadsman.

'By the deep six, muddy bottom,' from the starboard side.

William let out a sigh, and quickly covered it with a cough. He didn't want the crew to be aware of his concern.

The clouds now covered the sky, shutting out even a glimmer of moonlight. They were blind.

'Time?'

'Half hour sand just turned, Sir,' said the Second Mate.

William walked to the starboard side and tried to peer into the blackness. Where was the buoy?

'Keep a sharp lookout to starboard,' shouted William to the crew on deck.

'We need to find the buoy.'

The sound of three bells forward caused William to aim his telescope ahead of the ship. Three strikes of the bell told him that the lookout had seen something dead ahead.

'Something in the water dead ahead, Sir,' came the cry from forward.

'Steer——' shouted William.

A cracking sound forward, followed by a scraping sound interrupted him.

'We hit the buoy, Sir,' shouted the bow lookout.

'By the mark three, sandy bottom,' shouted the starboard leadsman.

William leaned over the taffrail on the starboard side in an effort to make out what had happened. The scraping sound grew louder, and suddenly the buoy came in to view as it banged its way down the side of the *Albatross*.

'Steer nor'–nor'–west.'

'Nor'–nor'–west, Sir.'

'Mr Austin, go with the carpenter and check for damage,'

ordered William.

He moved to the helmsman and checked the compass. It was nor'–nor'–west.

The tide was stronger than he anticipated. He had to make sure that they didn't go too far over to the other side of the channel, or they'd run aground.

'By the deep eight, muddy bottom,' called the larboard leadsman.

'Steer north, helmsman.'

'North, Sir.'

'The tide is stronger, Captain,' called James Austin, returning to the poop deck.

'Yes, the tide will run faster and faster as the ebb takes hold. Did you find anything?'

'No, Sir, all dry. The carpenter will do another round in an hour.'

'Thank you.'

'If we keep this speed, James, we should see the next buoy in a few minutes. When we reach it, I will alter course to due west. I suggest you have the crew on standby for the sails. We will not have much time as the gap between the buoy and the sand bank to larboard is very small.'

'Aye, Aye, Sir, the wind has freshened with the tide.'

William glanced at the sky, so dark that he couldn't even see the clouds scudding overhead. He quietly voiced his thoughts to his first mate.

'I would have preferred a moon tonight, but I suppose beggars can't be choosers.'

'We'll get through, Sir, don't worry.'

'Thank you, James.'

The First Mate saluted as he left to organise the crew for the change of course and sails.

A single stroke on the forward bell told him the lookout had seen the buoy.

'Where away?' called William.

'A point on the starboard bow!'

They were inside the channel.

'Standby, Mr Austin!'

'All ready, Sir.'

William moved to the starboard side again and strained his eyes to see the buoy.

'By the mark five, sand and mud,' called the larboard leadsman.

They were close to the sand bank.

'By the deep four, sandy bottom!' the larboard leadsman called again.

'By the deep four, muddy bottom!' called out the starboard leadsman.

They were running down the very edge of the bank. William still couldn't find the buoy.

He leaned further out over the rail in an effort to see better, when he felt rain. He glanced up at the clouds, now lit as lightning flashed. The roll of thunder was so loud he thought the ship had struck the bank. A second flash lit the sea astern, and in the instant of the flash, William saw the buoy as it bobbed in the rising swell of the storm, half a mile astern.

'Hard a larboard!' he bellowed. 'Put her over!'

William rushed to the helmsman as another peal of thunder put an end to anyone hearing his orders.

Reaching the helmsman, William pushed him aside and

pulled on the giant wheel to turn the *Albatross* to larboard. They were about to run into the sand bank, dead ahead.

The helmsman saw his Captain hauling on the wheel. He jumped up and added his strength to help turn the wheel.

'Now, Mr Austin, now!' bellowed William.

William watched the mainsails drop from the yards and fill in the wind.

'Have you got her?' William yelled at the helmsman.

'Aye, Sir, I have her now.'

'Steer west.'

'Aye, Aye, steer west.'

'By the mark ten, sand and gravel!' cried the starboard leadsman.

'Well, Mr Austin, it worked,' said William, with both relief and pride. 'We are clear of the river and the sand banks. When we are further out in to the Irish Sea, alter course south, which will take us clear of the Welsh coast.'

The *Liverpool Lass* sailed a week after the *Albatross*. Henry had the trade goods unloaded, and the slave quarters knocked down, so that more suitable goods for sale in Boston could be loaded. He used every stitch of canvas to catch the *Albatross*. The wind was fair, but Henry kept careful watch on the masts. He did not want the *Lass* to lose a mast in his haste to catch his quarry. He spent most of each day on deck, and refined the sails in an effort to get every bit of speed from the wind. The lack of female company onboard put him in a very poor mood.

The *Liverpool Lass* arrived in Boston thee days after the *Albatross,* and berthed some distance away. Henry did not wish to attract too much attention from William.

Henry met his father's agent, Mr Leather, and between them they organised an auction to sell the contents of the *Lass.*

'What do you know of the *Albatross,* and her Captain?' asked Henry of the agent.

'He has dealings with Abraham Judson, by letter of introduction from Liverpool.'

'I want you to keep an eye on him, and the Jew, Judson. I want to know everything they do, and where they go, and what cargo he carries.'

'He could be here for some time. There is little cargo at this time of the year for England. Perhaps later there will be some salt fish from the North.'

'I don't care what the cargo is, just get me the same, to make sure it carries me to the same place to which King is destined; I don't trust the man.'

'As you say, Sir, I will do my best.'

'Make sure your best fits my needs, or we may have a falling out.'

The agent made to speak, but stopped as he peered into Henry's eyes. He knew this man would hurt him if he did not comply with his request. He felt suddenly very hot, and a small rivulet of sweat from under his fashionable wig ran down the back of his neck.

'What kind of entertainment do you have in Boston?' asked Henry.

'It depends on what is your fancy, Captain, boys or girls.'

'I have some special needs, and I am not bothered which it is, but on the whole I have found I relax more with a woman.'

'May I enquire about your special needs, Captain.'

'You may not!'

'Captain, I do not wish to pry, but unless I know what you want, I cannot supply your needs.'

Henry's face softened as he realised the Agent was correct, and he must have some idea of his special needs.

'Shall we say I like to discipline my friends?'

'Exactly, Captain, now that I am aware, I will make enquiries and let you know tomorrow.'

'I am glad we understand each other; until tomorrow then.' Henry stood, picked up his hat and left the Agent's office without another word. The Agent mopped his brow, and with hands that shook, poured himself a large drink. After swallowing the rough rum, he realised how long it was since he drank before noon. Henry Nicholson's cold dead-fish eyes frightened him. He consoled himself that the drink was medicinal to calm his nerves. He then realised the dilemma that he was in; where would he find a woman with similar tastes to Captain Nicholson?

- CHAPTER FIFTEEN -

Proposal

Liverpool
February 1806

George King stood in front of a full-length mirror and admired his new clothes. He wore a plain dark green, single-breasted coat with a black velvet collar. It buttoned with a slight strain over his growing waistline. The tailor had persuaded him that a vertical broad striped waistcoat would make him appear a little slimmer. He turned from side to side to admire his image. His pants were of a light-coloured soft woollen cloth cut to the latest fashion of calf length, fitting well into his new Hessian boots. He fluffed up his white silk neck cloth and positioned a diamond stud to be visible, but not ostentatious. The tailor informed him that fluffed up neck cloths were last year's fashion, so he pulled his a little tighter to smooth out the excess cloth.

He felt well groomed and he cut a dash. He hoped Charlotte thought the same.

Donald had acknowledged that George would ask for Charlotte's hand in marriage today. George felt sure she would agree, but even so, he didn't want to leave anything to chance.

He absent-mindedly stroked his new hat while recalling the past few weeks. William was happy and enthusiastic about his future, and had sailed for America on Christmas Eve. It was a shame they could not work together, but George did not believe the end of the African trade would come about in his lifetime.

He could not understand why Charlotte had taken a dislike to William. She hadn't a good word to say about him. George hoped the two would become friends, after he married Charlotte.

A light tap on the door broke into George's thoughts. Alfred entered the room.

'The coach is ready, Sur'

'Thank you, Alfred. What do you think?' George gestured to his overall appearance.

'The perfect gentleman, Sur.'

'Are you implying unless I wear these clothes, I am not a gentleman?' The smile on his lips carried to his eyes.

'Sur?'

'Never mind, Alfred.' George placed his new hat on his head. 'Let us away, I have a very important appointment this afternoon.'

At the main entrance hall, the parlour maid opened the door. George could see the coach waiting outside. The brass work and the paint shone like new.

'You worked hard on the coach, Alfred, well done. Take the long way to Mr Nicholson's place.'

'Yes, Sur.'

Alfred climbed up to the coachman's seat after making sure that George was seated inside. George felt at peace with the world as the coach began to move. Heavy rain during the previous week had cleansed the streets of dirty snow. Even the sky had changed from a dull grey to a light blue, in support of George's important day.

George sighed as he watched the scenery pass. Duke Street was his normal route to town, but at the bottom of the street they would turn left into Paradise Street, and then left again into Park lane.

It was always a beautiful ride along Park Lane to the new Toxteth Park. The smell, in early spring, of the country and the river complimented each other. He loved the gentle climb up Park Lane to Charlotte's home, with its commanding views across the river and the anchored ships.

Donald Nicholson's nearest neighbour was St James's Church. The church bells were the only interruption to the overall tranquility of a Sunday. The Nicholson house had set a new standard in luxury.

The coach came to a halt in front of imposing colonnades, fashioned in the form of black slaves, holding up the roof of the porch area. Each time George visited this home; the house appeared grander than the time before.

Donald's household was a mixture of black and white servants. The only difference was that the white servants could leave if they wished, but the black servants were bound to the Nicholson family because they didn't have anywhere to go.

Donald Nicholson came forward, his hand outstretched as George stepped down from the coach.

'Welcome, George!'

'Thank you, Donald,' answered George, shaking his host's hand.

'How are you?'

'How do you think? I have never been so nervous.'

'If it is any consolation, Charlotte is also nervous, so you will be a pigeon pair,' laughed Donald. 'We will take tea in the withdrawing room.'

On entering the room George saw Charlotte, and her mother, intent on something in the garden. The large open glass doors allowed access to a flagged area. He could see a glass-topped table surrounded by four metal chairs. The table was laid for afternoon tea. The two women turned as the men approached.

'Good afternoon, Mr King,' said Sarah.

'Good afternoon, Mrs Nicholson.'

'I think we should do away with the formalities, don't you, my dear?' said Donald to his wife.

'If you wish.'

'Will you take tea, er, George?'

'Thank you, Mrs, er, Sarah.'

'Good afternoon, Charlotte,' said George, bowing his head.

'How are you, George?'

George gave her a weak smile and ran a finger inside the edge of his neck cloth. 'A little warm, but otherwise I am fine, thank you.'

'Do sit yourself down, George,' said Donald, full of bonhomie.

'You look very smart, George,' commented Charlotte.

'Oh, thank you.'

'Lemon or milk, er, George.'

'Lemon please, Sarah.'

The tea was poured, with great ceremony, into dainty teacups. Small ham sandwiches were handed around on a decorated china plate. The conversation did not seem to be going well. George did his best to ignore the small trickle of sweat that slid silently down his face.

'You appear hot, George, for such a time of year,' remarked Sarah.

'Well——' gasped George, trying desperately to think of something funny or lighthearted to say.

'Come, my dear,' said Donald, and offered his arm to his wife, 'I thought you wanted to show me the new work in the garden?'

'Work?' whispered Sarah, and gazed at her husband as if he had lost his mind.

'Yes, Dear, come along. Now is a good time to show me. You don't mind if we leave you and Charlotte. Do you, George? I have promised Sarah, for some time, that I will inspect the new work.'

'Not at all, not at all,' said George, as he stood to farewell Donald and his wife.

'We will be about half an hour or so, if it is all right with you. Do look after George, Charlotte.'

Donald and Sarah linked arms and disappeared down the steps that lead to the extensive garden.

'Well, well,' said George, and put down his plate of half-eaten sandwich. He pulled out a large green handkerchief and mopped his brow.

'We are alone now, George.'

'Yes, yes, indeed.'

'More tea?'

'I think I will.'

Charlotte poured the tea and placed a fresh slice of lemon in the cup. She sat back in her chair; her hands lightly clasped in her lap, and gazed expectantly at George.

'Thank you,' he said.

George finished wiping his face and returned the handkerchief to his pocket.

'Charlotte,' said George, wriggling in his chair.

'Yes, George.'

'Charlotte, my dear.'

'Mmm?' she said, and watched George while she made her eyes appear large and open. She placed a hand on his arm in an effort to stop him moving.

'We have known each other a long time, haven't we?'

'Some years now, George.'

'I have grown very, very fond of you, and I just wondered if my feelings were reciprocated?'

'Reciprocated, George? In what way do you mean?'

'I am a lot older than you, and I have been married before, but my feelings for you are very strong. I wish I was twenty years younger and that I could say what I want to say.'

'George, dear, I think you babble ......' she smiled to take any sting out of her comment.

'Babble. Oh dear, am I?'

'Just a little. Is there something you wish to say to me?'

'Say to you? Oh, yes, there is.'

'Well, George, Father will be back soon, and we will not be able to speak so freely if he is listening.'

'Yes, yes, of course, you are right. Do you like me a little?'

'I like you a lot, George. I always have.'

'Have you?' his hands flapped in his nervousness. 'I am so pleased.'

She sat and waited for him to make the next move.

To Charlotte, George was weak, but he could be manoeuvred to her advantage. A good life with a rich older man was more attractive than a young man struggling to make his way in the world. She would marry George, whether George liked it or not.

Their marriage would be her first step in revenge against William.

Her plan had been ruined when William refused to take her to his ship. Attending the *Albatross,* without a chaperone, would have so compromised William that he would have had to marry Charlotte. She would have gained the man, the hero of the hour, and she would have also gained access to his father's money by being the dutiful daughter-in-law. Charlotte marrying William would be the best of both worlds. Unfortunately, she would now have to marry the father, and block any chances of William having access to his father's money.

Charlotte forced the most beautiful smile she could muster and flashed it at George in an effort to force him to ask for her hand. She knew her father and mother would return within the next few minutes and ruin everything, so she had little time for George's dithering.

'You were saying, George?' she said as she affectionately stroked his hand.

George glanced down and watched her stroking his hand. He realised that now was the moment. He placed his other hand over hers and squeezed gently. Charlotte turned her hand and entwined her fingers in his, and let out a little sigh of pleasure.

'Charlotte, my dear, will you marry me?'

'Oh! Yes, George!'

'Yes?'

"Yes, George. What did you want me to say? No!'

'Oh no, my dear, I wanted a big yes from you.'

'You have it, George.'

'May I kiss you?'

'Oh, yes please, George.'

George leaned over and kissed her lightly on her lips, and

then again a little harder. He placed his hands on her shoulders and pulled her closer.

She closed her eyes and let him kiss her. She was not sure what would happen next, but she held her breath while the kisses grew harder.

She felt panic as the kiss lengthened, how long she could hold her breath.

At last George stopped kissing her and moved away. He sat with a lopsided grin on his face while he gazed, owl-like, at his future wife.

'When shall we marry?'

'A June wedding would be lovely, George.'

'Don't you think we are rushing it a little, my dear. It is already February and it may seem we have married in indecent haste.'

'If we are to marry, George, dear, then let us marry. Why delay?'

'I would like William to be my best man, but I am not sure when he will return.'

'Then we may not be able to wait for William, George, dear, and I don't want to delay any longer than we have to. I want you to be my husband and I do not want to wait for your son to join us. After all, William will have to fit his life around us. If he is at all concerned about you, dear, he would be one of your officers and not in command of someone else's ship.'

The comment came out stronger than she meant. She was frightened that she might scare him away, after so much planning.

She suddenly turned on her womanly charms and played the defenseless little girl. It had always worked when she used it on her father, and George was no different.

She stroked George's face, and said in a low voice, 'We will have to discuss it with Mother: she will know best. I am all of a flutter, such an exciting time.'

'Just as you say, dear, your mother will know best, and we should be guided by her. Please don't fret yourself on such a happy day for us both.'

Charlotte smiled. She could see George was concerned that he had upset her. She had won a small point, and knew she would win more in the future.

'You are a sweet man, George. I am so happy we will marry.'

The newly engaged couple gazed at each other and wondered what the other would be like after they were married.

—⚭—

'Well, that was nice; your Mother has done herself proud with her new work,' called out Donald Nicholson.

George and Charlotte jumped in surprise as Donald stumped his way up the garden steps, followed by his wife.

George blushed when Donald looked at them both and flopped down in the chair he had used before.

'Well, Charlotte, is there anything your Mother and I should know?'

'Donald, Sarah,' said George, and moved closer to Charlotte to hold her hands in his, 'Charlotte has agreed to be my wife.'

'Congratulations, George!' said Donald, as he pulled himself to his feet and offered his hand. 'It is about time someone took the girl in hand. She needs a strong hand, does Charlotte, and I am sure you are the man.'

'Father, what do you mean, a strong hand indeed. You make it sound like George has bought a horse!'

'Your father's advice is always given whether one wants it or not,' said Sarah, and kissed Charlotte on the cheek.

'You may kiss me, George,' said Sarah primly.

George leaned forward and gave his future mother-in-law a small peck of a kiss on her cheek. 'I hope you are pleased, Sarah. You know I will look after her.'

'I am, George, and I am sure you will.'

'This calls for a celebration,' said Donald, 'I am sick of tea; it doesn't have any body in it. Champagne is what we want. Sarah, my dear, can you get one of those girls to bring us a cold bottle in a bucket?'

A few minutes later a housemaid arrived with a tray, on which were four glasses and a bottle of champagne in a bucket of ice.

'Clear the tea away, girl, and put the tray down on the table. I will open it,' said Donald. He pushed aside some of the tea dishes to make room.

With a flourish he picked the bottle from the ice bucket and uncorked the sparkling wine. It flowed down the side of the bottle as he filled the four glasses.

'A toast, I think, my dear, to Charlotte and George!'

Donald and Sarah drank, and watched their child and George.

'To you both and especially to Charlotte,' George responded, raising his glass to each of them in turn. 'I only wish William was here to share in my pleasure. I am sure you will grow to love him as I do, Charlotte, my dear.'

Charlotte sipped her drink and smiled at George, 'I am sure we will get to know each other very well,' she replied ambiguously.

- CHAPTER SIXTEEN -

The Wedding

Liverpool
June 1806

In George's eyes, the preparation for the wedding took on a life of its own. The conversation in Charlotte's family was always about what the bride and her mother would wear, what George should wear, who to invite, and who not to invite. Donald insisted that some of the city councillors be invited, although George had only met some of them once, as well as friends, acquaintances and major political figures.

'Good for the future, George, you never know the future!' emphasized Donald, in an effort to win George over to his list of names, rather than Sarah's.

Not since his wife died, many years before, had George been the centre of so much attention.

The weeks progressed, and he and Charlotte were invited to various social occasions. On many of these occasions George did not know their host. Charlotte or Sarah and Donald, knew everyone. They were fussed over and feted by some who hoped for an invitation to the wedding of the year, and by others to show they had already been invited and that the bride and groom were close friends. Eyebrows were raised at the age difference between the bride and the groom. Friends made allowances, while those not invited made cutting remarks.

George was unhappy that he had not heard from William since he'd sailed.

Eventually the great day arrived. George sat at the long table in his dining room and sipped coffee. He stared at the breakfast food laid out for his pleasure, and felt his stomach contract. A large brandy and coffee would settle his nervous disorder, but decided against the alcohol, in case people could smell the brandy on his breath.

The dining-room door opened and in walked Morgan Brookes, a distant cousin of George, and apart from William, George's only blood relative. George had asked Morgan to be his best man, as he couldn't wait any longer for William. Morgan lived in Lancaster and traded in furniture to the Americas.

When Charlotte asked George for a list of relatives that he wished to invite, he sat at his desk for a long time in an effort to think of a friend and a relative. Being an only child, and both of his parents' dead, brought home how lonely his life had become. He scribbled down the names of business friends and acquaintances. Suddenly he remembered Morgan. He had not seen him for some years. At least he would have one relative on his side of the church.

It was Charlotte's idea to ask Morgan to be his best man. This was after George confided that he didn't have any other relatives or friends.

'Then you must ask Morgan to stand with you,' said Charlotte.

'I would prefer to wait until the last possible moment, my dear, just in case William returns in time.'

'Nonsense, George, we cannot wait on the chance that William will return. You haven't heard from him since he left. He could be anywhere, and because of his new anti-slavery friends, he may not even wish to return to Liverpool.'

'I am sure he wouldn't just sail away and not let me know.'

'How many letters did you receive during his time in the Navy?'

'Things were different then. He was in a fighting ship with little chance of communicating on a regular basis, especially on blockade duty off a French port.'

'Maybe, dearest, but the truth is you need a best man and time is short. I think the most suitable person is your cousin, Morgan. If William returns in time, perhaps you could ask Morgan to forgo the honour in favour of William.'

'I suppose so,' said George reluctantly.' I am sure Morgan would understand, in the circumstances.'

'I knew you would see sense in the end, my dear. You have to have a best man, and it would be easier if he were from your family. In the absence of William, Morgan has to be asked. Now please write to him and ask if he would do us the honour of attending as your best man.'

'I suppose you are right, my dear. It's just that I really wanted William.'

'I know, George, but he isn't here, and we do need to finalise the plans for the wedding.'

'Yes, you are right, as always,' said George, leaning over to kiss Charlotte on the cheek.

'George,' said Charlotte as she accepted the light kiss and smiled at him.

'Good morning, George!' shouted Morgan, making his way to the sideboard to inspect the breakfast food. 'Sleep well, Old Man? Your last night of freedom!'

'I did sleep a little,' said George in a quiet voice.

'Nervous?'

'A little, yes.'

'Not to worry, all will be well by this evening. You will be married again. Oh! Sorry, George, didn't mean to offend.'

'I am over that now. She has been dead for over twenty years, and time heals.'

Morgan sat opposite George. The smell of his breakfast caused George's stomach to give a growl of demand.

'Went to the church yesterday just to make sure I knew what to expect,' said Morgan.

'Which church?'

'Church of Saint James, the one at which you will be married this afternoon. You do know it is at St James?'

'Yes, of course I do,' snapped George.

'Sorry, George, just wanted to make sure.'

The day dragged. The ceremony was scheduled for 2.00 pm. By 1.30 pm he was standing with Morgan at the top of Quarry Mount, near the sandstone church of St James. Its large bell tower dominated the small mount. George inspected the arched entrance to the church grounds and read the inscription over the arch. *Built in 1775.*

'Morgan, wait here please. I want to walk off my nervousness,' said George and strode away from Morgan to the top of the mound.

'I'll accompany you, Old Man,' retorted his cousin.

George ignored Morgan and started to walk across the open ground to climb the last few feet of Quarry Hill. He wanted to be on his own. It was a beautiful day with hardly a cloud in the sky, a perfect summer's day to marry.

He reached the top and peered over the edge of a man-made cliff. Below him he could see a large sandstone quarry. The quarry was hidden from the road by the small mound on which he stood. The sandstone from the quarry supplied most of the construction material for the major buildings in Liverpool. He watched the people below; they were the size of ants as they worked on the quarry floor.

He turned away from the edge and breathed the clean air from the river. Glancing across to the church, he saw Morgan wave frantically. Slowly he returned. Today was his wedding day; nothing should mar his happiness, but why did he feel so sad?

'It's nearly time, George,' shouted Morgan as George drew near.

The two men walked up the path into the church and stood at the front pew on the right-hand side. George watched the various guests arrive. Each had to decide on which side they were to sit.

The remainder of the day was a blur to George. He remembered being asked if he would take this woman, and when he looked at Charlotte he felt a desire to run madly from the church, but he didn't, and gave the correct answers to the simple questions.

A warm breeze gently wafted the smell of the flowers tied

to the ends of each pew. The flowers were to mask the overpowering smell of the city if the wind changed. Although the church was further out of the city than George's home, a sea breeze would pick up the smell and blow it across Quarry Hill.

At last the service was over and he and Charlotte were married. She looked lovely when she threw back the veil of her headdress to allow herself to be kissed by her new husband. He looked into her eyes that sparkled in happiness.

Charlotte gazed at George and knew she had won. She knew that she would be the mistress of her home. No longer would she be required to do what her parents wanted. No longer would she be dragged around like a mare at auction. As the wife of a prominent Liverpool trader, she had a home to run; she had servants, power, and prestige in local society. Charlotte was very happy.

The only negative thought Charlotte had that day was about William. She was now his stepmother.

The wedding breakfast was at Donald Nicholson's home. The alcohol flowed freely. Toast after toast was made to the new Mr and Mrs King, to His Majesty, to the guests, to the city of Liverpool, to the African Trade.

Guests spilled out of the house into the garden. The evening retained some warmth of the day.

Eventually Charlotte became too tired for another dance, and too full of food and wine. It was unseemly for a lady to eat a hearty meal and her corset, which crushed her waist to produce an ample bosom, did not allow her to eat anything other than very small pickings. Her feet hurt after each male guest tried to dance *The Happy Captive* with the new bride. She tried the

Quadrille, twirled the two-step, until she could no longer keep cool by the use of her fan. She wanted to go home but she was home, in the only home she knew from childhood. She wanted to go to her new home to rest and sleep.

She knew that if she showed too much eagerness to leave, the guests would make lewd jokes. She was not looking forward to being alone with George. She was unsure of what would be required of her in the marriage bed. Her mother had tried to tell her, in a very embarrassed and not very useful roundabout way, what would be expected. Unfortunately, Charlotte could hardly make sense of it.

She felt confused as to what George required. She knew he would want something, but what it was she could not be sure.

It was after eleven o'clock when George suggested that they might leave for their own home.

'Yes please, George. I am very tired and just want to go to sleep.'

'Of course, my dear.'

Would she be too tired for him to claim a little of his conjugal rights. It occurred to him that perhaps he should wait until Charlotte became accustomed to the title of Mrs King. If he did not make an approach, Charlotte may think that he didn't love her, or that he was upset with her desire to go home so soon.

Arm in arm they bade farewell to each of the guests, after thanking them for attending their wedding. Eventually they said their goodbyes to Donald and Sarah. Donald, a bit worse for too much wine, shook George's hand over and over. Sarah cried. It was as if George was abducting her daughter and Sarah would not see her again.

The married couple climbed into the coach to the loud

cheers of the guests. Charlotte clung to his arm while she watched her mother shake a tear-sodden handkerchief towards them both. This brought Charlotte to tears. George put his arm around her shoulders in an effort to comfort her.

The coach swayed as it turned in to Kent Street, heading towards Charlotte's new home.

- CHAPTER SEVENTEEN -

The Wedding Night

Liverpool
June 1806

Charlotte was surprised that George made to join her in the master bedroom. She opened the bedroom door and yawned as she turned to face him.

George noticed the dark circles of fatigue under her eyes. He felt a wave of love as he realised his desires had made him selfish. His thoughts had been on his own pleasure, without any consideration for Charlotte.

'Perhaps you're right, my dear, we are both very tired. I will sleep in the guest room.'

She gave him a smile of thanks.

George bent to kiss her on the lips, but she turned her head in pretence of shyness and presented her cheek.

'Goodnight, my dear,' whispered George.

'Goodnight, George,' she said, and opened her bedroom door. Almost as an afterthought, she said, 'Thank you for today.'

'My good fortune, my dear, sleep well. You will feel better in the morning.'

'Thank you,' said Charlotte, and closed the door. She leaned back on the door and glanced around. A large bed dominated the room. Flames from a fire danced in the grate and lit the wall opposite.

She lit a taper and passed the flame to a lamp over the fireplace.

Undressing slowly, she let her wedding dress lie where it fell. She stripped off the remainder of her clothes and slipped her nightdress over her head before sitting at the mirror to brush her hair. After a few strokes she stopped and climbed into bed. She was too tired to blow out the lamp.

Her maid placed a tray of tea and hot water on the small table at the foot of the bed. The rattle of the crockery woke Charlotte. She peered around the room, puzzled, until the memory of the previous day returned. She was married and this must be her new home.

'Don't make so much noise!'

The maid tiptoed to the window and pulled open the heavy curtains to allow the light from a watery sun to enter the room.

'What time is it?'

'After ten, m'lady.'

'Who are you?'

'Don't you remember, m'lady? My name is Beryl. I'm your maid? Mr King hired me last week, before you were wed, so that I could be shown what you required and to take care of you.'

'Oh! Yes, I remember now, we spoke a few days ago.'

'Tha's right, m'lady. Can I get you anything else?'

'Run my bath.'

'Yes, m'lady, shall I put these clothes away first?' asked Beryl, picking up the expensive dress from the floor.

'Pass me my tea. Do what you want with the clothes, and don't ask so many questions. I don't feel well.'

'I'm sorry, m'lady.' Beryl stroked the wedding dress in an effort to remove the creases. She placed it over a chair and picked up the rest of the clothes. 'I'll have these washed later today, m'lady.'

'Do as you think fit. Bring me the tea and then leave me alone. Let me know when my bath is ready.'

'Yes, m'lady.' Beryl placed a cup of tea on the bedside table within Charlotte's reach, bundled the underclothes under her arm and collected the wedding dress from the chair.

Charlotte sipped the tea as her maid left the room.

She replaced her empty teacup on the bedside table and allowed her head to fall back on the pillow, placing an arm over her eyes to shield them from the light.

The crackling fire made her realise that somebody had entered her room while she slept, to either reset the fire or rekindle the ashes.

She went over the happenings of the previous day and suddenly realised she had made a mistake. She wanted George's money, but not George. He was old enough to be her father and although he appeared to be the handsome suitor before they married, last night he had become old. She could not understand how he had grown so old, so quickly.

She decided that she would play the sweet wife for outsiders, but not in private. She would become the epitome of a new wife and laugh at the right time to George's feeble jokes and fuss over the wives of George's customers. She would serve tea to those honoured by an invitation to their new house. Her energy would be directed into her new house and she would have it running like a well-oiled clock in no time at all. The staff would know his or her place, and what was required of them each day.

The guest room was cold. The fire had not been laid because all the staff expected him and his new wife to share the main bedroom.

Eventually George fell asleep. His dreams were full of William lost at sea, and he lost on land, ever parted from his son. In the dream he searched for his first wife, but every time he got close to her she would move and he'd start the search afresh. He felt a sense of disloyalty throughout the dream.

On waking, he realised the sense of disloyalty was to Charlotte, because he compared her to his first wife. He woke early in a cold sweat. It was still dark. He lit a lamp and studied his watch. It was only five thirty. He could hear the servants moving about downstairs. They would be preparing breakfast and relaying the fires. Would Charlotte be awake?

He knocked gently on Charlotte's door, but did not receive a reply. He turned the handle softly and pushed open the door.

The still burning lamp cast enough light for him to move about. He stepped over the clothes on the floor and saw that the fire was nearly out. He riddled the ash gently, so as not to make too much noise. Placing fresh wood onto the embers, he blew softly to encourage the small flame. The fire took hold as he watched his wife's sleeping face. Her face, framed by her hair, made him catch his breath as he realised that such a beautiful person had married him. The wood began to crackle as the fire began to consume the fresh fuel. With a final glance he quietly left his sleeping wife.

Returning to the guest room he rang for Alfred to run his bath and to put out some fresh clothes. The dressing room, attached to the master bedroom, had a door that lead off the main passageway. This allowed servants to prepare their master's clothes without disturbing him, if he happened to be in the master bedroom. Alfred would be able to obtain fresh clothes for him without his wife knowing.

Alfred's face did not reflect his thoughts. It was no concern of his what the white people did after they were married.

'Thank you, Alfred; I will be down for breakfast after my bath. Please tell Cook that I think Mrs King will be sleeping late today.'

'Yes, Sur.'

October 1806

George tried and tried to break down Charlotte's apparent resentment. For over four months they shared the same house, but not the same bed. He didn't understand what had happened or how he had offended her. She never had time for him. He was fortunate if he saw her one or two evenings a week at dinner, when they didn't have guests. Most of the time she took her meals in the master bedroom. He tried to talk to her and offered to join her in the bedroom for dinner, so that she didn't have to dress formally. She would not allow him to enter the bedroom, let alone eat with her in the room.

Charlotte converted the master bedroom into her own bedroom. The only concession she made was that George could still use the dressing room as long as he entered and exited via the door from the passageway.

On one of the rare occasions she shared dinner with George, Charlotte said, 'We have been invited to my parents for a family dinner.'

'Are we going?'

'Of course we are going, what a stupid question.'

He remained silent. He was not in the mood for another argument.

The dinner gathering was just family. Donald, Sarah, George and Charlotte. The early evening was pleasant enough, but it changed when they sat quietly enjoying a glass of port. The two men agreed not to leave the women at the end of the meal, so they all adjourned to the sitting room. The conversation turned to business and the forthcoming Christmas festivities.

The business was doing well. They had received two ships in the last six months from the Africa Trade. Both men complained of the idiots in Westminster, who did not know what they were talking about when they tried to ban the trade in Negroes. Times were grim, as it appeared Wilberforce's anti-slavery proposal would win a majority. Various resolutions had been put to Parliament and the new Whig Government supported abolition.

Both Donald and George feared that in the early part of the New Year of 1807, Wilberforce would introduce his Abolition Bill again, and this time it would become law.

'There may be a way around the problem, George,' said Donald.

'How so, if they make it illegal we will not be able to trade in slaves.'

'There is always a way. I understand the proposal is to make it illegal for British ships to carry slaves. If this is so, then we will own ships which are not British.'

'If we own the ships, surely that makes them British?'

'George, George, we must use our brains, and perhaps our connections. We will not personally own the ships, but we will damn well control them!'

'Mr Nicholson, have you forgotten yourself?' 'Such language in front of Charlotte and your wife—I am ashamed of you!' snapped Sarah.

'Madam, I apologise for the lack of respect, but this Wilberforce fellow is trying to put George and I out of business. If he does, you will have a lot more to complain about than an occasional overheard word. Our livelihood is in the Africa Trade and we have to find a way to trade. If they pass this Bill, it will increase the price of the slaves. They will be in short supply, and with any shortage, we will always have an increase in price. I am beginning to like the fellow already,' laughed Donald, draining his glass before reaching for the decanter.

'Do you think we will be able to control foreign ships carrying our cargo, Donald?'

'Rest assured, George, I have considered the problem for sometime and I have thought of ways to get round a number of possibilities. It all depends on the actual Bill. Once we know the details, then we will be able to plan accordingly. The use of a foreign-controlled ship is not something I would advocate. One cannot control the variables and, as you know, controlling the variables means profit for you and me.'

'A toast to Donald, ladies, may his mind never stop working, nor the profits dry up.'

'Donald,' whispered Sarah, who still smarted from her husband's comments.

'Father,' said Charlotte, and raised her glass.

What would he and George do if the trade became illegal? Would George still be a rich man if he no longer traded in slaves? She sipped her drink and glanced at her father.

'No more talk about bad business; this is supposed to be a family party,' said Donald, standing with his back to the fire surveying the three people before him.

'Let us talk of happier things. Is there perhaps a chance your mother can be a grandmother?'

- CHAPTER EIGHTEEN -

The Truth

*Liverpool
October 1806*

'Father!' Said Charlotte, blushing, 'it is not the sort of conversation we wish to pursue.'

'Why not? It is a reasonable question!'

'Donald, leave the poor girl alone,' said Sarah, 'she will tell us when she is ready. I can't believe you asked such a question in mixed company.'

'Mixed company, what are you talking about, woman? Mixed company indeed, I asked the question in front of my wife, my son-in-law and my daughter, the three closest people to me, and I am told I am in the wrong.'

'Well, you are. It is not a subject to be discussed. Look at Charlotte; she is blushing in embarrassment and it is your fault. You drink too much, that's your trouble.'

'Oh, so now we have turned the tables and I am the wicked person, and all I wanted to know was if you were going to be a grandmother. It is a question you asked me only the other evening, when we were on our own. Remember?'

'I asked the question in the privacy of our own rooms.'

'I have asked the question in the privacy of our dining room, to our daughter, in front of her husband. So what is the difference?'

'Donald, let's talk of other things,' suggested George.

'No, George, I like straight speaking. It is how I built the company and it is how I intend to carry on. The best way to find something out from your own family is to ask them, don't you agree?'

'In principle, Donald, yes, but I can't answer the question about you both becoming grandparents.'

Charlotte turned her head to her husband with a look that implored him not to say any more, and not to comment on their marriage being unconsummated.

George finished speaking without looking at Charlotte. 'In regard to the future of the family, I know as much as you in regard to your grandchildren.'

Charlotte buried her face in her hands and prayed the conversation would change, or God would strike her dead so that she would not have to listen to everyone discuss her.

'Donald,' said Sarah, 'no more. Can't you see you have upset Charlotte? George is ill at ease too. Please change the subject.'

Donald glanced at his daughter with her head buried in her hands.

He glanced at George, he did appear a little uneasy had he touched a nerve. His nose told him that things were not quite right. Perhaps George can't father a child, which could be reason why he was single for so long after his wife's death. Perhaps he can't function properly. He set the thought aside, to be worked on at a later date, and changed the subject.

'Did I tell you I have been asked to stand for Mayor?'

'Mayor? You never mentioned this to me,' said his wife.

'You were too busy asking me about grandchildren.'

'Congratulations, Donald, may I offer my hand?' said George.

'Thank you, George, will you be able to help if I require assistance?'

'Of course, old man, it will be my pleasure and privilege,' said George shaking Donald's hand.

Charlotte glanced at her father and her husband, feeling pleased that they had changed the subject. She felt it was time to reassert herself.

She bit down hard on her tongue to force tears from her eyes. She was determined not to have a child by George, but knew that she could not show her true feelings. She had to play the embarrassed fragile wife.

'Charlotte dear, what is the matter?' cried her mother as she moved to wrap her arms around her daughter.

'This is all your fault,' shouted Sarah at her husband.

'My fault, I have changed the subject, and told you of my good news. Because she is unable to discuss certain subjects with her parents, and her husband, she starts to cry.'

'You embarrassed her. The subject is not a fit subject for a young lady in mixed company.'

'I am still learning, George, after all these years. My fault, I suppose, for having a daughter.'

'I do think it would be best if I took Charlotte home, Donald. She is upset and perhaps I can calm her. I'll put her to bed when we get home.'

'You do, George,' adding in a whisper, and with a smile, ' and you make sure you bed her properly, because we want grandchildren. None of us are getting any younger, so make 'em twins, old man.'

'Come, Charlotte,' said George, and held his hand out to assist her to rise, 'I will take you home.'

Charlotte rose and rested her hand on George's arm as they made their way to the hall to collect their cloaks.

—⚏—

In the coach on the way home George tried to take Charlotte's hand to comfort her, but she pulled away and hissed, 'Don't you dare touch me!' and then lapsed into silence.

George looked at his wife and had the overwhelming desire to strike her. After some seconds of tense silence, George asked, 'Why did you marry me, Charlotte?' Charlotte gave no indication of hearing the question. The only sound was the clip clop of the horses. 'Did you hear me?'

'I heard you,' she whispered, and turned her head away so that George could not see her face. She peered out of the coach's window in to the black night.

'I'll repeat the question, Charlotte. Why did you marry me?'
'I don't know.'
'So you don't love me?'
'Love you? No, George, I don't love you. I never have.'

George felt as if a horse had kicked him in the stomach. He sat in the darkness and tried to comprehend Charlotte's words. He felt physically sick.

They arrived at their home in silence, each busy with their own thoughts, each condemning the other for the hurt they perceived they had been caused.

George followed his wife up the curved stairway to their respective bedrooms.

'Am I such a wicked fellow to live with?'

'No, George, you are not wicked, just dull.'

'Dull? I thought you liked a quiet life.'

'I do, George, but not so quiet that I can hear my blood flowing.'

'I thought you loved me for who I am. I know I am not a great person for parties, but can we rekindle the time when we looked forward to the future, and our marriage? Can we pretend that time is here again?'

'Don't be silly, George. I don't love you, and I don't think I ever will.'

'Then why did you marry me?' he cried in anguish. 'Why?'

'Why? A question I have asked myself a number of times.'

'Did you ever find the answer?'

'I liked you, George,' she said as she pushed open the door of the master bedroom. 'I thought I would grow to love you, but I don't think I can.'

'What do you want?'

'What I want now, George, and what I wanted earlier, are two different things. Now all I want is to be left alone so that I can get some sleep. Oh, by the way, I suggest you tell my parents you cannot have children. The fault lies in you.'

'Cannot have children!' George flustered. 'Who will believe me when I already have a son?'

'Well, think of something. Just don't blame me.'

'Perhaps I should tell them you are childless because you will not agree to your wifely duties. Few men would have waited this long. We have been married for nearly six months, and have I treated you in any way about which you can complain? Have I not supplied you with everything you desired? Isn't it true I have not forced myself on to you, nor demanded to share your bed? What I should say is that you should share my bed!'

'You have been a perfect gentleman, George, of that I have no complaint.'

'The perfect gentleman wishes you good night! I'm going to my room. I have a lot to think about.'

'Good night, George,' she whispered, and closed her door behind her.

Burning with indignation, George walked to his room.

'My room indeed!' muttered George to himself. 'It is nothing but the guest room. I have become a guest in my own home, and I am tired of being the decent fellow.'

He kicked the door closed behind him and threw his jacket on the bed.

Pulling back the bedclothes, he grabbed his nightclothes. He caught sight of his face in the mirror.

'Decent fellow! Decent fellow!' he shouted at his reflection. 'I have spent years being the decent fellow, and this time I am tired of the whole thing.'

He pulled his shirt over his head and dropped it on the carpet. His pants, shoes and underclothes followed. He dragged his nightshirt over his head and sat on the side of the bed to contemplate the future.

The house was silent. Had the servants heard the two of them arguing. Servants always know when a master and mistress fight. They must know he wasn't sharing his wife's bed.

He glanced around the room and saw the brandy decanter and a single glass. The single glass added to his frustration. Alfred knew more than he let on.

George poured himself a large brandy. He sipped the drink

and smiled as the familiar taste trickled down his throat. In his opinion brandy was the best thing that the French had ever produced. He sipped again as he sat on the bed.

It was common for married couples to take lovers when their marriage no longer worked.

He drank again and thought a little more. He didn't want a mistress when he had not yet taken his wife. He wanted to do things in the right order; take his wife before he took a mistress. He puzzled as to how he could take his wife when she would not sleep in the same bed with him. He day dreamed of forcing himself on her, but knew he couldn't go that far as he was a gentleman, and a gentleman does not force his way with a lady, even if she is his wife.

He drained his glass, poured a second, and tried to remember when he had last slept with a woman. All he knew was that it was a very long time ago. He sipped his drink and dreamed she was lying there now waiting for him to come to her. He disregarded this idea, as she would have called out if she wanted him to go to her. He drank once again and fantasized that she was shy, and didn't wish to wake the servants.

George lurched to the bedroom door and opened it gently, listening for any sound from across the hall. All was silent.

He took another drink, and placed his ear to Charlotte's door and listened.

All was quiet.

He raised the glass to his lips before realizing it was empty. Quietly he returned to his room and refilled the glass.

He knew she didn't love him. He was entitled to show her, and the world, why she didn't love him. If he took her tonight, the world would say it was his right as her husband. His problem was that if the World found out he waited six months to bed his own wife, he would be the laughing stock of Liverpool.

George listened once again at Charlotte's door, before entering. The room was very quiet. The only light was from the smouldering fire. Charlotte lay on her back, her head to one side.

He moved closer to the bed and watched his wife. He finished the remaining brandy and placed the empty glass on the floor.

Kicking off his slippers, he sat on the side of the bed and looked at his wife. She hadn't moved. Slowly he pulled back the bedclothes to allow himself to slide in to bed along side her. She grunted a little and sighed, but slept on.

George gently placed his arm over Charlotte in a gesture of protection. The extra weight caused her to roll towards him. He took this as a sign of affection and leaned over to kiss her lightly on the face. She whimpered a little, like a kitten. He kissed her again, a little harder. Charlotte moved, but this time onto her back. Her unconscious movement was not to escape George's arm, but to find a more comfortable position. To George it appeared she was making a movement of opportunity, for him to carry on in his lovemaking. He slowly moved the bedclothes back so he could see his wife's body. Her breasts rose at each breath, which he found fascinating as he watched the slow movement of her nightdress. He slowly moved his hand to her face and stroked it gently. Her silken skin, her perfume of scented soap, and her own female scent enveloped him. He sucked in the heady aroma, and made a memory of the time and place. He leaned closer to kiss her, but this time on the lips. His movement caused her to come partly awake.

'Is it you, George?' she asked in her half-sleep.

'Yes, my darling, it's your George.'

The taste of brandy on her lips brought her to full wakefulness.

'What are you doing here?' she cried, and opened her eyes. She saw George watching her with a strange glint in his eyes.

'Are you pleased to see me, my love?'

'You're drunk, George, please go back to your own room and let me sleep!' She pushed George with both hands.

'No, no, that's not what it is all about.'

'What do you mean? I just want to sleep. Please, George, let me sleep. I am very tired and we can talk of this in the morning.'

'I am not here to talk, my love, but to claim my rights as a husband. I have waited long enough.'

'No, George, this is not what you said.'

'What I said was out of love for you, but you have tried your best to kill my love, so now I will take what is mine!'

'You can't, George. You don't want it this way. This is not love.'

With his right leg across her to stop her wriggling, he held both wrists in a single grip and pushed up her nightdress with his free hand.

'Not love, I must agree, but we have not shared any love for these past months, so what does it matter?'

'You promised, George,' cried Charlotte, as tears filled her eyes.

'I promised to love my wife and to cherish her, but you have not been a wife to me, so I am free of all promises.' His hands pushed the nightdress above her hips to lay bare her slim legs. His eyes looked on the treasure Charlotte denied him. He pushed her legs apart with all the power in his right leg, as she tried to hold them together.

'George, this is not the way it should be,' she cried. He rolled over onto her and smothered her efforts to squirm away from him.

'Sleeping in separate beds, and separate bedrooms, is not what is meant either.'

He bent down and kissed her on the lips. She accepted the kiss without responding. She accepted the inevitable, knowing she could not beat George or deny him his rights as her husband. To whom could she complain? Her husband owned her for all intents. She knew she had been fortunate that, for the past few months, George had not forced himself upon her. She had hoped that she would be able to keep him at a distance, and that he would find himself a mistress or one of the women in the city. She decided the best thing to do was to think of something else while he had his way, and perhaps he would then leave her alone.

George forced open her legs and mounted her. It was not pleasurable, knowing Charlotte did not want it this way, but it was obvious she did not want it at all, and he was tired of playing the nice fellow.

Charlotte managed to release her hands and held her arms over her eyes. She did not wish see the expression on George's face or to look at him.

She suffered George as he grunted. She felt nothing emotionally, except an invasion of her private self.

Charlotte made her way to her water closet. George lay on the bed and stared at the ceiling, and thought of the last half-hour.

He was aware that the drink had taken over, and that she hadn't enjoyed his lovemaking. If he was honest, neither had he. Why couldn't she welcome him to bed, as other women welcomed their husbands?

He heard Charlotte returning, so he began to move some

of the bedclothes in an effort to make the bed a little more presentable.

'Please, do not waste your time. I will not use these bedclothes again. I will have them washed or even thrown away. I can't sleep in this bed after this attack.'

'Attack, attack, I never attacked you! All I did was try and make love to you, and when you refused, I took what was mine by right and by law.'

'You will never have a child by me, George!'

'A child, all I wanted from you was a little love.'

'You have lost any chance of that.'

George sat on the side of the bed and studied the floor, and thought of Charlotte's words. What chance would he have now for children, or for love? Perhaps he should go back to sea. Things were a lot easier to control at sea than his sham marriage. The more he thought about it, the more he became convinced that there was another man.

'Is there someone else?' asked George.

'There is always someone else, compared to you. Do you think you are the only man who has been interested in me?'

'Of course not, you are an attractive woman, a beautiful woman, and I am not surprised there is another man.'

Charlotte looked at George, what was he was talking about. Her spirits lifted as she realised that George thought her dislike of him was due to an infatuation for another man. It dawned on her that he could not accept the fact that she didn't love him. He had to invent another man. Her mind raced as she realised that George had just handed her the instrument with which she could make sure that he would never touch her again. No man likes to go where another has been.

'You are correct, George, there has been another man.'

'Who is the swine?'

'I can't say, George, I am too upset.'

'Upset! What do you mean upset, when I have lost my wife to this person? Who is he? I will call him out and we shall settle this.'

'No, George, you cannot do that. It would be murder and it may be you who is murdered. I would be careful whom I called out, if I were you!'

'Who is this person who goes around taking advantage of a newly married woman?'

'I can't say, George, and I will not say.'

'You will say, and I will know the scoundrel's name before this day is out. What is his name? Why will you not tell me? Do I know him?'

'George, I will not give you his name.'

'So I do know him?' said George, standing over Charlotte.

'I never said that!'

'You didn't have to. I could see it in your eyes!'

'Please, George, don't make me say anything. It will upset you.'

'What do you mean upset me? The only person to be upset will be this scoundrel when I get hold of him. Now tell me who it is, or do I have to take a strap to you?'

'You wouldn't dare strike me!'

Furious, George lashed out with the flat of his hand and struck Charlotte across the face. 'Does that satisfy you as to my intentions?'

Charlotte, knocked back on to the bed, held her hand over her face. Tears flowed down her cheeks. She touched her face gently in an effort to feel if she had been marked for life. She feared that she would be permanently damaged and ugly if he struck her again. Charlotte clenched her fists and wanted to strike George and hurt him, but she knew that George was too strong. She could never win such a contest.

Then it came to her; the winning blow.

She rolled across the bed to the far side, leaving its width between her and George.

'Do you really want to know his name? Are you sure you want to know?'

'Of course I want to know, and I want to know where he lives. I will have something to say to such a person, and I'll show him what happens to someone who meddles in another man's life.'

Charlotte watched her husband's eyes and the anger in them. He was ready to kill the person who cuckolded him. Now, she thought, is the time to push home the knife and to get my revenge.

'I'll tell you. His name is King.'

'King? That's my name! What are you talking about?'

'King! King! King!' she screamed at him, her face contorted with the effort.

'Are you stupid? King is my name. What are you talking about?'

'I am talking about your son, William King!'

'William? You lie! You and he have never been alone together!'

'You think not?'

'When?'

'The farewell party that you couldn't attend!'

'The farewell……'

'Yes, the farewell party, don't you remember? I asked old Mrs Johnston to take me.'

'What are you telling me?'

'I am telling you your son is a much better lover than you are. I didn't have to keep him waiting for over four months!'

George stepped backwards and collapsed into a chair. He stared at his wife, not able to believe what he had heard.

'William,' he whispered. The blood drained from his face.

Charlotte watched her husband. Had she gone too far? He appeared very ill. Her emotions swung from joy to sadness that George might die. She watched him as her feelings became less fearful.

George remained seated; he did not have the will to strike her again.

She watched his eyes fill with tears and overflow. He buried his face in his hands and gave out great sobs, his heart completely broken.

Charlotte made to go forward and comfort the broken-hearted man, but then remembered that she'd wanted this to happen. She stopped at the foot of the bed, in a position to rush out the door if George became violent.

George used the sleeve of his nightshirt to wipe his eyes. Using the chair as a support, he stood and thrust himself to the bedroom door. He pulled open the door and stepped into the hallway. The door closed quietly behind him as he slowly made his way to the guest room.

- CHAPTER NINETEEN -

Boston

Arriving Boston
February 1806

The *Albatross* butted her way south into the Atlantic Ocean. On the morning of their thirty-sixth day out of Liverpool, a welcome cry was heard from the masthead.

'Land Oh! Fine on the starboard bow.'

Sang had just completed the ritual of shaving William when they heard the lookout's cry.

Sang expected his Captain to rush on deck, but he did not move. William continued to drink his tea. It was as if William had all the time in the world and expected the land to be sighted that morning.

William was relieved, and happy with his skill at navigating. The thick cloud they had experienced recently had hidden the sun for the noon sight. He had been forced to estimate the *Albatross'* position.

William finished his tea, checked his image in the mirror, and noted that his hair was longer than he preferred.

'Sang, do your skills extend to cutting hair?'

'Have cut crew hair, Captain.'

'Perhaps after Boston I may allow you to cut mine.' William placed his hat on his head, checked that it was correctly positioned, and only then did he make his way to the deck.

On deck the Second Mate saluted and pointed ahead 'We have sighted land, Sir!'

'So I believe, Mr Fuller, thank you.'

'Good morning, Sir.'

'Good morning, Mr Austin, have we identified the landfall?'

'Not yet, Sir, the mist is still over the land, and even with the spyglass, I cannot get a clear image.'

William glanced at the shrouded landmass and then up at the high clouds.

'It'll be the best part of the day before we know our exact position.'

'Aye, Sir, I think you're right.'

The land grew more solid as they drew near. By early afternoon the heat of the day had dissipated the low grey land mist. It would be early evening before the *Albatross* would reach the coast.

William did not wish to enter an unfamiliar harbour so close to nightfall.

'Mr Austin, trim the sails, we will spend the night hove to. I want the sun behind me when we enter amongst the islands to pick up the pilot.

William waited while Sang smoothed the creases across the shoulders of his best uniform. He was ready to meet his main Boston contact, Abraham Judson. He hoped the agent would be as efficient as Owen. A fast turn around was required, with a profitable cargo for the return voyage.

William stepped on to the wharf from the *Albatross,* and read the hand-drawn map and the street address of Owen's contact once again. He glanced around and saw that warehouses covered most of the north side of the wharf. The warehouses supported a mixture of shops and small workshops. The sound of hammering carried on the still morning air. The street leading from the dock area was cobbled. A channel down the centre of the street carried sewerage to the waters of Boston harbour. He trod carefully around the sewerage as he scanned the buildings for Judson's name.

Each building was a mixture of warehouses and offices. A sign hung outside stating their business as a chandler or importer of various goods.

At the Judson premises, he pushed open a door and entered the ground floor warehouse. A well-dressed black man greeted him and asked if he could help.

'I wish to see Mr Abraham Judson.'

'This is Mr Abraham's office, may I ask who wishes to speak to him?'

'Please tell him Captain King, of the *Albatross.* I arrived this morning.'

The black man left William standing in the warehouse, which allowed him to study his surroundings. Part of the warehouse had been created as an office area where a group of whites and blacks worked. The white men appeared to be filling in ledgers or copying manifests. The black men waited until a writer called and sent them on an errand.

'Captain King, what a pleasure!'

William turned from studying the clerks to see a rotund man

making his way towards him. The man limped, and used a stick in his left hand.

'Mr Judson?'

'The same, Sir, the very same, how are you?'

'Well, Mr Judson, well. I would feel better if I could start work unloading.'

'All in good time, my dear fellow, all in good time, I have arranged for the labour to be at your ship later this afternoon.'

Owen had described Abraham Judson to William, and told him how Judson received the injury that caused him to limp.

Judson had fallen from the quay to the deck of a ship. He, and the ship's Captain, had sampled wine in Judson's office. In accompanying the Captain back to his ship, Judson missed his footing and fell from the quay. His left leg was shattered and his doctor offered him a choice, lose the damaged leg, or lose his life if gangrene occurred. Judson chose to keep his leg and asked the doctor to fix it as best he could. The doctor saved the leg, but it had healed twisted, and left Judson with a permanent limp.

'I am also searching for outbound cargo. Do you have any ideas?' asked William.

'Most ships sail in ballast to the West Indies and pick up molasses, sugar or coffee for England,' replied Judson.

'I am reluctant to carry any cargo produced by slaves. I hoped you may have some suggestions for an alternative.'

'I received a letter from Owen and he outlined your plans for this little enterprise. I am afraid there is little produced hereabout at this time of the year. In a few weeks perhaps salt cod from Newfoundland would be available. In mid-winter there is little grown to sell, but that's not to say we will not seek out what we can.'

Judson always liked to end on a high note, both verbally and mentally. His motto was never to disappoint a customer, as it may cost money.

'I would have written to Owen to inform him of the limited prospect of an outbound cargo, untainted by slave labour, but you have arrived before the letter would have even reached him. Never fear I am sure we will find something. Please follow me to my office.'

William followed Judson and listened to the agent chattering about the weather.

'The one good thing about the winter is the lack of mosquitoes, so even winter has its positive elements. We have a large number of lakes around Boston and I used to skate on them as a youngster. After my fall I put the skates away. I have enough trouble just getting about. Can't complain though, at least the Lord thought I was fit enough to stay on this earth. He must have some plan for me, but I do not know what it is,' laughed Abraham, his voice lifting at the end of the sentence.

'Here we are,' said Abraham, and opened a door to a large office. Large windows overlooked the approaches to the harbour. 'I like the view; it allows me to watch the comings and goings of the harbour. I saw you arrive this morning.'

'We arrived at seven o'clock, just about dawn.'

'Yes, I know. I like to get in to the office early. The sun rising over the ocean is a view of which I never tire – can I get you a drink?'

'Do you have tea?'

'Tea! In Boston, the last Englishman who asked for tea in this town lost a whole country. To be accurate, it was the taxes on the tea, not the actual tea. Yes, we do have tea.' He rang a small bell on his desk. The door opened and the black man who had originally greeted William stood in the doorframe.

'Tea, Elijah, please, for two.'

The black man bowed and withdrew.

'I know you don't like dealing with slave owners, and that you do not wish to carry cargo produced by slaves, but Elijah was a slave once. He is not anymore. He is a free man. He used to work on a plantation in South Carolina before he escaped and made his way to Boston, where I found him. Bounty hunters tracked him here, so I paid them off and kept him. I took him to England, where I met Owen and his friends, and they convinced me that Elijah should be free. Well, you know it is illegal to have a slave in England, and as I had become fond of Elijah, I asked him if he wanted to stay in England, or return to Boston with me, as a free man. He chose to return with me, so now he is my manservant and he earns a wage. All the other blacks downstairs are also free. Elijah hired them for me, and they all report to him. It took a few people in Boston a long time to get used to so many free blacks in the Company, but I don't care what others think if I'm making a profit.'

'Thank you for telling me, Mr Judson.'

'I trade with Cuba, where they have slaves under Spanish rule. I cannot see it doing me much good to follow your example, in this country. Many people have their own slaves, and if I refused to do business with anyone who owned a slave, I'd be out of business within a week.'

'Thank you for your honesty.'

'Ah, tea!'

Elijah placed a tray on the table between two armchairs and held the teapot, an unspoken question in his eyes.

'Milk or lemon, William?'

'Lemon, thank you.'

'Pity we don't have limes, what?'

'Lemon is fine, Mr Judson.'

'Please call me Abraham; my humour seems to have fallen flat.'

'Thank you, Abraham, and I did understood your humour,' replied William smiling.

The ice broken put them both as ease.

'When do you think we will complete unloading the *Albatross*?' asked William.

'I am hoping you will be ready for sea within a week, with a full cargo for England. As I said, I will have to search for a cargo, but at least you can load ballast and return via the West Indies, where you can pick up sugar or tobacco. I know you would prefer not to carry this cargo, but you may not have a choice, my friend. In the meantime, is this your first visit to our fair shores?'

'Yes it is. I have traded around the Mediterranean, and the Baltic, but never to America.'

'Then I must make sure you enjoy your stay! You must come to dinner at my home, *Mamre*, and meet my family. Please bring your First Mate.'

'Thank you, I will look forward to it.'

'I will arrange to have you collected this evening, let's say about six o'clock?'

- CHAPTER TWENTY -

Mamre

Boston
February 1806

The journey to *Mamre*, home of Abraham Judson, took a little over an hour. The sky was clear and the moon, high above the horizon, allowed the coachman to keep a fast speed as he skilfully negotiated around the numerous potholes.

William looked down upon a part-frozen river as the coach rattled over a covered bridge. The slow moving river made him pull his boat cloak a little tighter.

'It appears we are about there, Captain. I can see a large house lit up about two points to starboard,' commented James Austin.

William leaned out of his window and peered over the backs of the horses.

'Aye, I'll not be sorry to be indoors. This evening is cold, even without a wind.'

'*Mamre* ahead, Captain,' shouted the driver, ''bout five more minutes.'

'Thank you,' replied William, and bowed his head to regain

the inside of the coach.

The coach pulled to a stop at the front of a large colonial home. William could see Abraham Judson and a young woman waiting to greet them.

'Welcome, my friends, welcome to *Mamre*,' called Abraham, holding his hand out in greeting as Elijah opened the coach door for James Austin.

'Mr Austin, a pleasure to meet you,' said Abraham, pumping the First Mate's hand.

'Thank you, Sir, the pleasure is all mine.'

'William, I see you made the journey all in one piece.'

'A very comfortable ride, Abraham, thank you for the use of your coach.'

The young girl held back from joining in the enthusiastic greeting. She wore a dark blue-dress with a light shawl draped across her shoulders. Her hair shone in the light cast by the lamps of the house. Her nose appeared long and sharp, but William put this down to a trick of the light.

She offered her hand to William as he climbed the few steps to the front door. He kissed it in the Continental fashion.

'Captain King, welcome to our home.' Her voice reminded William of a light breeze through the ship's rigging.

'Thank you.'

'I am Ruth, Abraham's daughter. Are you English?'

'Yes, why do you ask?'

'No reason, other than the few Englishmen I have met don't kiss one's hand, but you did.'

'What do they do?'

'They just shake it, as they would a man's.'

'I learned a lot when I traded in the Mediterranean.'

'This must be your First Officer?' said Ruth, and turned to James Austin who was chatting with her father.

'My daughter Ruth,' said Abraham to James.

Ruth offered her hand. James shook it, 'I am English, and not one for the Continental ways.'

'How do you do, Lieutenant Austin?'

'I am well Ma'am, but I do not hold the King's Commission. I am only the First Mate of a merchant ship, not a naval ship. Please call me James.'

'Well, thank you, I will be pleased to call you James. Surely you can call me, Ruth?'

'Thank you, it will be my pleasure.'

William watched his First Mate escort the beautiful woman into the house.

'William, are you listening to me?'

'Pardon? Oh, sorry, Abraham, I was in a world of my own.'

'So I see. Perhaps you should have been a bit quicker?'

'Quicker? I never knew James could charm a lady so fast.'

'He is different from the other young men she meets.'

'How so?'

'Most of them are very flowery and kiss her hand.'

'As I did a few minutes ago?'

'As you did, William, many of the young men are very polite and treat her like a piece of china. She has helped me run the business since her mother died some years ago, and prefers the straightforward approach rather than the Continental, if you know what I mean?'

'I do now.'

'Shall we go in and join them for drinks?'

In the warm and friendly room, a large open fire blazed in

the hearth. William listened to Ruth and James as they talked about the dress mode of fashionable men in London. James was struggling as he had little interest in such things, but he was trying to be entertaining to Ruth.

William sat near the fire and offered his hands to the heat.

'What can Elijah get for you?' enquired Abraham.

'I'll have the same as you, Abraham, thank you,' replied William.

'Sherry for me, please,' chimed Ruth. 'James, what can we get you?'

'Brandy, please.'

'With ice?' asked Ruth.

'With ice?' queried James.

'Yes, some people like it cooled by the ice, others take water.'

'A small brandy, without ice, will be fine, thank you.'

Abraham turned to William. 'I have taken the liberty of inviting a couple of friends for dinner, so that you can meet them. Dinner will be just the five of us plus, of course, Ruth.'

'Are they also traders?"

'One has a lumberyard and supplies cut lumber to the town. He also sends logged timber to the southern states.'

'The other guest?'

'He trades in peppercorn. You may not be aware but Salem, which is north of Boston, is a major port for peppercorn. They bring it in from the East and resell it around the world.'

'I have heard pepper can be used as a preservative in a similar manner to the way we, in England, use salt.'

'Some say it preserves meat, but I am not sure.'

'I need a cargo to take us home. Do you think your peppercorn friend may have course to use us?'

'I doubt it. He has ships on charter and he'd be reluctant to change these arrangements for a single shipment.'

'I understand, but what will we carry? Perhaps I will have to load ballast. Is there gravel around Boston?'

'It is mined from the seabed, and then bagged. It can be expensive, but if I can't find a cargo, then we will have to pay for ballast. Perhaps you can sell it in the West Indies.'

'Who will want gravel for ballast when they can use sugar? I doubt any ship would sail from those islands in ballast. I'll just have to dump it, but doing that will be a drain on our profits.'

'Father!' interjected Ruth. 'Please, can we talk about something else other than trade in this or trade in that. I want to hear from William all about England.'

'I have been told, William,' said Abraham, and smiled. 'Perhaps you can entertain us with news of England?'

'I doubt I can entertain anyone about England, having spent nearly two years in the navy, on patrol off the coasts of France and Spain.'

'We heard of the great battle off Cape Trafalgar.' Ruth's eyes were bright with interest as she waited for William to speak.

William picked up his drink and sipped the golden liquid. As he tipped the glass, a piece of ice knocked against his lips.

'William, you were about to tell us about Trafalgar. Were you there?'

'No, but I hear it was a bloody day. We lost Nelson, our "Nel," the seaman's Admiral. A great man.'

'Did you meet him?'

'Meet him? No, I never met him.'

'Now, now, Ruth, enough of Trafalgar, no more questions about battles.'

'Perhaps later,' said William in an effort to placate Ruth, yet not to lose her interest in him.

Jacob Perkins apologised once more to William. He was very sorry he could not offer his peppercorns to the *Albatross* because he had contracts with a number of ship owners who operated from Salem.

He would be happy to discuss a regular trade between America and England if Captain King could guarantee a schedule. William thanked him and said he would discuss the proposal with his partners on his return to Liverpool.

Throughout the evening William's greatest pleasure was to sit next to Ruth during the meal. Afterwards, they all drifted towards the sitting room. William couldn't understand why she made such a point of favouring James. Had he offended her? Should he ask, or just let it pass and hope for an opportunity of becoming friendlier?

William felt strange being jealous of his First Mate. He knew he was being childish. Perhaps Ruth preferred older men. She was used to older men through business and knew how to handle them.

The men sat around the fire and helped themselves from the box of cigars that Abraham placed on a small table. Ruth took this as a sign that she should leave.

The talk drifted. Richard Savage, the timber merchant, complained about the amount of sawdust he had to get rid of each day. After a while Abraham said, 'William, Jacob is staying the night. It is late. Would you and James also care to stay the night?'

'Thank you, Abraham, but we cannot leave the ship overnight. At least one of us should be on board.'

'I understand, but the weather is good and *Albatross* is discharging rather than loading. Will you not reconsider?'

James Austin turned and said quietly to William, 'Perhaps, Captain, you can stay, if Mr Judson would furnish me with the means to get back to the ship.'

Abraham heard James' comment and said, 'If Mr Austin has been kind enough to offer to return, then perhaps this is the solution. I would like to discuss our options further, and if we travel together back to Boston tomorrow, we will not waste time.'

William hesitated, 'Well——'

'It is settled then. I will have Elijah take James back to the ship while you and I have a nightcap. Richard lives on the other side of Mamre Lake and his horse knows its way home, even if Richard is asleep!'

William slid into the warm bed and pushed the bed-warmer aside. He felt overwhelmed with tiredness. The strain of the voyage and the lack of outbound cargo worried him. As his head lay on the pillow, his mind drifted to the thought of ballast.

Had he been right in accepting the Captaincy of the Albatross? Was he arrogant, trying to prove to his father that trading to the Americas would work without the African trade? Would he be forced to carry sugar and tobacco so that the voyage could break even?

Eventually his fevered mind slowed and his body gave way to a disturbed sleep.

- CHAPTER TWENTY-ONE -

Mamre Lake

Boston
February 1806

William entered the dining room and was met by a strong aroma of coffee.

'Ah, William, I do hope you slept well?' enquired Abraham, who was seated at the table.

'Like a log, Abraham. Good morning.'

'What would you like to do this morning? I thought we might leave for Boston after lunch, perhaps about two o'clock. Hot food is on the sideboard. Help yourself.'

At the sideboard William studied the food.

'Just tell Noah what you want,' Abraham said. He will serve you and bring the plate to your seat. Make yourself at home.'

'Noah?'

'Oh, yes, all of my black employees have biblical names.'

'Old and New testament?'

'I am a Jew so we don't have much call for the New Testament,' responded Abraham, smiling.

'Err, I am sorry, Abraham, I didn't mean to be rude.'

'Don't apologise, we have the same God. I presume you are Christian?'

'I am sorry to say it has been a long time since the Lord saw me in His Church.'

'We both have that problem. At least I am accepted here in Boston for what I am, rather than being a Jew or a Christian. We do not have the same restrictive laws, which are current in England, concerning religion. Although when I lived in England everyone treated me well, and it is where I met your friend, Mr Wilberforce, and Owen. Both Jew and Gentile can object to slavery!'

'Amen,' said William as he pointed to some of the food for the servant to serve. After he had finished choosing, he joined Abraham at the table.

'When I built this house I named it after the place Abraham from the Bible settled, after the Lord gave him the promised land of Canaan. Abraham lived near the great trees of *Mamre*, near Hebron, which is why my home is called *Mamre*. If you glance outside at the rear of the house, you will see a row of giant trees that can be seen for miles. They act as a landmark. When I saw the trees I just had to call the estate *Mamre*. My family had wandered enough, and America seemed like the Promised Land to me, so I settled here some years ago. My Ruth was born here, but unfortunately my wife died here from the fever.'

'I am sorry to hear about your wife.'

'No matter, I am over the sadness now.'

A sudden change came over Abraham. He spoke as if a door had closed on the past.

'If you are fit enough, Ruth will be happy to show you

around our small estate. Do you ride?'

'Not for a number of years: there aren't many horses in the navy. Can you furnish me with riding gear?'

'I'll have Elijah layout some clothes for you.'

'Will Ruth join us for breakfast?'

'She will eat in her rooms, and join us a little later. '

Ruth, her maid Lydia, and William rode over the brow of the hill and viewed the frozen lake in the valley.

The cloudless sky and the clear sharp air refreshed William's mind and body. Every so often a small cloud would cross his mind when he remembered the lack of cargo to the West Indies, and the cost of ballast.

William gazed out across the large lake.

'Is this a fresh water lake or is it attached to the sea?'

'It is fresh water, and part of father's estate.'

'How thick is the ice?'

'At this time of the year, about two feet.'

'I had ice in my drink last night. Is this where it came from?'

'We harvest some of the ice each winter and pack it in to ice houses. It is then used throughout the summer. In some years we even have ice left over from the previous year. It all depends on how well it keeps.'

'Fascinating. Will the ice be thick enough for us to skate on at the moment?'

'I am sure it will, but we don't have any skates.'

'No, but we can slide! Come on, I'll show you.'

William dismounted and secured his horse. He offered his hand to Ruth, who slid down the side of her mount with practiced ease.

Ruth held his hand as he tentatively placed his right foot on the solid ice and eased his weight from the land to the frozen water. It held. He then placed his left foot on the ice and realised the whole of the lake must be solid. He slid his feet in a skating motion across the ice and turned to see Ruth watching him.

'Come on in, the water is lovely!' he called and headed back to the bank to take Ruth's hand, and to guide her onto the ice.

Time passed quickly as William pulled Ruth across the ice by the use of a strap from his horse. Their laughter carried across the frozen water.

Back on solid ground, Ruth smiled a sad smile as if she didn't want to leave.

It wasn't long before the large trees that marked *Mamre* came in to view. William wished the ride would last forever. He could not remember the last time he had felt so happy and free.

'Thank you, William, I had a lovely time.'

'Ruth, it has been my pleasure. I haven't laughed so much since I was a child.'

He fell silent as his mind suddenly found the solution to the problem of the ballast to the West Indies.

It was a wild idea, but it would be cheaper than paying money for ballast.

The fear of failing his partners in Liverpool began to fade.

Unconsciously he pressed his legs to his horse to encourage it to walk faster. He wanted to discuss his idea with Abraham. If it worked, he'd found a profitable cargo - and ballast.

'You must be in a hurry to leave *Mamre*,' called Ruth.

'Not leave; I have had an idea about an outbound cargo and wish to discuss it with your father.'

'You have the journey back to Boston to discuss business. I

have you for such a short time.'

'I am sorry, Ruth. How thoughtless of me.'

'I'll forgive you,' she said gently, and added in a near whisper, 'if you will promise to come back to *Mamre*.'

'It is a promise I am happy to make. It is such a beautiful place and so quiet.'

They stopped their horses and, resting in their saddles, studied the house on the small rise framed by the large trees.

The fields around the house were a patchwork of snow and green, as grass tried to push the snow aside.

'What a difference to Liverpool,' William whispered, more to himself than to Ruth.

Ruth gazed at him, enjoying the sight of her home through his eyes.

'Race you the last few yards?' shouted William as he prodded his horse into a slow trot.

Ruth let him gain a good lead before she kicked her horse into a gallop. She streaked past William as he attempted to get his horse to trot faster.

'See you in the dining room for drinks and lunch. Bye!'

An embarrassed ship's captain dismounted from his horse and handed the reins to a grinning servant. William summoned what little composure he could muster and walked into *Mamre* in time to see Ruth shake her head and allow her black hair to fall over her shoulders.

'Next time we will have a race out at sea!'

'On sea horses?' asked Ruth, and laughed.

'I give up. You win.'

—∞—

William felt sadness when the coach pulled away from *Mamre*.

He wanted to see a lot more of Ruth in the future. Perhaps he was wrong about the attention she gave James Austin.

'Well, William, did you enjoy your ride?'

'I had a wonderful time, Abraham, and cannot thank you enough for your hospitality. What a beautiful home you have. The countryside makes me compare Liverpool in a very unfavourable light.'

'We all do that, my boy, but home is where the heart is, not the physical building. Tell me more of the idea you touched on over lunch.'

William fell silent while he gathered his thoughts. He wanted to make sure he could communicate his idea in the best possible way.

'We don't have a cargo at this time of the year for carriage to England, nor do we have a cargo for the West Indies. To put it correctly, we didn't have a cargo until this morning.'

'This morning? Did you meet someone when you were out riding?'

'The last thing I wanted to do this morning was to share Ruth, with anyone else.'

Abraham scrutinised William, his eyes questioning, and raised his eyebrows in emphasis.

'Abraham, don't look like that. I like Ruth a lot, and we enjoyed a good time on the ice. It was a very special day for me because I got to know your daughter a little better than yesterday. I believe I have found a way out of our dilemma.'

'I do wish you would get to the point, or else we will be in Boston before I hear the idea!'

'We will carry ice to the West Indies!'

'Ice? Are you mad? Is this the brilliant idea I have waited for, ice to the Caribbean?'

'Think about it, Abraham.'

'Think about it, you are mad. Who ever heard of sending ice to the Tropics? It will melt before you get out of Boston harbour. You must think of something else, or take a lower profit and buy the ballast. The only other thing you could do is wait out the winter and perhaps carry a cargo of salt fish from Newfoundland to England.'

'I will not wait out the winter, as I don't have the time. My voyage was too well advertised. I can't allow all our efforts to stagnate while I wait for winter to pass.'

'But, William, the ice will melt and fill your vessel with water.'

'If we have melted ice in the ship, we will pump it overboard. We do that now when sea water enters the hold.'

'When the ice melts it will lighten your ship, and she will become unstable without ballast.'

'Insulation, my dear friend, insulation; you gave me the idea yesterday, but I did not realise it until I saw your frozen lake this morning.'

'How so?' Abraham's tone was no longer so negative.

'Last night you gave me a whisky that contained a piece of ice. I noticed it as it was not the first time that I have received ice in a drink.'

'They use ice in England?'

'To a small extent yes, but when on the Mediterranean trade I would visit father's agents and they would offer me chilled drinks in the summer; chilled by the use of ice. They harvested the ice in the winter and stored it on the coast in icehouses. The ice came from the Alps. So if they can carry ice from the mountains to the hot coast of the Mediterranean, and keep it frozen until the summer, then the few weeks to the West Indies should not be a problem.'

'Where will you get the ice?'

'The best place I can think of now is your lake, *Mamre Lake*. It is currently frozen to at least two feet thick. We can have it 'harvested' and transported to Boston. The weather is cold enough to stop it melting while in transit. I will have the *Albatross* insulated, based on what I can remember from my time in the Mediterranean.'

'If the ice survives the voyage to Jamaica, will you throw it overboard?'

'If I have to, I will, but I will first try to find a buyer. Whatever I receive for the residual ice is more than I would get for dumping the stones. There may not be a lot of ice left by time we get to Jamaica, but suppose we manage to reduce the speed of melting, what price ice in the tropics?'

- CHAPTER TWENTY-TWO -

Liverpool Lass

Boston
February 1806

Henry Nicholson drew deeply on his small cigar as he thought of the best way to make a profit and scuttle the efforts of William King. The idea of succeeding in both brought a smile to his cruel face. He glanced at the body next to him and gave it a hard kick with the heel of his foot.

'Get up, you!' he shouted.

The body moved and groaned. A woman's hand pulled down the sheet that covered her black face. She turned to face Henry and tried to smile. Her bruised lips turned the smile into a grimace. She gently raised her hand to her face and touched her mouth. The pain caused her to groan again.

'I said up!'

Henry pushed the young woman's body away from him, until she teetered on the edge of the bed. Another strong shove tossed her over the edge. The room vibrated as her body hit the floor.

'Mass'er, why you do dat?' she cried in a pitiful voice.

'Get out! Give me some peace.'

She slowly rose from the floor, but didn't make any effort to cover her nakedness. After last night, a sense of modesty would be laughable.

Henry studied the girl and remembered the pleasure he experienced with her. She was good and accepted his blows as part of lovemaking. Any other woman would have taken a knife to him. He felt aroused as he watched her collect her clothes. Perhaps one more session to start the day would put him in a better mood. It would be better than coffee and a brandy.

Hot ash fell from his cigar on to his chest. He jumped in pain and dropped the cigar amongst the bedclothes. He rolled off the bed and pulled the sheets back.

'Get out, this is your fault!' he yelled.

The girl drew her dress over her head and wriggled her feet in to her shoes. Smoothing her dress over her hips made her feel a woman again.

'You promised me a presen', Mass'er, if I did what you tol' me. I did what you tol' me las' night and you hurt me.'

'I'll hurt you a damn sight more if you don't get out of here,' said Henry with a low menace in his voice. He found the remains of the cigar smoldering in the bed.

The girl watched the black-haired Englishman and made the sign of the curse behind his back. She had realised that she would not receive a present, or money, for last night's efforts. Her hand gently touched her face to test the swelling of her lips. Some men were gentle, but others tried to kill her.

'You promised,' she said. A large tear rolled down her face. Without payment she knew she would be hurt again, because she hadn't taken some money home, however small the amount.

Henry drew on the ember to keep it lit, glanced at the girl

again and saw a pathetic figure shaking in fear. She had been good last night and perhaps he would need her again in a few days.

He picked up his discarded clothes and found some money. He threw the coins to the girl, but they fell short and bounced on the floor. She quickly dropped to her knees to gather the scattered coins. She had to stretch for the last few that had rolled under the bed.

He watched her dress ride up to show the back of her legs and ankles. He could see her dirty feet were calloused. He stubbed the end of the cigar out on the table, as the girl stood clutching the few coins she had collected. She backed away from him towards the door.

'Go!' he yelled.

With a draped shawl around her neck she pulled open the door and ran into the cold street.

Henry checked his pocket watch and realised there was enough time for breakfast before his arranged meeting with agent Leather.

Agent Leather opened the conversation by asking, 'I trust she was satisfactory, Mr Nicholson.'

'Aye, just,' snarled Henry.

'Good', replied Leather, relieved that Henry was a lot calmer this morning.

'Have you found out anything about King?' muttered Henry.

'He is to sail in ballast for Jamaica, Mr Nicholson.'

'When?'

'Soon. In the next few days I understand.'

'Have you found me a cargo?'

'I was not sure if you wanted a cargo for Jamaica, or for

England.'

'May the Saints preserve me from idiots. I want a cargo to make a profit. But, I want to keep in touch with King. Do I have to spell everything out or are you just stupid?'

'I——uh, I.'

'Don't stutter man. Tell me what I need to know!'

'I have sourced a cargo to England, which is cod from Newfoundland, but you will have to sail in ballast to Halifax to load.'

'Is King sailing to Newfoundland?' asked Henry, his voice cold and angry.

'No, Sir, to Jamaica.'

'Then why pray, do you wish me to sail to Newfoundland?'

'I thought profit was your main desire.'

'It is, but there are other ways to profit than just by making money. So, let me be very clear on what I want. Wherever King is heading, that is my destination. I want a cargo to carry to that destination. Have I made myself clear?'

'Abundantly, Sir, I will have some information for you tomorrow about the movement of King and about a cargo for your ship.'

'Thank you, you may leave now and start your work.'

'Yes, Sir,' the agent gathered his few papers and nearly ran from the room.

Henry Nicholson smiled as he heard the steps of the agent quickly receding. Fear, added speed to any man's steps.

After a bout of drinking in one of the local taverns, Henry spent the night on his own. He needed rest and another night with the woman would tire him. He liked to think that denying himself a woman was an act of decency on his part. He admitted it did not happen often, but when it did, he felt better the next day.

He woke before dawn, dressed, and broke his fast before the agent called.

'Coffee?' asked Henry, his back towards Leather.

The agent glanced at Henry and tried to work out why he was being offered coffee. He knew Henry had not taken the woman again last night. She had left town to heal her face. She was no use to her family with swollen lips and a bruised face. The pickings along the docks were small at the best of times. A broken face was a guarantee that she would not earn any money for a few weeks.

'Thank you, Sir, black please.'

Henry poured the coffee and pushed the cup towards the agent. He waited while the agent sipped the hot liquid.

Leather watched Henry over the rim of the cup and realised the silence meant Henry was waiting for a report.

The agent hurriedly placed the cup on the table.

'I have spoken to all my contacts around Boston town, and the only cargo we can produce is shingle ballast to allow you to collect a cargo out of Jamaica.'

'I heard the *Albatross* is loading cargo for Jamaica. If this is correct then I think I have the wrong agent working for my father's company.'

Henry's voice was very quiet, just above a whisper, which caused the agent to lean forward. Leather didn't wish to antagonize Henry by asking him to repeat himself. As he leaned further across the table Henry's right hand shot out and grabbed the luckless man by the neckerchief.

'Do you take me for a fool?' snarled Henry.

'Sir, Sir, please you are choking me!' gasped the agent as he clawed at his throat in an effort to release the pressure. He knocked the hot coffee over which ran across the table and soaked into his pants, burning his leg. He yelped and jerked from the pain, which broke Henry's grip on his throat. Leather stood and a made to pull the material of his pants from his legs in an effort to cool the burning sensation.

Henry stood away from the table to avoid the spreading hot coffee.

Leather pulled the neck cloth clear of his throat, breathed deeply, and tried to calm himself. He knew Henry did not suffer fools gladly, but he needed to retain the Nicholson agency.

His voice was a whisper as he coughed a number of times to clear his throat and muttered, 'Sir, you should have let me speak. I am aware of the cargo being loaded by the *Albatross*.'

'Speak up man, I cannot hear you!'

'The *Albatross* is not loading a normal cargo.'

'I don't care what she is loading, but I do care that she has a cargo and I don't!'

'Sir, please allow me to finish,' croaked the agent, 'the cargo is ice! Sir.'

'Ice? What do you mean ice?'

'Frozen water, Sir, she is loading ice instead of shingle ballast.'

'Have you lost your mind man? Nobody loads ice for ballast. That is the most stupid excuse I have ever heard. You are covering up for your own incompetence. To think you would have me believe such a tale.'

'It is true, Sir, it is true!'

The force of the speech from the frightened agent made Henry stop and think.

'Sit down, and calm down. Did the coffee cause much damage? Have another.'

'Thank you, no, Sir. I have had sufficient coffee for one day.'

'Have a brandy, you appear upset.' Henry poured a generous measure of brandy and handed the glass to the agent, who now sat at the table trying to dry the legs of his pants with a silk handkerchief.

Leather accepted the glass and drank deeply, savouring the liquid as it slid down his throat.

'They have cut the ice from fresh water lakes further inland and have secured a great deal of sawdust for insulation. They have done this to save money. The *Albatross*'s captain does not wish to spend money on shingle and then pay someone in Jamaica to unload the ballast.'

'The man is a fool,' said Henry, 'who ever heard of anyone shipping ice to Jamaica? It will melt before he reaches the Caribbean, never mind Jamaica.'

'Exactly my thoughts, Sir, which is why I did not wish to suggest you carry ice instead of gravel.'

'What cargo do you have for me?'

'I am sorry, Captain, but I tried to tell you. I have tried all of my contacts and I can't obtain a cargo to Jamaica. I can have salt fish for England, but you will have to sail to Newfoundland to load.'

Henry sat in silence. If King carried ice, then he must be a fool. On the other hand his foolishness could be an opportunity. If Henry sailed a day behind King and the ice melted before King reached Jamaica, the *Albatross* would become unstable. King would have to pump the melted ice overboard.

The *Liverpool Lass* would then arrive with the solution to King's problem. Henry would sell King some of the *Liverpool Lass* ' ballast, at a small profit of course. To do this Henry would have to take additional ballast to make sure he didn't suffer the same fete of instability.

Henry felt a cold sweat as he thought of what his father would say if he allowed the *Liverpool Lass* to be compromised, because he sold too much ballast. He would have to be careful. He wanted to destroy King, but not at the expense of his own vessel.

'Buy me enough shingle for a safe trip to Jamaica. Then buy enough to sell to the *Albatross* at sea, after her ice has melted!'

Agent Leather's mouth hung open as he contemplated what he had just heard.

To make sure his agent understood Henry said, 'The *Albatross* will be unstable after the ice melts and her captain will pay any price for ballast to keep her from rolling over and sinking.'

The agent drained the last of the brandy and placed the glass on the coffee stained table. 'I will leave you now, Captain, to arrange the ballast and the new cargo. A brilliant plan if I may say so.'

'You may. How soon do you think it will be before we are ready to sail?'

'Give me three days, Captain, and you will be ready to sail.'

'When is the *Albatross* due to sail?'

'The day after tomorrow, if they are able to keep cutting ice.'

'King's agent is a Jew, is he not?'

'Yes, Sir, I do believe he is a Jew. He lives with his daughter.'

'Good looking woman?'

'If I may say so, Captain, she is a beautiful woman, but not one I would like to cross.'

'So little likelihood of you paying court?'

'Oh, I didn't mean that I should court her, I meant in business. She is very astute and works with her father. He wanted a son to help in the business but his wife gave him a daughter. Miss Ruth decided she would learn the business and often attends meetings and negotiations with her father.'

'Does she really?'

'It would be more seemly if she married, like all good girls of her age.'

'Not married?'

'No, Captain, I have heard it said that the local young men are not strong enough for her. She waits for the right man.'

Henry smiled and thought of what he could do for such a woman and what she could do for him. It was a long time since he had enjoyed a white woman. Ruth Judson was a rich, educated woman. He would soon show her that she would not require fancy education in bed. He would teach her all she needed to know.

'How can I meet this lady?'

'Perhaps I could introduce you to her and you could pretend to buy the ballast from her father's company?'

'Capital idea, but I don't want to delay the loading of the *Liverpool Lass*. I just wish to meet the lady and if you have to use the gravel ballast to generate the reason, so be it.'

The following afternoon, Leather and Henry waited in the outer area of Abraham Judson's office. They made themselves known to one of the clerks.

They waited and watched the clerks scribbling away at various documents.

Henry paced the small reception area. He was not used to being kept waiting. In Liverpool all offices all were open to him and his family. He would not have been kept waiting in a Liverpool Jew's office. The ticking of the wall clock exaggerated the time they had already waited.

After three more minutes he would walk out. Damn them and their ice. He would finish William King some other way.

The clock struck the hour. Henry picked up his hat and, while placing it on his head, he heard the office door open and a clerk approach.

'I will show you in gentlemen,' said the clerk waving his hand towards the office where the door was ajar.

'Thank you,' said the agent. He lived in Boston and would not jeopardise the possibility of future business with the Judson's.

Henry grunted and removed his hat.

The clerk opened the inner office door and stood back to allow the two visitors to enter.

'Welcome, gentlemen, I am sorry I kept you waiting.'

Henry stopped suddenly when he realised the voice came from the woman who sat behind a large desk. The agent, close on Henry's heels, bumped him in the back and knocked him forward a little.

'Mind my back, damn your eyes,' barked Henry at the agent as he staggered forward. Then remembered Judson was a woman.

'My apologies, Ma'am, I was under the impression I was to meet Mr Judson.'

'My father is not too well at the moment and asked if I would attended to your needs.'

She smiled a smile of pure innocence, flashing her eyes at the visitors, but she appeared to keep a special smile for the tall stranger who cussed.

Henry regained his composure and muttered a greeting. His hands played with his hat.

'Please Mr Nicholson, or should I say, Captain? Please sit down and tell me how I may be a of service.'

Henry dropped into a large armchair in front of the desk. The agent sat opposite and watched.

'Well I——'

'How very rude of me, Captain, would you like a drink?'

'No, thank you, I have come to——'

'Perhaps your agent, Mr Leather, would like a drink?'

'I am sure he doesn't want a drink, either,' said Henry.

'No, Sir, thank you,' said Leather.

'Where was I?' sighed Henry, turning his attention back to Ruth.

Her eyes shone, which gave the impression that he was the only person for which she had time. For the life of him he could not remember why he had come. A beautiful woman and her warm smile would distract any man.

'I have come to ask you about the price of ballast. It appears we are short of a cargo, and we will be required to buy ballast. Mr Leather here, tells me you are the best company to speak to in regard to the purchase.'

'We do deal in ballast. We mine it ourselves so we are very competitive.'

Ruth allowed the silence to lengthen. Another clock ticked, Henry became impatient again.

This is no way to engage in a business discussion. He was used to dealing with men and shouting. Perhaps he should wait until her father is available.

'Are you going to tell me the price?'

'Captain, I am surprised you have come to my father's company for ballast. Mr Leather has his own arrangements with another company. He has never bought ballast from my father's company, yet he brings his Principal to a meeting which is normally dealt with, shall we say, at a lower level?'

Henry waved his hand as he realised he would have to be very careful around Miss Ruth. He was not comfortable discussing business with women and this one needed watching.

'Miss Judson, you are evidently a very clever woman and I see I will have to be honest with you. I know Mr Leather has a regular supplier of ballast and he can supply all my needs. I have seen you in the street and have tried to create an occasion where I might meet you, shall we say in the correct manner. I couldn't think of a situation, which would appeal to you, so when Mr Leather told me that you help your father in business, I decided the best way for me to speak to you was through a business connection. So here I am.' Henry flashed his teeth and smiled a disarming smile in an effort put Ruth at ease.

'I am flattered, Mr Nicholson, but why did you wish to speak to me?'

'This is my first visit to your fine city and I wondered if you would honour me by showing me around Boston. Mr Leather would have been delighted I am sure, but with the greatest of respect to Mr Leather I would prefer a beautiful lady to show me Boston.'

Ruth smiled, but felt uneasy at the flattering words rolling off Henry's tongue. His eyes reminded her of a reptile, they were cold and without feeling. 'Mr Nicholson, do you flatter the ladies in Liverpool in the same way?'

'In Liverpool, Ma'am, I know my way around so do not require the services of anyone.'

'I am sure,' said Ruth in a low voice.

The two of them watched each other.

'Well, will you show me Boston?'

'I am afraid, Mr Nicholson, I will not have the time to help you. My father is not too well at the moment and I am required here in the office.'

'Perhaps one evening you could show me some of the fine eating houses of which I have heard?'

'I am sorry Mr Nicholson, but each evening I dine with father since his wife, my mother, died some years ago. We only have each other. As I said, he is not too well, so I cannot see myself dining out with anyone at the moment. Perhaps next time when you are in Boston, I am sure father would be delighted to meet and dine with you.'

'Your father?—Oh yes, I will look forward to meeting him in the future.'

'Thank you, Captain, for coming to see us, it has been a pleasure to meet you. I assume you do not wish to purchase ballast?'

'No, thank you, Miss Judson, perhaps next time.' Henry stood and bowed. The meeting was over.

Outside the two men walked back towards the wharf and the *Liverpool Lass.* Henry growled at the agent 'I want to know all about their business interests.'

'Yes, Sir,' said the agent, not wishing to arouse his wrath.

Henry Nicholson strode up the small gangway and dropped lightly on to the deck of the *Liverpool Lass.* Agent Leather, feeling out of place, followed.

'Afternoon, Captain,' said the First Mate. 'Cargo has all been discharged and we are now waiting for fresh cargo before making ready to sail.'

'I'll tell you when we sail, damn your eyes!'

'Aye, Aye, Captain,' said the First Mate saluting.

'I want you to spend a few dollars on finding out all that can be gleaned about the Judson business and his family. I also want to know what King is up to loading a cargo of ice. We will load a little more than the normal ballast in the next day or so. I think I may have found a buyer for the stuff.'

'A buyer for shingle and stones?' responded the mate; a smirk briefly crossed his face.

'What's wrong in that?' snapped Henry.

'Sorry, Captain, I have never heard of anyone buying ballast to resell it.'

'Well you have now. I have arranged for a horse to be at my disposal so I expect it later on this afternoon. I will sleep ashore tonight, but I expect the ballast and the cargo to be loaded before I return late tomorrow afternoon. Is that clear?'

'Yes, Captain. When the horse arrives I'll let you know.'

Henry nodded and went below to change into clothes more suitable for horse riding.

The ride out to *Mamre Lake* was more pleasant than Nicholson had expected. The cold air and the soothing bounce of the horse gave him time to review everything. Henry believed that King was up to something. He would find out what it was and scupper his plans. There must be more to the information that the *Albatross* would be carrying ice. Although Henry didn't like King he wasn't going to under-estimate him.

The horse stepped daintily to the top of a small rise. Henry was then overlooking the full expanse of the countryside. He watched labourers below as they worked on the frozen water of *Mamre Lake*. Several wagons were being loaded with blocks of ice, obviously cut from the lake. Others were dragging fresh blocks to the shoreline.

Henry withdrew a small spyglass from his saddle pouch. He had to admit that the workers were efficient in cutting blocks of a similar size. If King's idea worked, and the blocks stayed frozen, then the ice would be cheaper than gravel.

The wind became stronger and chilled his neck. Henry closed the glass and kicked the horse in to motion.

—⁂—

Nicholson stepped down from the gunwale to the deck of the *Liverpool Lass*. The First Mate was waiting for him.

'Captain, a word please,' said the First Mate, saluting.

'Come below, it is too damn cold to speak on deck.'

The First Mate followed Henry to his cabin, waiting while Henry pulled off his outer clothes and poured a large glass of rum.

'Help yourself,' said Henry indicating the rum and glasses.

'Thank you, Sir, it's a cold tonight.'

'Well, Mister, what do you have for me?'

'What I can make out from the rumours, Sir, is that William King, and the Judson family, have gone into partnership over this ice business.'

'Damnable! King is supposed to be Christian and he gets into bed with a Jew?'

'Aye, Sir, so I hear'

'What else?'

'The *Albatross* sails tomorrow for Jamaica.'

'I guessed as much. Has she finished loading ice?'

'They will finish tonight, Sir, and be ready to sail on the morning tide.'

'When will we be ready to sail?'

'Some time tomorrow afternoon, Sir.'

'Good, I don't want to sail before her, nor do I want to be too far behind her. A good day's work, Mr Mate, this should cover your expenses.' Henry tossed a small bag of coins to his first mate. 'If there is nothing else I'll say good night to you.'

—∞—

Next morning Henry watched from the poop deck of the *Liverpool Lass* as the shore gang released the *Albatross'* stern lines. He could see King waving to someone on the wharf. Henry focused a spyglass on the small group of people and saw Ruth Judson. He also noticed a number of black men around her buggy, clerks finalising the paperwork for the vessel's departure. An idea suddenly came to mind of how to make a little more profit on the voyage to Jamaica.

'Mr Mate!'

'Aye, Sir?'

'Three good men around dark, I will have a little work for them.'

'We will have sailed by the time it is dark, Captain.'

'No, we will not. Have the *Lass* moved to an anchorage in the harbour and have a boat ready to take me ashore just before dark.'

'Aye, Aye, Sir.'

'Bosun,' called the First Mate and waited while the word was passed. He speculated that the Captain would want to grab himself a doxy for his special needs to keep him company for the voyage home.

- CHAPTER TWENTY-THREE -

Jamaica bound

Kingston
March 1806

William had packed a hundred and fifty tons of ice in Richard Savage's unwanted sawdust. Thanks to Abraham, he had been able to hire the Mamre estate workers, who usually spent the winter waiting for the spring thaw. There were carts, drivers and workers to cut the ice and load the carts. The cost of the men and the carts had been cheaper than buying stone ballast.

Abraham had set out the lake in a squared pattern to allow the ice-cutters to work in a methodical fashion. They did not cut too deep in case that made the lake unstable. The ice was thick enough for horses to be used to tow the large blocks to the shoreline. Other groups cut the ice to smaller sizes to be loaded onto wagons..

Insulation was not required for the journey from the frozen lake to the wharf, as the temperature was constantly below freezing.

In the meantime, William built an inner shell that mimicked

the hull of the *Albatross*. The space between the inner shell and the ship's side was filled with Savage's sawdust to insulate the ice. Additional bags of sawdust had been laid on top of the ice to slow the evaporation.

If any ice survived the voyage he would try and sell it. He and Abraham could split the profit or build a large icehouse near Boston. Stockpiling near the wharf would save time in the future, if the voyage were a success.

The *Albatross* drifted slowly alongside the main wharf at Harbour Street, Kingston. It had been three weeks since they had left Boston and William felt the tension flow from his body. He'd risked all on his limited knowledge of the Mediterranean ice trade.

'All fast, Captain,' his First Mate said. 'Ready to work cargo.'

'Thank you,' William answered. 'I will check the ice.'

William crawled across the top of the sodden bags of sawdust in an effort to estimate how much ice remained. The hold was cold. Even though some had melted during the voyage, it was not as much as he had expected. He estimated that he had about eighty tons left. The insulation would require a little work if he wished to slow down the rate of melting for the next trip. William smiled as he realised he was already thinking of the next voyage.

A wild concept came to him.

What if he only sold part of the ice and used the remainder to keep fruit fresh during the return voyage to Boston? Fresh fruit in a Boston winter would sell very well.

Climbing out of the hold he called to his First Mate.

'Mr Austin, I am going ashore and I will require a carriage. I want to see if I can sell the remainder of the ice. In this heat I don't expect it to last too long.'

' Bosun, a carriage for the Captain, lively now.'

William descended to his cabin to collect his hat. The heat below deck emphasised how little time he had left to sell the ice.

William's yellow carriage swayed and bounced over the rough road as it made its way along King Street, in the largest British town in the Caribbean. The bright colours of the carriages were a sharp contrast to the dull black of the hackney cabs of Liverpool.

Kingston felt alive. The hot sandy street was crowded with bullock wagons, two-wheeled open-topped carriages and single horsemen. The street appeared to be more a dry riverbed than a normal street. Horse droppings ground into the dirty sandy soil indicating the route taken by most of the traffic. The hot sun meant the day's work would have to be completed before it drained the energy from a labourer's very soul.

The smell of horses and the buzz of the flies reminded him of Liverpool in summer. William waved his hand to frighten the flies from his face.

The wagons ahead swayed while the drivers flicked long-handled whips over the bullock's ears. Every wagon was stacked high with goods. Outside some of the shops, gangs of black labourers unloaded wagons. Horsemen cursed the small naked black children running under the bellies of their horses. William laughed when a rider leaned over too far in order to strike one of the children with his riding crop, and was nearly unseated.

Smart army officers walked under the canopies of the brightly painted shops and offices. A well-dressed lady accompanied each officer, a hand resting gently on the officer's arm, the free hand twirling a parasol while studying the fashions of the other ladies.

Each two-storey building contained a shop at street level and offices or accommodation on the upper floor. The upper level was constructed in such manner as to hang over the walkway, providing shade to the passing strollers.

He reached *The Parade* and noticed two European women cross the street and disappear under the canopy into a shop. His carriage drew level with the shop and he was able to read its name, *Paris' Coffee and Sherbet House.* The memory of sherbet made his mouth water as he pictured a sparkling cold drink. He decided to stop.

Paris Aristotle poured the sherbet drink from glass to glass to create as many bubbles as possible. When he was satisfied, he placed the glass on a plate and made his way to the small table by the window.

'Your sherbet, Madam.'

'Thank you, Paris,' replied the well-dressed lady.

The sherbet should have been cold, but in Jamaica there was little chance of a cold drink of sherbet, or anything else.

Paris, chasséd back to the counter in the exaggerated fashion of a decadent Frenchman. His chassé was his trademark and part of the reason for his success with the ladies. He gently pushed a black girl behind the counter.

'Work, you harlot; what do I pay you for?'

'Yes, Mass'er,' said the young black girl, a smile on her face. She knew Paris would not harm her; she was his bed partner. The language he used to her in the café was for the customers, not for her. She knew what he liked in bed and she did not mind his abuse in public. It was all a game. She picked up a cloth and started to wipe the counter, making sure he could see her behind.

It wiggled inside the flowery skirt each time she stretched to clean the flat display area. She turned to see what effect she was having. It was just what she wanted. She was in control, just as her mother had taught her. First you must control his organ, and after that, said her mother, the rest is easy. Her mother was a wise woman.

Paris stood behind the small counter and surveyed the room. How fortunate he was to have come to Jamaica. Seven years had passed since he opened his first coffee shop.

He had been born in London but, as a child, spent many years in Paris. His ability to speak French without an accent convinced others that he was French by birth. Fortunately his papers proved his birthplace was London. He liked to play the part of a French aristocrat who had escaped the guillotine. It gave him that little bit of mystery that attracted the ladies. Only the Secretary for the Governor, Mathew Atkinson, knew his real identity. Paris did not wish to be thought of as a Frenchman by the authorities.

His air of mystery worked well. Most of his customers were English ladies who came to his coffee shop to discuss the latest fashion with their friends. He had added the name 'Aristotle' later. His exotic persona allowed him to eat well, and make a profit, from his tea and coffee house on the corner of South Parade and King Street.

He stocked fashion publications, which he placed singularly on each table to encourage the ladies to move to the next table to read the next edition. When they moved, they were obliged to buy a fresh cup of coffee.

Paris referred to his coffee shop as the fashion center of the Caribbean. He would often drop names of acquaintances, implying that they were famous French designers. He tried to make sure he only mentioned the names of people who he knew were dead.

Nobody in Jamaica could accuse him of lying; all his 'friends' in the French fashion world had met Madam Guillotine. How sad, he would say, the world lost such a great designer.

When the occasion required, he would add a large measure of rum to the coffee of a particular customer who felt sad. As his customers became aware of this additive, they would often complain about feeling sad. It was not ladylike to be known as a drinker of strong spirit. To have a 'sad coffee', as the rum-laced coffee became known, was one way of helping the ladies get through the day. There was little to distract them in their daily lives. Their husbands were either in business or ran a plantation, and the abundance of servants never allowed any of the wives to get their hands dirty.

All the ladies felt safe with Paris. After all, he could discuss fashion like a lady and he never became hot and bothered by working. He was a true gentleman, and fun to be around. His many stories about life in Paris before the war kept them enthralled.

Paris was always on somebody's list for dinner: sometimes as a single person, and other times as a partner for some visiting lady. He was in great demand and he knew everything about everyone. Most of his information came via the bedroom. It did not take long for a bored wife or daughter to fall for his sophisticated chatter. Within a short time he would strip his conquest bare of not just her clothes, but also information and general gossip. He was careful to make sure his black lady-friend never found out about the liaisons with the wives of the island.

Paris knew how fortunate he was to obtain the building in which his coffee shop now operated. His first attempt had been in the capital, Spanish Town, on the left bank of the Rio Cobre, a town sacked by the English pirates and eventually captured by English troops. Any town so easily captured made him nervous. He moved to Kingston and opened his new coffee shop under the guns of the fort pointing down King Street to the harbour.

Kingston's four main streets created the square, or centre, of Jamaica. This square was called *The Parade*. It was where everyone would find Paris. He often glanced out of the large front window to reassure himself all was well with his world. Across the road from his coffee house he could see Kingston Parish Church, which was the only place for everyone to be on a Sunday morning. After the service the congregation would stroll across the road to Paris' for coffee or sherbet.

'I love Kingston,' he said to the black girl, 'it is full of life.'

'Life?' questioned the girl. 'It is dusty and noisy.'

'You can't see the beauty of Kingston.'

'I am a slave, so I don't see beauty in anything.'

'Slave, bah! I treat you well; you aren't a slave. Have you forgotten all that I have given you? If you were a slave, would I have done that? No! Clean up, you ungrateful bitch.'

'Yes Mass'er,' smiled the girl as she wiggled her behind once again.

'Pull over, driver, and wait for me.'

The sudden change from the bright sunshine to the well-shaded coffee house caused William to stop inside the door to allow his eyes to become accustomed to the low light. The two ladies sat at a table to one side.

A long counter dominated the rear wall. Behind the counter stood a white man and a black woman. The man was obviously in charge, as he was in conversation with the two ladies. William could hear his Continental accent that did not sound quite right. It sounded affected.

William removed his hat and lodged it under his arm. The women stopped talking and watched the newcomer approach the counter.

'Good morning, ladies,' said William, bowing slightly.

'Good morning, Sir,' they responded together.

'Good day, Monsieur, how may I help?' asked Paris.

'Sherbet, please.'

'I am sorry, Monsieur, I cannot make a true sherbet as I do not have any ice.'

'No matter, the fruit and the cream will be fine.'

The odd Frenchman began to mix the drink. William asked, 'If you had ice, do you think you could make ice cream?'

'Of course I could, but I do not have any ice.'

'I have ice,' William said quietly.

'You have ice?' asked Aristotle, handing over the sherbet drink.

'Correct, and I have enough at the right price for you to make a lot of money.' William sipped his sherbet drink and watched the owner.

'I think, Monsieur, you play a little trick on me.'

'Can you get cream by this afternoon?'

'Oui, Monsieur, how much do you wish me to obtain?'

'How much do you think you can sell?'

'What happens if you do not return? I will have too much cream.'

The enthralled women listened to the conversation between the officer and Paris.

'Madam,' said William, turning to one of the ladies. 'Would

you be so kind to witness something for me?'

'I don't know you, Sir.'

'Forgive me, ladies, I am Captain William King of the *Albatross,* newly arrived this morning from Boston.'

'Captain, what do you wish me to witness?' asked one 0f the ladies.

'You have heard my suggestion to——' William turned, not knowing the proprietor's name.

'Paris Aristotle, Captain, at your service.'

'Ladies, you have heard my suggestion to Monsieur Aristotle. I will now give him two golden guineas for his trouble. If he buys the cream, and I fail to return as promised, then he is at liberty to keep the coins.'

William brought out his purse and counted out the promised cash. He held the coins in his hand and looked at Paris Aristotle and asked, 'Well, Monsieur, do we have a deal?'

'Oui, Captain,' replied Paris, and proffered his hand for the money.

William dropped the coins into Paris' hand and turned to the ladies.

'May I suggest, ladies, that you visit this emporium this afternoon. There will be iced drinks for sale, and if you wish to buy some ice, this will also be for sale. I bid you both farewell and look forward to meeting you again.'

As he finished speaking he put on his hat, saluted the ladies, and turned to Paris. 'Until later, Monsieur.'

On his return to the *Albatross*, William summoned his officers to his cabin.

He could hardly control his excitement.

'Gentlemen, I think we may be able to sell the ice!'

'Sell it? Who would want so much ice, Sir?' asked David Fuller.

'Anyone living in this climate,' growled Austin, under his breath.

Fuller blushed.

'I hope we can sell it to everyone in this town, Mr Fuller,' commented William.

'Sorry, Captain, stupid question.'

'Not at all Mr Fuller, those who do not ask, never learn. Sang! Let's have some cold drinks while we work out our plan.'

'Yes, Sorr.'

Within a few minutes Sang produced fruit drinks in which he had placed chunks of ice. He had bargained with a dockside fruit-seller and bought a mixed lot of fruit. He intended to crush it and offer it to the Captain as a dessert, but it occurred to him it would be better in a punch. Sang crushed the fruits, mixed in rum, and added chunks of ice. William was impressed.

'Does anybody know how to make ice cream?' enquired William.

'As far as I know, Sir, you just wrap the cream container in ice and let it go hard.'

'I don't think so, Mr Austin,' said William. 'I have tasted ice cream in the Mediterranean and I am sure they spend time stirring it before they serve it.'

William laughed and commented 'I have sold the idea of ice cream this afternoon, and none of us are sure how to make it!'

'Captain, Sorr, I can dooa ice crim!' interjected Sang quietly from the corner of the cabin.

'What?' said William, turning to face Sang.

'I can do ice crim, Sorr,' said Sang, a little louder.

'Where did you learn to make ice cream?'

'Sorr, in China, ice crim all time same, no problem, can dooa.'

'Gentlemen, it appears we have a saviour. Let's get a couple of carts and fill them with enough ice to make a big splash! If you'll excuse my little joke.'

The small audience laughed dutifully.

'I'll arrange the carts, Sir,' said the First Mate. ' Mr Fuller, make sure we only unload clean ice. It must be attractive, we don't want anyone to think that we are trying to poison them.'

'Aye, Aye, Sir.'

'Thank you, Mr Austin,' said William, 'I will return to the coffee house to make sure we have the right audience. Bring the ice as soon as you can. It is called Paris' and it's on King Street near the *Parade*.'

'Don't worry, Captain, I'll find it.'

'Sang, come with me and tell me what you will require.'

—⚬—

The unloading of the ice attracted the attention of every lay-about and wastrel for miles around. William was not concerned. He wanted word to spread that a cargo of ice had arrived in town.

He stepped from the carriage outside Paris' coffee shop to be met by a large crowd. There were too many to fit in the small shop.

'Stay close,' he commanded Sang, and began to push his way through. Every table was full and people stood around the walls.

'Captain, Captain, over here; do you have the ice?'

'It is on its way, Mr Aristotle, and will be here directly.'

'I have the cream.'

'Do you have my two guineas?'

Paris Aristotle extracted two guineas and handed them to

William.

'Thank you, now we must discuss the cost of the ice.'

'How much do you have?' asked Paris frowning.

'Enough for anyone with the right money.'

'So, what price are you asking?' responded Paris, his eyes fixed on William's.

'There are two prices, depending upon which way you wish to buy. You can buy by the pound, or you can become my agent here in Jamaica to sell the ice, and supply me with an outbound cargo. To my agent the ice is free.'

'Free?' blurted out Paris, astonished.

'Free to my agent, because a partner can't sell his goods to himself.'

'Partner?' echoed Paris, his French accent forgotten for the moment.

'I do hope you will not repeat everything I say, Mr Aristotle,' commented William with a sigh.

'Sang, what do you require to make the ice cream?'

'Big bucket and small bucket: cream go inside small bucket, small bucket then go inside big bucket.'

'Monsieur, can you supply my man with those items?'

'Oui, come,' replied Paris, his accent returning. He waved his hand for Sang to follow him to the rear of the shop.

William turned and studied the waiting crowd. He smiled as Paris' accent slipped.

A sudden roar from the crowd heralded the arrival of the ice carts. William pushed his way to the front of the shop.

There were several blocks on each cart. The ice, covered in canvas in an effort to protect it from the hot sun, was the centre of attention. Black children rolled under the cart and held their lips to the cold liquid dripping between the boards of the carts. The screams of the children and the chatter of the adults would ensure the whole island knew that the ice ship had arrived.

James Austin climbed down off the cart, saluted William, and asked where the ice was to be stowed.

'Take it through this shop. You should find an area inside.'

Three seamen from the *Albatross* each picked up a fifty-pound block of ice and pushed their way through the crowd to the rear of the shop. Hands caressed the ice and wiped the cold water over hot faces.

William followed the last sailor and saw Paris attack one of the blocks with a club. The block broke in to smaller pieces. Sang collected these smaller pieces of ice and placed them in the large bucket, inside which sat a smaller bucket containing cream. Sang then mixed salt with the ice and packed it tightly around the inner container.

'Is this how they do it in China, Sang?'

'Yes, Captain, ice an' salt make vewy cold, and cold goes in to crim. Must keep turning crim so all of it get cold!'

'Monsieur,' called William to Paris, 'I think my man wants someone to stir the cream as it cools.'

'Harlot! Come here!' yelled Paris.

The attractive black woman William had noticed earlier came into the shop from the rear. She saw the crowd and her eyes expanded so much that they appeared to fill her face.

Paris reached under the counter and produced a long-handled wooden spoon and handed it to the young woman. 'Keep stirring the cream with this.'

'Monsieur,' asked William, 'have you decided which way you wish to pay?'

'Captain, you have partner,' replied Paris, holding out his hand to confirm the deal.

'This means half of today's profit from the ice sales, and the sales of ice cream, is mine,' said William straight-faced.

'Captain, as partners we share everything; the successes and the failures, and please call me Paris.'

William shook the offered hand and said, 'Partners.'

'Now, Paris, I think you had better serve our customers before there is a riot.'

The next couple of days were frantic for William and Paris. The demand for iced drinks and iced sherbet far exceeded their wildest dreams. Queues formed from early morning alongside the *Albatross*. Hundreds of people wanted to buy ice. Ladies of quality, who had only visited the wharf area the first time they had arrived in Jamaica, sat quietly under parasols as their native servants loaded blocks of ice on to carts to be rushed back to their plantations, or their homes in town.

William heard the crack of whips encouraging horses into a gallop. Long lines of melted ice water followed the carts; the ground became small rivers of mud.

William kept a mental count of the sales and the amount of money he had collected. It was considerable. On the evening of the second day he stopped selling ice. His stock had dwindled and he still wanted to experiment with the carriage of tropical fruits to Boston.

The gap between the inner skin and the outer hull, packed with sawdust, had worked a lot better than he had expected. Now he needed to buy fruit, load it quickly, and keep it chilled with the remainder of ice.

Paris quickly sold out of ice cream and was now rationing the remaining ice to sherbet drinks. He had never known his small coffee house to be so full for so long. He opened early on the second day of the 'ice bonanza' because he wished to have the place cleaned. The dirt from the street mixed with the melted ice had turned to mud on the floor of the coffee house.

He hired four idlers to clean the place and had arrived early to make sure they worked properly. As he walked towards the front door of his shop, he could see a white man sitting in an open-topped carriage.

It was unusual for a white man to be out of bed so early.

As Paris approached the front of his premises, the white man descended from his carriage.

'Good day, Sir,' said Paris.

'I wish to discuss a matter of business,' said the man, touching his hat.

Paris held open the door for the man to enter the coffee house.

'How may I be of service?'

'I have heard the *Albatross* is seeking fresh fruit for a return voyage to America. Am I correct?'

'It has been discussed,' said Paris cautiously, not sure what the man wanted, although he did appear respectable.

'I have a plantation and, as well as sugar, I also grow various fruits, including forbidden fruit'

'Forbidden fruit?'

'Aye, it is a sour fruit larger than an orange——'

'Do you mean grapefruit?' asked Paris.

'Some call it that, and some have other names for it. I can

supply pineapple as well.'

'Why did you grow grapefruit?' asked Paris.

'Most sailors are aware limejuice counteracts scurvy, but limes are sour, whereas the forbidden fruit has a more pleasant taste,' answered the man.

'I will discuss your ideas with the captain of the *Albatross*. He may be interested in pineapples. What price is your fruit?'

'I will supply you with the lowest price I can, on one condition.'

'Condition? If we are to buy from you it will be cash for fruit.'

'My condition is simple; I want to be your supplier for all fruit that leaves Jamaica on the ice ships.'

'Ice ships, we only have one ship with ice.'

'One today, but tomorrow, who knows?——I am sure there will be more.'

Paris' mind was in a whirl, 'I will discuss your proposal with the captain.'

'I can assume our conversation is confidential?' said the man.

'You can, but I cannot guarantee that others will not have the same idea, and condition.'

'Perhaps, but I will match any price.'

Paris smiled and said, 'If you expect to be our sole supplier you must beat any price, not just match it. Now may I ask your name, Sir, and also offer you a glass of my famous iced sherbet while we discuss the matter further?'

- CHAPTER TWENTY-FOUR -

Return to Boston

April 1806

The hills behind Boston were free of snow. The air held a hint of warmth to herald that spring was not too far away. Long Wharf jutted arrow-like into the harbour as the Pilot conned the *Albatross* alongside.

A carriage drew to a halt at the *Albatross'* berth. William's heart skipped a beat as Ruth descended from the carriage.

When the last line was secure, he hurried to greet Ruth.

He kissed her hand and straightened to search her face for a sign that she had missed him as much as he had missed her. Something was wrong.

'What's the problem, Ruth? Is your father well?'

'He is as well as can be expected.'

'There is something wrong. What is it? Tell me.'

'We have lost four of our black clerks.'

'What do you mean 'lost'? Have they run away?'

'No, no, they have not run away. They are free men and they don't have to run away from anything. They have papers stating that they are free.'

'What do you think happened?'

'I suspect, but cannot prove, that they may have been taken by slave hunters.'

'Slave hunters?'

'Yes, hunters from the south come north in an effort to find runaways. They get paid a bounty to return runaways to their original owners.'

'But your four men didn't have an original owner. Your father bought them from the hunters. Did you report them missing to the authorities?'

'Who would be interested in four missing blacks? This happens all the time, but our people have been lucky as they usually go home together.'

'Where is home? Back at *Mamre,* or do they live in town?'

'They couldn't afford to live in town so Elijah takes them back to *Mamre* each night. On the day you sailed, the clerks returned to the office to make sure all the paperwork was in order.'

'I remember the clerks.'

'When Elijah went to the office to collect them in the evening, he was unable to find them. We questioned the other clerks, the whites and the blacks, but all we know is that they returned to the office after you sailed. They were last seen waiting outside the office for Elijah. They haven't been seen since.'

'How's Abraham?'

'He has been very tired of late and of course he has had to work extra hours to make up for the missing men. We have hired additional clerks, but the missing men had been with us for a number of years and they were reliable. They knew everything about our business. The new clerks try, but they have a lot to learn.'

'Did you see the *Liverpool Lass* during your voyage?' Ruth asked, suddenly changing the subject.

'No, should I have?'

'Perhaps. Henry Nicholson's in command.'

'When did she arrive in Boston?'

'A few days after you arrived last time.'

'I don't remember seeing her or Henry.' William felt concerned at the information.

'She berthed at the other end of the wharf.'

'I wonder why he didn't call. He must have seen the *Albatross*?'

'I don't like the man,' said Ruth quietly.

'Have you met him?' asked William in surprise.

'Yes, he came to the office and asked for the price of shingle for ballast. I think he was surprised to be talking to me and not father. His agent is Leather. You may have seen him around the wharfs. All the agents try and sniff out information.'

'Small man, thinning hair?'

'That's him, a quiet, unsettling person with wet hands.'

'Why did Nicholson try to buy ballast from you?'

'That's what I found strange and I don't know the reason. I heard he bought a lot more ballast than he required for stability. I also heard rumours he bought the extra to sell.'

'Sell?'

'I also found it a little odd, but I think I may have worked out why he bought extra.'

'Why?' asked William as he guided Ruth to her carriage. Ruth allowed William to assist her into the carriage before she answered.

'I think he found out that you carried ice as ballast. It was common knowledge and there were plenty of jokes made at our expense.'

'Not any more,' laughed William.

'No, not any more,' agreed Ruth, 'but if the idea had failed, your ship would have become unstable as the ice melted.'

'So Henry gambled he would find me at sea. He'd have been able to sell me some of his ballast at an extortionate price. He knew I wouldn't have a choice if I wanted to save my ship.'

'Exactly.'

'You're clever to have worked that out.'

'Don't underestimate me, William!' retorted Ruth as her eyes flashed.

'Underestimate you? Never. Now if you will excuse me, I have to see to the discharge of the *Albatross*. When I have finished, I will call at the office. Will you be there?'

'Yes, I'll be there, and father wants you to come to dinner this evening.'

'Do you want me to come?'

'Of course I do, what a silly question.'

'Then I will be happy to accept your father's invitation,' William said, raising Ruth's gloved hand and kissing it gently.

William had little time to think of the pleasure of the forthcoming dinner while he dealt with the numerous visitors and the requirements for replenishing the *Albatross*.

James Austin made sure the cargo from Kingston was unloaded quickly, before any more fruit spoiled. The demands on his time seemed endless. William received visits from most of the shipping agents in Boston. They had heard about the tropical fruit. All attempted to buy, but none were successful as Abraham bought it all.

The ride to *Mamre* gave William plenty of time to think of Henry Nicholson. Why hadn't Henry called when they were both in port? Why did he wait until after the *Albatross* had sailed before approaching Ruth for ballast?

During dinner Abraham informed William that he had prepared another cargo of ice for a second voyage to Jamaica. He had built an icehouse near the wharf and filled most of it with ice and still had enough room to accommodate the trial cargo of fresh fruit. He held bags of sawdust and peat in his warehouse for insulation.

The experience gained on the first voyage allowed them to work a lot faster preparing for the second voyage. William knew that they would not be able to complete a third voyage, as the spring thaw would melt the ice on *Mamre Lake*.

At William's suggestion, he and Abraham signed an agreement to operate as partners on the sourcing and shipping of any cargo out of Boston on any vessel William owned or controlled.

He spent every spare minute he could with Ruth. She helped him to such an extent that her father jocularly commented that she spent more time helping William run his company than she spent helping her own flesh and blood.

William felt great sadness as he sailed from Boston on the second ice voyage. First, he was aware that he had fallen in love with Ruth. Second, he had misgivings that he could not rationalise. All was not right with Henry Nicholson.

On his second arrival in Jamaica, William's misgivings came to a head. Paris Aristotle did not seem pleased to see him. As soon as the gangway was in place, Paris hurried to board.

'William, a good trip?'

'A fine trip and profitable; the fruit lasted longer than I expected, and brought a good price in Boston.'

'Can we talk?'

'Of course, but what seems to be the problem?' asked William noting that the French accent was not in evidence.

'Not here; in your cabin.'

William waved his hand to the companionway, and followed his fancily dressed partner.

As he closed the door behind him, William glanced at the open skylight.

'Keep your voice down. I do not want the whole world to know our business, but what is the problem?'

'The ice cream went well last time, didn't it?' asked Paris.

'Yes,' said William.

'The ice brought a much better class of customer. From the Governor down, everyone wants a cold drink with his own piece of ice.'

'I am aware of this, Paris, but please come to the point. I have a lot to do now we are in port.'

Paris sighed and appeared to gather his courage to speak.

'Why do you want me to run a brothel?'

'What!'

'Why do——'

'Yes, I heard you,' snapped William, 'please explain that remark!'

'Some weeks after you left I received a visit from a ship's captain. He told me that summer was approaching in the north and you would not be able to supply ice – but you did need to keep the partnership alive for next winter.'

'What captain?'

'He told me that you had sent him, and I should treat him the same as you.'

'I repeat, what captain!'

'Captain Nicholson of the *Liverpool Lass*.'

'Henry Nicholson?'

'I believe so.'

'Pray carry on, Paris, I will not interrupt again.'

'Thank you, he told me you wanted to keep an interest in my business and we should arrange for certain ladies to use the upstairs rooms for liaisons.'

'Carry on.'

'I objected as I do not wish to lose the customers I have. If they found out that sort of thing was happening upstairs, they would certainly leave me. We all know it goes on, but one never mentions it, and if you run a high class coffee shop, a brothel is the last thing it should be.'

William waved his hand to encourage Paris to carry on with the story.

'I objected and told Captain Nicholson that I did not wish to have my premises used for such a service. We eventually agreed the brothel would not be on my premises, but a little way out of town. I think Captain Nicholson became his own best customer.'

'Where did he get the girls from?'

'From Havana, in Cuba.'

'How did he know we were partners?'

'I think he got information from my black bitch. A little money goes a long way amongst the local blacks.'

'All he needed to do was to find out who you were dallying with and then pressure her for information.'

'I know that now,' answered Paris.

'Who knows you are involved in a brothel?'

'Not many: mainly common sailors. They are his best customers.'

'So nobody of rank?'

'No.'

'That's something, anyway.'

'Did you send Captain Nicholson to me?'

'No, I did not!'

'Then why did he tell me he came from you?'

'I am not sure yet, but I believe he wants to discredit me in England. Nothing to do with you, or the coffee house.'

'Why?'

'That is something I hope to find out.'

'I think he is evil.'

'You may be right,' William said. 'I am a member of a group of people in Liverpool who believe a profit can be made from trading to the Indies without the selling of slaves. We are against slavery.'

'Oh,' said Paris. William must surely be aware that without the slaves, there would not be any goods to export to England, he thought.

'Nicholson's family have made their fortune carrying slaves to here and Cuba.'

'The *Liverpool Lass* had come from Cuba,' commented Paris in a thoughtful voice.

'Where did Nicholson get the girls for the brothel?'

'He brought them with him; he didn't buy them in Jamaica. I don't believe he visited the local slave market. All this is according to my black bitch, and I believe her. She was frightened that she would be sold into the brothel, until I calmed her down.'

'Why was he in Cuba?'

'I don't know.'

'Is he still in Jamaica? I didn't see his ship in the harbour?'

'He sailed some days ago but I am not sure to where. He loaded a cargo of rum and sugar, so I can only presume he sailed for England.' Paris's face changed as something occurred to him. 'Wait a minute; he was in port for only a few days, which would have been too short to unload his ballast and load sugar. He must have loaded sugar in Cuba and topped off with rum from here.'

Paris watched his partner as he thought through the problem.

'What bothers me,' said William, 'is why he went to Cuba. It could not have been just to buy female slaves and sugar. He could have bought the females here, along with the sugar. It would have been less trouble for him to buy both here. If he bought slaves in Cuba, unless he bought off a slave ship, the price would have been a lot higher than buying from the slave market here in Kingston. What cargo did he carry from Boston to warrant a call at Cuba?'

'I don't know, but he definitely arrived from Cuba, not Boston,' Paris said, and quickly changed the subject. 'On a lighter note, my friend, we have been invited to a small gathering at the Governor's residence tomorrow evening. Many of the guests will be the cream of the island's society and most of them visit Paris' coffee shop, so I cannot refuse to go. I think you should also come. It will expand your circle of acquaintances.'

William sighed and said, 'If I must.'

The reception at the Governor's house allowed William to meet a number of influential people. During a conversation with the Secretary to the Governor, Mathew Atkinson, he heard of an American proposal to close American ports to British ships. It was all in retaliation for the way the British stopped American ships to search for British deserters.

'But the Americans will be the losers if they close their ports,' said William with indignation. They need our goods.'

'We have it on good authority, Captain King, that it will happen in the near future. For a trader, it could be a disaster. They also object to our blockade of Europe.'

'I have heard of the Fox blockade of Europe but surely, after Trafalgar, the French are not in any position to challenge us?'

'Not in open battle but they are encouraging the Americans to defy us when we search their vessels for war material.'

The conversation drifted to other subjects but William could not help feeling concerned that his trading venture could come to an abrupt end if America stopped him sailing his British ship into Boston, or any other American port.

Later during the reception, two independent traders approached him to discuss the shipping of ice to other islands. Their questions and interest convinced him, more than ever, that the trade in ice could be a success.

Within a few days, William had secured another cargo of fruit for the return trip to Boston.

- CHAPTER TWENTY-FIVE -

Proposals

Boston
June 1806

Winter became spring, which allowed Abraham to scour Boston for cargoes to the southern states. He wanted to take full advantage of the availability of the *Albatross* and run her down the coast as often as possible. William was very happy with the arrangement as the coastal trade kept him close to Ruth, and it was very profitable. Abraham couldn't help but notice how close William and Ruth had become. He only hoped that William was not just dallying with Ruth until the time came form him to return to Liverpool.

The evening before William was to sail once again to the Southern States, he was sitting with Ruth and Abraham on the porch of *Mamre*. The conversation turned to the missing clerks. It had now been six months since they had disappeared.

'Did you ever hear of the missing men?' asked William, puffing on one of Abraham's special cigars.

'I made enquiries, in and around Boston, but gained nothing of consequence. I did hear from Mr Leather, the Nicholson agent.

He claimed to have seen them talking to some English sailors on the evening of the day they went missing. I don't know if I should believe the fellow.'

'They wouldn't have shipped out, not after having worked for you, Abraham. They were not sailors.'

'I don't know what has happened to them, perhaps they will return one day.'

They both sat in silence, lost in their own thoughts, when William changed the subject.

'Abraham, I received some depressing news in Jamaica that America will close her ports to British ships in the near future, because the British Navy has been stopping American ships to check that the crews are not British deserters. I doubt the American Government will put up with this much longer.'

'I heard that a few days ago,' commented Abraham, 'are you also aware that the British will deem a cargo of grain from Boston to France as war supplies? How long will it take the French to follow the British? If this happens and America closes her ports to British and French ships, we will have a problem. Politicians have a way of fighting that an ordinary man finds a little strange.'

'I fear you are correct, William. What do you have in mind?'

'To protect us both, I propose to sell half of the *Albatross* to you for one dollar. If, for any reason, I fail to gain ownership of the *Albatross* upon my return to England, then you have only lost a dollar. If America closes her ports, this could be the end of the anti-slavery effort to show that a profit can be made without recourse to slavery.'

'A dollar, I see what you are trying to achieve, but as your partner, I feel a more substantial amount would be appropriate.'

'Father, I'm sure William has a good reason for this unusual transaction. Let's listen to what he has to say,' said Ruth, quietly.

'You are right, my dear. William, I will listen to your proposal.'

'We will have two sets of documents; one to show that you own fifty-one percent of the *Albatross,* and the other to show that I own fifty-one percent.'

'How can that be, William? There is only one hundred percent ownership in any business,' asked Ruth.

'A good question, Ruth, I said we would have two sets of legal documents, each dated differently. If the British Navy stops me, I produce the documents to show that I own the ship and that the cargo is already under British control. If an American ship stops me, I produce the other documents and state that, as I am the Captain of an American ship, they do not have the right to interfere in the voyage of an American-owned vessel.'

William's two listeners sat silently.

'The legal ownership, of course, is the later dated of the two documents,' said Abraham after some time.

'I know, my friend, but I will only produce whichever document allows me free passage in the circumstances. After all, we are only interested in profit, not in the squabbles between nations.'

'Father, this will mean we could take advantage of a British-owned ship to carry goods from a British colony, such as Jamaica, to England, which is currently not allowed to foreign-owned ships.'

'Yes, my dear, I realise that. Would you please get us another drink or ask one of the servants to do so?'

'Certainly, father.'

As Ruth left, her father leaned forward and, in a low voice, said to William, 'You are aware if you are discovered in the ruse, they will hang you?'

'I am aware that is what the British will do, but in my defense, I will not endanger England or her possessions in the quest to make money. On the other hand, the restriction of trade between America and England seems to me to be stupid, on the part of both countries.'

Abraham sat back in his chair and contemplated the young man in front of him.

'There is one other thing, Sir,' said William.

'Yes?'

'I wish to marry Ruth.'

'In one breath you acknowledge there is a strong possibility you could be hanged, and in another you wish to marry my daughter, and perhaps make her a widow in a very short time.'

'I don't intend to make her a widow!'

'No, I don't suppose you do.'

'The risk is small.'

'But still a risk.'

'With your permission, I would like to ask Ruth and let her choose.'

'I know what she will say.'

'How can you know, I have only just broached the subject?'

'I have seen the way she looks at you, and you at her, and I suspected you may speak of it tonight. You sail tomorrow, which is why I asked Ruth to fetch the drinks, to give you an opportunity to speak your mind. All I have to do is ring the bell to have someone bring me a fresh drink.'

William glanced at Abraham and smiled. A larger smile lit his face as he realised his future father-in-law agreed with him marrying Ruth.

'A little bit of advice to you, William; Ruth Judson is a very strong-willed woman. It will take a real man to control her, so you must start as you mean to carry on. What happens if you cannot get control of the *Albatross*?'

'I have an agreement with my associates that I can buy out their shares. If, for any reason, I fail to keep the *Albatross*, I will find a ship and return. I can't marry if I do not have a ship. It would not be fair on Ruth to ask her to marry someone without prospects.'

'If you fail to get the *Albatross,* then I will be happy to offer you a position in Boston.'

'Very generous of you, Sir, but I will return with a ship, even if it isn't the *Albatross*.'

The door opened and Ruth rejoined the two men she loved most in the world. 'The drinks will be here in a minute or two. I couldn't find Elijah.'

'I have a book I wish to lend to William, so you will have to entertain him while I go and find it.'

'Tell me the name, Father, and I will get it – I am sure you and William have much to talk about.' She began to rise from her seat.

'Sit down, child, I am quite capable of finding a book. I couldn't tell you where it is, as I cannot remember the name, but I will recognise it when I see it. Just entertain William while I am away.'

He laid his hand gently on her shoulder and squeezed a little. The gesture reminded Ruth of her childhood. The memories flooded back to give her a warm comfortable feeling that all was well with their world. Her father often made the gesture to calm her. It was a sign that told her that he loved her.

Abraham left the porch to the two young people and made

his way to his study. He pulled out his watch to check the time. An hour should be long enough. He smiled to himself as he remembered that it had not taken anywhere near an hour when he asked Ruth's mother for her hand all those years ago. However, people were different these days.

'It's a beautiful sunset this evening,' said Ruth and stared over the fields to the clouds flecked with the red of the setting sun.

William watched the sun's remaining rays dance on the low clouds. 'Red sky at night, sailor's delight.'

'What does that mean?'

'That it will be a fine day tomorrow and hopefully a calm sea when we sail.'

'When you sail,' repeated Ruth. She blinked tears from her eyes. 'How I hate those words; they carry all my happiness away.'

William left his chair and sat next to Ruth on the cane seat, which was large enough for the two of them. He held her hand and gently stroked the back.

'I'll be back as fast as I can.'

'Oh, William, do you have to go?'

'I am afraid I do, for a number of reasons.'

'You have a lady friend in Liverpool?'

'No, no lady friends anywhere except here.'

Ruth turned her face to him. 'Here?'

'Yes, here, at *Mamre*, Oh, Ruth, you must know how I feel about you?'

'Do I?'

He let his fingers slowly move up her bare arm and gently caressed her skin. His other hand held her two hands in her lap.

'Ruth. Ruth, I have something to say.'

'Yes,' whispered Ruth, her voice failing her.

William gazed into her eyes, at her mouth and her black hair falling around her ears. He could see the small sparkle of her earring as it caught the last of the evening light.

'You are beautiful,' William blurted out.

She blushed and her breathing quickened.

'Ruth, will you——?'

'Will I what, William?'

'Will you wait for me while I am in England. I'll return as quickly as I can, you know I will, don't you?'

'I think so.'

'Will you wait?'

'Oh, yes, William, I will wait,' she whispered. Of course she would wait. She had waited for William since the day she was born. Her fingers curled around his as she tried to will him to ask the right question.

'Would you do me the great honour of marrying me on my return?'

The world seemed to slow down for William as he realised he had uttered the words he had been thinking for so long. He was in uncharted waters. Had he been too quick? Perhaps he should have waited until he returned from his next trip. Also, she might not marry him because he was a Christian. Such a beautiful woman must have had a number of marriage offers from far wealthier men.

'My answer is yes, William, to both questions.'

'To both questions?'

Hearing William's unexpected response, it was Ruth's turn to have doubts. Perhaps he didn't mean to ask her; perhaps she answered too quickly, and perhaps she should have left him dangling until after his return from his next trip. If he withdrew the questions he would be ashamed and she would be embarrassed. 'I said yes, William. Is that what you wanted to hear?'

'You will marry me?'

'Yes, William, shall I say it again?'

'Yes, please, say it again,' said William.

'I will marry you, William, and I will wait for you. Is that what you wanted to hear?'

'Yes,' he whispered. He leaned over and gently kissed Ruth's slightly opened mouth. Her lips tasted sweet and the gentle waft of her perfume caused his head to spin.

She felt his lips on hers and she responded. She could taste the brandy, a slight smoky taste, then realised it would be the cigar he had smoked.

They drew apart and each looked lovingly at the other, as if for the first time. Ruth freed her hand from William's and ran her index finger down the scar on his face, trying to memorise it for the future. Her hand, soft and delicate, touched his face so lightly that he was not sure if she had actually touched him.

- CHAPTER TWENTY-SIX -

Havana Fire

Savannah ~ Cuba
June 1806

William felt frustrated that he was unable to carry through with his plans to develop the ice trade. The ice had melted at the end of winter and the icehouses had not been completed in time to store commercial quantities. He'd sent plans to his partner, Paris, to construct two icehouses in Kingston. One was to store fruit for export, and the other to accept fresh ice from Boston. The icehouses had to be large enough to hold enough quantities to extend the ice season to early summer.

He consoled himself that trading from Boston along the American coast made profits, and each return to Boston allowed him more time with Ruth.

―※―

It was early June when the *Albatross* sailed from Boston for Savannah, Georgia; with a cargo of timber the morning after William had asked Ruth to marry him. Savannah had suffered another fire, not as bad as that of 1796, but it had destroyed a number of buildings. The local sawmills could not cope with the demand for timber to rebuild and so supplies were ordered from all over the country.

After unloading the timber, William found it difficult to obtain a return cargo for Boston. He realised, reluctantly, that he would have to sail to the Caribbean to find a cargo for the return voyage. After studying his charts he decided that as Cuba was closer than Jamaica, he would accept a cargo of cotton Havana and risk the consequences of him being an Englishman in a Spanish possession.

He thought the voyage would give him an opportunity try out the new paperwork that proved he captained an American ship. Trading to Havana would save weeks of sailing to Jamaica. If all went well, he should be able to collect a cargo of hides for the return to Boston.

Another consideration on his mind was his crew. They had been away from Liverpool for nearly a year now and were eager to return home. They had been told when they signed on that the voyage would be six to nine months. Two voyages to the Caribbean and a number of small voyages along the American eastern seaboard had meant a longer time. William would make this last voyage to Havana his final voyage before returning to England.

Havana

A dark smudge of land slowly rose from the sea as the *Albatross* drew closer to Cuba. It eventually hardened into soft green hills giving an impression of peace and tranquility. William focused his telescope on a dark area at the base of one of the hills. Houses jumped into view; it was Havana.

William was aware of Cuba's turbulent history. The island had been attacked and captured by pirates, the Spanish, and then by the English. In its latest change of ownership, it had been transferred from England to Spain in exchange for Spanish Florida in the America. William saw two white-sail vessels emerging from the narrow entrance of the harbour and spreading canvas to pick up the fresh ocean winds.

The *Albatross,* flying the American flag, drew closer to the gap denoting the entrance to Havana harbour.

'Stand by the halyard, Mr Mate.'

William focused his telescope once again, moving the glass slowly to the left of two forts dominating the harbour entrance. He noted the Spanish flag, on Morro Fort on the eastern bank of the harbour entrance, moving gently in the morning breeze.

He felt tense as the *Albatross* entered the gap between the two forts. He wanted to wipe the palms of his hands to rid himself of sweat. He knew he must not show anxiety in front of the crew. The *Albatross* could be fired upon any moment – if those inside the forts did not believe she was an American vessel.

'Dip!' he called out as the *Albatross* came abreast of the Spanish flag. The flag of America slowly lowered to half-mast. The soldiers of the fort answered the salute as they lowered their flag a similar distance. A few seconds later the Spanish flag rose to the top of the mast.

'Haul!' called William, feeling enormous relief. Courtesy had been completed and his ship hadn't been fired upon.

The speed of the *Albatross* dropped as she passed Morro Fort headland. The *Albatross* tacked back and forth across the ever-widening harbour in an effort to use every breath of wind. The last puff was enough to push his ship to within a couple of hundred yards of the wharf.

'Prepare to anchor. We will wait for the authorities to come to us.'

It was early afternoon on a hot humid day before the *Albatross* received permission to move alongside. The speed of the Spanish authorities' decision-making was no faster in Cuba than in Spain.

The attitude of the official brought back memories of William's time in Spain. The Spanish took an eternity to come to the point. If he interrupted the official by discussing the voyage from America, the weather or the war in Europe, he would just prolong the agony. William sat quiet, sipping rum and lime juice and trying to smile at the appropriate moment.

At last he was allowed to weigh anchor and move towards the yellow and blue stucco houses of Havana. Once alongside, William left the *Albatross* under control of James Austin and made his way to the warehouses. There he would find a shipping agent for his cotton cargo. He would also, he hoped obtain good rates to carry hides, and perhaps dried meat, back to Boston.

It didn't take him long to find the agent for the cotton. All he needed now was a return cargo (as long as it wasn't sugar.) The Savannah agent gave him names of several companies that specialised in hides. William decided to visit each of them.

Rows of two and three storey buildings dominated the cobbled streets. They cast cooling shade over the walkways and each time William stepped down from the carriage, he tried to stay in the cool shadows.

As the afternoon progressed, small white clouds gathered above the surrounding hills. Eventually they became storm clouds and drenched the town in tepid rain. Within a few minutes the rain stopped and was followed by a hot, drying sun. The cooling of the air by the rain was short-lived. The sun quickly dried the damp streets and added the vapourised rain to the humidity, and to William's discomfort.

When visiting each of the offices William communicated in English and broken Spanish. It had been some years since he had called at a Spanish port. At each office he went through the same pleasantries required under Spanish business practice. To complement the pleasantries, he accepted lime juice laced with rum, which he realised was beginning to affect him even though he sipped as little as possible. A refusal to accept the drink would cause offence. Each time he left an office, the sun felt stronger and he felt weaker. By evening he ached with tiredness, though he was pleased he had only one more company to visit. It was disappointing that no one seemed able to offer him a full load – but by accepting a few bales of hides from each, along with sacks of dried meat, he had been able to accumulate enough freight for the voyage to Boston.

His last stop was 107 Muralla Street, across the road from the bustling market of the Plaza Nueva. The mixture of the rum, heat and the noise from the market square made him feel ill. Still, he marveled at the beauty of 107 Muralla Street. A covered gallery hid the windows from the heat of the day and the noise of the market. From his carriage, he walked slowly into the shade of the gallery leading to the main door. Inside the gloomy interior, he found the office pleasantly cool.

'Senor, may I help you?' said a small man from behind a desk.

William replied that he had a small amount of space left on the *Albatross* for hides or dried meat for his return voyage to Boston. When he mentioned Boston, a Negro sitting at another desk glanced up from his work and met William's gaze. He felt he knew the Negro but couldn't think where he had seen him before. Perhaps he resembled one of the many he had seen during the afternoon. Havana was full of Africans.

'Perhaps we can help you, Senor, would you please follow me?'

William followed the man to the rear of the building and up a flight of stairs. As they reached the last door of a row of offices, the Spaniard tapped lightly and called out. The only part William recognised was his name and the word Boston.

'*Entrar,*' called a voice.

William was greeted by a clean-shaven, well-built man who appeared to be in his early forties, standing behind a desk covered in a mass of papers. He was unlike many of the local Spaniards that William had spoken to that day. His face was deeply tanned. He peered from behind heavy eyelids that hardly moved. William had the impression that the man had spent his life staring across a vast glittering ocean that reflected the glare of the sun back into his face. The shuttered eyes gave his face a cruel appearance, as did his thin lips. The man gently placed a quill on a rest near a small pot of ink.

'Senor, how may I help you?' said the man as he offered his hand.

William repeated what he had said downstairs.'

'You are American, Senor? You sound English,'

'I was born in England but now have business interests in Boston.'

The man shrugged his shoulders as if he didn't care. 'Please be seated. I am Amancio Cardenas.'

'My pleasure to meet you, Senor Cardenas.*'*

'We may be able to help you, Captain. It is odd, but in the

past few weeks I have received two American Captains looking for cargo.'

'I am sure you must sell to many American ships, Senor, why do you find this odd?'

'Some weeks ago another Captain came to see me, and he sounded like you. How do you say it in English? His accent sounded similar to yours. Perhaps he also was born in England and has business interests in Boston.'

William felt the hair on his neck rise while he listened to Cardenas. He kept his face neutral.

'There must be many Englishmen who have now settled in Boston.'

'That is true, that is true, but I have a fine ear for dialects and accents and it has seldom failed me in the past. I also was a sailor. I sailed in ships bringing slaves from Africa to Cuba. I have also visited your country and your great city of Liverpool. Of course this was before the latest little trouble between Spain and England.' He sighed as if there would never be an end to the war. 'Napoleon will ruin good businesses,' said the Spaniard, making a spitting noise when he said Napoleon. 'I have left the sea and changed to trading.' He waved his arm to illustrate that all around was his.

'You trade in many things, Senor?' asked William.

'If there is a profit, then I will trade.'

'Perhaps I may know this other Captain,' ventured William, in an effort to appear polite.

'His name Nix-son.'

William felt himself go cold as he realised the Spaniard had tried to say 'Nicholson'. His face did not show any emotion but his mind was in turmoil as he tried to make sense of why Henry would visit Havana.

'I am afraid the name means nothing to me, Senor. Perhaps we could discuss terms for a cargo. I wish for a fast turnaround. We are currently discharging the cargo we brought from America.'

'Cotton, I believe, Captain, from Savannah?'

'You are well informed, Senor.'

'Information is profit, Captain. Now let us to business, as I can offer you both hides and dried meat.'

'I also wish to hire extra labour,' said William.

Heavy with fatigue, William returned to the *Albatross*. Why had Henry Nicholson called at Cuba? He felt certain he was out to damage him. A damaged reputation would make gaining the *Albatross* a much harder task.

The unloading of the *Albatross* had stopped for the night. He flopped into his chair and opened his shirt to let a little cool air circulate around his body. He closed his eyes and sat thinking.

William sensed, rather than heard, Teng Sang as he moved about the cabin, picking up the clothes William had dropped.

'Sang?'

'Yes, Cap'n'

'Ask Mr Austin to join me'

'Aye, aye, Sur.'

A few minutes later the First Mate knocked on the door.

'Come in, James, come in and sit down.'

James knew his Captain was worried; he seldom called him by his first name.

'How can I help, Sir?'

William explained about visiting the agents. He went into

more detail when he reached the final agent, Amancio Cardenas.

'I have a feeling that all is not as it may seem with Senor Cardenas.'

'How so, Captain?'

'I am not sure and I do not know why I feel so uneasy, but I thought I recognised one of his Negro clerks this afternoon. When I left Cardenas' building, I searched for the man, but I didn't see any black that I recognised. I must have been mistaken. I have never visited Cuba before and perhaps, like Chinese; blacks all look the same to us. It is just a feeling I cannot shake.'

'Do you plan another visit to Senor Cardenas?'

'Yes, tomorrow: I have agreed to carry his hides and some sacks of dried beef. He has an agent in Boston. Mister Leather. I would value your help tomorrow. I want you to come with me when I visit Cardenas. Mr Fuller is capable of supervising the unloading of the last of the cotton.'

The two officers approached Senor Cardenas' building and stopped a short distance away to study the layout of the area.

'Mr Austin, I'll go in the front door and engage Senor Cardenas in conversation. I would like you to explore the area and then join me and make out you have a problem. This should allow us both to leave.'

'Aye, Sir.'

Before entering the building, William closed his eyes for a few seconds. His eyes adjusted immediately to the low light within the office. He scanned the clerks' area for the Negro he thought he had recognised.

'Captain King, how nice to see you again,' said the familiar voice of Senor Cardenas.

William watched Cardenas approach with his hand out in greeting.

'Senor Cardenas, good morning, I called in to confirm our arrangements of yesterday.'

'But I thought all was arranged. Is there a problem?'

'No, no problem, but as you know, I wish to make a fast turnaround, so perhaps we could use an extra gang to speed up the loading.'

'I have arranged for two gangs to load your vessel when she has finished discharging the cotton. I was under the impression you wished to keep your costs down. If I am mistaken ....,' said Cardenas, and smiled with his lips but not his eyes, 'if you wish an extra gang, it will not be a problem. I will arrange one immediately.' He turned and spoke in rapid Spanish to the man who had greeted William the previous day. The man's head bobbed up and down as he acknowledged Cardenas's words

'*Si, comprendo, Senor*'.

While Cardenas issued his instructions, William casually glanced around the office and spied the black man from the previous day. The Negro was writing what appeared to be a ship's manifest. He raised his eyes and met William's gaze. His mouth twitched as if he was about to smile, but changed his mind and resumed his work.

'All arranged, Captain.'

William quickly looked around in case Cardenas saw him staring at the Negro. His mind tried to place where he had seen the black man before. Some sixth sense warned him not to ask a direct question to Cardenas.

'I am obliged, Senor, and thank you for your help.' William offered his hand to close the conversation. Cardenas gripped

William's hand and held it longer than required.

'If there is anything else you wish, you have only to ask, my friend.'

There was no sign of friendship in Cardenas' eyes. William pulled his hand free and turned to leave. At that moment the outer door burst open and James Austin stood in the frame.

'Mr Austin, is there a problem?'

'Aye, Sir, may I speak to you outside?'

'Isn't it strange, Captain, how problems can manifest themselves in such a short time? Don't tell me you need a fourth gang to work your vessel,' said Cardenas.

'Thank you for your time, Senor; I will return to my ship.'

The Captain and his Mate walked quickly away from Cardenas' building towards the wharf.

'What have you to report?'

'I think we have found the missing blacks from Boston, Sir.'

William stopped and grabbed his First Mate's arm. 'That's it, James, I remember now. Inside the office is a black man making out a manifest and he recognised me. I couldn't remember where I'd seen him before. He must be one of the clerks who were on the *Albatross* to check the paperwork when we left on the first voyage from Boston. He is one of the four that went missing.'

'I think I have found the other three, Sir.'

'Tell me, man, tell me.'

'After you entered the Cardenas' building, I wandered around the back and found a large warehouse near the canal. The canal must allow barges to be worked if a ship is at anchor in the harbour. In the warehouse were a number of blacks stacking bales of cotton and generally working freight. I thought I might be able to talk to one of them just to get an idea of what the company did for trade. As I entered the warehouse, one of the blacks fell from a stack of cotton bales and landed nearly at my feet.'

'Did you recognise him?'

'I did not pay too much attention because I just thought he was a clumsy oaf and should be more careful. His clothes were the worse for wear, but appeared to once have been of good quality. They were the type passed down from a plantation owner. You know how the plantation owners pass old clothes to their favoured slaves?'

'Yes, yes, James, I know,' said William sharply, 'please get to the point.'

'Well, Sir, he gets up from the floor and started to brush himself down, when I heard him mutter something in English. So I asked him if he knew if the boss-man was around. He peered at me and pointed to a small office area I had not seen. It was then the black said '*Mr Austin, Sir*'.

'He recognised you?'

'Yes, Captain, he did, and I don't know who was more surprised, him or me!'

The two men stopped speaking while they exited the town through one of its eleven gates. The armed guards on the gate gave William a limp salute. The effort of a proper salute was evidently too much. William nodded and they passed through to the wharf.

'Carry on!'

'Well, Sir, it appears this black, and three of his mates, were shanghaied in Boston and shipped out on the *Liverpool Lass*!'

'How did they end up here?'

'It appears they were not too good at being a sailor, so the Captain of the *Liverpool Lass* sold them to your Spanish friend.'

'He's no friend of mine.'

'I bet the *Liverpool Lass's* Captain got a good price for them because they are all educated and they can write in English. The black I met in the warehouse was not happy. He finds the work hard compared to Boston.'

'I am not surprised, he used his brain in Boston and now he has to use his muscles.'

'Captain, ——I, emm.'

'Speak up, James, what is on your mind?'

'Well, Captain, I don't think it is right we leave them to work for Cardenas. Not as they are free men and have been stolen away from Boston.'

'What do you propose?'

'Can we rescue them, Captain?'

'When will we finish loading the outbound cargo?'

'In about a week.'

'Then we can do nothing until we are ready to sail. I will not risk a successful voyage and put the crew and the ship in jeopardy.'

'Aye, Captain I understand, but it does give us time to make a few plans!'

'Plans we can make, so remind me about the guard gate curfew,' said William.

'According to the Savannah agent, the guard gates are closed at nine each night, after the firing of a cannon. The gates are not opened again until after another cannon is fired at dawn.'

'Thank you, James, this will take careful planning.'

William crossed the gangplank and dropped down onto the deck of the *Albatross,* his mind awhirl with information.

Now it was clear what Henry Nicholson had been doing in Havana, he thought. He had kidnapped Abraham's clerks and sold them to Cardenas, bought female slaves and sailed to Jamaica. No wonder Cardenas recognised my accent.

- CHAPTER TWENTY-SEVEN -

Rescue

Havana
June 1806

An anxious week passed. William thought it would never end. No matter how many times he climbed into the holds to check on the progress of the loading, it was never fast enough. The stench from the bales of hide permeated every nook and cranny of the *Albatross*. Would he ever rid his nostrils of the overpowering smell? Coupled with the odour from the hides, the crew had to suffer the constant attention of tiny flies that were attracted to the sacks of dried meat.

William felt sure Cardenas' spies were on the quay. He could feel their eyes watching the slow progress of loading.

'The last of the battens are in place, Captain,' reported James Austin. 'We should be ready to sail within the hour.'

'Thank you, Mr Austin, how are our other plans?'

'In hand, Captain, and the four blacks have been warned it will be tonight. We passed the word to them earlier today. I visited Senor Cardenas' office in the normal course of my duties and was able to pass a message to the blacks in the warehouse.'

'It is fortunate they all sleep on the premises.'

'Aye, Captain, but they are locked in a cellar of the warehouse at night.'

'A problem I am sure we will be able to overcome. Who volunteered to come with us?'

'Mr Fuller wanted to come but I told him he is to secure the ship. If anything goes wrong, we need him to make sure the ship is cleared from Havana. He wasn't happy about being left out, though.'

'You were right, Mr Austin. Who else?'

'We have four of the crew, all reliable and all able to handle themselves with a pistol or cutlass. They have seen action in the past.'

'What about the bosun?'

'Like Fuller, he was of the opinion we couldn't do without him, but this time I told him he and the Second Mate are in charge.'

'Excellent. When it is dark, have the *Albatross* moved from the wharf to an anchorage, and ready to make sail. Issue pistols and cutlasses to the volunteers, pistols and our swords for you and me. We may need a lamp, so have someone responsible for it and make sure it has enough oil, and whoever you appoint carries flint to light it.'

'I think Sutton will be the right man; he's a steady hand and has initiative.'

'Captain, Sur?'

'Yes, Sang, what is it?'

'Sang come as well.'

'It could be dangerous, Sang, and people could get hurt.'

'I am your servant, Sur, so I go with you!'

William smiled. Four crew, James Austin, plus himself and now Sang. They would fill the small ship's boat when they added the four blacks. Sang could watch over the ship's boat. 'You can come, Sang, but only if you do just as I say!'

Using their oars, the crew pushed the small boat away from the comfort of the *Albatross*.

'Oars out, and give way together,' whispered William.

The four volunteers gently dipped their oars into the still waters of the harbour and began to row. An oily swell lapped the boat. William glanced behind at their wake and felt confident that the shadows cast by the three-quarter moon would cover their movement, yet leave enough light for him find his way through the city. He had waited until it was dark and the noise ashore stilled. It would be unlikely that the owners of the warehouses would be about at this time of night.

William went over the plan once again in his mind. His idea was not to approach the harbour facilities directly but to land his small force in the mangroves on the landward side of the city wall.

The small boat glided gently through the mangroves until the vegetation was too thick to allow further use of the oars.

'Hold her steady, lads. Jenkins, off with you and see if there is anyone about.'

Jenkins slid over the bow into the black water and waded silently ashore.

William turned to his steward and said, 'Sang, you stay here. Guard the boat and wait for us.'

Sang, who wanted to be at his Captain's side in case of trouble, could tell by William's voice that it would be useless to argue.

'Right men, over the side and drag the boat closer. Turn her around and have her ready for a fast exit. Keep your pistols dry and make sure none of them are cocked. We will have wasted our time if any of you shoot yourself in the foot.' William was serious, but managed to lighten the comment and generate a few smiles as his crew slid over the side and pulled the boat the last few yards to the shore.

The small group gathered on the path that ran alongside the mangroves. William glanced back but could no longer see the boat or Sang.

'Mr Austin, mark this spot if you would, so we will know where to enter the water on our return.'

'Note this plant,' Austin whispered to the men, 'it is the only one of its type. It grows white cloth! When you see it, the boat is directly in front in the reeds.'

Jenkins jogged quietly back along the path having checked ahead for any unwelcome visitors.

'All clear up to the city wall.'

'Thank you, Jenkins, now listen, men, if we are separated, make your way back to this spot. If you are challenged by one of us waiting here, our password is 'ICE'. Understand, the password is ICE!' emphasised William. ' Carry on, Jenkins, we will follow you.'

'Aye, aye, Sir.'

The small group quickly moved in single file towards the city. The moon had nearly set by the time they reached the foot of the city wall.

'Gather round,' whispered William. 'Mr Austin and Holt will stay here amongst the trees to cover us if required. You three will come with me. The warehouse is just over this wall. Hopefully we will have four extra men on our return and they may not be able to move as quickly as us. Some of them may have been mistreated and they will all be frightened. Follow me.'

William and his three men kept to the shadows as they ran quietly along the base of the wall that curved towards one of the city's gates. He peered around the curve of the wall and saw a guard patrolling in front of a large city gate. The only sound they could hear was the insects amongst the distant mangroves.

William's next move, if it failed, would see him shot. He could not ask his men to do it. He rose from his hiding place and walked boldly towards the guard. He managed to approach within ten yards before the guard heard him and turned. The guard raised his musket and challenged the stranger. William pulled a handkerchief from the sleeve of his jacket and wiped his brow, at the same time speaking to the guard in Spanish. The handkerchief muffled his words and gave him enough time to cover the last few yards. The guard, unsure of what the officer said, hesitated. William could smell the garlic on the guard's breath when he brought the pistol down on his head. The guard collapsed and dropped his musket. William felt for a pulse. He couldn't find one. He held his breath and listened, in case the noise of the falling musket had attracted anybody's attention. All was quiet.

A wave of his arm brought the rest of his crew out of hiding.

'Chapman, over the gate and see if they have posted a guard inside.'

The other two crewmen made a stirrup from their hands and pushed Chapman high enough to grab hold of the top. He slowly raised his head and peered over, then lay along the top, listening for the tread of a guard. The area remained quiet. He slid over and allowed his body to hang down inside. William and his men heard a soft thud and a grunt from Chapman as he hit the ground. They held their breath and listened.

A scraping noise followed by a bump could be heard behind

the gate.

'They must have a beam across the inside of the door, Sir. Chapman may not be strong enough to move it on his own. If you, Sir, and Sutton, give me a leg up, I can help him,' said Jackson.

'Good idea, Jackson; Sutton, lend a hand.'

William and Sutton linked hands and bounced Jackson as high as they could. He gripped the top of the gate and pulled himself up and over.

The scrape of the beam as it was moved became distinct. Within a minute, the sounds moved to the far end of the gate and a small space began to open between the two giant doors. On seeing this, William and Sutton threw their weight against the door to widen the opening.

They were now in the city. William ran quietly across a road and into the shadows of a building. The street was quiet. He waved his arm for his men to follow. Hugging the shadows, he moved quickly away from the area around the gate. He could hear the others as they followed. The beat of his heart filled his ears. He stopped at the junction of two streets and peered around the corner. It was Muralla Street. He could see the lights of the market in Plaza Nueva.

He was close to Cardenas' warehouse; he could see a faint glow from it. He slid around the corner and, staying close to the walls of the building, ran quietly towards the dim lights ahead.

On reaching the warehouse, he pressed himself against the wall. The others joined him. 'This is the building where the blacks are being held. Sutton, see if you can find an entrance other than the main door,' whispered William.

The seaman padded off, his shoeless feet silent in the night.

'Windows?' whispered William to Jenkins.

Before Jenkins could answer, they heard a low whistle.

'Captain, this way.' Sutton stood at the corner of the building. 'I can hear talking from inside but can't make out the words.'

'With me,' whispered William to Jenkins and Chapman.

They followed Sutton to the canal side of the building. As they reached a spot near a large double-door, Sutton waved his hand for silence.

William moved around some bales of cotton stacked near the warehouse entrance. He placed his ear to the door and heard muffled voices. He stepped back and studied the wall. He could see a window above the doors that lead into the warehouse.

William waved beckoning for Jenkins to join him. He indicated the window and whispered, 'I want those bales to be built into a ramp so I can see inside.'

'Aye, aye, Sir,' came the whispered acknowledgement.

He kept watch while his three men stacked the large bales. At three high, William climbed to the top. He peered through the dirty glass into the warehouse and could see three Cubans around a table, drinking.

'We have to get the Cubans to open the door,' he said, climbing back down to his men. 'I doubt we could break in without them hearing us.'

'We could pretend to be drunk and persuade them to open the door,' suggested Sutton.

'Too noisy,' commented Jenkins, 'we have to do it silently. We don't want to attract attention.'

'Sutton,' said William, 'hand me your lamp. Jenkins tease out some of the cotton and place it round the base of the door. Chapman, give him a hand.'

With their knives, Chapman and Jenkins slit handfuls of

cotton from the bales and teased the strands apart before placing them around the base of the door. Sutton handed his lamp to William.

William gently removed the glass cover and unscrewed the wick holder. He sprinkled the oil around the cotton and motioned his men to move back. Sutton produced a flint, stacked a small pile of oil-soaked cotton near his hand and struck the flint. The spark jumped to the pile and caught alight. He blew gently on the infant flame until he was satisfied that it was large enough and quickly flicked the burning cotton onto the larger pile near the door. As the cotton burned it gave off heavy black smoke. Sutton used his shirt to fan the smoke and blow it under the doors of the warehouse. William climbed to the top of the stacked bales and watched.

The three Cubans looked tired. They were ready for sleep, but one of them had to stay awake, even if they didn't expect any trouble.

Two of the guards allowed their heads to fall forward as they dozed. Suddenly one moved his head and sniffed, closely followed by the second guard.

'*Humo*,' yelled one, as he sniffed the smoke. '*En fuego,*' shouted his companion and pointed to the bottom of the double-door, which was now ablaze.

All three jumped up and glanced around as they waited for someone to give them instructions. William could hear one of them speaking rapidly in Spanish, but his words were too fast for him to understand.

The three Cubans ran towards the double-doors. William dropped to the ground and drew his sword.

'Not a word is to be spoken except by me! I do not want

them to know we are English, understood?'

'Aye, Sir,' said all three, as they fingered their cutlasses.

'No killing unless you have to; we are not murderers. I want them to be secured and blindfolded so they cannot see us. The smoke will help, as it will confuse them.'

The Englishmen hid among the bales of cotton. They could hear the bolts being drawn, and the large doors dragged open.

First one and then another came out of the warehouse, rubbing their eyes. William stepped forward, and with the hilt of his sword, knocked the first Cuban to the ground. Sutton hit the next man in the abdomen, causing him to double over. The third Cuban, who was not as fast, carried a large, heavy wooden bucket, evidently to carry water from the canal to the fire. He saw what had happened to his comrades and stopped, dropped the bucket and grabbed the door in an attempt to close and bar it. Chapman charged the door, hitting it with his shoulder, which knocked the Cuban to the ground. The Cuban yelled at his attacker, grabbed the heavy bucket and swung it at Chapman's legs. The solid wood hit him on the knees, throwing him off balance.

The Cuban ran back to the table and grabbed a sword hooked over the back of a chair. He flicked his wrist, which released the sword from its scabbard, and turned to attack Chapman.

Chapman tried to get up, but the Cuban kicked him and Chapman collapsed to the ground. The Cuban drew his arm back for a killing blow. Chapman tensed and tried to move sideways in an effort to save himself.

A clash of steel caused Chapman to twist around in time to see his Captain block the downward thrust of the Cuban's sword. The two swordsmen were now locked, face to face, in a struggle of strength. The Cuban grabbed William's hair and pulled hard in an effort to unbalance him. William's eyes watered and his vision blurred. His natural reaction was to pull back from the grip on his hair, but he knew that if he broke contact, he would be at a disadvantage and would not be able to focus if the Cuban made a thrust. He remembered a trick he had learned in his Liverpool childhood and suddenly shot his head forward and hit the Cuban across the bridge of his nose with his forehead. William heard a sharp crack and a scream. The bridge of the Cuban's nose had snapped and burst, causing blood to flow. The Cuban lost his grip on William's hair and tried to step away. William thrust with his sword arm and forced the Cuban to retreat away from Chapman. Jenkins ended the fight with a blow to the Cuban's head. William rubbed his eyes free of tears.

'Can you walk?' he asked Chapman.

'With a little help, Sir,' Chapman groaned. William helped him to stagger from the burning building.

Meanwhile, Sutton, using rope from the cotton bales, had finished securing the Cuban he had captured. He used another piece of rope to secure wads of cotton over the prisoner's eyes.

William saw that the Cuban he had struck was regaining consciousness. He indicated this to Sutton, who nodded and cut another length of rope from a bale and proceeded to tie the Cuban and bind cotton over his eyes.

The flames had now taken hold on the doors and threatened the stock of cotton stacked outside. It wouldn't be long before the flames attracted the attention of others in the area.

'Jenkins, secure the man inside and bring him out here,' William said as he helped Chapman to sit on a bale well away from the flames.

Jenkins cut more rope and bound the Cuban with the broken

nose, covered his eyes with wads of cotton and dragged the man outside into the fresh air.

By the light of the flames, William could see a door under a staircase that he presumed was a back way to Amancio Cardenas' offices. It was locked. Jenkins scooped up a bunch of keys from the table and handed them to William. The first key did not fit. The smoke from the fire made breathing difficult. William wiped his streaming eyes and tried another key. The door swung open. He could see a flight of steps that lead down to a cellar.

'Are all the Cubans outside and bound?' William asked Jenkins.

'Aye, Sir, they are,' said Sutton, joining his Captain and Jenkins. Suddenly they heard someone shout from the cellar.

'Light,' demanded William.

Sutton thrust the lamp he carried before him, and made his way down the short flight of steps.

'Wait here, Jenkins,' said William, and followed Sutton to the bottom.

'Captain, Sir, we is here. We smell smoke!'

Sutton moved the light towards the voice and saw four black men cowering in the corner of the cellar.

'Captain, Sir, we belong Mr Abraham's people.'

'Can you walk? We have come to take you back to Mr Abraham.'

'Captain, to get out o' here, we happy to run!' smiled the man that William had recognised in the office of Cardenas.

'Come up now. Sutton, help them, and meet me at the canal.'

William returned up the stairs and saw the flames were now near the roof. 'Jenkins, help Chapman and try and make your way back to the boat. Use the canal side of the building; I expect company in a few minutes.'

'Aye, Sir.'

William covered his face and ran through the flames that enveloped the doors. He wanted to see if they had company, and if the Cuban prisoners were far enough away from the fire to be safe. As he ran through the flames he crashed into a man organising a fire bucket party in a vain attempt to control the fire. William grunted at the man in Spanish, which seemed to satisfy him that William was Spanish. William glanced around and watched a party of ten men attempt to drag the burning cotton from the doorway. He turned and saw Jenkins helping Chapman down the road towards the city gate. Sutton had moved the Cuban prisoners well away from the fire and hidden them among a pile of cotton bales.

Fortunately the night was dark, the only light being from the fire. He could no longer see Jenkins. The smoke from the burning cotton covered the whole area. He wrapped his jacket around his head and ran back through the flames. The men outside appeared to be concentrating on the bales rather than attempting to stop the fire spreading. As he entered the building again he felt the searing heat.

'Sutton! '

'Aye, Sir, here!' The fire sounded a dull roar as it reached the roof of the warehouse.

'This way!' shouted William, and grabbed hold of Sutton. 'Are they with you?'

'Yes, Sir, I have one by the hand and I told the others to hold the hand of the man in front. If they break their grip, they will not find their way out!'

'Keep me in sight and get ready to run!'

William could see the dull glow in the smoke of the fire around the door. He groped forward until he could run through the last flames to the outside.

'They will have to run through the flames or else they will die here!' He moved back past Sutton to the first black man and told him to run for the flames and keep going until he came outside to fresh air, and then to run to his right.

'Sutton, you go and wait in the darkness further down the road until I can join you with the others. Give us a couple of minutes, and then make your way back to the boat. Do not wait more than fifteen minutes! That is an order. Now go!'

Sutton grabbed the hand of the first and second black men and pulled them with him as he ran for the wall of flames.

They passed through the flames, the heat causing them to scream in pain. They emerged with Sutton's hair alight, causing the group outside to drop their buckets and run in fear. The sight of a white man on fire, accompanied by two wild-eyed screaming black men was too much for the superstitious locals, who evidently thought they had come from the bowels of hell. Sutton grabbed one of the abandoned buckets of water and poured the contents over his head. The two blacks glanced back at the building as the Captain and their friends emerged from the wall of flames. Sutton picked up another bucket of water and threw it over his Captain, whose clothing was smouldering.

'Which way, Sir?' called Sutton.

'Thank you, Sutton, along the road and keep in the shadows. Quickly! I can hear horses!'

'Follow me,' said Sutton to the Negroes, as he started to run towards the dark area under the walls of the next warehouse.

'Go, go, go. Run!' William urged.

Lights appeared in the houses as the noise from the fire spread. The fugitives moved quickly between the deep shadows, avoiding lighted areas. More and more people were coming on to the streets as the towns-people realised the fire might spread.

Finally, William and his men reached the last building before the city gates. William peered into the gloom around the gate. He couldn't see anything.

'Wait here,' he whispered to Jenkins, conscious of the deep breathing of his crew as they gasped for air. Taking a deep breath in an effort to stop his own heaving chest, William ran lightly across the road into the gloom around the gate. He expected to be challenged. He fingered his weapon and made sure it slid easily in its scabbard. The gate was still open a little. The guard had not been missed.

A sudden roar from the direction of the fire told him it must have touched off some barrels of oil. A large flame shot high in the air, shedding enough light for him to see that the gate guard was still on the ground. William turned and waved his arm to signal his party to should follow him.

William stood back while Jenkins helped the limping Chapman through the gate. Sutton and the four blacks joined William.

'Sutton, when we are through, close the gates and make it appear that it has always been locked, then climb over and join us.'

'Aye, aye, Sir.'

'You four follow me!' said William to the Negroes, and made his way through the town gate.

On the outside of the town walls, the smell of the smoke was not as heavy. The air seemed cleaner and even the smell of rotting vegetation was a pleasant relief.

A figure moved from the blackness of the trees and made its way towards the small group. William drew his sword and waited. The figure stopped, crouched, listened and watched.

'ICE,' hissed William.

The figure moved towards them, but stayed low.

'ICE, Captain; Austin here.'

'Thank God, I thought you were a guard! Report.'

'Chapman and Jenkins found their way back and I sent them to the boat. I think Chapman has a broken knee. How many with you, Sir?'

A figure dropped from the gate and landed softly.

'All in order, Captain,' said Sutton.

'Sutton and four blacks, Mr Austin.'

'Right, Sir, follow me.'

'Sutton, follow behind Mr Austin, I'll bring up the rear.'

William touched each of the Negroes and pointed to Sutton. 'Follow him!'

The First Mate ran towards the trees, keeping low, followed by Sutton and the black men. William waited until they had nearly reached the trees when he stepped away from the cover of the gate to follow his men.

- CHAPTER TWENTY-EIGHT -

Escape

Havana
June 1806

'*Cargar!*' William heard, and saw four mounted men. The horsemen spurred their horses into a gallop.

Cargar was a word he had heard during his time in Spain. He racked his brain for the meaning; '*Cargar*' was the order to charge!

He watched the horsemen raise themselves a little from their saddles and then he heard the sound of swords being drawn. The horsemen were concentrating on the group of Negroes. He realised the horsemen had not seen him. He was behind them. William ran towards the point he estimated the horsemen would reach the Negroes. The horsemen were dark shapes of night, but the noise they created made them easy to follow.

Austin and Sutton gained the edge of the trees as the lead horseman reached the slowest Negro. The horseman passed the running man, and slashed with a backhand movement. The sword sliced through the facial bone of the Negro who gave a high-pitched scream, and fell backwards into the path of the second horseman. The galloping horse tried to avoid the man and shied away to cannon into the third rider. The third rider pulled his horse up sharply to avoid being dismounted.

The first horseman raised his sword again to attack the next black man. The Negro ran screaming before the drumming hooves of the horse.

James Austin drew his sword and turned to face the horsemen. Holt stepped forward and used both hands to steady a pistol aimed at the charging cavalryman. The horseman raised himself to slash at the running man and became a clear target for Holt. A sudden flash and the ball from the pistol hit the horseman in the chest, driving him back. The sword flew from his hand as he rolled from his horse to the ground. The horse galloped away into the darkness.

In the flash of the pistol shot, William saw the black men in the trees: James Austin standing with sword drawn and Holt with his arms outstretched, holding a smoking pistol.

William thrust his sword on the blind side of the second rider. He felt the blade scrape along the man's chest. The rider dropped his reins, twisted in his saddle to find his adversary, and raised his sword as William pulled his sword back to defend his head. The rider slashed down. Sparks flew as the two swords met. The rider raised his sword again. William thrust his sword into the rump of the horse. The animal screamed and attempted to turn away from the pain of the stab. The rider lost control and was thrown. William kept running towards his men.

'Captain, this way!'

William recognised James Austin's voice and swerved towards the sound.

'Well done, Holt,' gasped William as he reached the safety of the trees. 'Retreat to the boat, Mr Austin, and take command;

make ready for a fast exit.'

'Aye, aye, Sir.'

'Holt, Sutton, with me as a rearguard.'

William and his two crewmen walked steadily along the path, making sure nobody followed. After a few minutes William could see the white cloth that indicated the position of the boat. He could make out the shape of James Austin and Sang.

'All's well, Mr Austin?' asked William as he slid his sword back into its scabbard and prepared to climb in the boat.

'Aye, Captain.'

William felt a slight vibration of the ground and turned to peer back down the path. The vibration was followed by the sound of galloping hooves. The two horsemen he hoped had forgone the fight were returning, and it sounded like they had company. Before he could draw his sword, he was knocked to the ground as four horsemen thundered past.

James Austin ran forward and drew his pistol.

'Jenkins, to me, to me', yelled Austin. Holt and Sutton turned to meet the riders' charge.

Sparks flashed from the clash of Sutton's cutlass and the sabre of the first horseman. Sutton's weapon fell to the ground, his arm numb from the shock of attack. The first horseman passed Sutton and the next was upon him.

Holt fired his now reloaded pistol into the back of the second horseman, who was attempting to bring his sword down on to Sutton's undefended head. The horseman's scream matched a scream from James Austin. Austin had aimed at the third rider, but before he could fire, the horseman slashed. The sword cut deeply into the First Mate's arm. Without feeling in his fingers, his hand opened and the pistol fell to the ground. Slowly he fell to his knees, holding his wounded arm.

William, still on the ground, rolled away from the charging horses. As the last of the horsemen passed, he rose and drew his sword. He ran the few yards to the ship's boat. He saw Jenkins smash a boat oar across the face of the third horse. The animal reared in pain and threw the rider. Jenkins drove the handle of the oar into the rider's face.

Sutton recovered his cutlass and raised it to challenge the fourth horseman. The rider pulled hard on the horse's reins with his left hand in an effort to aim his sabre and to crash through Sutton's defence. Sutton dropped to his knees and lunged at the leg of the horse with the flat surface of his cutlass. Its damaged leg collapsed, throwing the rider off balance. He tumbled from the horse and William buried his weapon deep in the man's chest.

The first horseman, realising he was the only survivor, pulled his horse's head around and galloped off away from the city walls.

William looked back down the path, turned to Sutton and said, 'Guard the path.'

'Aye, Sir,' the man replied.

William then turned to Sang. 'Sang, help me with Mr Austin.'

'Give way together,' said William, as Holt and Sutton dragged the overloaded boat into deeper water. The stink of disturbed mud assailed their nostrils.

An agitated David Fuller greeted the rescuers and freed black men as they climbed wearily over the side. Fuller counted the Negroes, his eyes questioning.

'We left one behind, killed by their cavalry,' William commented. 'Mr Austin has been wounded; rig a line to swing him aboard. He is unconscious and has lost a lot of blood.'

Crewmembers were standing around, drawn to the spot by the sight of the wounded and exhausted survivors. William barked, 'Don't stand there like stranded fish. All hands make sail. Make sail, God damn you!'

'Aye, aye, Sir,' responded Fuller. 'Bosun, rig a cradle for Mr Austin to be swung aboard. Hoist the ship's boat inboard and make ready to get under way! Lively now, lively!'

Men ran to the capstan to bring the anchor hove short, while others gently swung the First Mate inboard. Two of the crew then bore him to his cabin.

William had spent time the previous day studying the harbour. He had taken a bearing of the fort that dominated the harbour and would use this to guide their escape. The fort would not fire on them at night incase the ship was Spanish. The fire had caused many vessels to move away from the quay for safety. One extra ship moving in the harbour would not be noticed. The chart indicated good depth of water.

The *Albatross* slowly gathered speed and headed for the gap between the two forts at the mouth of the harbour.

William focused his telescope on the fire. It appeared to be spreading as neighbouring buildings were now alight. The whole town was in an uproar. In the confusion he hoped to slip out to sea. He felt that the soldiers who manned the forts would be watching the fire, and perhaps men may have even been sent to help control the fire.

The *Albatross* drew close to the eastern fort and William waited for the telltale flashes from the muzzles of the Spanish cannon.

'Larboard a point.' He wanted to get close under the guns of Morro Fort. If he sailed close enough to the shore, the fort's gunners would be unable to depress the guns low enough to fire on him.

The steady chant of the leadsman in the chains was the only sound from the British vessel.

They slid past the fort and the feel of the ocean swell told William they were nearly through the heads. The slight breeze from the ocean brought the sweet smell of the sea, blowing away the stench of Spanish Cuba. They were through the heads and safe.

'Make all sail,' he shouted as his ship rose to the ocean swell.

- CHAPTER TWENTY-NINE -

Regrets

At sea Havana to Boston
June 1806

'Mr Fuller, you have the watch: I am going below to see, Mr Austin.'

'Aye, aye, Sir.'

William found Sang and the young cadet, Dylan Howell, trying to make Austin as comfortable as possible.

They had stripped him of his clothes and bandaged his wound, but the blood kept seeping through the bandage.

'Have you placed a tourniquet above the wound?'

'Yes, Sir,' replied Howell, 'but Sang is frightened that if we cut all the blood from the lower arm, Mr Austin's arm will die.'

'Let me see the wound.' William gently peeled back the bandage and saw a bloody mess with flecks of white bone mixed with raw flesh. 'The arm has been broken,' he said more to himself than Sang and Howell.

James Austin groaned when William replaced the bandage and laid his friend's arm across his naked chest.

'Pass the word for the Bosun, Mr Howell.'

William looked at the strained white face of his friend.

'You sent for me, Sir?' asked the Bosun.

'Bosun, I want a mess table scrubbed as clean as you can get it, hot water, sail makers' needles——', the finest the sail-maker has, and four volunteers to help with Mr Austin. I intend to try and save his arm. The volunteers are to hold him down. Understand?'

'Aye, Sir. A clean mess table, sail makers' fine needles, and four of the crew.'

'As quickly as you can.'

William turned back to his friend and lifted the bandage again. James groaned.

'Sang, get some rum, and try and make Mr Austin drink as much as he can. I want him asleep when I move him.'

'Mr Howell, find some sheets; make sure they are clean, and cut them into strips for bandages. Also have a bucket handy.'

Alone with his first mate, William knew he had to do something. The blow from the sword had nearly severed the arm. William wiped sweat from his forehead. Did he have the skill to save the arm, or should he remove it completely?

He'd seen the surgeon on the *Belleisle* wash his instruments in hot water.

William turned as Sang entered the cabin with a beaker of rum. 'Get him to drink as much as possible. '

William stepped over the conning and breathed deeply of the salty air. It tasted sweet and healthy, unlike the smell below.

'Table scrubbed and all ready, Sir,' said the Bosun, knuckling his forehead.

'Ask the carpenter for his smallest saw and the next one up and have them cleaned and placed in boiling water.'

William climbed the small ladder to the poop deck. He

checked the compass, the sails, and the wind.

'Mr Fuller: in a while I want you to alter course and run before the wind. I want the *Albatross* to be as steady as possible while I try and fix Mr Austin's wound.'

'Aye, Sir, but running before the wind will carry us into the Atlantic, away from Boston.'

'I am aware of that, Mister.' As soon as William spoke, he regretted his tone. Fuller was only doing his job. William felt tense as he thought of what he was about do, and the consequences if he failed.

'Bosun,' shouted William, 'rig the scrubbed table in my cabin and bring your volunteers, and the tools I asked you to collect. Tell Cook I want boiling water at all times.'

―⚓―

Sweat dripped from his face as William wiped the blood from around the wound. Even though James had drunk the best part of a pint of rum, he twitched and groaned as William probed his flesh to remove as many pieces of bone as he could find. William could see that the main bone had been broken. He did his best to bind the broken pieces together.

'Hold him still,' cried William, as he stitched the open wound together.

At last it was finished. William bound the wound and placed two splints to hold the broken arm ridged.

'Sang, give Mr Austin laudanum, it'll calm him and help him sleep. Just a few drops, not too much.'

―⚓―

On deck William stripped off his shirt and used it to wipe himself down. He stood on the weather side in an effort to cool down.

'Mr Fuller, resume our course for Boston, and I want all sail on her. We must get Mr Austin to a doctor.'

'Aye, aye, Sir.'

The effect of laudanum, rum, and shock caused James to sleep for nearly twenty hours. Sang and Howell split watches to sit with him. William stood watch and watch with the second mate, yet he didn't feel tired. He was too concerned. On the hour, every hour, he had the tourniquet eased for five minutes to allow blood to flow to the arm. He had no idea if five minutes was too long or too short. All he was concerned about was that James did not bleed to death.

Although James woke after his twenty-hour sleep, he was delirious with fever, and sweating all the time. Sang and Howell washed his face and body in an effort to keep him cool.

It was five days after the operation when William, sitting in James' cabin and dozing between sleep and wakefulness, became aware of a strange smell. He thought it was from the bilges.

He suddenly stood, eyes heavy with fatigue. He leaned over James' wound, sniffed, and then yelled for Sang. He had smelt the same thing on the *Belleisle*.

'Captain?'

'Find the Bosun and tell him to scrub the table again. Have Cook boil water and send the carpenter to me – and be quick.'

'Yes, Sor.'

A few minutes later the Bosun knocked on the cabin door.

"I believe the first mate has gangrene. His arm will have to come off if we are to save his life. I have sent for the carpenter. I'll need his saws after all, and I need cook to heat a flat iron as hot as he can make it.'

William unwrapped the bloody bandage and caught his breath as the smell of putrefaction assailed his nose. Low groans emanated from the two volunteers holding James' upper body.

'Breath through your mouth,' gasped William, 'tighten the tourniquet until the blood stops. Keep the pressure on, and stand by his head. I need the space to cut.'

William grasped a sharp knife and slowly slit the flesh above the damaged area. The knife scraped against bone. James groaned and bit down on the leather mouthpiece. A large dose of laudanum had put him to sleep, but he was not so deeply asleep that all pain was hidden.

Placing the knife to one side William took up the cleaned saw and began to cut off James' arm. Sweat streamed down William's face. Suddenly a dull thud let William and his volunteers knew that the arm had hit the deck.

'Sang, get this out of here and throw it over the side and tell Cook I am ready,' snarled William as he swallowed his gall in an effort not to be sick.

Sang dragged the arm by the hand and pushed it into a bucket and quickly left the cabin.

William cleaned the wound. The Cook arrived with a large red-hot cleaver, gripped in layers of cloth.

William could feel the radiated heat from the glowing blade as he pressed it on James' open wound. The blade hissed as the flesh cauterised. James let out an animal like scream and fainted.

'Release the tourniquet and let's see if the wound leaks.'

William held a lantern close to the wound and watched for seepage of blood. The raw end, now black after the heat of the knife, was holding.

'Good. Mr Howell, bandages please.'

James Austin lived for another eight days, before dying peacefully in his sleep. He never really regained consciousness. The eight days were a time of screams, as James faced his own demons. William did his best to make his friend comfortable. When the laudanum wore off, his friend tossed and turned with the pain from a phantom arm. The poison from the gangrene had won, but he was now in peace.

The *Albatross* hove to for the funeral. William watched the sail-maker pass the last stitch through James' nose. A final check that he was dead. His body was weighted with two round shot before sliding gently down the plank into the ocean upon which he had spent most of his life. The small splash was the last sound James made.

Sixteen days had passed since leaving Havana. Each of the three rescued Negroes clung to the rigging by one hand and waved with the other to the men who waited to catch the mooring lines. William watched one of the shore-side labourers run towards Abraham's office. Obviously he wanted to be first to carry the news that lost staff had arrived home.

As the last lines were secured, he heard the cry of a coachman urging his horses to greater speed. Elijah was driving Abraham's coach as fast as he could along the wharf. It came to a dusty halt near the small gangway. Abraham climbed out of the coach. A long line of Abraham's employees was running towards the *Albatross,* all wanting to share in the joy of their missing friends return.

In the excitement of the *Albatross'* return and the safe rescue of the three Negroes, Abraham insisted that only a dance would suffice to crown such an achievement. It would be held at *Mamre* the following weekend and all the crew were invited to celebrate the safe return of the missing Negroes.

'It will be a feast, William, a feast. You look strained, my boy, do you wish to tell me what ails you?'

William told Abraham of the death of the fourth Negro, and the death of James Austin. When he finished he sat in silence and stared into space, seeing again the shattered body of his first mate.

'The dance is to be in the grain barn, Captain,' called Elijah over the noise of shouting servants carrying chairs from the house to a large barn. The place was noisy as carts of ice were dragged to the barn.

'For the wine, I hope,' said William.

'I expect so, Captain,' replied Elijah.

Smoke from the kitchen chimney told William that the cooks were busy baking. A large pit had been dug and alongside stood cords of wood for cooking the meat. He smiled to himself at the anticipated luxury of unsalted roast meat. He entered the open door of the main house and quickly jumped aside as a large table propelled by four men came sliding across the floor.

'William, how kind of you to come early,' called his host from behind the accelerating table.

'My pleasure, Abraham, the place is a hive of activity.'

'I am happy you are here. Let's remove ourselves to the library for some peace and quiet, and a drink.'

The two men sat quietly for a few minutes while Abraham poured the cold wine. 'A little luxury in the summer months, cold wine kept cool in our own ice house,' said Abraham, handing a glass to William.

'The ice business is going well in Jamaica,' commented William. 'They will soon come to rely on a regular supply.' He sipped his wine.

'I am glad it worked out well; especially after we all thought you had lost your mind. You appear older, William. Do you wish to talk about the voyage?'

'Did I do right, Abraham, in my attempt to rescue your people? After all I am no longer in His Majesty's navy, and don't have the right to risk the lives of my men. They are merchant seamen, not soldiers. Was the cost worth it?'

'Each of the three blacks you brought back know you did the right thing. To them the cost was worth it.'

'I am not looking forward to telling James' family he died while saving blacks. Liverpool is still a slave town, and the death of a white man rescuing three blacks will not be accepted easily.'

'James volunteered, didn't he?'

'Yes, but it doesn't alter the fact that if I had loaded hides and dried beef and left Cuba as planned, he would still be alive.'

'All the blacks who work for me consider you and your crew to be heroes. They are sad for your loss, as they are sad for the loss of one of their own, but I can assure you they are very grateful for your actions.'

William fell silent and twirled the remains of the wine in his glass as he remembered James Austin. He found it hard to accept that he was right in rescuing the blacks, and found it difficult to reconcile James' loss with their freedom. Had he rescued the blacks because they had lost their freedom, or because he wanted to impress Ruth?

Abraham allowed his friend the silence. There was little he

could do, as the clock could not be put back.

The sounds involved in preparing for the dance began to lessen. The lack of loud voices brought William back from his depressing thoughts. He lifted his head and stared at Abraham.

'Thank you, Abraham.'

'What are friends for?' said Abraham, as the door opened and Ruth entered.

'We are ready, father, and the fire for the meat is lit. The guests have started to arrive and the musicians are playing.'

'Thank you, my dear, sit awhile with William while I greet some of the guests.'

Ruth sat on a chaise-lounge and studied William. 'Talk to me, William, tell me what bothers you.'

William sighed and started to talk. He did not go into too many details of the rescue and made light of their escape from the fire.

Ruth watched his face. He was still sunburned from the voyage, yet he seemed a lot older than she remembered. James' death had affected him more than he would admit.

She felt disappointed, yet pleased, that he would shield her from the full details of the incident. She wanted him to share his feelings, but knew instinctively that he would always protect her from the ugly side of life. He would stand up for her against the world, but she would not always know his thoughts. In a perverse way she knew she would always try to fathom his mind, yet she didn't want him to be completely open. She wanted to peel away the layers like the layers of an onion.

―⁂―

The dance was a great success and William could not remember ever feeling so happy. He danced most of the evening with

Ruth and enjoyed the feel of her warm body in his arms as he breathed in her perfume. They talked and talked of their future and his plans for a shipping company to rival any in existence. His energy and enthusiasm carried her along. She felt aware of a small cloud in her sky of happiness. The building of this wondrous new life would be from Liverpool, or the deck of a ship. How could she be happy with William away building his company?

Abraham found a cargo of smoked fish in Newfoundland. As Newfoundland was within the control of the British Crown, William would not have a problem loading the cargo, and topping off with timber.

William had to return to Liverpool to meet his colleagues and clarify ownership of the *Albatross*. What ever happened in Liverpool would decide his next course of action.

- CHAPTER THIRTY -

Home at last

Liverpool
December 1806

To arrive home was always a great moment. Families of the crew would be waiting on the dock and William hoped his father would be amongst them. He had much to tell his father about Ruth, and the ice shipments. Perhaps he could try the same cargo to Liverpool–ice from Norway.

'Reduce sail if you please, Captain,' said the Pilot as they approached the entrance to the basin leading to George's dock. The *Albatross* turned to larboard and brought the spire of the sailors' church dead ahead. It towered over the turning basin.

William scanned the buildings. The place hadn't changed from nearly a year ago. The *Albatross* slipped quietly into the turning basin and moved slowly to starboard to enter George's Dock, which was packed with vessels from all over the world. Some were berthed three and four deep along the quays.

'They have arranged for you to be berthed alongside the quay and not alongside another vessel, Captain.'

'Why do we deserve such special treatment?'

'I understand the arrangement was between the Sheriff's office and Mr Johnston.'

William felt cold at the mention of the Sheriff's office. Moored alongside the quay, with perhaps other vessels berthed alongside the *Albatross,* would leave little hope of escape, if the need arose.

The families on the wharf shouted and cheered. Lines were passed ashore where willing hands pulled them to the bollards. Even the ship herself seemed to know that this was the time for rest. She gently touched the stone quay and the lines secured her alongside. She was once again home in Liverpool.

William searched the shore but could not see his father. He could see Owen Johnston, hopping from one leg to the other, obviously eager to hear all about the voyage. The gangway was manhandled in to place and the crowd surged forward.

'Mr Fuller, what are the arrangements for paying off?'

'As soon as you are ready, Captain, we can close the ship's books and pay off the crew.'

'Allow that gentleman to come aboard,' said William, pointing to Owen Johnston, 'and then have the crew muster for signing off.'

'Aye, aye, Sir.'

Owen bustled aboard and made for the Captain's cabin.

'Are you well, my friend?' asked Owen, a look of sheer pleasure on his face.

William grasped Owen by the arms and squeezed gently, 'All is well. Sit down and tell me what news you have.'

'Good news, and very good news; the Bill to abolish the slave trade will go before Parliament again in the New Year and this time we are confident of success.'

'That is great news.'

'Mr. Wilberforce is being fêted all over the country for his good work.'

'How are he and his colleagues?'

'They are all well. They were in Liverpool last month. We anticipated you would arrive before Christmas, so wanted to make sure everything was in order.'

'Is everything in order in Liverpool?'

'Ah--hmm, oh yes,' said Owen.

William felt that Owen was hiding something

'Then perhaps this is an appropriate time for us to talk about my purchasing the *Albatross?*' suggested William.

'I know how keen you will be to see your family, so perhaps tomorrow or the next day would be the right time.'

'Where are you staying?' enquired William.

'At the Pen & Whig; will you join me there after you have seen your family?'

'I would be delighted,' said William, his heart not fully accepting the joy of being home. He felt disappointed that his father had not come to the quay to greet him. He would have known the *Albatross* was due today. The families of the crew knew of their arrival.

'I will leave you to finalise things here, while I return to the Pen & Whig. I only wanted to make sure you were well and to let you know of the work being accomplished at home.'

'What of the Sheriff's office?'

'I have convinced the Sheriff to allow you to land your cargo and finalise your arrival details. I am guarantor that you will not abscond before the investigation.'

'I am innocent of the charge of slave trading!'

'My friends and I know you are innocent, and that the charge is a false accusation. The problem is that you didn't stay to answer the charges.'

'We would have lost the opportunity to prove that a Liverpool ship could make a profit without the Trade. If I had returned to Liverpool I would have still been here and our enterprise would have failed.'

'The sheriff will be down tomorrow with lawyer Snelgrove, who is acting on behalf of his client.'

'And may I ask who that is?'

'Thomas Nicholson!'

'That damn family again. Am I never to be free of them?'

'I will be here in the morning to bear witness on your behalf.'

'Thank you, Owen, you are a true friend.'

'Well ......'

'Well, what?'

'Nothing. Nothing. Just well ...... it is nice to see you.'

'You seemed troubled, Owen, has something happened? What is it that I should know?'

'No, no but ......'

'Owen, you are making me angry. What are you hinting at?'

'I don't know anything for sure. It is all rumours.'

'Rumours, what rumours?'

'Perhaps you should ask your father.'

'Ask him what?'

'When do you plan to see him?'

'As soon as I can get some sense out of you, and sign off the crew.'

'Then I will leave you to finalise the crew. Goodbye, my

friend.'

'Goodbye? Now hold on, Owen, I need to know what you are talking about.'

Owen rose and walked to the cabin door. He paused and turned. 'William, all I can say is that I suggest you visit your father as soon as possible.'

Owen stepped through the door and without looking back allowed it to close behind him. William could hear Owen's footsteps as he hurried up the companionway ladder.

William sat at his desk and pulled the muster book towards him, knowing that the crew was waiting to sign off. A light tap on the cabin door made him glance up, thinking Owen had returned.

'Come in.'

David Fuller stood on the threshold.

William waited while a sad-faced First Mate said, 'Mrs Austin is topside, Sir.'

'Show her down, please, and make sure we are not disturbed.'

A few minutes later David Fuller showed a middle-aged woman into the cabin. William stood and moved a chair close to his desk.

'Mrs Austin, Sir,' said Fuller.

'Mrs Austin,' William said, 'won't you take a seat?' She had been crying.

'I want the truth, Captain King. I hear that my James has been buried at sea.'

'I cannot soften the truth, Mrs Austin, but James was buried at sea between Cuba and Boston. I can show you on the chart the exact spot if it will help.'

'How did he die?'

'He was wounded in Havana. We tried our best for him, but

his wounds didn't heal properly and he became ill.'

'Did he suffer?'

'No, Mrs Austin, I can assure you James was not in any pain. Most of the time he slept. He slipped away peacefully one night, and was given a Christian burial with the ship hove-to for the service.'

She couldn't stop her tears running down her face. She sobbed.

'What is going to become of our Michael? He is a growing boy and we had high hopes for him, but now I will not be able to earn enough to hardly feed us, never mind clothe him properly. James wanted him to get an apprenticeship, but I don't have the money for an apprenticeship bond.'

'Mrs Austin, you will be paid the balance of James' wage; the amount will be the same as if he signed off in Liverpool. Normally his wage would cease the day he died, but I like to think of him as a friend. He meant more to me than just the *Albatross'* First Mate. How old is Michael?'

'He be twelve this year. Why?'

'I will be happy to accept him as an apprentice on my ship.'

'No! You are trying to get out of paying me James' wages, because I will have to give it back as a bond for Michael's apprenticeship.'

'No, Mrs Austin, you do me a disservice. I have no intention of charging you a bond for Michael.'

'I'll not have him going to sea and ending up like his father,' screamed Mrs Austin, standing up quickly and knocking her chair over. Her face contorted with fear for her son, grief for the loss of her husband, and the lack of money for food and rent. Her whole world had collapsed around her and she couldn't bear the thought, or the possibility, of losing her son to the sea.

William stood quickly and reached out a hand to her in an effort to stop her from falling over the chair.

'Mrs Austin, Michael is old enough to leave home and the sea can be a good life for a boy.'

'No, I will not let him go to sea!'

She grabbed the cabin door handle, pulled it open and fled from the man who had offered to take her son.

William stood in the doorway of his cabin. Could he have phrased certain things a little better? Perhaps he should have waited a few days before making his offer to take on James' son as an apprentice. Michael might not even wish to be a sailor. He sighed, picked up the overturned chair and closed his cabin door.

Charlotte stood at her bedroom window and watched the traffic moving slowly up and down the road.

She knew the *Albatross* was due in the morning. She even considered meeting it at the quay, but it wouldn't have been seemly without her husband.

The relationship between her and George had deteriorated since she lied that his son had been the first to bed her. George hardly spoke to her now.

She moved from the window and sat at her writing desk while her mind considered the problem of George.

William hadn't, of course, touched her. She wanted to wound George for striking her and to end any further ideas he may have of sharing her bed.

She let her mind drift to the day after their lovemaking. It was Charlotte's practice to eat breakfast in her room but this day she decided to share breakfast with her husband in the dining room. George never liked to eat breakfast in his bedroom. It was uncivilised and it gave the servants extra work. Charlotte's opinion was that she paid good money to lazy good-for-nothings, so they could serve her in her bedroom and like it, or she would know the reason why.

This day George was not at breakfast.

Later in the morning, she'd visited George's room with a vague idea of offering him an apology. It would allow them to start again, if he'd leave her alone in bed. She had knocked on his door and placed her ear to the panel. She couldn't hear anything, so knocked again - still silence. She turned the handle and slowly pushed the door open. George was lying on the bed with an empty bottle of brandy clutched in his arms. She looked around and considered waking him. Then she saw the pistol. It lay cocked on the table near the bed. Had he planned to shoot himself? It was fortunate that he had fallen asleep before he could carry through the deed. A terrifying thought struck her that perhaps the gun was for him to use on her! She moved into the room and gently picked up the pistol. Holding it in her hands, she looked at her drunken husband. She could shoot him and then placing the gun in his hand. It would not be difficult to play the bereaved widow and she would have George's wealth to keep her company after the funeral.

George grunted and rolled over in his sleep. She jumped in fright at the sudden movement, then realised she still had the gun in her hand. She un-cocked the weapon and put it back on the table. She couldn't shoot him; the servants would hear the shot. Giving him one last glance, she silently made her way from the room.

The next time she met George, he was a changed man. He was more pleasant to the servants than he was to her. He would be very polite to her in front of the servants or their friends, but when they were alone he never showed her any affection. She made an occasional effort to show her willingness to try to get back together again, but he would never allow the conversation to get any further than civilised politeness.

Her mother brought up the subject of their relationship. 'Even your father has noticed that things are not as they should be, and for your father to notice anything outside of making money is very unusual.'

'George and I are having a few problems, Mother, so I would rather not talk about it because it is between George and myself.'

'I am only trying to help, dear.'

'I would prefer it if you and father didn't try and help. Any interference might make the problem worse.'

He mother sniffed, which said more than any words 'How we can make things worse, I don't know?'

'Mother, I have asked you not to mention it again, so if you wish me to stay for tea, I do not wish to discuss George and myself anymore, otherwise, I shall have to leave.'

'Very well, but you can't stop me from being concerned for the two of you. I had my doubts about the marriage and your age difference before you even married him, but no, you got your own way as you always do and——'

'Goodbye, Mother, I am leaving. Give my love to father.'

'You said you would stay for tea if I didn't mention George again, and I haven't. I only commented on what my thoughts were at the time of the marriage. Your father is making a special effort to be home to take tea with us this afternoon. He will be disappointed if you are not here to greet him.'

'This is the last time, Mother; you can discuss the weather or anything else, but not George and myself, nor the possibility of grandchildren.'

'Grandchildren,' sighed her mother, 'I so want a grandchild.'

'It will be a long time before that happens, so perhaps Henry can satisfy that need for you, because I cannot. Talking of Henry, where is he? Has he returned to Boston?'

'It appears your step son, William, has started a house of ill-repute in Jamaica.'

'I doubt that very much, Mother. William is more interested in trading and shipping than in women, but if you had said the same of Henry, I would have believed that.'

'Charlotte! To say such a thing, and about your own brother, I have never heard of such a thing.'

Charlotte sighed, pushed her chair back from her writing desk and stood at the window to gaze at the traffic once again.

A hackney cab stopped at the main gate. She watched a dark-haired man emerge from the cab and start to walk towards her house.

- CHAPTER THIRTY-ONE -

Father's house

*Liverpool
December 1806*

William paid the cab driver and stood at the gate to his father's home. He could have been driven to the front door, but he wanted to savour the moment of his homecoming.

He had changed from his uniform into a dark green single-breasted cut away coat that showed off his white breeches. He had also chosen a pair of black boots that Sang had shined to a mirror finish.

William pulled his waistcoat down tighter and began to walk towards the house. The noise of the crushed gravel beneath his boots disturbed the tranquil setting. He noticed that the lawns were neat and trim, but the borders were bare of flowers. The flowerbeds appeared ready for new growth in spring. The house was well maintained and appeared to have been painted recently. Marriage must suit father.

Charlotte watched the confident man stride to the front door. He was very handsome, with a lot more confidence than the last time they met. It was obvious that command had changed him.

He had a presence about him that was not there last year.

She heard the doorbell and the sound of a servant answering the call. A murmur of voices preceded the front door closing. Charlotte moved away from the window. It would never do for the servants to know that she had watched the visitor's arrival. Charlotte returned to her desk and opened a book to give the impression that she was deep in thought.

'Come in,' called Charlotte in answer to the maid's knock.

The maid dropped a small curtsy. 'There is a gentleman in the library asking of the Master, Madam.'

'Thank you, Beryl, please inform him that I will come down and speak with him.'

Charlotte inspected herself in the full-length mirror and absent-mindedly brushed her clothes to smooth the creases in her dress. Her face felt a little flushed, as she thought of the man downstairs. He was technically her son, yet only a few years older than herself.

William was intent on the books, neatly filed on the library shelves, when he heard the door open and the sound of a dress as it brushed against furniture. He turned to see Charlotte in a bright yellow dress that clung to her upper body and flared outwards from the waist. He made an effort to remember the details of the dress, as he was sure Ruth would wish to know all about the latest fashion.

Charlotte glided towards him and extended her hand to receive a kiss.

'William, what a delightful surprise; are you well after your voyage? How long has it been?'

'Nearly a year.'

The last letter he had received from his father was not long before he sailed for Liverpool. It had informed him of his father's marriage to Charlotte.

'I assume you do not wish me to call you Mother?' said William accepting Charlotte's proffered hand.

'You're correct, William, I am not old enough to be a mother to anybody!'

The tone of her voice told him a lot more than he had expected. He accepted her hand but instead of kissing or shaking it, he leaned forward and kissed her on the cheek. 'Welcome to the family, even if I am a little late.'

Charlotte felt his lips and the sensation burned. She blushed and pulled her hand back from his grasp.

'William, you mustn't.'

'Why ever not? What have I done wrong but kiss my father's wife on the cheek?'

Charlotte moved away in a fluster, ill at ease.

'Where is father?'

'He's, um——he's at the office.'

'Do I assume he was unaware the *Albatross* was due in this morning? He must have known! I saw the signal arms flapping as we entered the river. The crowd on the quay confirmed that the crew's families knew of our arrival, yet nobody greeted me.'

'I am sorry William, but I don't know why your father did not meet you. I don't normally go to meet my own father or my brother. I wait with Mother at the house.'

'I never expected you, but if we were in port, it has always been normal for either my father or myself to welcome the other back. It grew into a tradition.'

'Would you like a drink. Tea, perhaps, or something stronger?'

'Nothing, thank you, I will go to the office and see if I can find father.'

'He has been under a lot of strain of late; perhaps you should wait until he returns home.'

'Is he ill?'

'No, not ill, but I can tell he is worried about the possibility of the anti-slave bill being passed.'

'If he had done what I wanted a year ago, he wouldn't be worried today.'

'Pray what did you want him to do last year?'

'I advised him to stay away from the slave trade. He didn't need it. He had a healthy business in trade goods; he didn't need to carry salves.'

'The Trade is still legal, William, and my family have a proud heritage in that business, so much so that my father has been asked to stand for the office of Mayor. If the Trade is wrong, do you think the business leaders of Liverpool would have asked him to stand for such high office?'

'Liverpool was built on slaves, or the Trade, as you say. It is not a history of which to be proud.'

'That Wilberforce fellow may be the death of Liverpool,' snapped Charlotte.

'If the city cannot make a living without selling black Africans into slavery, then it doesn't deserve to survive. I think you underestimate your fellow citizens. This town will survive, and it will flourish through genuine trade and not that of slavery!'

He watched as Charlotte drew in a deep breath to calm herself. It seemed that each time they met, they quarreled.

He bowed to his stepmother and said, 'I apologise, Ma'am, for my temper. I am sorry and did not mean to upset you so.

Perhaps slavery is a subject we should avoid in the future. I do not wish to upset you or my father. I will leave now and attempt to find him.' He moved to the door, placed a hand on the knob and bowed again to Charlotte. 'Your servant, Ma'am'.

Charlotte heard his footsteps as he crossed the entrance hall. She picked up a small cushion from the chaise-longe and threw it across the room with such force that it hit a vase of flowers, knocking it to the ground. The vase cracked with a loud snap and water flowed across the floor, soaking into the carpet. She clenched her fists and shook them over her head in anger as she watched the cushion roll off the table in to the ever-widening pool of water.

'Damn the man, damn, damn, damn!'

'You called, Madam?' asked Beryl, entering the room.

'No, I didn't, but now you are here, clean up that mess and try and dry the carpet.'

Beryl glanced at the broken vase, pool of water and the flowers scattered across the floor.

'Yes, Madam,' said Beryl, and bent to pick up the flowers.

By the time William had calmed down, he had walked the length of the drive to the road.

His father would have allowed him the use of a carriage to return to his ship. If William had realised that his father was not at home, he would have retained the cabby. He refused to return and ask for the use of a rig to get back to town. He realised he would have a long hard walk ahead of him and stepped out to begin the journey back to town, when he heard a carriage approaching. Turning he saw his father's coach, driven by Alfred, who pulled on the reins and stopped alongside William.

'Missues King tol' me to drive you to the city, Mr William.'

If he refused, it would mean a long walk, which would be stupid as he would be the loser.

'Thank you, Alfred, Mr King's office, please.'

'Yes Zur, Mr William,' replied Alfred.

William climbed aboard, while Alfred flicked his small whip.

He had a feeling that all was not quite right between his father and his stepmother, but he didn't know what it was. Perhaps the age difference was too great, or his father was working long hours and leaving his young bride alone for too long. Charlotte wasn't the type to be left alone for long. He would have to approach the subject with caution next time he spoke to his father.

William stepped down from the hackney at the Company office and registered the sign over the offices. His father used to be very particular about the office sign. *A good clear sign tells the world what we are about, and a dull sign tells the world we don't care,* his father used to say. The sign was dull, and the paint had peeled in areas. Did this mean his father no longer cared?

Pushing open the door, William was aware of the clerks as they scribbled, and the strong smell of ink. Someone had to make out manifest, but he was glad it wasn't his responsibility. A movement at the rear of the office caught his eye and he saw Chief Clerk Watkins, coming towards him.

'Mr William, may I be of assistance?'

'Mr Watkins, I am looking for my father. Do you know where he is?'

'I think Mr King said he may go to his club for luncheon, but I do not know what time he will return.'

'Thank you, which club and where is it?'
'The *Athenaeum*, Mr William, on Hanover Street.'

—⁂—

William bounded up the steps to the door of the *Athenaeum Club* and entered. A large fat man, dressed as a head butler, moved quickly to attend to the young intruder. The fat man's expression gave away his thoughts; a gentleman did not enter the *Athenaeum Club* in such a manner.

'May I help you, Sir?'

'I am looking for Mr King.'

'Does Mr King know you are looking for him?'

'I doubt it.'

'Then, Sir, I am afraid I will have to ask you to leave.'

'I am not leaving until I see Mr King. Please be good enough to tell him William King is here to see him.'

'Are you related, Sir?'

'Mr King is my father, and that is the last question you will ask me. Go and do as I have asked!'

The cold edge to William's voice caused the fat man to step back in surprise.

William watched the man's expression. He was obviously not used to being spoken to in such a manner, particularly by someone who was not a member, or even a guest of a member.

'I will ascertain if Mr King wishes to see you.'

'You will ascertain, as you say, if my father is here, and if he is, you will then show me to where he is. Do I make myself clear?'

The fat man gulped and nodded his head.

William placed his hat on the table alongside the latest newspapers from London and began to pace the Club's foyer with his hands clasped behind his back in much the same way as he did on the *Albatross*.

He had completed ten circuits of his make-believe ship's deck before the fat man returned, his face red from the unaccustomed effort of moving quickly.

'Sir, your father will see you in the dining room. Please follow me.'

'Thank you,' said William, and collected his hat.

In the dining room he saw his father seated near a window, and realised he was not alone. On closer examination he saw that the other man was Charlotte's father, Donald Nicholson.

'Father, I have found you at last! I have been to the house and the office. It was beginning to feel like a game of hide and seek,' laughed William, holding his hand out to his father.

George glanced up at his son and waved his hand, which held a fork, towards an empty chair opposite. Gravy flicked from the fork and landed on the snow-white cloth in front of William's chair.

'Sit down,' said George, 'do you want anything to eat?'

The weak sun through the window highlighted his father's face, which appeared to William to be old and tired, with the possibility of sickness.

'Are you well, Father?'

'As well as can be expected!' snapped George.

Donald Nicholson appeared a little embarrassed.

'How was the voyage, William?' asked Donald.

'Profitable, Mr Nicholson.'

'That is the main thing, my boy; no point in sailing around the world and not making a profit, –– eh?' William smiled and glanced at his father again.

'How is everything with you, Father? You appear tired.'

'I am tired. I am tired of people asking me why I am tired! I have asked you if you want anything to eat?'

'What do you recommend?'

'We had the roast. Wine?' asked George in a quieter voice.

'Thank you,' said William.

'Some wine here!' shouted George.

The waiter scurried over in response to the shout, and poured a glass of wine for William.

'I hear you carried an unusual ballast from Boston to Jamaica,' said Donald, ripping a piece of bread to mop up his gravy.

'Mmm,' said William, and raised his glass to his lips.

The sound of his father's knife and fork hitting his plate stilled the other diners in the large room. The napkin followed the cutlery, as he pushed his chair from the table.

'Forgive me, Donald, but I must speak to my son.' He glared at William and said, 'Follow me!'

William rose from the chair; his meal finished, and followed his father to the exit.

'You!' yelled George to the fat man at the door, 'find me a small room for a meeting. Now!'

'Yes, Sir,' said the man, and moved quickly to the reception area. 'Please follow me, gentlemen.'

They entered a small room lit by a cheerful fire. The furniture consisted of two large chairs facing the fire and a small table under the window, on which a lighted oil lamp had been placed.

'May I get you gentlemen a drink?' asked the man in a very subdued voice.

'No, just get out and leave us alone until I call!' said George King, collapsing into one of the chairs.

'Sit down, damn you!' shouted George at his son.

William slowly sat in the other chair and wondered what calamity had happened. He was about to speak, but decided to let his father open the conversation.

'A good voyage?'

'Yes, Father, as well as could be expected.'

'Did you make a profit without trading in slaves or carrying products produced by slaves?'

'I was forced to trade in a few cargoes produced by slaves, which was unfortunate, but overall the majority of the trade was in cargo not produced by slaves. It can be done, Father, if only people would try.'

'Poppycock. You have just admitted to me it can't be done without carrying cargoes produced by slaves.'

'This was the first attempt, Father, and I think it was a success. We managed to get most of our profit from goods not produced by slaves. It will take time, but I believe that one day we will produce sugar, rum, coffee, and many other goods from free labour. It will happen in my time, I am convinced.'

'You don't seem to realise those damned friends of yours in Parliament may win the next vote on slavery, and if they do, how will I be able to keep the *Margaret* and *Elizabeth Rose* in work?'

'Surely you haven't taken both ships off the Mediterranean and Baltic Trade?'

'I was forced to when you left. I had little choice because the Irish traffic didn't make a profit and I was unsure of the best action for the future. There was no one in whom I could confide. My son had left on a harebrained scheme.'

'Don't blame me for your misfortune. If I had had my own ship, this would not have happened!'

'It is all in the past, and now I have to think of what I should do if the Trade stops.'

William remained silent and watched his father stare into the fire.

The silence grew longer. Perhaps his father was asleep. William's stomach rumbled as the smell of food seeped into the room. His mouth watered as he picked out the type of food attached to the different aromas, from the roast meat to the boiled cabbage.

'I met your new wife earlier today.'

George's head shot up as he turned to stare at his son. The expression he gave William was of hatred. Then his face collapsed while he focused on the fire again.

'Why didn't you tell me?' whispered George.

'Tell you what, Father?'

'Don't make me spell it out to you.'

'I am sorry, Father, but I have no idea what you are talking about.'

'I am talking about Charlotte, before we were married.'

'Before you were married? I am sorry, Father, either I am very stupid or something has happened of which I am not aware.'

The fire spluttered as a piece of wood collapsed in a shower of sparks. His father ran a hand across his face and brushed at a watery eye.

'You knew Charlotte before I married her?'

'Yes, I met her at your house the evening I returned from Trafalgar.'

'I don't mean then; you knew her later,' he whispered, 'and you never warned me.'

'Warned you about what?'

'I thought we were more than father and son; I thought we were friends and could confide in each other.'

'I have great love and respect for you, Father, but of late I have found my desire to stand on my own two feet has clashed with your desire to keep me always under your command!'

'What are your feelings for Charlotte?'

William remained silent. Why was his father asking such a question?

George waited as time dragged. He turned his face to William and demanded, 'Well?'

'I am not sure how you mean.'

'It is a direct question that requires a direct answer.'

'I don't have any feelings for her, except for respect as your wife. I am sorry, Father, but she will not replace the image I have of Mother, nor can I accept her as my mother, if this is to what you allude?'

'You never knew your mother.'

'The image I have is the one you gave me over the years. I am aware I never knew my mother.'

'So you have little or no feeling for her. This gets worse.'

'Father, you have something on your mind about Charlotte and me, and I can tell you now, I find her an attractive woman to the eye, but not a woman I would wish to marry.'

'Perhaps you don't want to take a bite of the same fruit twice.'

'This conversation has gone on long enough. You either tell me what is on your mind or I leave now. I don't know what you are implying, but I do know your new wife has come between you and me, and I don't like it. Ever since you became involved with the Nicholson family our relationship has deteriorated.'

'If I was a younger man I would call you out, son or no son.'

'I wouldn't fight you, Father. I couldn't hurt you, which is why I don't understand your line of questioning!'

George struggled to his feet and stood in front of William, his hands opened and closed in preparation to fight his son. His face became bright red in anger.

'I will ask you once, and once only, William, did you bed Charlotte before I married her?'

The question shocked William to silence as he realised the reason for the line of questioning.

George watched his son's face as it flushed with blood.

William responded through clenched teeth, 'So this is why you are so upset. Do you really think I would have done such a thing, knowing you were interested in the lady?'

'Answer the question, William.'

'Who is my accuser? Who has put such an idea in your head that has poisoned our relationship?'

'Answer the question!'

'Do you believe I am capable of such a thing? You must if you ask the question!'

'Well?'

'If I refuse to answer, what will you believe? Will you believe I did or I didn't? What now? The trust between father and son is obviously broken!'

'William, I must know for peace of mind, my mind!'

'When am I supposed to have done such a deed?'

'On the *Albatross* the night before you sailed from Liverpool last Christmas Eve.'

'I was at a farewell dinner that evening, a farewell dinner you refused to attend.'

'Was my wife there?' George watched his son's eyes as William cast his mind back.

'Yes, she was.'

'Did you leave with her to show her around the *Albatross*?'

'No, I didn't. Charlotte wanted me to take her to see the '*Albatross*', but we didn't have a suitable chaperone to accompany us. I refused to take her without a chaperone.'

His father studied his face and sat down again in his chair. He let out a long sad sigh.

'Who accused me of bedding Charlotte, Father?'

'She did.' The two words seemed to rip from his heart. His body sagged with despair.

William dropped to one knee and took his father's hands and held them in his left hand. With his right hand he stroked his father's head. He had become the father. He remembered all the times George had stroked his head when he was a child. His father's strokes had soothed away all of his pain.

His father gripped his son's hand, realising how close he had come to losing the last link to his first wife. 'I'm sorry I doubted you, Son.'

'It's in the past now, Father,' replied William, his voice calm. 'I will take care of everything. Don't you concern yourself any longer.'

- CHAPTER THIRTY-TWO -

Accused

Liverpool
December 1806

William helped his father to the carriage and ordered the driver to take them home to Kent Street. He left the old man in the library and made sure the servants knew what was required. Satisfied that his father was safe, he left to find his stepmother. He was thankful that she was not home; he was not sure what he would have done in anger.

Donald Nicholson gave him a cold, blank stare as he informed William that Charlotte was away visiting her maiden Aunt in Manchester, who had been taken ill suddenly.

William didn't believe a word. He knew Charlotte had left Liverpool so that there would be little chance of him speaking to her after he found out the truth from his father. He would wait his time for the reckoning.

The following day in his cabin, William met with Owen to discuss the purchase of the *Albatross*.

'I apologise for being a little obtuse the other day, when

you asked me about purchasing the *Albatross*. I did not wish to distract you from visiting your father, as he hasn't looked well of late. How is Mr King?' asked Owen.

'He is fine, a little tired, but in good health.'

'And Mrs King?'

'She is in Manchester looking after an elderly relative. Owen, may we discuss the *Albatross*?'

'Of course, dear fellow: I have scrutinised the accounts of the voyage and I am pleased to say it was a very successful venture. A large portion of the overall profit was due to the shipments of ice that you carried. The cost of the ice was minimal, but the sale price was excellent. Taking everything into account, I am pleased to offer you the *Albatross* as your share of the profits and your wages for the voyage. You only owe for the expense of fitting her out for the voyage and we are happy to defer the payment until you return from your next voyage.'

'Owen!' exclaimed William with pleasure. 'What can I say? You and your associates are very generous. The ship is mine?'

'Yes, William, she is yours and here are the ownership papers.' Owen smiled as he handed over the documents to William.

William accepted the papers and opened them to read that Captain William King was the owner of the sailing ship *Albatross*.

William gently folded the documents, placed them in the draw of his desk and whispered, 'Thank you, Owen, you have no idea what this means to me.' He could now return to Ruth, as promised, with his own ship.

As he closed the drawer, there was a light knock on the cabin door. It creaked open and Sang's head appeared.

'Captain, people to see you.'

'That will be the Sheriff and lawyer Snelgrove,' said Owen.

'Show them in, Sang.'

The door opened and Pilcher entered, followed by a round-faced fat man. The fat man's waistcoat buttons strained under pressure of his chest and stomach. His face was ruddy from the effort of climbing from the quay to the deck of the *Albatross* and walking the short distance to the Captain's cabin. Holding a leather case under his arm, the fat man mopped his brow with a large silk handkerchief.

'An exceedingly humid day; Captain, my card.'

With a flourish the fat man withdrew a card from a small pocket in his waistcoat and presented it to William.

William accepted the card and glanced at the printed words. They were so embellished with scrolls and fancy lines he found it difficult to decipher the name.

'Lawyer Snelgrove, at your service.'

'Thank you, Mr Snelgrove, may I offer you a chair?'

'Thank you, yes.' Snelgrove flopped down on the only other chair in the cabin.

'Good morning, Mr Pilcher,' said William, ' have you met my associate, Mr Johnston?'

'I have, Sir, I have,' said the sheriff's man as he nodded to Owen.

'To business, gentlemen, to business,' said lawyer Snelgrove, opening his leather case.

'I have here a sworn statement that the *Albatross,* with you, Captain King, in command, did sail from Liverpool last December with a slave known as Ben Liverpool on board. The statement also states that it was your intention to sell this slave upon reaching the West Indies.'

'Mr Snelgrove, I have never traded in slaves. I have a simple question for you as a man of the law. Where am I supposed to have obtained this slave, Ben Liverpool?'

'I am sorry; I do not have the information as to where you obtained the slave.'

'You may not have that particular information, but you will be aware that no man can be a slave in England. I could not, therefore, have purchased a slave, nor stolen one, as they don't exist in England.'

'Clever words will not change the statement. A black man was secreted aboard this vessel with the intention of being sold in the West Indies.'

'Ben Liverpool, you say?'

'Yes,' said the lawyer, wiping his face once more.

William opened the drawer where he had placed the ownership deeds for the *Albatross* and lifted out a heavy ledger.

'Mr Snelgrove, are you familiar with a ship's log?'

'I am, Captain, but I fail to see any connection with the charge made against you.'

William opened the logbook and turned to the pages for the previous December. 'The log states that we found a stowaway, a man called Ben Liverpool. Here, read it for yourself,' and he pushed the logbook towards the lawyer.

The sheriff's man, Pilcher, leaned across to also read the log.

'You will note that the stowaway agreed to sign on this vessel as a sailor. He was a free man when he made his mark. Alongside the mark you will see the signature of the First Mate and myself. In addition I have a full crew who will swear that what I am telling you is the truth.'

'He was still a slave when you sailed.'

'Mr Snelgrove, he was a free man when we sailed and was

later found on this ship as a stowaway. The poor devil didn't even realise he was a free man until I explained it to him. He was free on two accounts.'

'How so?' asked Pilcher.

'I have already stated that one cannot be a slave in England, not since 1772. Also, according to Ben Liverpool's statement to me and to other persons on this vessel, his previous *owner* promised Ben his *freedom* if he hid himself on this ship. He did hide on this ship until we found him. By his act of hiding he therefore won his *freedom,* being the bargain between his *owner* and himself. He completed his part of the bargain. So you see, gentlemen, when we left the quay in Liverpool, Ben was a free man, so we could not have broken any laws. At the time we sailed, after being wrongly detained, Ben Liverpool, a free man, volunteered to sign on the *Albatross.* The act of signing onto this vessel would have made him free, if ever he needed such freedom. We are an English ship and we were in English waters. I have the crew muster book if you wish to examine it.'

Lawyer Snelgrove mopped his face once again and stuffed the handkerchief into an inside pocket of his jacket. William glanced from the lawyer to Pilcher and waited for a response.

'I think, Mr Snelgrove, we have outstayed our welcome,' said Pilcher. 'I would be obliged if you would accompany me back to the office, where we may discuss this incident in private.'

'You don't think I have done any wrong, surely?' blurted Snelgrove, perspiration once again appearing on his brow.

'Wrong? Mr Snelgrove, you are a lawyer. You can't do anything wrong, but I am sure you would wish to see that justice is done. I need to talk to you about the person who swore out the statement that instigated this evidently spurious charge.'

The tone of the Sheriff's voice left Lawyer Snelgrove in no doubt that he should comply.

William stood and held his hand out to the lawyer. 'Give my best wishes to Mr Nicholson, both Mr Thomas and Henry. Tell Henry if he has any other black freemen that he doesn't want, I will be happy to offer them a berth in one of my ships.'

Ignoring the proffered hand, the lawyer scowled at William and waddled from the cabin. Pilcher smiled and shook hands with William and followed. The sudden sound of a slammed door was a relief valve to Owen who burst out laughing and slapped his knee in glee.

'How I kept my face straight, I will never know, William.'

'Lawyers are time-wasters. If my handshake is not good enough, I will not do business; any lawyer will break another lawyer's contract. Forget him, Owen - down to business. We have lost enough time.'

'What are your plans for the *Albatross* now, William?'

'I think I will return to Boston.'

'May I make a suggestion?'

'Please do.'

'The Prime Minister has introduced the Foreign Slave Trade bill, the aim of which is to forbid any British ship to carry slaves. The bill to go before the House of Lords within a few weeks, after which we expect it to be passed.'

'Owen, I am aware of what has been happening, even though I have been out of the country for nearly a year.'

'Quite, quite, my, dear fellow, I am coming to the point. Please bear with me.'

'At your service,' said William.

'Everyone is aware that if the anti-slavery bill goes through, and is ratified by His Majesty, it will become illegal for a British ship to carry slaves. Although British citizens will still have slaves on their overseas plantations.'

'Owen, I am also aware of this. Please come to the point!'

'I am surprised you have not yet picked up on the point, William.'

'Enlighten me, please.'

'What will the current owners of British slave ships do to generate income for their ships?'

William stared at Owen without blinking, for over a minute, as the logic of Owen's point became obvious.

'Carry on, Owen.'

'Thank you, my friend; my point is that without trade contracts and contacts outside of the slave trade, many will have to sell their ships. There will be a glut of ships on the market and we will be able to buy one or two at good prices.'

'Are there any in port for sale now?' enquired William.

'There may be, but once people know we are in the market, the price will rise.'

'Then we must poison the market and play down the desirability of an ex-slave ship.'

Later that day William met his father in the company' office.

'It is agreed then, Father. I will control both the *Margaret Rose* and the *Elizabeth Rose?*'

'Yes, do what you think is right. I'm tired and I have lost Charlotte. Will you keep the crews?'

'They are still your ships, Father; my involvement will be as manager to make sure they operate profitably, without being involved in the Trade. To answer your question; yes I will keep the crews, if they are willing to sail on a ship that is not involved in the Trade, but they will be on lower wages. I cannot match the wages earned on a slaver. It will be up to them.'

William watched his father in the chair near the fire. He was tired and looked old.

George stared into the fire. He had been happy when he married Charlotte, but now he felt a fool for believing that she felt the same about him. The shock of losing her, although he had known he had lost her the minute he forced his attentions on her, had caused him to despair.

He shivered, as if he was cold, each time he thought how close he had come to losing his son. George was happy to allow William to control both of his vessels, even at the risk of a rift between him and Donald Nicholson.

'Father, I must attend to matters elsewhere. Will you be alright?'

'What? Aye, I'll be fine. Will I see you at home this evening?'

'I will do my best to be there.'

'Go and attend to business then; you have been away from it far too long.'

William climbed the stairs to Owen's rooms and felt happy. His father had showed confidence in him by allowing him to control the two *Rose* vessels.

As he raised his hand to knock on the door, it opened.

'Thought I recognised those footsteps. You appear happy with the world,' said Owen smiling.

'I am, Owen. Father has given me control of his two ships.'

'Marvelous. When are they due in Liverpool?'

'The *Elizabeth,* before Christmas, and the *Margaret,* early

January.'

'I have some news as well. I have found a slaver and the owner has read the signs of change in the same way that we have; he has agreed to sell her. She is currently at anchor in the river.'

'The problem is, Owen, I have little money left after paying my partners for their share of the *Albatross*.'

'Hmm, well, I have a large investment in stock, and in the factory in Manchester. I also have to find other markets.'

'What do you propose?'

'That I buy the ex-slaver, but that we jointly share the cost of sailing her. She would carry my cargo and I would act as your agent in England. We would jointly share the profits, but you could use your share to purchase her from me sometime in the future. I am not interested in owning sailing vessels. I own the factory where the goods your ships will carry are manufactured – that is enough responsibility for me.'

'We have a deal, Owen! My hand on it.' Owen smiled and accepted the partnership on a handshake.

'So what kind of vessel is this slaver?'

'She is three masted barque and her name is the *Blackbird*. I understand she is fast.'

'We must change her name, Owen. I'll not feel right sailing an ex-slaver with such a name!'

'I heard that it was bad luck to change the name of a ship.'

'It is, but I think I can get round that little problem.'

'How?'

'We will call her the *Black Swan*, which is a black bird, is it not?'

Owen shook his head and laughed. 'I should have known you would dream up the right name.'

'The next problem is to gain ownership. How much does the owner want?'

'I will ascertain the amount and let you know. I do know the owner is not too well at present. He has picked up some disease during his ventures in the African Trade.'

Ten days later Owen purchased the *Blackbird* and renamed her the *Black Swan*. The figurehead on her bow was altered to be more like a swan. She was a low-drafted vessel, built for speed and for navigating the rivers of the African coast. Her hold was rigged to carry the maximum number of slaves.

William arranged for her to be pulled out of the water and checked on a slipway. The tiers, for the slaves, were ripped out and replaced with cargo holds. Gangs of labourers cleaned her and painted the inside with lime-wash in an effort to kill the smell and return some dignity to such a fine vessel. Her sails and rigging were in good order. The previous owner had looked after his ship so as to make a good profit from his human cargo. A fast passage from the west coast of Africa would mean his cargo would be in better condition on arrival, which meant better prices from the slave market.

William studied her lines and visualized her in the water. A good wind on her quarter and she would fly. She would be ideal for the ice trade from Boston to Jamaica and for carrying fruit on the return trip.

Owen organised the cargo from his factories in Manchester and also sold space on the *Black Swan* to those merchants who wished to take advantage of a fast passage to Boston. He arranged for William to act as their agent in Boston if they didn't already have one.

To return to Boston and to Ruth was the driving force in William's mind in the final few weeks of 1806.

As expected the *Elizabeth Rose* arrived in Liverpool the week before Christmas. Many vessels now sailed on their own as the threat from the French had subsided after their defeat off Cape Trafalgar.

William re-equipped the *Elizabeth Rose* and sent her to the Mediterranean to reactivate her old trading patterns. His instructions to the Captain were given as owner of the vessel.

The *Albatross* was made ready for her next voyage, but this time without William in command. William appointed David Fuller as First Mate and hired a new Captain who had not been involved in the Trade.

She sailed the second week in December for Boston, and for another winter on the ice trade.

- CHAPTER THIRTY-THREE -

Boston Again

Boston
Late January 1807

After the Pilot disembarked at the mouth of the River Mersey, William ordered all sails and with the wind on the *Black Swan's* starboard quarter, she almost flew down the Irish Sea and out through the St George's Channel to the open Atlantic.

He tested the crew, and his new ship, to their limits. She was a beautiful vessel to handle.

It was nearly dawn on the twentieth day of the voyage, and the sky was clearing after heavy overnight rain. William had spent most of the night on deck, but didn't feel tired.

He rubbed a hand across his face and realised he needed a shave. He tried to remember the last time he had shaved himself, and came to the conclusion he hadn't shaved his own cheeks for over a year. Not since the day Sang took him in hand.

'Eight bells, Sir.'

'Thank you, Mr Austin, please make it so.'

Michael Austin struck the ship's bell eight times. At the sound of the first strike, the off-watch crew came on deck to take over from the duty watch.

William watched as twelve-year-old Michael Austin made his way below. He remembered the conversation with Michael's mother on the day before they were to sail. Sang had knocked to say a lady wanted to see him. At first he thought it might be Charlotte, until the frail figure of James Austin's wife entered the cabin, followed by a young boy. He was tall for his age and had the stance and facial features of James Austin.

'Mrs Austin, a pleasure.'

'Captain King, I will come to the point. This is Michael and you told me that you would train him to be an officer.'

'That is correct, Ma'am.'

'He,' said Mrs. Austin, and pointed to her son, 'wants to go to sea and has been pestering me for days. I have agreed, but only for one voyage, after which I want the truth from you, Captain, as to his suitability for the sea. Of course, if of his own accord he wants to come ashore after the voyage, that is another matter. I want him to work in an office and have a proper job.'

'Being at sea, Mrs Austin, is a proper job. I was Michael's age when I went to sea, now I command my own ship. There is no reason why Michael can't do the same, if he works hard.'

'Thank you, Sir.'

William heard Michael's voice for the first time. 'Do you wish to go to sea?'

'Aye, Sir, I do!'

'Mrs Austin, we sail tomorrow. If Michael is to join us, he has to report aboard no later than six o'clock this evening.'

—∞—

When the *Black Swan* hit the Atlantic rollers, the young apprentice became seasick. It was over a week before he found his sea-legs and was able to keep food in his stomach. He showed courage by reporting for duty each day at the correct time. He lost weight and appeared as pale as his father just before they sewed his body into a hammock.

—⚓—

Twenty-eight days after leaving Liverpool, William once again gazed on the snow-white backdrop to Boston harbour.

After berthing the *Black Swan,* he stepped down to Long Pier and was met by Elijah, who beamed a large smile with his strong white teeth. The warmth of the greeting was never more genuine.

'Morning, Captain.'

'Morning, Elijah, Miss Ruth in the office?'

'She sure is, Captain, she waitin' for you in de office now. She not sure when you comin' ashore.'

William climbed into the carriage and sat back to enjoy the short ride.

Elijah hauled on the reins and brought the carriage to a halt outside the offices of Abraham's building. William jumped down and ran through the main door of the building to take the stairs two at a time.

Ruth heard the main door bang and the rush of feet of someone running upstairs. She examined herself once more in the mirror and smoothed her dress. A quick glance around the office to make sure everything was neat and tidy just before the door flew open and William stood in the doorway, grinning at the woman he loved. She stood rooted to the spot, not sure how she should greet him.

Her hands fluttered to her neck with indecision. William entered the office and wrapped his arms around her, trapping her hands between their bodies. He gently lifted her face to his and kissed her lightly on the lips. His kiss was enough to vanquish any negative thoughts. She kissed him back and surrendered to the strength of his arms. Her knees felt like jelly as he kissed her again.

Eventually he eased his crushing hug when he realised she was finding it difficult to breathe. He stood back and stared at her face and stroked her hair. Her perfume invaded his mind and all he wanted was to hold her again and not let her go.

His silly grin made her laugh.

'What's so funny?'

'You, my love, you have a grin on your face that tells the world what you think of me.'

'Is that wrong?'

'No, no, not wrong, in fact it's very pleasant and comforting to me. I won't share that grin with anyone else. Therefore I will have to give you a gentle kick if I see it in company. It is not a grin for others, only me.'

'Only for you, my sweet,' he hugged her again, but not as fiercely this time. There were plenty of days ahead.

'How is your father?'

'He is well and looking forward to seeing you tonight at dinner, if you can come.'

'I'll certainly be there, with the utmost pleasure.'

She moved to the mirror and tidied her hair with her hands. As he watched he had an urgent desire to stroke the small fine hairs he could see at the back of her neck. He brushed the back of his fingers gently, so very gently, along Ruth's skin. She shivered and jumped a little, the delicate touch sending shock waves through her body.

'You jumped. Don't you like me doing that?'

'Oh yes, but I can't control the way my body moves when

you touch me.'

The welcome William received at *Mamre* could not have been warmer. Abraham greeted him as the long lost son he had always wanted. Discharging of the *Black Swan* had commenced that afternoon, under the control of John Leigh, the First Mate. He was a capable young man and William felt it was time that he showed confidence in him, and so decided to sleep ashore at *Mamre*.

Abraham, Ruth and William talked half the night about the political problems in England and America. It appeared the two countries, from the same roots, could not stop arguing over trade.

The *Black Swan* was placed on the same agreement as the *Albatross* with Abraham's company. Abraham did not argue this time just solemnly hand over a dollar to William.

After dinner Abraham made an excuse to leave Ruth and William alone in the drawing room.

'Do you still wish to marry me?'

'When?' asked Ruth, her voice soft.

'My father has two ships on the slave trade, but I have persuaded him to allow me to control them. He has agreed and I was fortunate to be in Liverpool when one, the *Margaret Rose*, returned from her last trip. I have had her stripped and refitted for cargo and ordered her to the Mediterranean. The other vessel, the *Elizabeth Rose*, had not returned before I left for Boston. I left instructions that she was also to be refitted and to follow the *Margaret Rose*. I am concerned for my father, as I believe his new wife has caused him much heartache. Her family is powerful and they are very influential in Liverpool. I know they will take advantage of him if he becomes too ill to manage his company. I don't trust them at all. I think you met their son last year; Henry Nicholson.'

'I remember Mr Nicholson. I didn't find him to be a very pleasant fellow.'

'Has he called in to Boston recently?'

'I don't think so, but Boston is growing. I used to know all the ships that visited, but nowadays I am not sure what vessel is in port. I only have dealings with ships linked to our company.'

Only later did he realise that he had not answered Ruth's question about when they would marry.

William was busy the following week making sure the goods he had brought from Liverpool were landed safely. Abraham searched for an outbound cargo for the *Black Swan*.

'William, you know the cargo will not be ready for some weeks?' said Abraham at the end of the *Black Swan's* first week in port.

'Yes, I do. What do you have in mind?'

'Ice.'

'To Jamaica? The *Albatross* has already sailed there with ice.'

'I have received word from a contact in Savannah. He wants to try selling ice locally. He heard of your venture last year, and tried to do it himself, but I wouldn't sell any ice to him. I wanted to make sure I stocked enough to supply your ships,' laughed Abraham.

'Savannah? Not this time, Abraham, when the *Albatross* returns from Jamaica, you can send her to Savannah. I trust you and her captain will ensure it is a profitable run.'

'My problem is that I gave my contact my word that when the first ice ship arrived in Boston, I would dispatch a full cargo for him.'

'Your word?'

'Yes.'

After a few moments William said, 'Is Savannah warm at this time of the year?'

'Thank you, William.'

'After Savannah, do you intend to return to Jamaica?'

'No, not this time; I want to load the *Black Swan* with as much ice as possible, because I intend to sail to Calcutta in India.'

'Calcutta! William, have you taken leave . . .'

'On the contrary, Abraham, I intend to take your clean frozen water to the hot climes of the East and make our fortune.'

'A fortune, I doubt that, William. Calcutta is a lot further than Jamaica and you suffered ice loss on each of the Jamaica voyages.'

'I know, I know, but I am convinced there is an opportunity for ice to Calcutta. I have spoken to sea captains in Liverpool and I understand that they don't have clean ice in India. At first I presumed they would have collected the ice from the mountains, similar to the people of the Mediterranean, but it appears the mountains are too far from Calcutta. In addition they do not have the roads to allow for insulated wagons. We have learned a lot in Jamaica and if we can reach Calcutta with a commercial load, then there is no reason for the British in India not to have the same desire for cold drinks as the British in Jamaica. There are a lot more British in India and one never knows what opportunities may arise for cargo back to Boston, or at least back to Liverpool.'

'As long as it is not tea from China!' said Abraham.

'No, it will not be tea; the Honorable East India Company have the monopoly on tea to England and I do not wish to cross them. They could put us out of business. I have plans for spices from Sumatra, though; pepper!'

'Bring pepper back here and I will sell every last ounce for you.'

'I expected nothing more, Abraham,' laughed William, clapping Abraham on the back. 'The *Black Swan* is ideal for this trade. She will make a fast passage to India. We will see how fast she really is on the round trip to Savannah. On my return, I will load for Calcutta to take advantage of the winter.'

'In that case you can sail for Savannah as soon as you are loaded, William. I have the wood shavings and the peat for insulation. Also, if you require them, I can obtain carpenters to build you a false wall in the *Black Swan's* hold. On your return we will work around the clock to clean, and make good any repairs for your voyage to Calcutta.'

- CHAPTER THIRTY-FOUR -

Fever

Boston
Early March 1807

The *Black Swan* edged closer to Long Pier near Abraham's warehouse. The voyage from Savannah had taken an extra week, due to light winds.

William focused his telescope on the window of Abraham's office. He could see Abraham watching the slow progress of the *Black Swan* creeping towards the wharf. William swept the glass across the other windows of the building in the hope of seeing Ruth. He refocused on Abraham and waved. Abraham acknowledged the wave and then moved away from the window. The *Black Swan* was home.

'Come in, my boy, come in. Make yourself comfortable,' shouted Abraham.

William entered and quickly glanced around for Ruth; she was not there. A large fire gave off so much heat that he threw off his cape and placed it over the back of a chair.

Abraham struggled to his feet; leaning on the desk for support, he offered his hand. William grasped it and realised it was just fragile skin and bone. The hand felt like parchment, dry and frail. He studied Abraham and felt a sudden dread as he realised it would be only a matter of weeks before Abraham would be too weak to stand. His friend was wrapped in heavy clothing in an effort to keep warm, despite the heat from the open fire.

Abraham pulled his hand from William's grasp and collapsed back into his chair. His breath came in short sharp gasps. The act of breathing seemed too much for him. His pale face was tinged with yellow around the eyes.

'How are you my friend?' asked William, dragging a chair closer to the desk. The old man waved his hand to dismiss any concern for his health and wheezed as he gasped for the breath to answer.

'I am fine, just a little tired. A busy year, this year,' whispered the old man. He closed his eyes as if wanting to sleep.

William waited quietly.

'I see you are flying the American flag, William,' wheezed Abraham.

'Yes, I heard about the Embargo Act in Savannah.'

'America will be the loser. This Act forbids the importation of British goods, but where are we supposed to obtain alternative suppliers? I do hope next year is a better year.'

'Our agreement——'

'Fine, fine,' whispered Abraham as if listening had become too much for him.

'You should be at home in bed, not here in this office.'

'Too much to do,' whispered the old man.

'How is Ruth?'

'She will be here later; she had to go into town earlier, before we received the information about the *Black Swan's* arrival. If she knew you were about to berth, she would have never left. As to your question, she is well.'

Abraham sat back in his chair and pulled out a large handkerchief and coughed into it a number of times. The effort drained him of his strength. He let the handkerchief fall to the floor and closed his eyes.

William rose from his chair, opened the office door and shouted for Elijah. The urgency in his voice produced the sound of running feet as Elijah bound up the stairs.

'Captain, you called?'

'Yes, Mr Judson is very ill. He should not be here. It would be better if he went home and to bed.'

'I tol him, Captain, not to come to work this morning, but he do'wn listen to me any more.'

'Where is Miss Ruth?'

'She out in town, Captain.'

'Send someone to find her and have the coach made ready to take Mr Abraham home to *Mamre*, quickly now.'

'Yes, Captain.' He turned and ran down the stairs, yelling for someone to ride like the wind and find Miss Ruth.

William went round the desk to get a closer look at Abraham. The old man was sweating and shivering at the same time. He was either asleep or had fainted. William moved the chair so that he could pick up his friend. The lightness of Abraham surprised him. The layers of clothing had given the appearance of him being heavier.

William placed his old friend gently in the carriage and made sure he was well wrapped in a blanket.

'Elijah, take us home as fast as you can, but be gentle!'

'Yes, Captain, I's be gentle as I can.'

William sat back in the carriage next to Abraham and placed an arm around his friend to cushion any shocks.

Arriving at Mamre, William allowed the servants to put Abraham to bed. He sent a fast rider for the local doctor and the carriage back to town to collect Ruth.

The doctor arrived within an hour to examine Abraham. The news was not encouraging. Abraham had a fever, and other than keeping him warm, there was little else the doctor could do for him. The doctor left various potions, which he said might help, but William held little faith in them. If his friend could fight off the fever, perhaps he would have a chance, but being an old man, William felt it would be only a matter of time before the fever would take Abraham's life.

William sat in the library of *Mamre* with a glass of brandy in his hand. The servants hadn't been allowed to light the lamps, as he wanted to think.

He was sipping his drink automatically, not tasting the fiery liquid, when the door opened and Ruth entered. He rose from his seat and felt his spirits lift at the pleasure of seeing her again.

'Why are you in the dark, William?'

'I have been thinking of today, and Abraham. Do you want a drink?'

'Thank you, a small sherry please.'

He poured Ruth a drink and refreshed his own.

'How is he?' he asked quietly, as he handed Ruth her drink.

'Sleeping.' Ruth sat in a chair close to the fire and watched the flames.

William returned to his chair. 'Do you want the lamps lit?'

'No, it's pleasant in the semi-darkness with just the fire,' answered Ruth without turning her head.

'What are your plans now, Ruth?'

'Plans? I haven't any. I'm not sure if father will get through the night.'

'I think you should make plans.'

Her head came up and she half-turned to study William. 'He's not dead yet!'

'Ruth, you know I didn't mean anything by my comment. I just think you should consider your future.'

'With or without father?'

'I suggest you consider both possibilities.'

Ruth sat back in the chair and stared at the fire again. 'I am practical in most things, having always taken care of father. Even as a young girl I often felt more mature than him.'

William didn't speak; each lost in their thoughts. It was not an embarrassed silence, but a silence of friendship and companionship. It comforted Ruth.

'Father is of a business mind and can deal with most things in business, but he would rely on me if he felt unsure about an individual. He would ask me to join him when he was not sure about someone with whom he wished to do business. If I was invited to join him and his guest for dinner, or for a few drinks here at *Mamre,* I knew he was in a dilemma. My presence would cause the other person to be less aggressive and I am fortunate that I have the ability to usually judge a person's character on first meeting with them. I have made an occasional mistake, but most of the time I am correct about people. I suppose with mother not being here for him to discuss ideas, he has relied more and more on me.'

William nodded and sipped his drink.

After a short time Ruth put her empty sherry glass on the small table near her chair and glanced at William. 'So you see there are many things to consider.'

'I have no doubt there are, and I don't wish to burden you with extra problems, but——' Before he could finish a great commotion began in the hall. They could hear wailing and shouting. William rose quickly, strode angrily to the library door and pulled it open, to be met with three crying black women.

'What is all this noise about?' William asked in a loud whisper. 'Are you unaware your Master is ill and trying to sleep?'

The noise of wailing grew as the youngest woman tried to speak between great sobs and gasps. William felt Ruth behind him and stepped aside to allow her to see what was happening.

'Calm yourself, Sarah, and tell me what is the matter.'

'Ms Ruth, I been to see Mr Abraham and I tried to tidy his bedclothes and my hand touched his cheek. He didn't move; he was cold.'

Ruth ran up the stairs, closely followed by William. She reached the first floor landing and hurried down the corridor to her father's bedroom. The door was still open after Sarah's excited exit. Ruth entered and saw her father in bed, his arms on top of the bedclothes. She stopped and pressed a hand to her breast in an effort to slow her heartbeat. She moved quietly towards the bed and the still body.

William, following, saw Ruth standing by the bed with one hand outstretched towards her father.

'Ruth, wait! Allow me!'

She turned towards William, her arm still extended. William gently touched the old man's hand; it was icy cold. He placed his ear close to Abraham's mouth and listened. He felt sure he could hear a slight movement of air passing. He moved his hand under the bedclothes and felt around Abraham's chest. The body felt cold.

'Please bring me a small mirror.'

Ruth allowed her arm to drop to her side and watched her father. She glanced at William and felt that everything was happening as if in a dream, and she just hoped she would wake from it soon.

'A mirror, please!' said William, a little louder.

'A mirror, yes,' said Ruth, leaving to do William's bidding.

A few moments later she returned with a small hand mirror from her bedside table. She handed it to William, who wiped it on his sleeve and placed it close to Abraham's mouth. He watched the glass as it fogged and then showed the glass to Ruth.

'He is still alive,' whispered William, and pointed to the fogged section of the mirror

Ruth sat on the side of the bed, covered her face with her hands and burst into tears. William knelt and placed his arms around her in an effort to share her grief. Her hair felt like silk. Time passed and she slowly regained her composure. He removed his arms when Ruth smiled gently at him. She pulled a small handkerchief from the sleeve of her dress and dabbed her eyes.

'What'll happen to him?' she asked.

'I don't know, Ruth, he's very frail at the moment. He may get over the fever, but then he may not.'

'What happens if he doesn't?'

'You will have a number of decisions to make.'

'Will you help me?'

'Yes, my love, I will help you.'

William felt a great surge of love for Ruth as he watched her dabbing her eyes. He wanted to take her in his arms and protect her from the whole world.

'Can I get you a drink or something to eat?'

'Thank you, William, but I couldn't face food at the moment.'

'You must eat or else you will lose your strength. You will not be able to help your father if you become ill.'

She glanced up at William's face and tried to smile. 'I suppose you are right. I don't think my mind could cope with such a simple task as eating.'

William smiled and placed his hand under Ruth's elbow and gently raised her from the bed. 'We will let your father sleep. Sarah can sit with him while we have something to eat, or would you prefer to eat in here?' William waved his hand towards the small table across the room.

'In here would be nice,' replied Ruth, smiling at William's thoughtfulness.

He led her to a comfortable chair and positioned it so she could see her father as he slept. 'Sit here while I go down and speak to the servants.'

—⁓—

Dinner was a sombre affair and far removed from the dinners William and Ruth usually attended. He did his best to take her mind off her father, but the occasional sigh from Abraham would interrupt their attempts at conversation. At each sigh they fell silent, was it Abraham's last.

Ruth curled up on the chair and fell asleep in the knowledge that William would keep watch. He sat at the table and puffed slowly on a small cigar. The servants had not been called to clean away the remains of their meal, as Ruth didn't want to disturb her father. William watched the ash fall from his cigar onto a small plate and thought of the night he had refused a cigar in his father's house, because it had been produced by slave labour.

The grey light of dawn attempted to get round the edges of the thick curtains covering the windows. William stubbed out the remains of his already extinguished cigar. His mouth tasted sour and his eyes felt gritty. He rubbed his face in an effort to wake, stood and stretched while rubbing his lower back to relieve cramp. He moved to the curtains and gently pulled them apart. The day was coming to life and it looked miserable. It was drizzling, which made him think of a bath and fresh water for his mouth.

'You let me sleep through,' said Ruth, stretching her legs.

'I thought there was no point in both of us losing sleep.'

'How is he?'

'Still making those small sighs every now and then. The doctor is due later this morning.'

Ruth paused, then said softly, 'Thank you, William.'

'For what?'

'For all you did yesterday and last night.'

'I did nothing. Do you want breakfast?'

'No, do you?'

'I need a wash and a shave and perhaps I may borrow a clean shirt.'

'I'll speak to Elijah'

'No, it's all right, you stay here, I will find Elijah.'

Soaking in the bath eased William's aches and pains. Elijah had brought him hot coffee, which he sipped as his body absorbed the heat of the water.

Later, as he shaved, Elijah brought a choice of shirts from Abraham's wardrobe and laid them across a small table. He dressed in one of the borrowed shirts and was arranging his jacket when he heard Ruth shout his name.

He ran along the corridor to Abraham's room and found Ruth standing over her father, the small mirror clasped in her hands. William moved to her side and looked at Abraham. One glance was enough; Abraham was dead.

Ruth, her voice wavering, said, 'I was just about to check that he was still breathing by using the mirror. I hadn't heard him sigh for several minutes.'

William took the mirror from her and placed it on the table. He helped her to the chair in which she had spent the night.

Abraham's flesh felt clammy and cold to William's touch. He pressed his finger into the dead man's cheek. The indentation stayed. William gently pulled the bed sheet over his friend's face.

'Come with me,' he said to Ruth and offered his hand for support.

- CHAPTER THIRTY-FIVE -

The Future

Boston
Early March 1807

Abraham was buried in the bottom area of *Mamre* amongst the trees he loved so much. The gathering of his friends surprised William. He knew Abraham had many friends, but he didn't realise just how many. They arrived from all over Massachusetts and from as far away as the Canadian border. Fortunately the cold weather held, allowing the funeral to be delayed a little longer than normal, which meant more of his friends could pay their last respects.

William and Ruth fell into a pattern of walking after breakfast. They always seemed to drift towards the fresh over-turned earth that marked the last resting place of her father.

'I must leave soon,' said William, standing below the trees near Abraham's grave. 'Spring is nearly upon us and I must return to Liverpool.'

'Must you go so soon? I thought you planned to go to Calcutta?'

'I am sorry, my love, but your father's death forced me to change my plans and there are things to attend to in Liverpool.'

He hesitated as he held both of Ruth's hands in his own. He stared at her and waited until she turned her face.

'What, William?' Her eyes searched his face.

'I have to leave. Will you come with me?'

'To Liverpool?'

'Yes, to Liverpool. I will leave my father in charge of things there. We could be married and——'

'But what about the business here?' interrupted Ruth. 'We have a large business here.' Tears sprang to her eyes as she realised she had said 'we', meaning her and her father. William placed his arm around her shoulders and she leaned against his chest. 'William, I can't leave *Mamre*.'

'You could appoint a manager to oversee the company and we would visit frequently.'

'Where would I find the right man to manage the company? A lot of information is in my head. I have grown up in the company and I can't see how a manager could make it work.'

'I want you with me, Ruth. I want to marry you!'

'Oh, William, how can we marry? You will be on the other side of the world.'

'I want you with me. Sell the company and join me!'

'Sell father's company! How can you think of such a thing?'

'I think of such a thing because I love you and want you with me!'

'No, no, I couldn't sell the company and have strangers in father's chair. What would I do about our Negroes? No, I couldn't sell.'

'Sell to me. I will buy the company.'

'You? What do you know of trading in Boston?'

'I will appoint a manager and your Negroes will be taken care of because they will be working for me. If you marry me, they will still be working for you!'

'But I will not be here if you want us to live in Liverpool. How do I know they will be well treated by this manager?'

'Because if they're not, the manager will answer to me!'

Ruth leaned forward and allowed her head to rest against his chest. She let out a great sob and her body started to shake. The strain of the last couple of weeks had become too much for her. Her tears flowed freely. William wrapped her in his arms and rocked gently back and forth, making soothing sounds while he stroked her. He didn't say anything, he just held her tight.

'Dinner is served, Sir,' said Elijah to his Mistress and the Captain. He bowed his head a little and closed the library door quietly. It saddened him to see such a lovely couple just sitting, his mistress staring into the fire and the Captain reading a newspaper. They should marry.

'Thank you,' said William to the closed door and folded the newspaper before placing it on the small table. 'They are ready for dinner, my love.'

He watched Ruth raise her head and push herself up from the chair. She allowed William to link her arm with his as they made their way to the dining room.

Ruth had hardly spoken since leaving her father's graveside. She didn't say a word during their return to the house. William found it a strain trying to make conversation in an effort to divert her mind. Finally he too lapsed into silence. He had guided her to the library knowing there would be a welcoming fire. Ruth stood near the flames and rubbed her hands together.

For most of the afternoon William read a newspaper and kept a watchful eye on Ruth as she sat quietly gazing into the fire. He realised that she may be in shock, having seen similar reactions in some of his crew after capturing the *Nancy*.

Eventually she slept. Although the fire gave off a large amount of heat, he placed a shawl around her shoulders to keep her warm.

The last lines linking Boston to the *Black Swan* were released. They splashed into the dirty water and the crew hauled them aboard.

Ruth sat in her open-topped carriage and waved while the ship slowly moved away from the land.

It was the end of March and the last few days had been hectic. She and William had agreed on a one-year separation prior to marrying. A year didn't seem such a long time until she watched the *Black Swan* move further and further from the shore. Which ever way she thought of the separation, twelve months or a year, they both added up to a lifetime.

On board William felt sick, as his stomach churned.

He tried to convince himself that he felt sick as a result of bad food, but he knew in his heart the real reason. He didn't want to leave Ruth. Seeing her in the carriage made him want to jump the ever-widening gap between his ship and the land.

The *Black Swan* pointed her bow towards the ocean.

'Make sail, make sail!' shouted the First Mate. The crew raced to the yardarms to release the lashings. Sails tumbled free, followed by a dull thud as the offshore wind filled them.

'Haul away!' yelled the Mate, 'sheet home!'

The *Black Swan* heeled gently, and began to pick up speed.

William stood on the poop deck and focused his glass on the diminishing image of Ruth now standing on the wharf and waving her headscarf. The breeze blew her hair as she brushed it out of her eyes. He lowered his glass and held his hat high in acknowledgement of Ruth's frantic waves.

His thoughts were drawn back to the frank discussion during their last meal together.

—⚞—

'Do you feel better?' William asked as they entered the dining room

'A little; I am not so cold,' replied Ruth.

'Hot food is the best medicine for cold; and to lift one's spirits.'

William pulled a chair from the table.

'Thank you,' she whispered and sat down.

William moved to the other side of the table to take the chair offered by Elijah.

'When will you leave?' asked Ruth.

The question surprised him, as she had not appeared to be thinking of anything in particular. 'That depends on you.'

'William, I can't marry you if you want me to go Liverpool. I can't sell my father's company, which is mine now. I intend to stay and manage it myself.'

'But you are a woman!'

'Yes, I am a woman. Do you see that as a problem?'

'No, I don't see your being a woman as being a problem, but I can foresee problems with the company. Running a company, and a shipping company at that is not a feminine role. In my opinion running a company is better done by men.'

'Why should men have all the pleasure of business? Why is it acceptable for a woman to be Queen, and to run a country, but unacceptable for a woman to run a company? Think about your country's history. Wasn't Elizabeth a woman?'

'She was different, as well you know, Ruth. She was born to the position, so there isn't any comparison between Queen Elizabeth and a woman running a company.'

'Why not? If she could run a whole country then my running a company shouldn't be too hard. And as far as being born to rule, may I remind you that I was born into this company and have spent years learning its management from my father.'

'But I love you!'

'Enough to give me the chance to run my own life?'

'Ruth, my place is where the expansion of my company will take place, and that is in the East.'

'I fear that I can see myself taking second place to your company.'

'But you can help me build the company. Think on it, both of us together, building the company and running it between us!'

His enthusiasm for the company was infectious. Ruth could feel herself starting to waver. She picked up her glass and drank some of the wine. It helped calm her nerves. She wanted to end the conversation. It was going nowhere.

'William, I am sorry but I cannot marry you if you wish for me to live in Liverpool. I wish to stay and run my company here in Boston.'

'Is that your final word, Ruth?'

'I am sorry, but it is.'

William picked up his glass and swallowed a deep draught of wine and watched her over the top of his glass. He could see her eyes and he knew she would not give in to him. Perhaps another way could be found. He would do anything to keep Ruth. He loved her and wanted to marry her, but he could understand her reluctance to give up her father's company so soon after his death. On the other hand he had business in Liverpool to make sure the Nicholson family was not taking advantage of his father. He had to return to Liverpool. If Ruth could keep her company going until his return, he would live in Boston if she would marry him. He estimated that he would be away for between twelve and eighteen months. Would her love for him stand an eighteen-month separation?

He placed the glass on the table and dipped a finger in the remains of the wine and ran his finger around the rim of the glass, causing it to give off a high-pitched hum. He made a decision. He removed his finger from the rim and reached across to take one of Ruth's hands.

'Let us have an understanding.'

'An understanding of what?' asked Ruth as she leaned forward to assist William to hold her hand.

'Each of us will build and run our own company for a year. After that time I will come back and ask you to marry me again. I want to marry you, Ruth, and so I will move to Boston. First of all, though, I must return to Liverpool to make sure my father is not ill or being taken advantage of by the Nicholson family.'

Ruth listened to William's plans for their future, and to his plans for hiring a managing agent in Liverpool. While he spoke, she gripped his hand tighter as the realisation dawned on her as to how much he loved her.

'Oh! William, I do love you. Thank you. Yes, yes, I will wait for you.'

She withdrew her hand from his grasp and picked up her

wine glass. She saluted him with the glass and drank.

'A year,' she said and waved for Elijah to refill her glass.

William picked up his glass and toasted, Ruth, replying 'A year.'

He felt the *Black Swan* shudder as she met the first of the Atlantic rollers. Spume flew across the deck, turning to spray before splattering William and drawing him back to the present. The wind was strengthening and he heard his First Mate shout for more sail. The shoreline had become a smudge on the horizon.

- CHAPTER THIRTY-SIX -

Charlotte's return

Liverpool
April 1807

Charlotte picked a piece of thread from her cape and flicked it to the floor of the coach. She hated herself today. Her body was not her own. She felt tired and every bump of the coach reminded her of how ugly her body had become. She hated George King and his son.

The coach rattled over cobbles and swayed, causing Charlotte to fall sideways on to the woman next to her. She groaned as she felt the child kick. The other female passenger smiled in pity at Charlotte and helped her to sit up again.

'Are you alright, my dear?'

'Thank you, I'm fine,' snapped Charlotte, brushing her cloak once again.

The other woman sighed and glanced at Charlotte's large body. 'Do you have long to go, dear?'

'To Liverpool.'

'No, dear, I meant——,' and she pointed to the large bulge

under Charlotte's cloak.

'Oh, that; I have another six weeks, according to the doctor. Not that he knows anything, being a man.'

The other passenger smiled in sympathy. She gazed at her sleeping husband. 'I know what you mean.'

'How much longer are we to be tortured by this coach?'

'Not long now, dear; we have passed Prescott, so we should be in Liverpool in less than an hour.'

Charlotte jammed herself into the corner of her seat and closed her eyes in the hope that she would be left alone. At the moment the whole world annoyed her. Even her Aunt Dorothy annoyed her by questioning why she was visiting without her husband, George.

Aunt Dorothy should have been happy that she had even come to visit. After all, she had to go somewhere once she realised that George would confront his son about her lie. Even her mother had been surprised that she wished to visit Aunt Dorothy. Charlotte hadn't answered her mother's question. She'd just whispered that she was expecting a child. The news had distracted her mother from any further awkward questions.

Being locked away with a maiden Aunt in the hills behind Manchester was depressing. Aunt Dorothy didn't think it proper for a lady in Charlotte's condition to attend dances without a chaperone. Charlotte was never allowed to be alone. Her Aunt's fear of men taking advantage of a young woman annoyed her, when every man could see she was going to have a child. As Charlotte grew, her Aunt Dorothy insisted that they both withdraw from society so as not to offend people. Charlotte considered that the most offended person was herself, particularly when she looked in a mirror. Eventually her Aunt's fussy ways and limited social connections caused Charlotte to pack her bags and return to Liverpool. She preferred to be in Liverpool than pretend any more to her Aunt. She wanted to be rid of the child, so as to get back to her shape before George attacked her. She planned to bring up the child herself, with a lot of help from the servants. The child would always be clean and quiet in her presence. She was not interested in motherhood, unless she had an audience.

'We are here, dear.'

Charlotte felt her arm being gently shaken. She opened her eyes and realised that she must have fallen asleep. The coach stopped and the smell of Liverpool assailed her nostrils. She was home. She allowed her traveling companion to assist her down from the coach.

'Thank you, would you ask the coachman to find me a carriage?'

'Aren't you being met, dear?'

'No, I want to surprise my husband.'

'How romantic!' fluttered the woman, 'Coachman! A carriage for the lady and be quick about it!'

—※—

Fanning herself in an effort to cool her face in the warmth of spring, Charlotte studied the house on Kent Street as the carriage turned into the driveway. It was drab and the gardens were not to her usual standard. The place needed a good woman to take care of it, and she was that woman. She would bring the house and the garden back to her standards.

The carriage stopped under the covered entrance area created by the Ionic columns. Alfred approached.

'Open the door, Alfred, and help me out.'

If she weren't so tired she would have burst into laughter at the expression of astonishment on the servant's face.

Walking up the few steps to the main door of the house, she turned to Alfred. 'Is Mr King at home?'

'No, Ma'am, he out.'

'Have my things taken to my room.'

'Yes, Ma'am, but which room?'

'Which room? The room I have always occupied!'

'Yes, Ma'am.'

It was early May when the *Black Swan* picked up the pilot off Anglesey. The river was crowded with shipping as they approached the basin for George's Dock. William studied the various vessels and tried to imagine if any were for sale or charter. He knew Owen would have all this information at his fingertips.

'William, it is good see you safe and sound.'

'Did you get my letter, Owen?'

'Yes, I did. By the smell of the *Black Swan,* you have a good cargo of fish!'

'Salt fish, timber and a few bales of wool. I assume you will be able to sell them at a good profit.'

'We will get rid of the fish quickly and I will sell the rest at the exchange.'

'I have plans, Owen.'

'Plans?'

'I intend to move my main operation to Boston.'

'What about Liverpool? I've bought another ship, a barque slaver like the *Black Swan*. People were trying to get out of the slave trade last year and there was an opportunity, which I took. Did you hear the great news?'

'What?'

'Parliament passed Wilberforce's Antislavery bill, 283 to 16 ¾ a massive majority. Royal assent was given last month, 25th March. We won!'

'I am pleased for you, Owen.'

'Is that all you can say, you are pleased for me? After all, you helped prove that a ship could make a profit without recourse to slaves.'

'Small contribution, Owen, and I am glad slavery has been outlawed, but the islands of the West Indies are full of slaves. What of them?'

'All in good time; we are already working on abolition across the Empire.'

'You know you have my support, but today I am interested in ships. Where is she?' smiled William, 'I saw a number of vessels in the river. If she's like the *Black Swan* I'll buy her.'

'What are your plans for Liverpool?' asked Owen.

'My plan, dear Owen, is to ask you if you wish to be in control of my Liverpool office.'

'What about your father? He would be the obvious choice for you.'

'My father is an old man and I want someone who will push ahead – you!'

'I'll think on it and let you know in the next few days.'

'Where is she?'

'She, William; I do not know of any young lady in Liverpool for you?'

'Owen, you are being obtuse. The ship, man, the ship! Where is she?'

'On charter carrying emigrants from Ireland to Liverpool.'

'There is no money in that trade!'

'Perhaps not in your mind, but when I mix the revenue from the emigrants from Ireland with the offer of board and lodging in Liverpool while they wait to buy a ticket from me for the voyage to the Americas, the new ship does make money on the Irish run.'

William burst out laughing once he understood the business Owen had created from one ship.

A knock interrupted their conversation and Sang's head showed appeared.

'Yes, Sang, what is it?'

'Mr Austin, Sur, he want to speak you.'

'Send him in.'

'Mr Austin, how are you?'

'Fine, thank you, Sir.'

'I am glad to hear it. You are off now, on leave?'

'Yes, Sir, I wanted to say thank you for everything.'

'Goodbye, Mr Austin, my respects to your mother and be assured there will be a berth for you if you so desire, after you have finished your leave. We expect to be in port for around three weeks.'

'Thank you, Sir, thank you, I will be back before you sail.'

—∞—

George King wanted to be at the wharf when the *Black Swan* arrived. He ordered his carriage to be ready and made sure his clothes were brushed and his boots polished.

He left his carriage at the main road, and with the aid of his cane, walked slowly along the cobbled wharf, breathing in the smell of the river. The rotten seaweed, the smell of the tar and hemp, it all came back to him. He missed the sea. He missed the feel of a ship as she moved in a gentle swell.

George could see the gangway from the *Black Swan* to the dockside. He made his way towards it.

'Father!'

George glanced up at the shout and saw William coming down the gangway, a small man following behind.

George swayed when the cane slipped and jammed in the gap between two cobbled stones.

William moved quickly to his father and held him tight. 'Father, how are you? I am pleased you came down to see me.'

'I wanted to,' whispered the old man, his son's arms crushing him.

'Perhaps, William, a slightly lighter hug; I have not been too well.'

William stepped back and held his father at arm's length and studied his face. 'What has been the problem, Father?'

'I have not been too well and the doctor suggested I take things a little easier.'

'Why did you walk? Where is the carriage?'

'I wanted to experience the docks again. The damn fool of a doctor wants me to sit around while my blood slows to a halt.'

'You should do what the doctor says and take things a little easier. I am home now to help you!'

'Are you giving up the sea?'

'No, no, but I will be around Liverpool for some weeks, so I will be able to help you.'

'Oh,' said George, disappointed that his son would be leaving again so soon.

'May I introduce Owen Johnston? Owen, my father, George King.'

'I had the pleasure of meeting Mr King a couple of years

ago. He kindly invited my mother and myself to dinner to mark the occasion of his new home in Kent Street.'

George leaned forward and studied Owen's face. 'I believe I do know this gentleman. I certainly know your mother. I knew your father very well before his passing.'

'Owen is selling for me,' commented William.

'Oh, I see,' said George.

Once he had gone, George said, 'Strange fellow you have as a friend.'

'How so?'

'I distinctly remember him at my house, before I married. He didn't drink the toast Nicholson made. I thought then that he was strange.'

'Not strange, Father, just different. The toast was to damn Mr Wilberforce by calling him a butterfly. Mr Wilberforce is a very close friend of Owen.'

'Aham ! Maybe so, but he is still a strange fellow.'

'No more, Father, I do not want to quarrel with you. I have been away a long time.'

'When can you leave? Will you come to dinner tonight?'

'I will be ready in an hour or so. Perhaps I should meet you at home.'

'You know Charlotte will be home? She came back last month.'

'I didn't know, but then why should I after so long away?'

'I have forgiven her.'

William studied his father and saw a thin old man, his face lined, and with the worries of the world on his shoulders. The man he knew not so many years ago was gone. His will to enjoy life had left him. William felt an overpowering love for his father and placed his hand gently on his father's shoulder. The gesture made George look up into his son's eyes.

'I felt lonely and she wanted to come back.'

'I will keep my own counsel on Charlotte, for your sake.'

George made an effort to stand straight. He pulled himself up with the aid of his cane. 'I am happy you are home and safe, my boy. Come to dinner tonight and let us all start again.'

'I will look forward to dinner, Father, and I will not cause any upset tonight. I will be pleasant to your wife, if it is what you want?'

'It is what I want. I am tired of fighting. I want to put the past behind, and Charlotte has been a little more attentive to me since she returned from Manchester.'

'How long was she away in Manchester?'

'Several months,' whispered his father. 'I was very lonely and saw little of Donald Nicholson. He used to be my only friend before Charlotte left home, but I can understand him not wishing to spend too much time in my company. Some days I would only speak to the servants or the staff in the office.'

'You have me. I am your friend and your son.'

George appeared to shake off his bad memories. 'I must be going, William, to make sure all is in order for tonight.'

George moved back from William, waved his cane and walked slowly away. He turned after a few feet and said, 'Until tonight then.'

'Until tonight,' answered William, watching his father walk slowly down the wharf, trying to make sure the cane did not slip on the cobbles.

- CHAPTER THIRTY-SEVEN -

Dinner

*Liverpool
May 1807*

William stepped down from the carriage in front of his father's house. 'Thank you,' he said to the tall black man holding the coach door open. 'Alfred, isn't it?'

'Yes, Sir, thank you, Sir.'

William saw his father and his stepmother waiting at the top of the short flight of steps leading to the front door. One look at Charlotte and he realised why his father had taken her back. She was eight months pregnant.

'Father, how are you?' said William and offered his hand.

'Fine, my boy, fine.' His father leaned forward a little on his cane and clasped his son's hand.

'You remember, Charlotte?'

William released his father's hand and turned to Charlotte. 'Ma-am, your servant.' He bowed a little.

'So formal, William, am I allowed to kiss my stepson?'

'If you wish.'

Charlotte kissed him lightly on the cheek.

'We start afresh, William, if it is your wish?'

'I will do whatever I can to ensure father is happy. A new start then,' and he leaned forward to return the kiss. He could smell her expensive perfume and noticed her skin was still flawless. 'Congratulations are in order, I perceive.'

'Thank you, William,' his father said. 'Perhaps it will be a beautiful little girl, like her mother.'

William saw Charlotte blush. Had she changed after all?

Charlotte placed herself between the two men and hooked their arms in hers. 'Two handsome men in the one family, I must be the luckiest girl in Liverpool,' laughed Charlotte.

To William it sounded light-hearted, so he allowed himself to be marched into the house.

On entering the library, Charlotte released her hold and moved to a table on which stood a row of bottles and glasses. 'Drinks are ready. What would you like, William?'

'Brandy, please.'

'George, darling, what would you like?'

'The confounded doctor doesn't like me drinking, you know.' George said to his son, 'but I will outlive them all! Brandy, please.' Charlotte picked up a decanter and poured a generous amount in to one glass and a smaller amount in another.

'I'll serve the drinks; we don't need servants interrupting us.'

'Thank you,' said William as he accepted his drink and sat in an armchair near the fire. He watched Charlotte fuss over his father's drink. She was still a very attractive woman. The emerald-green dress matched her blue-green eyes. He remembered that the first time he had seen her; he thought her eyes were blue.

Charlotte felt someone's eyes on her. She turned quickly and saw William looking at her. She smiled to herself as he quickly looked away. She was still attractive to men, she thought, satisfied, even with her excessive mass.

'Do tell us of your adventures, William,' said Charlotte as she smoothed the silk dress and sat near her husband.

'Not much to tell really.'

'Come, my boy, what about Boston?'

'The town is growing quickly and has a large deep-water harbour. I intend to expand and open an office there.'

'An office; who will manage the Liverpool office?' asked Charlotte.

A small note of caution entered William's mind. The best way to answer his stepmother was to be vague. 'I will have someone to oversee my interests while I am away.'

Before Charlotte could say anything the library door opened, 'Dinner, Sir, it's ready.'

'Thank you, Alfred,' said George. 'William, Charlotte, shall we retire to the dining room?'

On standing, Charlotte again made a point of holding on to each of them as they made their way to the dining room.

The meal progressed pleasantly, and with the help of a number of glasses of wine, there was a great deal of laughter. William was pleased to see his father enjoying himself, especially after their last meeting at his father's club.

Charlotte's eyes flashed between the two men. The wine made her daring and she concentrated her gaze more and more on her stepson. Her face became a little flushed and her laughter a little louder as she consumed more wine.

William felt relaxed for the first time in months. Had he been wrong about Charlotte and perhaps she wasn't as wicked as he first thought? Perhaps the forth-coming baby had made her happy to be the wife of an older man.

'Should we ask the lady to leave?' asked George as the meal drew to a close and Alfred brought in cigars.

'I would give the lady the choice, Father.'

'This lady is not leaving just because you two wish to smoke,' Charlotte laughingly told them.

George selected a cigar, clipped the cap and held it gently while Alfred waved a flame near the unclipped end. George drew on the heat and dragged in the taste of the cigar smoke. He checked the glow at the end, satisfied himself that it was even, nodded at Alfred and settled down to enjoy the smoke and his first glass of port.

William refused a cigar.

'Still not smoking, William?'

'No, Father, I only smoke occasionally.'

'I wish I could smoke,' whispered Charlotte as she rolled a cigar through her fingers.

'Not a lady-like skill, my dear.'

'George, darling, let me try yours.'

'How is the business, Father?'

'Business is good. If you are interested, we no longer send our ships on the African Trade.'

'I am glad to hear that; are they back on the Mediterranean and Baltic trade?'

'Yes, it is much easier to trade in those areas now that Napoleon has lost his fleet.'

'George, darling, did you hear me?' asked Charlotte peevishly.

George sighed. 'Yes, my dear, I did, but you are not to smoke and that is final.'

Charlotte pouted and quickly drank her small glass of port.

She banged the glass down and waited for William to pass the port decanter. William pushed the decanter across the table towards his stepmother. Charlotte poured herself another glass, spilling some on the tablecloth. She glanced up guiltily to see William watching her.

Everything was funny, as well as moving in slow motion. Why hadn't the men laughed when she spilt the wine? She dipped her finger in the spilt port and pressed her wet finger to her mouth and sucked on the tip while staring at William. Men had all the fun, but she knew how to control that fun.

Placing her finger in the pool again she watched her son-in-law as his eyes followed her finger to her mouth.

'William, you are not listening to me!'

'Sorry, Father, what did you say?'

'I am thinking of selling the *Elizabeth* and the *Margaret*. I am too old to worry about them.'

'But you are only in your fifties, Father.'

'I am tired and——'

'You haven't mentioned selling the ships, George,' interrupted Charlotte. Her hand suspended in midair allowing a drop of port to run down her hand and drip back to the table.

'I made up my mind this evening, after seeing William again.'

'But why?' she demanded. 'You have many years left in you. You're not ill.'

'I am tired and want to rest.' He tapped his cigar, allowing the ash to fall into the ashtray.

'Have you received any offers?'

'No, as I said, I have only decided this evening.'

'George, darling you can't sell! What will we live off?'

'I have been successful with the company and have money

set aside, so we will not want for much.'

'The ships are old, Father, and I fear that their best years have past.'

'Aye, I know, but someone will always buy them if they can still sail.'

William sipped his port and looked at his father. He did seem older than his years. Perhaps he was sick. He couldn't imagine Liverpool without his father. The idea of the *Margaret Rose* and the *Elizabeth Rose* being sold to someone who may treat them as nothing more than coal hulks, or worse, was not something he wished to think about.

His mind sifted several thoughts as he calculated the cost of the two ships. The average cost of a new ship was about fifteen pounds a ton. Using the *Albatross* as a comparison at 162 tons, she would have cost about two and a half thousand pounds, new, but he bought her cheaply on a falling market. His father's ships would be worth about seven or eight hundred pounds each. He decided that if he used them on the American east coast trade they would return a fair profit.

'Father, I'll buy them both.'

'Both! Where will you get the money to buy two ships?' asked his father.

'If you want the two *Roses* to be taken care of, then I am the person who will do it.'

'But, father was going——' interrupted Charlotte.

'But?' asked William, scrutinising Charlotte, 'do you wish to buy them?'

'Of course I can't buy them, what would I do with two ships?' Her voice rose in anger.

'Calm yourself, my dear, William didn't mean anything.'

Charlotte sat back in the chair, aware of a tightening in her chest as she tried to control her anger. She stared at William and lips shrank to a thin line. One day, she thought, I will have my revenge.

The thought calmed her a little, so she allowed her fists to slowly unclench and placed her hands palm down on the tablecloth. She would wait for the right time.

She studied William, who had not looked at her since asking if she wished to buy the two ships. Slowly her face relaxed. She opened her eyes wider in an effort to reflect innocence.

The two ships were destined for her father. Donald Nicholson wanted to use them on the slave trade to Brazil. For a small fee, his Portuguese agents would be happy to acknowledge that the two vessels were theirs. When George died, the ships would pass to Charlotte to do with them as she pleased. She knew that George's health was deteriorating fast. William's concerned looks over dinner had confirmed her thoughts. If he sold the ships now, Charlotte doubted there would be enough money to build or buy two new ships for her father.

'You are quite correct, George, I am sure, dear, William didn't mean to upset me.'

'If I did, I am sorry,' said William, turning to look at Charlotte.

'Not worth falling out, William, dear; let's forget it ever happened.' She smiled with her large round eyes.

William found himself reflecting her smile. 'Thank you,' he said, and nodded his head.

'How will I be paid for the ships if you don't have the money?' asked George, breaking into William's thoughts.

'I will pay you interest until I have paid off the debt. I will be leaving for Boston on the *Black Swan* in the next few weeks, so the *Swan* and the two *Roses* can sail in convoy. The *Roses* will trade around the American coast and down to the West Indies. I will be away for about a year so. On my return I will pay you the money I owe, plus interest at, say, 5%. Of all the potential buyers you know, you will be paid by me.'

'But suppose something happens to you, heaven forbid,' said Charlotte in her best little-girl-lost voice.

'I will leave instructions that the ships are to revert to father on my death, unless I pay for them beforehand. Also, if you can find a cash buyer for them before I sail, I will relinquish claim to them and you can sell to that buyer.'

'That seems fair, my dear. William, I think I will sleep on it and let you know tomorrow. I assume you will stay the night and not go back to your ship?'

'If you wish, Father. The *Black Swan* has instructions that if I am not back by midnight, they are to assume I have stayed the night.'

'Then I am off to bed. I feel very tired. First, the excitement of your being home and second, I have sold the *Roses*. Goodnight, my dear. Goodnight, William.'

'Goodnight, Father.' William stood and placed his arms around the old man and hugged him.

'Good night, George, darling,' whispered Charlotte.

'Goodnight, Charlotte, don't keep William up too long.'

The door closed behind the old man.

'Do you know why he wishes to sell?' asked William.

Charlotte pushed her chair back and stood up. 'If I knew that, I would understand him a little better. He never mentioned it to me.'

'Is he well?'

'He never complains about feeling ill.'

William moved about the room, touching the furniture and letting his fingers run along the backs of the chairs. He studied the pictures on the walls, particularly one of a four-mast ship being tossed about in a wild storm. Do all naval families surround themselves with pictures of ships in storms or battles?

Charlotte watched him. 'You seem to have made a success of trading and being Captain of your ship.'

'I thought all I wanted was to be Captain of my own ship. I now have two ships, a possible third about to join, and I have committed to buy my father's. I can see I will spend less and less time as a ship's Captain. I can't run a trading company from the deck of a ship. I have to put down roots.'

'Roots in England?'

'I am not sure at the moment.'

'You will need a good woman to help you.'

'I have a good woman; she's in Boston.'

'Beautiful?'

'Very.'

'You haven't mentioned it to your father.'

'I have been waiting for the right moment.'

Charlotte filed away the information and wondered what kind of woman attracted William. She surmised that with William's ambition, she would be a woman of substance, if not rich.

'Is she accompanying you on this trip?'

'No, she's in Boston, and she is waiting for me to return. Her father died recently and she couldn't leave the business.'

Charlotte smiled. William confirmed her suppositions.

'How is your father?' asked William.

'A quick change of subject, William! He's fine. I am sure he would want me to pass on his best wishes to you.'

'Thank you; please reciprocate my felicitations to your mother as well.'

'Hmmm.'

'How is Henry?'

'He is at sea.'

'When did he sail?'

'I believe he has been away for over a year. Why do you ask?'

'I heard he visited Boston; perhaps I was mistaken.'

'Yes, you must have been.'

'What is your father doing, now the African trade is illegal?'

Charlotte sucked in her breath. Why had William asked such a question? 'He trades here and there. He offers a broking service and buys space on other ships and sells it to those who wish to buy. Why do you ask?'

'No reason, I know father was a partner with your father until recently, and with the current anti-slave laws, I felt curious as to how your father managed the change.'

'He is successful, as one would expect of my father.'

'I'm sure; well, I think I will go to bed. May I escort you to your room?'

'Thank you, no. I wish to have a few words to the servants before I retire. Please don't let me delay you.' Charlotte moved towards the door and opened it as if about to leave. She held on to the door handle.

At the door, William waited for Charlotte to exit the room. She didn't, so he placed a hand on the door and pulled it gently towards him. Charlotte released her grip and allowed the door to open. She did not move.

William was forced to pass close to Charlotte, and in doing

so, breathed in her perfume. His gaze couldn't help but pass over the exposed tops of her breasts. He stopped halfway through the doorway and stared into her eyes, 'Goodnight, Charlotte.'

'Goodnight, William,' she replied, allowing her tongue to brush gently over her lips. 'I will see you in the morning.'

'Until the morning,' he answered, and pushed through the narrow gap.

- CHAPTER THIRTY-EIGHT -

The Invitation

Liverpool
May 1807

It was over a week since he had made his offer to his father to buy the two *Roses*. Word had quickly spread that the ships were for sale. Would anyone match or better his offer? William stamped his feet in an effort to generate some feeling in them. He and Owen stood on the small rise that dominated the turning basin into George's dock.

'She is due in this morning.'

'Owen, you have been telling me that for the past hour.'

'She is regular and I am surprised she hasn't arrived yet.'

'Perhaps a contrary wind held her back.'

Owen turned to the sound of singing that came from St Nicholas church behind where they stood.

'I'd forgotten it is Sunday.'

'See the spire on the church, Owen?'

'Yes.'

'It can be seen for miles downriver. It is an excellent marker for those coming up river.'

I believe so. I am cold. She is due in this morning.'

'Owen!'

'Sorry, William.'

William watched the river traffic and half-listened to the singing from the church. He found himself humming the tune of the hymn.

'Owen, look.'

Owen followed William's gaze and saw a strange craft punching its way across the river. She was a small vessel with a paddle wheel in the middle of her hull, which gave the impression that the bow and stern were two small boats. The paddle wheel appeared to cut her in half.

'She's the *Etna,*' said Owen. 'Operates from Tranmere across to Liverpool. She is one of the new steamboats, or floating kettles, as some call her. I have seen her some days covered in so much steam that you'd think she was on fire. I heard the Poole family started the service as competition to the sailing ferry service from Birkenhead. She's been in service a couple of months.'

William watched the small steamboat battle her way across the river. The wind and the tide didn't affect her progress. He felt he was watching the future unfold.

'There's the *Lady Ann*!' cried Owen.

William shielded his eyes and stared out across the river. 'A fine ship.'

'Aye, she is,' answered Owen, hopping from one leg to the other in excitement.

William heard the sound of someone snorting. He recognised the sound and turned to see Donald Nicholson a few feet behind.

'I thought it be you, King. Saw you as I came out of church.'

'Good morning, Mr Nicholson, how are you?'

'I'm fine.'

Turning to Owen, Nicholson asked, 'Owen Johnston, isn't it?'

'Good morning, Mr Nicholson, you are correct. I am he.'

'And what are you two taking such an interest in this cold morning?'

'Watching the traffic on the river, Mr Nicholson,' said William quickly.

'William,' snorted Donald Nicholson, 'please don't take me for a fool. I think you have been waiting for the arrival of the *Lady Ann* from Ireland. I see she is closing the bank now.'

'Perhaps, Mr Nicholson.'

'Perhaps, my foot; I am aware Mr Johnston bought the *Lady Ann* a few weeks ago. Nothing gets by me in Liverpool.'

'Glad to hear it, Mr Nicholson, at least I know where to come for information,' said William in a clipped tone.

'It has been some time since we spoke, but I remember you sailed off to America. Grand ideas, I heard, of trading to the Caribbean and not carrying slaves. Telling everyone a profit could be made by trading in non-slave commodities.'

'You have a good memory, Mr Nicholson. I believe I have proved it can be done.'

Donald Nicholson snorted once again. 'That is a matter of opinion, a matter of opinion, but all in the past. I came down to ask if you two gentlemen would honour me with your company this evening? I have invited your father, William, and Charlotte. Just a few drinks between friends.'

William glanced at Owen and tried to read his mind.

'You are included in the invitation, Mr Johnston.'

'I——I would be very pleased to accept your kind invitation, Mr Nicholson,' said William as he watched Owen.

'And I, Mr Nicholson, will be honoured to attend.'

'That's settled, then. Well, I can't stand here all day; must be off. The ladies will wonder where I am.'

'Goodbye, Mr Nicholson,' chorused William and Owen.

Owen replaced his doffed hat, and when Nicholson was out of earshot, turned to William and whispered, 'I don't like that man at all.'

'Not many do, Owen, but don't let him bother you. What about the *Lady Ann*?'

The two friends stood and watched the *Lady Ann* as she began to turn to larboard in the river. She began her swing through 180 degrees to stem the flood tide. She was slowly turning to face the North Pier when a gust of wind caught her bow and halted the swing. Her sails were in the process of being hauled round to the other tack, to allow her to complete the turn, and berth. The sudden gust of wind had the effect of pushing her back from whence she came. She began to fall off. She had missed her chance to stem the tide. She was on the cusp of falling back to starboard, out of control.

'She is in irons! She can't swing either way now. He's losing her. He'll not have enough time to set his sails to gain control. Anchor, man, anchor!' yelled William, unable to control his concern.

Owen stared at the *Lady Ann,* and then at William's face as he called out instructions. He knew the Captain of the *Lady Ann* could not hear William's shouts, and becoming agitated, began to jump from one foot to the other.

'What can we do?' asked Owen.

'Nothing but watch.'

Suddenly the *Lady Ann* began to turn back towards the North

Pier. She was carrying through with her original turn. The men in the yards frantically tried to reset the sails back to the original tack. Slowly she swung to larboard. William watched her Captain as he bellowed orders and exhorted his crew to haul tight on the braces. She came under control of the sails as she increased the speed of her swing. William watched her complete the manoeuvre and stem the running tide, which gave her Captain the control he needed to bring the *Lady Ann* alongside North Pier. Lines snaked out from the vessel to secure her to the land.

Owen grabbed William's arm and shouted, 'Look!' He pointed to a cloud of steam moving away from the *Lady Ann*.

'The *Etna* must have pushed her bow around,' said William in astonishment.

Owen released his grip and stared open-mouthed at the scene on the river.

'A fine ship, Owen!'

'Aye, she is. Come on. As soon as she's discharged her passengers, she will move from the Pier to an anchorage in the river. The fees are cheaper than leaving her alongside.' Owen started to run down the path to the pier.

William watched the crew assist the passengers ashore and single the mooring lines. He kept recalling how the *Etna* had pushed the *Lady Ann* out of serious trouble. It was something to remember. He checked over the side for any damage to the *Lady Ann,* but apart from some scratched paintwork, she appeared to be in order. William and Owen stayed on the *Lady Ann* while she manoeuvered into the river and anchored off Birkenhead.

It was obvious that the *Lady Ann's* crew was well trained. They were smartly dressed in a makeshift uniform and worked with a will. The captain must have paid for some of the clothing himself. No owner would put his hand in his pocket to spend money on uniforms for his crews. William could see the pride the crew had as they went about their duties.

On boarding, Owen had spoken to Captain Shaw and introduced William as his nautical advisor.

While Owen stayed by the Captain, William made his inspection. She was dry below decks and the hold had been whitewashed to help mask the stink of her slaving days. As with the Albatross, he used his knife to satisfy himself that she was sound. He would ask if Captain Shaw had been the Captain when she sailed as a slaver.

He heard the splash of the anchor as it hit the water and continued his inspection. He did not ask permission to enter the crew's area in the forecastle; he wanted to see what it was like without announcing himself. It was clean and neat, a sign of regular inspections by the Captain.

On deck, he leaned back to study the masts and watched as the crew furled the sails. If the standard of maintenance of the hull and the crew's accommodation had been carried through to the masts and sails, there was little to worry about.

William climbed the short flight of steps to the poop deck and watched Captain Shaw salute Owen before making his way below.

'She is a fine ship, Owen!' called William as he stepped onto the deck.

'Glad you think so. I visited a number before I bought the *Lady Ann*. I am told she is fast.'

'Who told you? The previous owner, before you bought her?' William asked with a smile.

'No, Captain Shaw did, after I bought her.'

'Owen, I'd like to rename her.'

'I thought that was supposed to be bad luck?'

'Only for those who believe in luck, I don't have the time for luck. When can she sail?'

'What name, William?'

'*Black Hawk,* a bird of a different style to the *Black Swan.*'

'Call her what ever you like, as long as she is profitable!'

'She will be profitable, or else I'll change the Captain. From what I have seen, I don't think I will have much trouble with a Captain who evidently spends his own money on his crew.'

'What will you use her for?'

'Are you joining me, Owen?'

'I suppose so, William, but if you want me to keep up with you, don't run too fast building this trading company.'

William smiled at his friend and offered his hand. 'A partnership in England.'

'In England,' repeated Owen, and shook his friend's hand.

'Her use, Owen, will be on the ice trade; if not to the Caribbean, then to India!'

- CHAPTER THIRTY-NINE -

Nicholson dinner

Liverpool
May 1807

'King!' called a voice from across the room.
He turned and saw Henry Nicholson, and nodded his head in acknowledgment. Nicholson approached William.

'What a shame, that we missed each other in Boston.' The cruel smile never left Henry's face.

'A great shame, Henry.'

'Perhaps we missed each other because I became so preoccupied with Miss Ruth Judson. A lovely woman, don't you think?'

William's face drained of blood at the thought of Ruth being assaulted, even verbally, by Henry Nicholson. William realised he was being baited, and even as a guest in Donald's house, he felt the urge to smash the cruel smile from Henry's face. He tensed, ready to attack.

'Sir,' interrupted a waiter offering a tray of drinks.

'Thank you,' said William, barely containing his rage.

'Henry, don't say another word about Miss Judson in my hearing, is that understood?'

Henry Nicholson cracked his face into a smile and bowed his head in a mock salute.

'Have I touched a nerve, Captain? I do hope so! Until the next time,' and he toasted William with his glass of rum.

William felt himself tremble in anger. Henry moved away to circulate amongst the other guests. In an effort to calm down, he sipped his drink and moved slowly around the room looking for his father. He found him deep in conversation with Charlotte, and a portly man whom he recognised as Thomas Leyland. He remembered that Leyland used to be a slave trader who had made a fortune before becoming Mayor of Liverpool. How had his father become associated with people in such circles?

'William, why so much interest in Mr Leyland?' questioned Owen, who had sauntered over to stand behind William.

William turned. 'Owen, you escaped from the thin-faced lady?'

'No thanks to you; if you knew I'd been shanghaied, why didn't you rescue me?'

'You seemed so happy, my friend,' laughed William.

'Why are you so intent on, Mr Leyland?' asked Owen, pressing his earlier question.

'Oh! Just wondering what his business interests are now, that the African trade has stopped.'

'Banking!'

'Banking?'

'Yes, he and a partner, a Mr Bullin, have started a bank. They have new offices in York Street, near his old offices in Henry Street.'

' Why is father talking to him so closely?'

'Perhaps he is discussing the sale of his two ships or asking advice as to their likely value.'

'I don't like the look of it at all!'

As William watched, the small group parted. Charlotte moved away from her husband and glanced around the room. She saw William watching, raised her glass in a small salute, and began to move towards him.

William followed her graceful glide across the floor. Her dress hid most of her pregnancy, so that she seemed just a little over-weight. As she moved, she acknowledged people with smiles and allowed a number of men to kiss her hand in greeting. She appeared to be in charge of every greeting. William could see how men were grateful for the small acknowledgment from Charlotte that they were still in her coterie of friends and acquaintances.

'A beautiful lady, William,' murmured Owen as they watched her progress.

'Yes, but dangerous.'

'William,' called Charlotte, 'I didn't know you were coming to this gathering.'

'Charlotte, good evening; I didn't know either, until this morning when your father invited me.'

'Oh, yes, he did say something about meeting you. Outside the church, I believe. I never took you for a church attendee, William.'

'I'm not. You know Owen?'

'We have met before. Good evening, Mr Johnston.'

'Mrs King;' bowed Owen and kissed Charlotte's hand, 'an honour.'

The crash of a gong rolled around the room, bringing immediate silence.

'Ladies and gentlemen, dinner awaits; pray take your partners!'

Charlotte glanced about because she wanted to choose the right male to take her in to dinner.

'Charlotte, my dear,' called her husband as he crossed the room.

The flick of her fan gave William an indication that she was not pleased to be escorted to dinner by her husband, not when there were so many handsome young men in the room.

'Come, my dear,' said her husband, holding out his arm.

'William, my boy, a pleasure to see you.'

'And you too, Father.' William watched his father and stepmother join the crowd entering the dining room.

'I have promised to escort Miss Cross to dinner,' mumbled Owen, his eyes averted from William's.

'Miss Cross?'

'The lady you called thin-faced.'

'My dear fellow, I had no idea——'

In a semi-whisper, Owen quickly said, 'Stop, William! Say no more. Miss Cross is behind you. Miss Cross, my arm?'

Owen held his arm out for the young lady and followed the other diners.

William smiled at Miss Cross and bowed slightly as she was whisked away by Owen.

Finishing his drink, William waited for the crowd to thin around the doorway to the dining room. Being single, he anticipated he would be seated at the furthest point away from his host and hostess, allowing him to watch the other guests without the necessity of making pointless conversation.

―⚬―

William ate and drank little. The noise in the room grew louder as the wine and brandy took control of the guests' tongue.

Gazing around, he wondered how many more saddles of lamb or stuffed birds could be brought out. After the food on the *Black Swan,* he found the Nicholson's food to be too rich.

His neighbours asked a few questions of him, but lost interest when they realised he did not have any gossip to contribute. He was pleased to be left alone, as it allowed him to think of Ruth.

The servants set down decanters of port on the table and waited for the ladies to leave before offering the gentlemen cigars and snuff.

William contemplated how to make his escape. Some of the male guests were leaving the dining room with the ladies. He glanced around for Owen, but could not see him. Then he heard his voice.

'William, I think there is going to be a meeting. Those of us who are not involved have been asked to help entertain the ladies. I have been informed that I am one of those not invited to the meeting.'

William's head shot round in surprise Owen. 'You startled me.'

'I did not wish to advertise my thoughts.'

'I'll see you after, then?'

Owen nodded and moved quickly to join the last few guests leaving the dining room. A servant stood by the door, and as the last guest left, he closed the double doors and turned a key in the lock.

William replaced his chair close to the table, having decided to tell his host that he did not feel well, and would beg his forgiveness for leaving such a splendid party earlier than intended.

He felt a soft touch on his arm and turned to see his father standing beside him.

'William, would you like to join us?'

'For what, Father?'

'A glass of port, and a chat about the future; there may be something in the conversation of interest to you, now that you wish to buy the two *Roses*.'

William watched the remaining guests gathering near the top end of the table. At the head of the table, drawing on a cigar, sat Donald Nicholson, with his son alongside him. Banker Leyland was passing the port decanter to two men William had not seen before.

'If you wish me to, Father,' responded William quietly.

'It is only right you should hear the alternative ideas for the two ships.'

'I thought you agreed to sell them to me?'

'I asked advice of Mr Leyland and Donald. I trust you, my boy, but I am not absolutely sure that I wish to sell the ships at all.'

Donald Nicholson waved his hand expansively when William approached. He indicated a chair across from his son, next to Mr Leyland.

'William, it's very kind of you to attend my little gathering this evening. The food to your liking?'

'An interesting evening, Mr Nicholson, thank you.'

'Gentlemen, this is Captain King, George's son. The good Captain is an up-and-coming trader in Liverpool and has interests as far as Boston.'

A murmur of greetings came from the two strangers and the banker.

'Gentlemen,' nodded William, and sat down.

'Help yourselves, Gentlemen. The port is from Lisbon, as are these two gentlemen. Senor Emmanuel Rodrigues and Senor

Pero Essa.'

William poured himself a small glass of port and sipped the ruby-red liquid. It was excellent.

'Senor Essa, would you give us your proposals?' asked Donald Nicholson to one of the two foreigners.

'Thank you, Mr Nicholson,' said the Portuguese, glancing at the other guests before saying, 'my friend and I trade wine and cork to England from Portugal, and we also trade to Brazil. Napoleon's army threatens my country. If we cannot stop him, our King will flee to Brazil and set up his court in Rio de Janeiro. Many will follow, and as a result we will have expanded trade between Brazil and Europe. To supply the needs of my countrymen in Brazil, we need ships, which is why I am here. I heard that Senor King has two ships for sale.' At the mention of George, the Portuguese waved his hand towards William's father.

William's mind was in a quandary at being included in the meeting. If his father had been offered a higher price for the ships, William expected him to take advantage of the offer.

Donald Nicholson's voice broke into his thoughts. 'Mr Leyland spoke to me about investments for his new bank. I was aware of Senor Essa's requirement for ships, so I invited him to meet Mr Leyland. Senor Essa does not wish to buy the ships outright, but to charter them. Now, George, here, wishes to sell his ships and not have them chartered.' Turning towards the Portuguese he continued, 'Please carry on, Senor Essa.'

Pero Essa sipped his port as he gathered his thoughts. 'I require sound ships and experienced crews. I wish to have a Portuguese Captain and the ship must appear to be Portuguese. It will make things a lot easier when we reach Brazil if the ship is, or appears to be, Portuguese. We are willing to pay a high rate to charter the ships, but we do not wish to own them. We are traders, not ship owners.'

Donald Nicholson interrupted the Portuguese speaker again. 'This is the heart of the proposal.' He waved his hand around the table. 'To assist George to gain cash for the sale of the two ships, I propose that we buy the two ships and charter them to Senor Essa and his partners.'

'How do you propose to split the cost of purchasing the ships?' asked Henry.

'We will offer shares in ownership of the ships in the same manner that we offer shares in cargo when we trade.'

Henry leaned back in his chair. 'I cannot afford to invest in trading ships. I have my money committed to other investments.'

'Mr Leyland will take the majority of the shares. George, and also myself, can take up the balance, if George wishes to invest. After all, he will have the cash once he's sold the ships to us.'

Thomas Leyland laughed at the idea of someone selling something they owned and then buying back a small share.

At this point William had a feeling of disquiet. 'What cargo will you be trading to Brazil, Senor Essa?'

'Why, slaves, Captain King; they are desperately needed in Brazil.' William saw the expression on the face of the Portuguese. It was an expression that told him that with the money involved he was stupid to consider any other cargo. 'Father,' said William, turning to his father, 'for a British ship to carry slaves will be illegal.' The scar on William's cheek became prominent as his anger grew.

'My boy, there are ways around a stupid law,' said Donald Nicholson.

The patronising comment further inflamed William's anger.

'It is the law, Father; you cannot allow the ships to be sold to a slaver.'

'We are not buying the ships, Senor,' said Essa misunderstanding William's comment.

'Father, sell the ships to me. We agreed, don't——'

'It is not your decision, William,' said Donald quietly.

William glared at Donald Nicholson. 'Why did you invite me to this meeting?'

George responded. ' It is only right that you should have the opportunity to make an investment, and a profit from the sale of your family's ships.'

'Father, you will be allowing our ships to be sold into an illegal arrangement. If they are stopped at sea by our navy, and it comes to light that they are British ships, and you knew what was happening, then you will be ruined.'

'The navy,' sneered Henry Nicholson, 'why would they stop a Portuguese ship?'

'My father's ships will not be Portuguese; they will be, and are, English! Don't be like the French and underestimate the British navy.'

'William,' shouted his father, 'we have the opportunity to make a lot of money from this venture. The slave trade is still legal in Portugal and in Brazil. We will not be breaking their law. The ships will be under Portuguese control and will fly their flag.'

'They will be owned by an English partnership and you will risk losing them altogether. If the moral issue cannot persuade you, then think of the loss to the family if they are seized by our navy.'

'Moral issue,' sneered Henry Nicholson, 'since when has the Trade been a moral issue?'

'From the beginning of time,' shouted William, pushing back his chair and standing. He leaned on the table and glared at Henry Nicholson. 'Some of us have woken up to that fact earlier than others.'

The group sat in silence, watching William and waiting for his next comment.

'Mr Nicholson,' William said in a calmer voice to Donald, 'thank you for dinner. I believe I can no longer stay under your roof. What is proposed here this evening is illegal, immoral and doomed to failure, so I bid you all goodnight. Father, will you accompany me?'

He waited for his father and prayed that he would join him, and leave the meeting.

'I have agreed to sell the ships to Mr Leyland.'

'You had already agreed to sell them to me, Father,' said William in a quiet voice.

'Yes, and in a year I might get paid.'

'You will get paid and you will earn interest on the outstanding amount until I can pay the agreed price.'

'William, I want the cash now.'

'So be it, goodnight gentlemen.' William turned and strode towards the locked door.

'In your opinion the slave trade is a moral issue?' called out Henry Nicholson.

William stopped, half-turned and glanced back at the faces of the small group that watched him.

'If you cannot see that, then there is little hope for you,' William replied.

'It must be very pleasant to pick and choose your moral issues.'

'I do not despise the Trade because it is immoral, but because I have seen the result of people being dragged from their homes and shipped across the sea.'

William watched the face of Henry Nicholson as it twisted in hatred. The broad bridge across his nose seemed to swell, which made his eyes appear smaller.

'Because you have seen the slave ships, you think you can now judge the rest of us?'

'The Trade breaks up families and villages, and the whole way of life for the African. It is cruel and barbaric.'

'So it is fine to be a slave in one's own country, but not to be one overseas.'

'Of course it isn't fine to be a slave, regardless of where one is. I have no more desire to discuss this with you, as it would be a waste of time. Goodnight once again, gentlemen.'

The group around the table sensed something was about to happen. They watched as Henry baited William again.

'I don't see why you shouldn't join us; after all, you have contributed to the slave trade in the last year.'

William turned and stared at Henry Nicholson and said, 'Unless you can prove that, I will call you out.'

'Do you deny you stole four blacks in Cuba?'

'I do deny being involved in stealing blacks in Cuba, or anywhere else. Goodnight.'

'Goodnight, Captain King, and next time you are in Boston, count the number of blacks working for your friend, the Jew. Your agent in Boston is a trader and also a user of blacks who are in servitude. It appears you are the only one who isn't aware of this small fact.'

'Abraham Judson is——was, a fine man, and he only employed

free men, black or white.'

'Yet think of this, each day he transported his blacks from his estate to work in Boston, because only the blacks slept at his estate. If they were truly free, why didn't they live in Boston? Was it because he didn't actually pay his blacks in money, but just fed and housed them in the same manner as is done with blacks on the Jamaican sugar plantations? Go, Captain, and think on that!'

William, ground his teeth tightly, opened the door and left the room in a fury.

- CHAPTER FORTY -

Hatred flows

Liverpool
May 1807

William ducked his head and entered the large cabin. Henry Nicholson stood with his back to the windows. Sunlight bounced off the water of the dock, causing his figure to be but a dark shape.

'Captain King, is this a social call?'

'It is not, and I would like you to arrange a retraction of the lies printed in today's *Gore Advertiser*.'

'What has it got to do with me?'

'I believe you, or your father, arranged for those lies to be printed. You know damn well that I have never taken part in The Trade.'

'I did hear that you stole four blacks in Havana, and lost one before you reached your ship. Kidnapping blacks is trading in slaves, as far as I am concerned.'

—⚭—

William was curious as to how Henry had found out about the rescue in Havana. 'Will you retract this article?'

'No, I believe it to be true,' Nicholson said as he moved towards his desk.

William tensed, not sure what Henry Nicholson was about to do.

'Have you learned to smoke?' asked Henry, and opened a box on the desk to remove a long thin black cigar.

'Nicholson, no more delays; this has to be settled.'

'Are you challenging me?'

'Yes!'

'As the one challenged, I have the choice of weapons. I choose pistols.'

William nodded at Nicholson, then turned to Owen.

'Owen, will you be my second?'

'My pleasure, William,' said Owen, doing his best to stand still. He could feel the hatred between the two men and knew that it would be pointless to interfere.

'Millers Dam, at sunrise?' Henry proposed in a low voice.

'Millers Dam,' repeated William.

The two men stared at each other with hate and loathing.

'Until tomorrow, Captain Nicholson.' William inclined his head in a small bow, turned, and followed Owen.

—⚜—

'Sang! Rum, chop, chop!' shouted William.

'William, are you really going to fight Henry Nicholson?' asked Owen.

'Of course, why do you ask?'

'Because I hear that he is very good with a pistol.'

'I must admit that I would have preferred swords. I have had plenty of practice against the French with swords, but he picked pistols, so pistols it must be.'

'Are you a good shot?'

'Not bad; steady in the arm and not too bad at accuracy.'

'Captain, Sur, rum as you ordered.'

'Thank you, Sang, please have my green jacket and white pants brushed and ready for tomorrow. I have a meeting at dawn.'

'Aye, Sur.'

'After we finish this drink, Owen, will you wait here for me? I wish to see my father.'

'Yes, William, I'll wait,' replied Owen in a subdued voice. Would his friend be killed in a stupid duel?

After William had left the *Black Swan,* Owen sat in silence thinking of all the things that had happened in the last couple of days. He sighed as he realised there was no way he could stop the duel in the morning.

'More rum, Sur?'

'Thank you, Sang, just a drop more.'

'I hear you and Captain talking about duel. I sponge Captain's coat and lay out clean shirt for fight tomorrow?'

'He will like that, Sang, thank you. Have you seen a duel?'

'No, Sur, I have seen Chinese man fight and I have seen Captain fight in Havana, but not seen a duel.'

'They will stand about twenty paces apart, aim their pistols, and each will fire in the hope of killing the other. Such a waste.'

Sang stood holding the Captain's green jacket and studied Owen. 'What happen if Captain lose?'

'Father, have you seen the paper?' asked William.

William's father sat at his desk with the *Gore Advertiser* spread in front of him.

'I was just reading it.'

'Henry Nicholson is a liar.'

'That may be so, but what can be done about this?' replied George, waving his hand across the open pages.

'What can be done, will be done tomorrow morning.'

'So will the *Advertiser* print a retraction then?'

'I don't know about that, Father, but I do know that I have called Henry Nicholson out, and will meet him at Millers Dam at dawn tomorrow.'

'NO!' screamed his father, making William jump in his chair. 'You can not fight him!'

'Cannot, Father? Why can't I fight him?'

'With what will you fight?'

'Pistols.'

'No, William! Call it off, sail now, but please don't fight him.'

'Why?'

'He is the best shot in Liverpool. He has already killed two men in duels. The only reason he is not in prison or has not been hanged is because of his father's influence. After each duel his father made sure that Henry sailed on the first tide. By the time he returned the duel was forgotten.'

'I have no intention of being shot,' stated William with more confidence than he felt.

'How many duels have you fought?'

'None!'

'Then be guided by me. I fought one when I was a young man and the strain of standing and waiting to be shot at is far greater than that in battle. It is so cold-blooded and Henry Nicholson is the coldest-blooded person I have ever met.'

'Father, I will not back down and Henry will not retract his accusations, so we will fight tomorrow. I came to inform you and to say that if anything goes wrong, I want you to send the *Black Swan* and the *Albatross* to Boston. Ruth Judson will be the owner. Her father and I had a business arrangement. He has already paid me a token $1 dollar for half of each vessel. I want Ruth to have the opportunity of paying you the balance of the cost of each vessel. I have left my share of the two ships to you, but I have detailed what I would like to happen in this letter. There is a share of the ice trade to Jamaica, which I have left to Ruth along with all my money and goods. Once you meet her you will understand why I have left her everything except the two halves of the ships.'

'Why didn't you leave the ships to her father?'

'Abraham, her father, died last year and Ruth is now in control. My plan is to marry her after I have seen that you are settled. Charlotte has returned and she is about to have your child. I am happy for you. If I survive tomorrow, I intend to leave for Boston and marry Ruth. I will operate our two companies from Boston as a single combined company.'

'What of me?'

'Of you, Father?'

'If you are in Boston, I will not see you again. What of us?'

'When your child is old enough to travel, I would hope that you and Charlotte will come out to visit. If Charlotte cannot or will not, you come, as there will always be a place for you.'

'Can't I persuade you to sail now? Please, son, go back to Boston and give up the idea of this stupid duel.'

'I am sorry, Father, but Henry has gone too far this time. He ridiculed all the good men involved with the *Albatross,* and the reason for her being. Even if not for myself, I must fight him for the others. They have been insulted and besmirched by him too.'

George King struggled to his feet and moved around the desk and held his arms out. William's arms folded around his father and the two men stood close, each locked in their own thoughts of yesteryear and things that might have been.

His father eventually let his arms fall, breaking the embrace.

'I am very proud of you, William, and pray that all will go well tomorrow. Come to the house as soon as it is over.'

'Yes, Father, I must go. There are things to arrange.'

'Keep well, my son; now go!'

George King turned his back to his son, but not before William had seen his father's face wet with tears.

'Goodbye, Father,' whispered William closing the door behind him.

- CHAPTER FORTY-ONE -

Millers Dam

*Liverpool
Late May 1807*

William stepped down from Owen's carriage at Millers Dam. He pulled his cloak tighter in an effort to retain some warmth.

He glanced around, and was heedful of the mist hanging over the lake on the Earl of Sefton's estate. It was a good location for a duel, being a few miles out of town, yet close enough that the journey did not take too long. Tracks across the wet grass indicated others had already arrived.

'Ready?' Whispered Owen.

'Yes, I'll wait for your instructions,' answered William, untying his cloak and tossing it into the carriage. He smoothed his jacket for the umpteenth time. It did not feel quite right, as if it no longer fitted correctly. He peered down and saw that Sang must have altered the buttons. They were lower and made the jacket gape at the top.

William watched Owen make his way to the small group of men. He heard the group greet Owen, but could not make out their words.

After a few minutes Owen turned and waved to William to join him. William shrugged his shoulders in an effort to make his jacket fit a little more snugly and stepped out to meet his second.

'How do you feel?' asked Owen as they walked side by side to the dueling area.

'Owen, stop worrying; I feel fine.'

'I have checked both pistols and they are loaded. Henry, being the aggrieved, has the choice and has chosen his weapon. I have yours here.'

Owen handed the butt of the pistol to his friend.

'Thank you, Owen.'

'You can still stop this madness.'

'The time has passed for talking; let us have an end to it one way or the other.'

'Stop,' said Owen as they reached the centre of the area designated by both seconds.

Owen moved forward to greet Henry Nicholson's second and they both agreed upon the spot where the two duellists would begin their walk.

'Henry,' called Nicholson's second.

'William,' called Owen.

The two men called moved slowly towards the centre of the area. A stranger moved into the little group.

'I am here to see fair play. I also have a doctor in my coach if either of you are in need of one later. You will stand back to back and on my count, you will step out ten paces. Upon my order to turn, you will turn and then be free to fire your pistols. Is that understood?'

'Understood,' the two duelists replied in chorus.

'Right. Seconds, move away if you please.' The two seconds walked back to their respective carriages.

The stranger spoke again, but this time to the duellists. 'For the last and final time, will you both drop this madness and walk away from each other, and attempt a reconciliation?'

'No,' said William.

'No reconciliation,' said Nicholson.

'Turn, gentlemen, and stand back to back.'

The two duellists did as ordered and each held his pistol pointing to the sky. The stranger stepped backwards, away from the duellists.

William's mind drifted as he took note of the morning rays of sunlight through the trees. He could see the river, the occasional white cap in the early morning breeze as diamond points of light flashed in the sunlight. How long would it be before Ruth found out that he had been killed? At least, he thought, he had parted on good terms with his father. Would they miss him, if things went wrong in the next few minutes?

The breeze, heavy with the heady fragrance of the dew-wet grass, caressed his sweating face. He lifted his head and breathed deeply of the clean fresh air, a sharp contrast to the stench of Liverpool.

He realised the sunlight would be in his face as he took aim. Nicholson would be a dark shadow with the sun behind him. He pulled his jacket once more as he heard the order.

'Gentlemen, start your walk!'

One, two, three, four … eight, nine, ten; now for it thought William and turned.

Nicholson turned to see his opponent lit by the sun. He aimed at the top button of William's coat, which all men traditionally positioned over their heart, and fired. His pistol kicked up and he waited for the smoke to clear to witness the result of his shot.

William staggered.

A smirk grew on Nicholson's face as he saw William in distress, his pistol still unfired.

Nicholson's heart skipped with joy as he saw his enemy stagger. It's over, he thought, as he waited for William to fall to the ground. He would do the right thing and offer his regrets to William's second, Owen Johnston, when it was all over. Now there would not be a problem with who inherited the two ships in the King family, he thought. They will pass to Charlotte when her husband dies and we will use them on The Trade.

Henry began to feel a little uneasy when William failed to collapse to the ground. He watched Owen Johnston rush towards William, but knew that the duelling rules would not allow Owen to touch William until he had fired his pistol. If Owen did touch William, Henry would ask Owen for satisfaction, which Henry thought would be a perfect ending to a perfect day.

'No! Owen, stay away,' shouted William, and waved Owen away as he closed on him. William staggered again in an effort to stay on his feet. The pain felt as if a red hot poker had been thrust into him, but he knew that he had to stand and fire.

Slowly William straightened and raised his right arm, his hand still gripping the pistol. He took aim at the dark silhouette of his opponent, who waited to see what would happen next.

William pulled the trigger. The pistol's kick made it fall from his fingers as he collapsed to his knees. He fell face down in the soft wet grass as the comfort of blackness overtook him.

He did not see Nicholson double over when the ball struck him.

Slowly the blackness cleared and the pain returned. William groaned as he felt fingers probe around his left shoulder blade. He was lying face down on a bunk, naked.

'Owen,' he whispered.

'Lay still, Captain, or I will not be responsible for your health,' said a voice he did not recognise.

'Where am I?'

'On the *Lady Ann,* William; this is Owen,' said a familiar voice.

'Owen, what happened?' gasped William.

'Don't talk or move; the doctor needs you to be still.'

'Tell me, what's happened' William demanded in a coarse gasp.

'We brought you back to my ship in case the authorities searched yours. The news of the duel is all over town.'

'What happened; will I live?'

'Only if you be still, Captain,' came the commanding voice of the doctor.

'William, the ball hit the top button of your jacket and ricocheted down your left side. It went round your rib cage and is lodged in the muscle just under your left shoulder blade. The surgeon is trying to remove all traces of cloth before the wound festers, and then he will remove the ball.'

William felt Owen wipe his brow with a wet cloth. It felt delightfully cool.

'Nicholson?'

'He's dead. When you were struck by Nicholson's ball, I don't know how you kept on your feet.'

'I'd have stayed on my feet to kill that pig of a man, even if he had shot me in the brain.'

William groaned as the doctor probed the wound.

'Owen,' whispered William, through waves of pain, 'send the *Black Swan* to sea right away. Send her to Ruth in Boston. Tell Father——'

His voice faded as he fainted from the pain.

—⚓—

Charlotte sat in the library and listened to the man in front of her. He told her of the duel earlier in the day and that her brother had been killed.

'And the other man?' she asked quietly, trying to hold back tears for her brother.

'I understand, Ma'am, that he was hit by your brother's ball and has since died.'

—⚓—

Her mind tried to grasp that her brother, who was so full of life, was dead. She couldn't understand how William had been able to kill her brother; he was no match for Henry. She looked at the man again through tear-filled eyes and thought perhaps the man was confused, and that it was William that had been killed, not her brother. Even in her grief, she couldn't help thinking of the benefit to her, and her family, if William was dead. She would be able to put the two '*Roses*' on the Brazilian trade without any interference. Henry would have to be spirited aboard again, to avoid the authorities, and if he stayed away for some years, on her father's death, she would control both companies. Oh, what a happy day, she thought.

'I do appreciate your coming and informing me of the sad news of my stepson's death.' Charlotte dabbed her eyes. 'You must be mistaken as to the death of Henry Nicholson.'

'Perhaps you are correct, Ma'am; I am only repeating what I have been told. I know your brother, Henry, and find it hard to believe that he was killed. He is an excellent shot.'

'Thank you, Mr - err?'

'Grange, Ma'am, Charles Grange, at your service.'

'Thank you, Mr Grange, would you mind? I feel distraught at hearing of poor William's death. I am sure his father will be devastated. William was my husband's only child.'

'Of course, Mrs King, how stupid of me to overstay, but one of the seconds asked me to let you know the details. I offered to be the bearer of such sad news, out of friendship to Henry.'

'You are most kind, Mr Grange, but I feel I must lie down.' Charlotte reached for the small bell and rang it. 'Show the gentleman out, Alfred. Thank you again, Mr Grange.' Charlotte offered her hand. The messenger stood, and bowing over her hand, kissed it lightly.

She waited until she heard the sound of Grange's coach depart.

'Alfred, have the carriage brought round. We are going to see Mr George at his office.'

—⁂—

Chief Clerk Watkins held the door of the office open, allowing Charlotte to enter the building without hindrance. All of the staff stood by their desks and bowed as she entered. She waited while the Chief Clerk quickly moved ahead of her, to lead her up the stairs to her husband's office.

Watkins knocked on George's door, and at the sound of his voice, opened the door to allow Charlotte to pass.

'Charlotte, my dear, what a pleasant surprise; what has brought you into town?'

'Thank you, Watkins; close the door as you leave, if you please.'

'Ma'am, please call if I can be of assistance.'

'What's happened?' asked George.

'Sit down, George, I have some bad news.'

'William,' George said, and collapsed into his chair.

'I am sorry, George, but I have been told he was killed this morning.' Charlotte sat opposite her husband and began to remove her gloves.

George stared at his wife with disbelief.

'I know, George, and I am sorry. I always liked him, even though we didn't always agree.'

'This cannot be true. I had Owen Johnston here not five minutes ago and he informed me that it was Henry who was killed, and William was only wounded, but he will live.'

'Surely Henry lives. He is such a good shot and has never lost a duel.'

'My dear, I believe that Henry fired first and wounded William, who was still able to return fire and killed Henry.'

'No!' screamed Charlotte, and hid her face in her hands as her world crashed around her.

George moved quickly around the desk to console his wife.

'Don't touch me!' shouted Charlotte as she felt George's hand on her shoulder.

'My dear, I am so sorry. You must go to your mother and help comfort her. I assume you did not dismiss the carriage. I will accompany you as far as your parents' house, but I do not think I will be welcome in their house today. I will return to Kent Street and have your maid pack a few things, in case you wish to stay with your parents for a few days.'

Charlotte allowed George to guide her downstairs to the waiting carriage. They rode in silence to the Nicholson's imposing house.

George helped her from the coach and watched as she walked slowly up the short flight of steps to the front door. The door opened and Charlotte stepped through. She didn't turn to farewell her husband. As the door closed, George climbed back into his coach and ordered Alfred to return to Kent Street.

'He needs tending to on a regular basis, which will be difficult on a ship,' stated the doctor.

'Thank you, Doctor, but he will not stay ashore, as he wishes to return to Boston,' responded Owen.

'Mr Johnston, I have given you my opinion. I have cleaned his wound and I have removed all traces of cloth, and the ball that was lodged under his shoulder blade. Fortunately for him, the pieces of cloth and a small part of his jacket button were carried with the ball as it passed around his rib cage. As far as I can make out, no cloth or pieces of button have been left in his body. I must say it is unusual to have the top button so low on a jacket. A new fashion, perhaps?'

'No, I have ascertained that his steward heard that Captain King's opponent would aim for the top button of his jacket, this being Captain King's duelling opponent's usual style. The Captain's steward moved all of the buttons three inches lower so if he were struck, the ball would enter the Captain's body three inches below his heart.'

'A clever and devoted man, that steward.'

'Aye, he is. He will do anything for the Captain. So you see, the nursing of Captain King can certainly be entrusted to his steward.'

'Still, I would feel more confident of his recovery if he were ashore.'

'Be that as it may, Doctor, the *Lady Ann* sails within a couple of hours. May I offer you a seat when I am rowed ashore?'

'Thank you, Mr Johnston, I will accept your kind offer!'

'Drink some more, my dear, it'll help the pain,' Donald Nicholson said to his wife, who lay on the chaise longue in the library.

'Where is Henry?' whispered his wife.

'He is upstairs in his room. He is at peace now.'

'I want William King dead, and his father. I hate that family; they have brought us nothing but misery since you invited the father to become involved in our family.'

Donald remained silent at the accusation as he helped his wife drink some more brandy.

'He murdered my son!' cried Sarah Nicholson as she pushed the brandy glass away from her.

Donald heard the library door opening and turned to remonstrate with anyone who dared to enter after he had given explicit instructions that they were not to be disturbed.

'Daddy, tell me it is all a lie.'

'Charlotte, I'm glad you've come. Is your husband with you?'

'No, he brought me to the front door, but wouldn't come in.'

'I should think not, indeed,' said Sarah as she rose slowly from the longue and held her arms open for Charlotte.

Charlotte moved into her mother's arms and allowed her feelings to overflow in tears. 'How could he lose to William King? He was such a good shot,' sobbed Charlotte.

'Look after your mother, Charlotte, I have to go out.'

'Out, at a time like this when we need you here,' cried Sarah.

'Sarah, I have business to attend¾¾'

'BUSINESS!' yelled the two women.

Donald jumped.

'Yes, Madam, business, and do not shout at me! I am going to see about William King.' The two women renewed their crying at Donald Nicholson's rebuke. They didn't hear his comment about William.

- CHAPTER FORTY-TWO -

Wanted

Lady Ann, at anchor off Birkenhead
Late May 1807

'Captain shaw, you are now working for me. The *Lady Ann* is now part of my fleet,' gasped William, trying to breathe without causing any pain.

'Aye, Sir, Mr Johnston explained everything to me.'

'You will find that I am a fair man and that I reward those who are loyal.'

William grimaced and tried to make himself a little more comfortable in his bunk. Sang fussed around his Captain to ease the strain of movement.

'Don't fuss, Sang, I'm not dead yet,' said William. He closed his eyes in an effort to think. 'Are we ready to sail, Captain?'

'Yes, Sir, although we don't have a cargo as yet, it is my understanding that we are to load an outbound cargo for Ireland.'

'We are not going to Ireland. I want you to sail in ballast to Lancaster. When we're there, we will load furniture, sailcloth and candles. We should be able to buy them cheap, as it saves the good people of Lancaster sending their goods to Liverpool. I must leave

Liverpool quickly and perhaps, after a few months or so, I will return. We will also obtain fresh water and supplies in Lancaster.'

'Mr Johnston is due aboard later today. Are we to wait for him?'

'Yes, but I believe he will not be sailing with us. Just let me know when you see him approach the ship.

'Aye, aye, Sir.'

'William, I have a surprise for you.' Owen's head appeared around the cabin door.

'Owen, I need you to find out about my father, never mind a surprise.'

'That's the surprise, William. I have brought your father with me.'

As he finished speaking, Owen pushed open the cabin door to reveal George King.

'Father,' shouted William, and groaned in pain with the effort.

'William, my boy, how are you?'

'I have been better,' hissed William, pain shooting through his body.

'Lie down and rest. I have come to let you know that I have ordered the two *Rose's* to sea. They will sail on this tide for Boston. I have told the Captains to report to Ruth, and to wait for you.'

'So you haven't sold them to banker Leyland and his Portuguese friends?'

'No, I fear I will not be a welcome guest at the Nicholson's house for a long, long time. Our relationship is over. I have decided to wait for the money from my son.'

'Thank you, Father, I'll pay you as quickly as I can. What of Charlotte?'

'Charlotte is with her family. I doubt that she will be back in Kent Street for many a month. Her time is near, and the upset over her brother may cause complications. I will stay in Liverpool until after the birth; perhaps Charlotte and I can start anew, with the child.' There was a long silence as if George was debating with himself about the child. 'We will see,' he said, with a forced smile. 'The main thing now is that you are alive. What are your plans?'

'Perhaps Owen, can aid me in that matter. Owen, how are things ashore?'

'Many people know of the duel. It is an open secret. Donald Nicholson has sworn out a statement that you murdered Henry. The authorities are making an effort to find you. They are aware of the duel and they don't believe you murdered Henry. Donald has a lot of influential friends in Liverpool, so the charge has been recorded. I think they know you are going to escape and the rumour is that you have already left for London.'

'Who put that rumour about?' smiled William.

'I have no idea, William. Let us say that I didn't enlighten anyone as to their mistake.'

'We will sail for Lancaster, obtain a cargo and make for Boston. I intend to marry in Boston, so it may be some time before I return. I believe that there is an opportunity to create a regular service carrying peppercorns from Asia and trans-ship them over to Boston.'

'I can handle anything you send, William,' said Owen quietly.

'Father, why don't you come with me to Boston? Leave Liverpool and start again. I am sure Ruth would appreciate your help, and your knowledge would be a great asset.'

'I am sorry, William, but I must stay here at least until after the birth of the child. If I were to leave, the Nicholson's would make sure that I would never see my child. As it is, I think I will have to fight to gain access to it. I doubt that Charlotte even wants it, but her father can be very vindictive. If I am not here, I may lose all contact with your new brother or sister.'

'Well, Father, you know that there will always be a place for you in Boston. If things don't work out for you, please join me in America.'

George King withdrew a large handkerchief from his sleeve and blew his nose loudly, then quietly said, 'Thank you, William.'

William turned to Owen. 'In the meantime, Owen, if you wish to accompany us to Lancaster, you are welcome, but if you wish to make the shore today, I suggest you leave the *Lady Ann* now. We will sail on this tide.'

Owen smiled. 'I will forgo your generous offer of a sea trip and bid you farewell. I will write to you within the week, after I have ascertained further details of the hunt for you. In the meantime, take care, my friend.'

Owen stood, shook William's hand and left the cabin.

William watched his father return the handkerchief to his jacket sleeve.

'I am very glad you came to see me, Father; thank you.'

'Take care, my son. Perhaps I will see you again in Boston.' George leaned forward and kissed his son on the forehead. 'I am glad we are friends again.'

William leaned back against the *Lady Ann's* taffrail and folded his arms. The clean salt air filled his lungs as he watched the everyday tasks of the sailors at sea. The sound of laughter was a sign of a happy crew. He felt at peace with the world.

Six weeks had passed since he collapsed after being struck

by the ball from Henry Nicholson. Six weeks of pain and fever. He didn't have any memory of the ship sailing from Liverpool, nor loading cargo in Lancaster. In his fevered dreams, the one constant face had been Ruth's.

'Sur, your medicine.'

'Thank you, Sang.' William took the small glass of foul tasting medicine and tipped the contents down his throat. He handed the empty glass back to Sang and accepted a large glass of green tea. The tea would wash away the taste.

The late June sun warmed him as he began his daily exercise of walking the weather deck of the poop. Although he had only been exercising for a few days, he already felt fitter and healthier.

Walking in the fresh air helped to clear his mind. He still experienced a tightening of his throat when he thought of his father. Would they see each other again? Even as he walked he could feel the strength of his father's embrace as they said their goodbyes before the duel. Would his father join him in Boston? Perhaps, after the birth of the baby, Charlotte might soften and accompany his father to Boston. William lived in hope.

He turned at the forward part of the poop deck and watched the dark clouds gathering. He glanced around the horizon; they could be in for a blow. His knees bent to compensate for the easy roll of the *Lady Ann*.

William watched a young seaman ring out the end of the watch. The man reminded him of Michael Austin, which brought to mind Michael's father, James Austin.

Did I do right, thought William, risking everyone's life to rescue the Boston Negroes? A shiver ran down his spine as he remembered his attempt to save James' arm on the *Albatross*. Had he done enough to save his friend? Perhaps he should have removed the arm immediately and not tried to save it. Would this have saved James' life?

The *Lady Ann* heeled a little as the wind freshened. Turning once again at the taffrail, fine spray, carried on the wind, cooled him. The salty taste on his lips was good. He felt clean and refreshed. He was free of the old world, and of Liverpool. Free from the Nicholson family, free of the land. He was heading for a new life, in a new country, with the woman he loved. Their lives, as well as their companies, would be entwined. They hadn't been apart for a year; just four months.

The wind strengthened. The *Lady Ann,* as if in sympathy, increased her speed. Thunderhead clouds, tinted with glowing shafts of sunlight, rolled up from the horizon. As the dense clouds covered their world, the sun fought a losing battle.

Captain Shaw approached William, saluted and said, 'I intend to reduce sail, Sir.'

'Thank you, Captain Shaw, you are in command; do as you think fit.'

'Aye, aye, Sir.'

William watched as the crew climbed the ratlines to the yards and began to reduce sail.

A peal of thunder, followed by a great flash of lightning, heralded the rain. Torrential vertical rain drenched everything and everyone within seconds. The crew on the yards hung on for their lives and tried to shield their faces from the driving rain. William leaned forward in an effort to breathe without sucking in water. The wind through the rigging gave off a high-pitched howl. The howl was so loud that any attempt at speech was useless.

Then, as suddenly as it started, the storm ceased. The dancing rain on the ocean surface indicated the movement of the squall. Flashes of lightning lit the sky. William looked up at the men clinging to the yards and noticed that the masthead and tips of the yards were glowing with the blue light of St Elmo's fire.

He burst out laughing as he remembered the *Margaret Rose*. St Elmo looked after sailors at sea. The blue glow was a sign that the storm was over, and life could begin anew. For William, that new life would be with Ruth.

The End

Lightning Source UK Ltd.
Milton Keynes UK
30 September 2010

160558UK00001B/2/P